# The Moon Maid

# and Other Fantastic Adventures

## Adventures

# R. Garcia y Robertson

GOLDEN GRYPHON PRESS ▾ 1998

Copyright © 1998 by Rodrigo García y Robertson

PUBLISHER'S CATALOGING-IN-PUBLICATION DATA
García y Robertson, Rodrigo, 1949–
   The moon maid and other fantastic adventures / R. García y Robertson. — 1st ed.
     p.     cm.
   ISBN 0-9655901-8-6 (hardcover : alk. paper)
   1. Fantastic fiction, American.   I. Title.
813'.54—dc20   1998           97-73940

To Jim Turner

And to my Celtiberian grandparents:
Sara Casasnovas y Unamuno and Benigno García y Rodriguez

And my Angloceltic grandparents:
Cora May Williams and James Cicero Robertson

# Contents

# Preface

Paramount Pictures optioned "Gypsy Trade" for a movie, which was especially exciting because the story is based on a hitchhiking trip I took to Nijmegen in the '80s. So the middle section is all real—aside from a few name changes. And we got to fantasize about who was going to play "us," and how the movie would compare to memory. For a long time, all I had was the opening scene until I thought of the hook that would tie the parts together— Nijmegen in the 1500s, 1980s, and 1940s—a travelogue moving through times, rather than places.

I went to grade school in San Francisco, living close enough to Chinatown that my playmates went to "Chinese school" after regular classes. The neighborhood was so multiethnic that when I got a blond-haired friend I remember thinking, "He looks like the kids in books." So "Four Kings and an Ace" is an attempt to tell the story of San Francisco, between the Gold Rush and the Great Quake. Improbable characters like Stanley Lealand and Mama Love are real people—slightly altered. The hook for the story was the final hand of cards, which was based on a famous Gold Rush poker game. But the main purpose of the story was to remind the reader that slavery existed in California long after it ended in Alabama and Mississippi. But the victims were Chinese and Indians, so their story is not often told.

"Cast on a Distant Shore" was written to sell to *Fantasy and Science Fiction* — a magazine I had never sold to at the time. To my surprise and delight, they made it a cover story. It was one of those stories that started with the ending. Knowing how it would end, I was free to write whatever I wanted. I decided to set it in a world where humans were at the bottom of the food chain. The result was a story that remains surprisingly popular. People continue to tell me, "I liked the diver story."

"The Moon Maid" is another *Fantasy and Science Fiction* cover story, written years later. Having them published side by side makes for a neat comparison. They were conceived very differently. For a long time I wanted to write a Bronze Age story from the point of view of a real historical Amazon. Amazons have become stock fantasy characters, and people often treat them as a myth — or as modern feminist wishful thinking — which only shows how misogynist standard history can be. Actually the Amazons are repeatedly mentioned in historical sources, their graves have been unearthed in the Ukraine, and the original name for the Don was the Amazon. As a result, "Moon Maid" is one of those stories where the far-out "fantasy" elements are actually based on the historical sources, while the more "realistic" plot elements are all invented by me. But we tend to view history not as it was, but as we think it should have been.

When this collection was proposed, I was surprised to see "Gone to Glory" on the list. I thought there were other, better stories to take its place. But when I reread it, I was struck by how smoothly and well it read. And "Gone to Glory" is meaningful in other ways. So many of my stories are historical, but this one is contemporary. I did not invent the ecological disasters on Glory. I just substituted "Azur" for "Aral" and "Saber-tooth Steppe" for "Kalahari." We are all trapped on an overtaxed planet, with billions of new "colonists" on the way.

"The Wagon God's Wife" is just the opposite — it is the one story I lobbied onto the list. It remains one of my favorites, and it is the only story in the collection that is a fairly strict retelling — based on an incident in the *Flateyjarbók*, the Saga of Olaf Tryggvason. I ran across it in a book of Norse mythology and thought, "This is a great story." Of course I gave it my own spin, but I tried to keep the flavor of Viking times. And modern times, for that matter — I've been to Copenhagen, and Danes do still look on Swedes the way Gunnar did.

"The Other Magpie" is inspired by an incident in another epic — though it is not a strict retelling. Instead of Norwegians and Swedes it deals with whites and Crows, and the epic is not the

*Flateyjarbók* but the Little Big Horn. The Other Magpie and Finds-and-Kills really did fight for the U.S. Army at the battle of the Rosebud. The story came out just as women and gays in the military emerged as a hot topic — and the idea of a teenage girl and a transvestite scouting for the Army was too good to pass up. Women and gays have in fact been fighting for us ever since the Revolution; their contributions are just routinely ignored. While the people are real, most of the story — except for the two women's heroics at the battle of the Rosebud — is pure invention. "Other Magpie" is one of the few stories where I went out on a limb, adopting a totally non-European point of view. But much of the charm of the story comes from the down-to-earth reasonableness of the Crows, compared to the alien antics of the Army.

The last story, "Werewolves of Luna," has no justification except to be a rip-roaring science-fiction tale, with rocket ships, aliens, space werewolves, and virtual vampires. It is one of those stories that started with just the title, and later the opening scene. For a long time it stayed that way. Suddenly the tale took off, turning into one of my most popular stories.

I never intended to write short stories. First I meant to be a history professor. Then I wanted to write novels. Short-story writing was one of those things that just snuck up on me — but I am glad it did. In part because it is fun, and in part because it lets me write about history in a meaningful way. The stories are meant to entertain, and to involve people with the characters. Yet at the same time they let me talk about history to an audience that extends far beyond the university, an audience that is free to accept or reject what I am saying, and one that does not need to be graded afterward. Good luck, and good reading.

# The
# Moon Maid
## and Other Fantastic Adventures

# Gypsy trade

*It is easier to hold an eel than a Gypsy.*
—SPANISH PROVERB

Dieter entered the sixteenth century carrying a 7.65mm pistol, a flat ugly Walther PPK semiautomatic. He hated to show distrustful karma, but 1591 was not a good year, and Dieter was badly out of costume. He was dressed in the uniform of a Waffen SS officer, complete with peaked cap, swastikas, lightning flashes on his collar tab, and an Iron Cross at his throat. Papers in his tunic pocket identified Dieter as Lieutenant-Colonel Walter Harzer, commander of the Ninth SS Panzer Hohenstaufen Division. The papers meant nothing in 1591, but the uniform was odd enough to attract attention. This late in the sixteenth century, it did not pay to look odd, or out of place.

Dieter glanced about. Nothing. Just the cold flat field, drear and empty under gloomy skies. In some centuries, the field was a swamp; in others, it was drained pasture or meadow. Right now, it was dyked and level plowland—flat as Dutch farming could make it.

Ruefully, he holstered the Walther. No sense being overly dramatic.

It was dusk. He had arrived facing west. Twilight silhouetted the dark mass of the Groesbeek heights. Kneeling down, he discovered that his jackboots had scattered the cards. Feeling carefully about, he found each one, counting them, wrapping them in their square of black silk. He slipped the pack into his rucksack. Without the cards, he would be stuck in the sixteenth century, a period whose most popular contributions to Western culture were syphilis and the artillery shell.

Shouldering the heavy rucksack, Dieter took a deep breath, sniffing smoke from a Gypsy fire. He could always count on Gypsies using the field. Sometimes a single wagon, or a tiny *karawan*. Sometimes a great Romany carnival. But always, even in the worst of times, there were Gypsies about.

He set out upwind, guided by the smoke. Goats bleated. Someone strummed a guitar. A small fire cast dancing shadows on gaily striped tents and a painted wagon sheltering under the first trees of the Reichswald—the dense black wood that straddles the border between Spanish Flanders and the Duchy of Cleves. A good spot. Dieter approved—silver reales from Flanders could be traded for cattle lifted in Cleves. Borders were great gifts to people who never obeyed them.

Raucous children played around the fire, like a flock of unkept birds, plaguing an old Jew in a black coat and broad-brimmed hat—laughing, capering, yanking at his beard and earlocks. The Jew merely tried to keep warm and fend off the children.

Dieter sat down beside the Jew, dropping his rucksack. It rang against the ground. He waved at the children. "*Bassak*. Enough. Stop bothering. Bring us food. Wine, if you have it." He started counting to show he was serious, "*Jek, duoi, tren, shtar . . .*" Children are the tyrants of a Gypsy camp.

Startled to hear a stranger using the Caló, dirty urchins disappeared into the tents and painted wagon. Older siblings came out of the tents to look him over. Girls in wide embroidered skirts grinned at him, showing off glistening teeth, intrigued by his strange uniform and familiar manner. Dexterous boys gauged the weight of his rucksack. Dieter grinned back, glad to be home. He had never been to this part of the sixteenth century before, but for a Gypsy, home is hardly ever a place, or a time—it is a people, a life, the Caló.

The Jew began to pour out his troubles in Yiddish and German; he was Isaac ben Jacob, a native of Den Haag, trying to get home through the Spanish lines. Half starved, he had no money. "*Kein gelt.*"

Dieter half-believed him. Isaac ben Jacob of Den Haag did not say what brought him to Catholic Cleves in the first place. Yet everyone had secrets worth keeping; Dieter certainly did. And small lies flow naturally around a Gypsy fire. "You're in luck." Dieter nodded at the barely visible heights. "Nijmegen is not far off." It amused him to be giving directions so soon after arriving. "In two days, Maurice of Nassau will be here to take Nijmegen from the Spanish. When he does, you may walk across the Waal bridge into Holland." He waved toward the tents and wagon. "I'll tell these people to feed you until then."

Astounded and pleased, Isaac thanked him generously, not the least put off by the Nazi uniform. All that lay in the future.

Dieter shrugged. "I can take no credit. Thank Maurice of Nassau when he arrives."

The guitar started up again. Bolder girls began to dance, giggling at Dieter over bared shoulders, twirling colored sashes and kerchiefs, showing dirty feet beneath swirling skirts. Bells on their ankles rang in time to the strumming. Dieter watched, knowing he would get nowhere with these girls. This dance was pure distraction. He sat and admired, keeping a jackboot firmly planted on his rucksack strap — a negligent attitude toward one's possessions invites theft.

A black-bearded giant, wearing knee breeches and a bright sleeveless coat, descended from the wagon. He had gold hoop earrings, oiled lovelocks, and a yellow silk bandanna. Very Gypsy. Jabbering children steered him over to Dieter.

"*San tu Rom?*" The man sounded suspicious. "Are you Gypsy?"

"*Da tchte san, pralo.* Yes, I am, brother," Dieter replied.

"You don't look it."

Dieter spread his hands apologetically. He had dark curly hair, but his skin was fair, his features very Aryan. Dyed blond, he could have posed for a Wehrmacht recruiting poster. Nor was his SS uniform very Gypsy. But the Caló was his best proof. Romany was an impossible mix of Sanskrit, Macedonian Greek, Persian, Armenian, Romanian, and a half-dozen other tongues. No one but Basques and Gypsies spoke the Caló fluently. Not in 1591.

"What does the wandering Jew want?"

Dieter shrugged. "What does any man want? To eat. To walk the earth, to not lie under it." He winked at the big man. "*Piavta.* Let's drink. Feed my friend Isaac out here. We have business inside. Gypsy business."

Black eyes narrowed.

"*Da.*" Dieter nodded. "I am the one."

"*Da. Piavta.*" The caravan leader produced a wineskin and

shouted orders to the children. "I am called Bratu. Come meet my woman."

Mounting three short steps, Dieter doffed his muddy jack-boots at the entrance to the wagon. Children jostled by him, shrieking with delight, carrying half a boiled chicken and a big three-pound loaf of *pan de munición*, the wheat and rye bread issued to the Army of Flanders. He heard them taunt Isaac, calling the bread ham and the chicken piglet. The insults were in Romany, so Dieter doubted that the hungry man minded overmuch.

Bratu drew aside the braided rug that served as a door. A single brass lamp cast dark shadows over brightly woven colors. An empty cushion was set out for Dieter, just inside the entrance. Bratu's woman, Draga, sat cross-legged facing the cushion, wearing a flounced skirt and embroidered jacket. She had full hips, a narrow waist, and a hatchet face. Her wrinkled eyes were old and knowledgeable—her clear intense scrutiny reminding Dieter of a queen's sculpted head he had seen in the Cairo Museum. As he sat down, she asked, "Are you the one?" staring suspiciously at his Nazi uniform. "You are very fair."

"Yes, I am fair."

"And oddly dressed." She did not like the dark SS tunic.

Dieter shrugged. "I come from far away."

"And young," she added.

Dieter nodded. He had known women like Draga all his life. Powerful, intense, worldly-wise. Wealthy and openhanded enough to serve meat to a strange Jew—but closefisted with her secrets, cool as a tigress if she distrusted you. The grandmother who had trained Dieter was so much like Draga that they had to be related. Which made Draga his ancestor too. "I am from a time and place where Gypsies come in all colors, and camp where we wish."

"*Da, da.*" Draga was unimpressed. "And gold escudos grow on trees. Save your stories, pretty boy—use them on the young and foolish."

Bratu closed the flap behind him. "Dark, fair; young, old. What's the difference? So long as he gets it done."

Draga made the sign for silence. "Three women have been taken from us, locked behind stone. . . ."

"Maybe tortured too," muttered Bratu.

Draga hissed.

"Where?" asked Dieter.

"Where were they seized? Or where are they kept?"

"Both." Dieter needed details to work his magic.

"They were taken by *genitors*, at the crossroads below the Groesbeek. The Spaniard in Nijmegen has them." Draga spat.

"He won't bring them out except to burn them," added Bratu.

"What Spaniard? What is his name?"

Draga and Bratu looked at each other. "Ask the Jew," Draga decided. "A Jew would know."

They brought Isaac in, and Dieter asked him.

Isaac pulled at his long straggling beard, looking from Gypsy to Gypsy. "The Spanish commander in Nijmegen is Colonel Mendoza de la Coruña, a nervous *gallego*. He buys art. But he may not have your women. There is a young witch-hunter hereabouts, a Jesuit named del Río." Isaac ben Jacob had not been just blundering about after all—he at least knew who stood between him and safety.

"We'll start with Mendoza." Dieter hoped that he didn't need to deal with del Río—"Jesuit Witch-Hunter" didn't sound inviting. "Who are the women?"

"My wife's mother, Marga." Bratu spoke without looking at Draga.

"And my Aunt Gan," Draga added.

"Those are the main ones." Bratu took a swallow from the wineskin. "The third is a cousin. Tinka. Young, not so important. You know the type. All tits, always in trouble. . . ."

"It is better to be all *prick*, and pigheaded?" Draga waved three fingers at Dieter. "They have lost three women. We want three women back, *tren*."

"*Tren*," Dieter nodded. He would not think of leaving Tinka. Tinka was already essential to the pattern. "I will do what I can do. But I need a nice-looking horse—not a cart pony. A gentleman's horse."

Bratu smiled. "I know where such a one can be stolen."

At dawn the next day, Dieter rode up to Nijmegen on a gorgeous chestnut mare whose only defect was that she kept turning her head, trying to take the road back to her stall in Cleves. He presented himself as Colonel Walter Harzer of the Holy Roman Reich, bearing crucial dispatches for Colonel Mendoza de la Coruña. Waiting by a high postern gate in the wet gray morning, he studied the solid *trace italienne* bastions and deep ditches. Below the fortress, he could see the stone bridge, and the big sweeping S-curve made by the Waal.

An English ensign wearing a Neville badge and the Cross of Saint Andrew led him to Mendoza's quarters; the Army of Flanders was not just Spanish and Flemish—Italians, Burgun-

dians, Austrians, Germans, even Scots and Irish served in its ter-
cios. A United Nations in miniature faced Maurice of Nassau.
Colonel Mendoza was dark and pensive, with deeply solemn eyes,
a trim beard, and the bearing of a professional soldier. Looking
more Gypsy than Dieter did, the Spaniard spoke corrupt Dutch-
German with a Latin accent. His oak-paneled quarters were
decorated with block prints and engravings. Dieter noted a woodcut matching one he had seen in Berlin. "Is that a Dürer?" He
praised the active composition and vivid classical lines.

Mendoza preened, offering his guest steamed chocolate. "I
bought it in Antwerp. He is still quite popular there."

The Spaniard sipped his own chocolate, looking dubiously at
Dieter's Nazi *Ausweis*, SS identity card, and papers stamped with
the Sword and H insignia of the Hohenstaufen Division. Dieter
hastened to explain. "The 'Colonel' is strictly honorary. I am on
detached service from the Reich."

Mendoza nodded. Germany was currently awash with free-
captains, condottiere, and military contractors—fighting for all
sides and for themselves. "So we are only speaking colonel to colonel?"

"Exactly." Dieter bet that he could best appeal to Mendoza as
a soldier. "Colonel to colonel, I can tell you that Maurice of
Nassau will be here before breakfast tomorrow, bringing enough
cannon to batter his way into Nijmegen."

Mendoza set down his chocolate, not nearly as pleased by this
news as Isaac ben Jacob had been. "Maurice of Nassau is before
Antwerp. He took Hulst only a month ago."

"He has loaded his army back onto boats and barges. The cannon that took Hulst are headed here." Dieter enjoyed wielding the
truth. A single truth well-told did the work of a dozen lies.

"He could do it," Mendoza admitted. The Army of Flanders
tried to keep Maurice pinned in the low flat Heart of Holland, between the forks of the Rhine and the sea. But interior lines and
command of the rivers let the Dutch move about at will. "Do you
expect a reward for telling me this?" Mendoza eyed him cau-
tiously. The warning was not worth much—alone and isolated,
Nijmegen was the last Spanish stronghold in Gelderland. Mendoza was at Maurice's mercy if the Dutch decided to act.

"No. The *warning* is free. I expect to be paid for saving your
*city*. With my help, you can beat Maurice of Nassau. Without me,
you won't last the week."

"Silver reales for saving Nijmegen?"

"Gold escudos—two or three hundred—I'm hardly greedy.
And three women you are holding."

"Ah, of course. *Las Gitanas.*" The Spaniard lifted an eyebrow. "It becomes clear. You do not look *Gitano.*"

"How else would I know what will happen tomorrow?"

"How else?" Mendoza sipped his chocolate and considered. "You understand, these women are being held for Father del Río. I am merely a jailor."

Mendoza seemed embarrassed. Dieter detected a northerner's distaste for the clergy. Good, he could use that. "On what charge?"

"Witchcraft."

Dieter had guessed as much, but it was still terrible to hear. There was no legal defense against the charge — torture guaranteed conviction and execution. To the south, in Trier, judges who refused to send victims to the flames were themselves burned. Flanders was only beginning to ignite. He tried to sound unconcerned. "As their jailor, you need to look in on them. Let me see that they are alive, and I will show you how to save Nijmegen from the heretic."

Mendoza nodded; to visit the cell cost him nothing. The Spaniard seemed sufficiently skeptical, but Dieter planned to be utterly convincing.

Gypsies say that every jailor serves a life sentence — Dieter never felt that more strongly than when he was in a dungeon. He followed Mendoza down stone steps into a dank hole, reeking of mold and urine. The women were huddled in a single cell. Mendoza held a scented handkerchief over his nose, trying to hurry Dieter through, but Dieter insisted on taking a lamp right up to the bars.

The cell was dirty and smelled of diarrhea, making Dieter want to gag. Draga's mother Marga looked frail and limp. Her sister Gan was more robust — hawk-faced, steel-haired. Tinka, the busty young cousin, did not strike Dieter as a troublemaker, just scared and woebegone. Leaning against Tinka was a Dutch or German woman, young, blonde, blue-eyed, looking harried and exhausted.

He whispered in Romany, "The cards have sent me. Tomorrow you sleep under the stars."

Even the blonde's eyes went wide, seeing her cellmates' reaction. She could not know what was said, but Dieter saw her trying to guess if she was included in the good news.

"*San tu Rom?*" Draga's mother demanded.

Mendoza coughed behind him. Dieter nodded. "Tomorrow night." Staring straight at him, the blonde woman managed a weak smile.

Back in the sunlight, the Spaniard tucked his handkerchief

into his sleeve. "I am hardly happy with this. At home, Jesuits do not hunt *Gitanas*. But here in Flanders, they take the new Witch Decree seriously. *Too* seriously, some would say. You have met Father del Río? No? Ah, then you have that delight ahead of you."

An interview with del Río was now inevitable; Dieter had shown an interest in the prisoners, enough to make him suspect. Witchcraft was a highly contagious crime. "First I want to show you what is at stake." Dieter aimed to convince Mendoza, colonel to colonel, before meeting del Río. "Do you have a firing range?"

"Nothing fancy. I will show you the midden heap the musketeers use as a butt." Dieter declared that that would do splendidly. The Spaniard led him to a stone court separating the fortress kitchen from the stables. It stank even by sixteenth-century standards. Dieter collected some broken pots and chipped plates, standing them upright in the midden. Crockery made spectacular targets. Opening his rucksack, he took out a black angular submachine gun. It was a factory-fresh Wehrmacht MP40, 9mm, the replacement for the older semiautomatic MP38. Dropping to one knee, Dieter fit the folding stock to his shoulder.

He took aim and squeezed off a couple of dozen shots. For the time it takes to count to twelve slowly, the gun banged like a metronome gone mad, two beats to the second, shattering every target.

"Mother of God!" Mendoza was awestruck by such offhanded destruction. "Where was that pistol made?"

"In Germany." Dieter traded the gun for a fresh one from the rucksack, one with a full clip. Soldiers, cooks, and harlots, drawn by the noisy demonstration, stood in hushed silence.

"Why have I seen nothing like it?" Mendoza demanded.

"A military secret. Watch this." Setting the second gun on full automatic, Dieter held down the trigger, blasting off an entire thirty-two-round clip in a deafening burst of sound. Manure, offal, and ceramic chips flew wildly about. The torrent of gunfire lasted less than four seconds. Terrified gasps, then an enthusiastic cheer, came from the shaken spectators. Nothing remained of the original plates.

Dieter handed the empty gun to Mendoza, who hefted it gingerly. "It weighs less than an arquebus!"

"And fires five hundred times as fast. A man with one of these is more than equal to a company of musketeers."

"How many do you have?"

"Enough. I will trade you a half-dozen of these guns for the three Gypsy women in your dungeon. And Nijmegen is saved for the faith."

"*Ave Maria.*" Mendoza turned the weapon over in his hand.

"You must meet the good Padre del Río." Whether or not Maurice's army arrived on the morrow, Mendoza wanted to know more about automatic weapons.

The witch-hunter was staying in a fortified manor, an increasingly popular type of residence in sixteenth-century Flanders—for those who could afford one. The *Schloss* sat like a small castle on a wooded spur, halfway between Nijmegen and the Groesbeek. Tower windows looked out over the treetops, toward Nijmegen and the Waal. Riding up the heights, Dieter explained in a general way the workings of a submachine gun. Mendoza was able to grasp the basic principle of a gas-operated gun, and how the blow-back mechanism worked, but he remained thoroughly amazed.

Grooms took their horses. The castellan ushered them into a stone-vaulted library where del Río was going over Greek translations. The young priest was barely out of his teens, with a bookish pallor and big eyes that made him look even younger. He sat at a wheeled desk, a combination writing-table and tricycle, allowing him to scoot from one folio volume to another as they talked. Mendoza had warned Dieter that del Río was a sort of prodigy, a Renaissance priest, accustomed to doing several things at once. "He never stops working, knows nine languages and a thousand authors. Published an edition of Seneca while still in his teens. Devoted to the Virgin. Very pure."

Dieter could well believe it. Especially the last part. Del Río looked like he had never made love to a woman, or a man either, for that matter. The idea of this weirdly arrested adolescent ordering up tortures and passing judgment on Marga, Gan, and Tinka made Dieter's asshairs curl. He listened as Mendoza elaborated on the menace presented by Maurice of Nassau and their precarious military situation. The Spaniard concluded, "Colonel Harzer has brought strategic information vital to the defense of Nijmegen. In return, he wishes to relieve us of certain prisoners, whose security I can no longer guarantee, given . . ."

"Do you mean the witches?" The young scholar stopped wheeling between volumes of Plato.

"*Sí*," admitted Mendoza. "The *suspected* witches."

"There is no suspicion." The boy's eyes bulged in an unhealthy fashion. "Three of them were taken with witch's paraphernalia—cards, crystals, dried herbs, and a goat. Their guilt is obvious. The other comes from a notorious nest of witches in Trier. Her whole village was infected, and had to be burned down to the roots." Dieter remembered the blonde German girl in the cell, with the searching blue eyes.

"She was convicted of witchcraft and condemned to death six

years ago," del Río informed them. "But the Prince-Bishop merely had her flogged before her parents' fire. A misguided show of pity toward a witch child. Now she is of age. She escaped from Trier, but she shall not escape the flames."

Colonel Mendoza objected that Maurice of Nassau might appear with an entire army of heretics. "By all means, burn the German girl—since she has had her trial. But give me *las Gitanas.*"

"You have guns. You have men." Del Río gripped the tricycle desk. "Would you save Nijmegen from heresy by giving in to *witchcraft?* Beware, Mendoza! There is the smell of deviltry about this dark-garbed man!" He wagged a finger at Dieter's SS tunic. "Across the border in Cleves, accomplices of Satan pose as Catholics. Patronizing heretics. Preaching toleration. Do not fall into that pit."

Dieter thought of the Walther in its saddle leather holster. The trigger pull was feather-light. Three-fifths of a second to draw and fire. He had practiced the movement. By putting a 7.65mm bullet in this boy's forehead, Dieter would be doing the sixteenth century an immense favor. But he would have to shoot Mendoza too—a real pity there. Then what? Killing Mendoza and del Río would not get Marga, Gan, and Tinka out of their cell. And it would not be very Gypsy.

"Burn them *all,*" the boy declared, "let Satan take the guilty. God will greet the innocent."

Mendoza protested, "By that logic, everyone is better off burned."

The stunted boy smiled. "Perhaps. But pity is a snare, and leniency is a sin." He lifted a pasty finger. "Yet, be merciful! If any of these women truly and wholeheartedly confesses, if she repudiates her crimes and shows real repentance—*strangle* her first." Throttling was the most common anesthetic administered to witches at the stake. He returned to reading Plato.

Mendoza rolled his eyes and showed Dieter to the door.

They stayed up half the night, drinking Spanish brandy and admiring the colonel's woodcuts, while Mendoza blasted the vicious stupidity of the clergy as only a Spaniard can. "Our padres are as damnable as the Dutch! Swindling drunkards, extorting money from the dying, selling amputated limbs as saint's relics. I know a company chaplain with a stable of fine horses *and* a strapping young son!"

"A most enterprising cleric." Dieter far preferred horse-fancying womanizers to sadistic eunuchs like del Río.

"As for our Flemish bishops, I was never blessed by one without feeling the need of a bath." Mendoza gave Dieter a dubious glance, "You know, I do not look forward to a Dutch attack. But if nothing happens *mañana*, if you are merely some mad doomsayer, imagine my embarrassment."

"Imagine *mine*." Dieter poured himself another brandy. "We shall know by breakfast tomorrow."

Next morning, Maurice of Nassau arrived, erasing Mendoza's doubts. Little Dutch battalions and big siege guns landed from boats and barges, moving like disciplined clockwork toys. Dieter was pleased. Timing was never a certain thing in the sixteenth century — calendars were being reshuffled, chroniclers were corrupt or inept. Mendoza glared from the ramparts, alarmed and hungover. "The Dutch are such energetic demons — it is a headache just to watch them work!"

Dieter offered him a pair of aspirin. "Take these — they thin the blood. We must do business now, before they blockade the town." With the Dutch still scrambling out of their boats, this was the moment to bargain.

Mendoza swallowed the aspirin. "You swear there is no deviltry in your guns."

"No more than in a musket. By the Blessed Saints and the Holy Virgin, I am no demon, just a *Gitano* and a sometime Catholic. But hurry," he insisted. "Maurice will waste not a moment. He plans to blast holes in your enceinte, then throw in his infantry. With my guns, you can hold any breach, slaughtering the infidels as they come on." Dieter warmed to his sales pitch.

"Enough." Mendoza held up his hand. "It is far too early in the morning to talk of slaughter. I will pay you right out of the company chests." Each captain had a chest, or *caja*, used to advance money during the long periods when regular pay was in arrears. A few hundred escudos was nothing, really, not with Nijmegen at stake.

"And I want the woodcut. The Dürer."

"The Dürer?" Mendoza looked as shocked as when Dieter had first fired the machine gun.

"Give it to me, or give it to the Dutch."

"Done," Mendoza agreed, "before you want my hose and doublet as well! Six guns. For the Dürer, the gold, and three women."

"Four women." Dieter pictured knowing blue eyes. If he left the young German woman for del Río to burn, her gaze would haunt him from century to century. "The German too. The one from Trier." Mendoza grimaced at what the boy Jesuit would say — but in the midst of stark calamity, what was one woman more or less?

"*Tren.*" Draga held up three fingers in the shadowy lamplight of her wagon, glaring at Dieter. "I said three women, and you return with *four!* You can't send a man to do the simplest task, without him coming back drunk. Or in love."

"I am not in love." Sitting cross-legged on a cushion, Dieter defended his decision.

"Then you are drunk."

"I just could not leave her." This was the bare truth.

"You were not there, Draga." Mother Marga lay in the back of the wagon, tended by Gan and Tinka. Wretched food and prison water had given her a violent fever. "You would have done the same." Gan and Tinka agreed.

"But what will we do with her?" Draga was not going to be silenced, even by her mother—not in her own wagon. "She is not Gypsy. How will we hide a pretty blonde fugitive? The first people to spot her will think that we stole her. And that *he* is fucking her." She nodded toward Bratu. "And they will be right, because my man also thinks with his pecker."

"Shave her head," suggested Bratu. "Make her ugly. It is all the same to me."

"Pig!" She spat in his lap. "So what do we say when the *genitors* come for us? All is well, kind sirs—she is only a witch?"

"I will take her with me." Dieter had expected this.

"Indeed, you will!"

"I can take her to a place where witches are not hunted."

"And Gypsies roam free." Draga snorted. "Just try not to promise her true love and a pot of gold. Then when you leave her somewhere far away, she won't be so shocked."

The blonde woman had been sitting by the entrance flap the whole time, wide-eyed, watching the conversation. Without knowing the Caló, she must still guess what was being said. The sharp-faced woman did not want her here. The men were going to give in to her.

Dieter settled down beside her. He smiled. By now, he knew that her name was Kathe, and that she had no one. Her parents, grandmothers, sisters, and aunts had all been burned. The family she had been staying with in Flanders had been scared senseless by her arrest.

"These people," Dieter indicated Draga's clan, "can take you only as far as Cleves." Cleves was a haven of sorts. Gypsies and witches were not tolerated there, but they were not hunted, either. Yet safety there was tenuous. The Erasmian Duke of Cleves was old and childless. When he died, the duchy would go to whoever was strong enough to take it.

"The Dutch will soon have Nijmegen," Dieter added, explaining that Mendoza was doomed. "The normal unit of fire for a submachine gun is eighteen hundred rounds. I brought only enough shells for each gun to be test-fired — not enough to bother Maurice of Nassau." Dieter shrugged apologetically. "A Spaniard should have known not to trust a *Gitano*." It was the true Gypsy genius to find people with more than they needed, then get it from them for free.

Dieter went on, "I do not know if Maurice of Nassau burns witches. I do know he means to be prince of all Holland. At Hulst, he shot the first soldier who mistreated a woman."

She stared calmly back at him, outwardly unruffled by his strange talk. Six years of horror and hiding seemed to have toughened her immeasurably. "But I am neither Dutch, nor a reformer." She appeared to have thought this out. Maurice of Nassau was at best an unknown quantity, at worst a bigoted tyrant and Protestant fanatic. Kathe seemed to be more concerned, sensibly enough, with the man in front of her.

Dieter nodded. "I can take you to where you will be safe. But the haven is far away. You must start a new life in a foreign land, a time and place that are incredibly different. Do you understand?"

She looked directly at Dieter. It was easy for him to guess what she must be thinking: This man has saved my life. Why? Does he want me? He is clearly a warlock, steeped in dangerous magic. Is he also a demon in human form? She studied every detail of his SS uniform, examining the lightning slashes, black crosses, and birds of prey, worry-lines crinkling around her eyes. Only the swastika seemed to reassure her — the crooked cross was an ancient symbol of well-being. She shook her head, "No, I do not understand."

"How could you?" Dieter agreed. "Will you come anyway?"

"Yes." Clearly she had no choice. The Gypsies did not want her. Dieter had snatched her from the fire. Whatever he planned for her, it could hardly be worse than what del Río intended.

They waited while Gypsies wrapped Mother Marga in a fur coverlet. Her fever was worse. Fire made her shiver. She complained that the night air felt hot. But the old woman was as determined as her daughter. She insisted on having her family carry her, leading Dieter and Kathe to a spot in the center of the field, under a great net of stars. There Marga asked to be put down, and patted the ground with her hand. "A good place to lay the cards."

Gan set down a brass lamp that might have belonged to Aladdin. Dieter took the square of black silk out of his rucksack. Inside was a Gypsy tarot deck. He handed them to Kathe. The cards felt cold and alive.

"What are you doing?" Draga demanded.

"Let her spread the cards." Dieter spoke softly. He was taking a risk—anger these women, and he was stuck in a thoroughly dismal century. "I am sure she has the Talent."

"So what if she does? She is not Gypsy!"

"But she is going with me. It will be better, safer, easier, if I have a woman with me who can spread the cards. I know the patterns, but . . ." He let the last word hang. Knowing the patterns was never enough, not if you were a man.

"You want too much." Draga shook her head. "I know what you think. You have got yourself a blonde witch. Scared. Thankful. Trusting. She will spread the cards for you, cook your meals, keep your bed warm—then you won't need tough old Gypsy women anymore. There are reasons why you men don't have the Talent. *Good* reasons."

"Be still, Draga," Mother Marga interrupted. "Be quiet. Be thankful." Marga sat wrapped in her coverlet, supported by Gan and Tinka. Her gray hair had come out in clumps, showing patches of scalp—her voice sounded ragged. "Dieter has done us a great service."

"I *am* thankful," Draga insisted. "But thankful is not stupid. Thankful is not throwing power at a man's feet!"

"When you are as old and as close to death as I am, you will care less about power, and more about balance, about life." Marga placed thin fingers on Kathe's wrist, then looked to Dieter. "Will you tell her exactly what I say?"

"Of course, Mother Marga."

"Tell her first to be brave, as brave as she was in the Spaniard's cell. Tell her that I am giving her a great gift, a power beyond imagining. Explain that you can teach her the patterns, but that you cannot lay the cards. Explain that no man can. Tell her that this is a Gypsy gift. Given in exchange for the kindness and trust she showed me in the cell—and because I am going to die. But tell her that no Gypsy gift comes free. If she uses it well, if she does right by the gift, Gypsies will *still* get the best of the bargain. Tell her all that."

Dieter told her.

Marga helped her lay out the cards. First the great circle that is the wheel of power. Then the pattern in the center that directs the power. When they were done, Marga said farewell.

Dieter shouldered his rucksack, and clasped hands with Kathe. They stepped together into the center of the circle.

And were gone.

# THE DUTCH SCHOOL

*Life without danger is as empty as life without love.*
—GYPSY PROVERB

Kathe stepped from a damp October night into blazing summer sunlight that smelled of new mown hay. Draga, Marga, Gan, and Tinka were replaced by yellowing wheat, lush green trees, and tall dykes—a Brueghel landscape, brimming with color. In the middle distance, a Dutch farmer stood beside a thatched barn, shading his eyes, trying to make out the two figures who had suddenly appeared in his field. Only Dieter remained the same, totally at ease with the astonishing transition. He gave her fingers a happy squeeze. "I knew you had the Talent. I could tell by your eyes." Letting go of her hands, he bent down to collect the cards.

*She* had done this? Kathe's mother had taught her cures, her aunts had cast spells, but this was raw supernatural power—none of the doomed women in her family could have come close to matching this Gypsy magic. "I cannot really believe . . ."

"Oh, you did it, all right." Dieter straightened up, wrapping the cards in black silk. "I have tried the patterns. I imagine that every Gypsy boy does, hoping he will be the one, the man who has the Talent even though he is a man. To me, they are only cards." He handed her the deck, then looked about. "You have brought us to a very safe moment—a brand-new century. Nijmegen is now part of the Netherlands. There is a truce with Spain. No war. No witch-hunts. Not for the moment." Wonder on top of wonder. He stared into the breeze blowing down from the Rhine—centuries passing over his face. "It won't last. It never does. All over Europe, nations are sharpening their sabers." Dieter had the true Gypsy contempt for governments, plunging their people into one holocaust after another, calling each new disaster leadership. Or statecraft. "The Thirty Years' War is coming." Dieter smiled and shouldered his rucksack. "But we won't wait around for it."

He led her through the wheat and across the stubble, to where a small horde of Gypsies was camped under the trees, with their children, dogs, and wheeled caravans. A buxom matriarch in a carnival tent dress met them at the steps of her yellow-green wagon, throwing arms around Dieter, greeting him in Romany. She grabbed Kathe next, hugging her, calling her Kathe.

"What is she saying?" Kathe was astonished to hear her name used by this wild Gypsy woman.

"She's happy we've come. They've been waiting for us."

"But how does she know me?"

"All part of the pattern," Dieter answered airily, delighting in her mystification. The big woman dragged Kathe into her painted wagon. Gypsies brought out food, drink, and fiddles—a party erupted. Hustled from dungeon to daylight, and steered through two Gypsy camps, Kathe wanted only to sleep, but people pushed food at her, demanding in Romany that she eat and enjoy. Men were showing Dieter paintings—he bent forward, studying brush-strokes and signatures, setting canvases aside.

"What's happening?"

"I visited here before, and gave them the names of artists whose work could be stolen or bought for next to nothing." Dieter showed her a pair of landscapes and a gentleman's portrait. "From Antwerp—the landscapes are student works by a young court painter; the portrait was done by a wife-beating sot. They are scandalized that I am paying good gold for them." She watched him count out some of Mendoza's coins, big heavy Spanish *escudos de a doce reales*. In ecstasy, Gypsies passed the gold about, admiring its weight and feel.

Kathe squinted at the paintings. The two landscapes were pretty, but the portrait was extraordinary, strikingly real. Yet each detail done with a touch of humor. She wanted to finger the lace on the man's cuffs.

"The landscapes are early Rubens—not so rich, not so Italian. The portrait is by Frans Hals, priceless."

Kathe nodded wearily. "He looks ready to stroll off the canvas."

Dieter patted her hand. "You must be wrung out." Tired as she was, Kathe found his touch thrilling—this strange gallant Gypsy was the first man in a long time who was not hell-bent on mistreating her. Of course, that could change.

Dieter called out in Romany. The Gypsy matron grinned, leaped up, and led Kathe to a couch in the back of the caravan, quickly and casually turning back the coverlet—Kathe guessed the woman was giving up her own bed. Burrowing under the bedclothes, Kathe motioned to Dieter. "Please thank her. I cannot believe how kind she has been."

He said something that made the big woman's breasts jiggle with amusement. "You really don't recognize her, do you?"

Kathe shook her head.

"This is your old cellmate, Tinka."

Kathe gave Tinka a weak smile. "Of course." Within the woman, Kathe could see vague outlines of the girl, her merry eyes and soft mouth, all half-hidden by folds of flesh—the teenager she had parted from last night was now a grandmother. *Decades* had passed in a flickering. Feeling immensely old herself, Kathe drifted into sleep.

She awoke the next morning remembering a dream. She had seen herself as a child, walking hand-in-hand with her mother and her youngest aunt, down a long muddy road. Each time they came to a puddle, the two women would swing the child into the air, saying, "Oopla." Then they would set her on her feet again. Kathe ran up to warn them about the burnings, but none of them knew her because she was a Gypsy. All Kathe could do was sob, begging them to be happy. "This is the best time of your lives!" she cried, feeling like one of those strange crazy women who cry over little girls. Before she could stop crying and collect herself, Kathe woke up.

Dieter was already at work, sewing a canvas-and-leather case to carry the rolled-up paintings. Tinka presented them with clean traveling clothes. Kathe got a peasant's dress with a tight bodice, turned-down collar, white apron, and gathered skirt. Dieter got some Dutchman's shirt and doublet, and stiff leather breeches. His Nazi uniform went to pad the paintings.

When it was time to be off, Dieter explained the pattern in detail, telling Kathe the significance of each card, having her try out different arrangements. She felt more confident, more in control—knowing what to expect. The result was the same. She stepped into the pattern, and half a century passed.

Her elation at controlling the patterns was tempered by aching emptiness. Tinka was now long dead. So was everyone Kathe had ever known, talked to, seen, or heard of—except for Dieter. The Gypsies who greeted them were gruff and unfamiliar. To them, Dieter was not the eternally youthful hero he had been to Tinka's people. He was a kind of legacy whose coming had been long predicted, needing to be fed and sent on his way. Kathe got even less of a welcome. This band had been hunted out of Germany, where legal opinion on Gypsies was divided between tradition-alists who favored flogging and hanging, and enlightened jurists who thought that flogging was inhumane, feeling that hanging alone would be enough to rid the Reich of human vermin.

Kathe felt that all she knew of the world now was Dieter and this Dutch field. He sensed her loss. "I warned you it would be hard. Look, for a while we will travel without the cards." The man was in perpetual motion, pure Gypsy, a moving target that might never stop, not even for her.

Walking, or riding in peasant carts, they passed through Nijmegen. Kathe saw a moderately prosperous Dutch town, built of stone and brick, with red-gray roofs, spires, chimneys, bridges,

and boats. Beyond the Waal bridge was the level expanse of farm-
land between the forks of the Rhine; a flat island in the land,
green polder dotted with windmills and tiny clusters of houses—
Lent, Elst, and Dreil. Kathe moved like a ghost through the low
dyked landscape, seeing faces she assumed she would never see
again. At Arnhem, Dieter booked passage on a barge to Rotter-
dam. From there, it was a short sail to Delft.

"Born in Delft, lived in Delft, died in Delft," Dieter recited.
"The life of Jan Vermeer. He is a favorite of mine."

Kathe was awed by Vermeer's studio. Paintings glowed with
pearly white light, like canvas windows into a luminous world
where calm graceful women worked at solitary tasks; on the walls
behind the women were miniature paintings-within-paintings,
tiny portraits and landscapes done in vivid detail. Each canvas reminded Kathe of the magic that is in everyday life.

Vermeer's house was more like a Gypsy camp, overflowing
with children. The painter was flattered that Dieter and Kathe
had come some distance to see his work, saying that he thought
he had no reputation beyond Delft, and a poor one even here.
Vermeer had Kathe sit for a portrait sketch, showing her how he
used a camera obscura to produce crystalline mirrorlike images,
capturing the many subtleties of reflected light. Dieter bought
two paintings that no one in Delft had wanted.

They returned to Nijmegen by barge and canal boat. In the
field, Dieter helped Kathe lay out a completely new pattern, all
coins and cups, different by far from any he had shown her. They
clasped hands, but instead of stepping into the pattern, they stood
for a long time, hand in hand. The thrill of contact, the feel of
flesh on flesh, was so strong she knew that Dieter enjoyed it too.
During her years of flight and hiding, Kathe had never allowed
herself to love. She had gotten scant encouragement. Twice she
had bought freedom with her body. Once she had been raped by
a *Reiter*, who claimed he was a knight exercising *droit du seigneur*.
She wondered what it would be like to make love with a man that
she did not detest. But aside from saving her life, while being gra-
cious, friendly, and giving, Dieter had made no moves to seduce
her.

She could feel him searching through words. Finally he told
her, "We must go even farther, far into the future. When all this
will be only a vague memory."

"Why? Already I feel like a living ghost." Did this Gypsy ever
settle down for more than a day or two?

"We must travel to where these paintings are worth something. To a place where you may be truly safe, and to where I can

complete the pattern." He frowned, as though one goal contradicted the other.

She held tight to his hands. "I am afraid of going even farther from everything I know. Stepping into the circle is like destroying the world—the cards almost make me feel like a mass murderer."

"We are not killing anyone." He gave her his most rootless Gypsy smile. "We are just moving on."

Kathe sighed. Already she felt as rootless and cut off as Dieter —she had not been born a Gypsy, but war and intolerance had made her one. She had had no true place ever since men in iron destroyed her village and burned its women, turning her life to ashes. Now she must go on with Dieter, or give in and be consumed by tides of fire. She looked around her. This world too would pass away, but she would somehow survive.

They stepped into the pattern. Vermeer, his studio, the children who played in his yard, the peasants in the field, the Gypsies who had fed them, all disappeared.

The field did not change. It was still summer, but the air felt different. Burnt oily odors seasoned the drowsy pollen scent. Kathe wrinkled her nose. Hot air vibrated with distant rumblings, like thunder or a far-off cannonade. The Dutch farmhouses had grown more numerous and more substantial, with shingle roofs and big glassed windows. Only a barn or two looked familiar.

"Brace yourself," Dieter advised, leading her up to the road that ran atop the nearest dyke. She was startled to find the road perfectly flat and unrutted—small pebbles were pressed into its pitch-black surface. Standing atop the dyke, she saw a silver speck, high in the blue, trailing a long thin cloud behind it. Too big to be a bird, more like a low-flying angel.

She tried to show Dieter, but he grabbed her, telling her to watch out, pulling her off the roadway. The dull rumble turned into a roar. A gleaming mass of painted metal shot by, shining with chrome and spewing fumes. The steel vehicle sped along like a cannon shell, propelled by some inner magic. Children riding inside pressed their faces against curved glass windows. Dieter waved to them.

"What was *that?*" Kathe watched in numb disbelief as the magic vehicle disappeared down the blacktopped dyke.

"A car. You'll get used to them. They own this century."

She saw another "car" coming. Dieter gave a cheery wave, sticking out his thumb. The vehicle roared by. Three more flashed past. Dieter shook his head. "The Dutch aren't being hospitable today." He gave up hitching, and they set off toward Nijmegen.

To Kathe's immense relief, they never got a ride, walking the whole dozen kilometers into town. She saw innumerable cars, and many, many people. The traffic circle at the top of the heights was a scene out of Dante. A hot haze hung over the Waal, filled with smoke from the cars—people, laughing and talking in light summer clothes, dodged the cars that went careening by, nearly colliding. She held tight to Dieter. The Dutch smiled at her peasant dress, and at Dieter's breeches and doublet. Dieter returned cheery greetings, thoroughly enjoying himself.

He took her to a coffee shop off the main square—all chrome and glass like the cars. Big block letters spelled out DEN PLAK. Dieter steered her to a small table by the door. A honey-haired young woman came to serve them, wearing a thin shirt knotted at the waist, sandals, and the briefest sort of pants—without a hint of underclothes. Nipples pressed against her shirt fabric. Long legs were browned by the sun. Kathe had never seen so much public flesh outside of paintings.

The seminude woman leaned forward, casually resting elbows on the table, fascinated by Kathe's very ordinary dress, commenting in a flood of Dutch. Dieter showed her one of Mendoza's gold escudos, which fascinated her even more. Taking the coin, she returned with mountains of food, fried potatoes, rolls stuffed with meat and vegetables, salt, sugar, strange condiments, and black cups of steaming coffee. Dieter grinned between bites. "Well, we've arrived!"

They had indeed. Kathe stayed speechless. Afterward, he walked her down quiet brick-and-cobble streets, shaded by tall trees. People rattled by on clattering black bicycles. Dieter stopped at a house with wide stone steps. A string hung out of a slot in the door—he pulled on the string, and the door swung open. Dieter called out in Dutch. An attractive dark-haired young man appeared in the doorway, inviting them in. He had broad muscular shoulders, an agreeable smile, and seemed to know Dieter.

The house was full of light, like the Vermeer paintings in Dieter's canvas bag, but the decor was not Dutch. Rattan mats covered the floor. Strips of oriental calligraphy hung from the ceiling. Everything smelled of strange spices. Children lay in the front room, staring at a strange box that made noise and showed pictures that moved.

The young man's name was Guido. He spoke Dutch with Dieter, and a peculiar sort of clipped German with Kathe, taking them into a back bedroom that opened onto a sunlit patio. Kathe stared at a curious picture hanging on one wall—a "movie poster," Guido said—that showed a tall handsome man wearing a uniform that reminded her of the one in Dieter's bag—decorated with swastikas and eagles. Guido laughed, asking if she recognized the man in Nazi regalia.

Kathe shook her head.

"Ronald Reagan," Guido explained. He saw the name meant nothing, and added that Reagan was President of "*die Vereinigten Staaten.*"

Of Holland? Both Guido and Dieter found her question funny. "*Nein, von Amerika!*"

"*Amerika?*" Kathe had heard of that place across the sea, inhabited by Spaniards and painted savages. Ronald Reagan looked like neither. Dieter brought out the paintings. Guido studied them, loading a small black pipe with hashish, saying that Dieter had outdone himself. Passing the pipe back and forth, the two men plotted an art show while Kathe napped on a chair in the patio.

The art show opened at midnight, in the basement of an abandoned brewery—a decaying building taken over by Krakers, who had turned the basement into a bar and coffee shop called the Krakcafé. Kathe asked Guido what *Kraker* meant.

He brought his hand down sharply in a chopping movement, saying to Kathe that *Kraker* came from the crack a lock makes when it is broken. She could hear banging going on above, and Guido told her that the squatters were busy constructing a theater, homeless shelter, and community center.

Art students had framed the paintings, hanging them alongside posters with incomprehensible slogans like STOP THE NEUTRON BOMB and CATCH THE DUTCH DISEASE. The Krakers were impressed —a few were even aghast. A visiting Dane wearing a lightning stroke BZ T-shirt demanded to know if the paintings were real.

"Touch them," Dieter suggested.

The Dane frowned. "I mean, are they really Vermeers? Is that an actual Dürer woodcut?" Dieter admitted that they were.

"Millions of guilders are hanging on the wall." Young people stared at the artwork hung on peeling concrete, awed by the Dane's claim.

"Are they stolen?" asked a wide-eyed punk with a hash pipe in her hand. She was wearing a leather jacket, blue jeans, and patriotic orange hair. A black circle-A was inked on her left cheek. Kathe could barely believe how Dutch women wore whatever they liked, and spoke as they pleased—in Trier, women had been tied to stakes and burned alive for far less.

Dieter accepted the pipe. "I know for a fact that the artists were paid."

"That is all that matters," concluded an aging Provo with gray in his ponytail. "Only the painters deserve to be paid, for their labor, minus the cost of paints and canvas."

"But what collections did they come from?" The Danish squatter in the BZ T-shirt remained a skeptic.

Dieter shrugged. "The Dürer came from the collection of a Spaniard named Mendoza, now deceased. The two Rubens and the portrait by Hals came from a Gypsy named Tinka. I bought the other two from Vermeer myself."

Everyone laughed, but they could get no sensible answer from him. The Dane was sure that something illegal had gone on, but no *Danish* laws had been broken. As for Dutch law? — the squatter was himself staying in Holland without a passport. The debate delighted Dieter. He repeated the main points to Kathe by candlelight in their room in Guido's basement. They lay on a narrow pad, sharing a single sleeping bag. "I cannot keep the paintings here too long," Dieter concluded. "White Mice might come nosing about." Dieter and Guido called the Dutch police "White Mice" or "Mr. Polite."

"What will you do with them?" Under the woozy spell of wine and hash, Kathe was enjoying Dieter's warm solid presence beside her on the sleeping bag. Surely this was the night they would make love.

"I need to take them where they will do the most good."

"Where?" It sounded like he would be traveling again.

"Somewhere dangerous," Dieter mused. "Gypsies have no word for duty, but we do have the pattern — and what we owe to the dead. You'll be safe enough here."

"I'm supposed to send you into the pattern alone?" Kathe was shocked. "How will you return?" Having lost so much, she was not about to lose Dieter too.

For once he seemed very serious. "I brought you here because I like these people. They are not Gypsies, but they are genuinely done with war and nations. They are Dutch, Danes, Germans, Americans, and whatnot — whose fathers and grandfathers killed each other with carefree abandon — but they have given up fighting. You can't get them to kill anyone — not Russians, not even Arabs. And they are more to be trusted than Gypsies when it comes to homeless young women." Dieter kissed her. "Especially pretty ones."

The kiss was a delicious shock. The prospect of loving Dieter both excited and terrified her. She had never made love to a man she even half cared for — except perhaps for the son of the family she'd stayed with in Flanders. But even with that boy, she had held back; after her arrest, the poor lad must have endured the

pangs of hell, finding out that he had been finger-fucking a witch.
"I don't feel safe here — just confused. I want to be with you."

Dieter frowned. "Impossible. You don't know how risky and
savage this twentieth century can be."

She looped her arms around his neck, locking her fingers to
keep her Gypsy from getting away. "Have you forgotten where
you found me? My whole life has been one great risk."

"Give this time and place a try," he insisted. "You could do far
worse." He kissed her again, slower this time. She responded,
stroking his tongue with her teeth, expecting him to lift her skirt.

Instead he took her upstairs to Guido's big tiled shower. "I will
show you the greatest luxury of this century — it almost makes up
for the two World Wars." Turning on the hot water, he sprinkled
bath herbs on the tiles. The stall filled with scented steam. Slowly,
he undressed her. Kathe's skin was stark white under the electric
light, smelling of excitement and caked with dirt; in the whole
time they had been together, Kathe had bathed only once, in the
cold waters of the Rhine.

He positioned her under the hot cascade from the shower noz-
zle, her bare hips pressed against the hard warm tiles, her feet
braced in the corners of the stall. Dieter scrubbed both their
bodies with spiced soap — his hands slid down her breasts and between her legs. Kathe realized that the sixteenth century had a lot
to discover about sex and cleanliness. Intoxicated by the wine, the
hash, the mad flood of steaming water, the clean spicy aroma, she
felt him slip inside her, thrusting harder and harder. Breath coming in ragged gasps, Kathe held fast, vowing never to let go.

The paintings hung for nearly a week. Kathe soaked up as
much of the twentieth century as she could, sitting with the
children in the living room, watching *Dallas* and *The Dukes of
Hazzard* with Dutch subtitles. She learned that America was an
amazing place, where beautiful people raced about in fast cars,
stopping only to make love or shoot at each other. *Dallas* was all
about J.R. — a rich and handsome man, second only to Ronald
Reagan in the nation's esteem. Kathe's interest delighted the local
children — she was the first adult they'd ever met who was genuinely eager to learn from them. She would stay up until dawn
with Guido and Dieter, talking, smoking hash, and listening to
Randy Newman records — *Little Criminals* and *Sail Away*. Then
she and Dieter would go down to the basement to make furious
love, and fall asleep. After school, Dutch children would tiptoe
down the stone stairs to see if Kathe was awake. She would slip
out of the sleeping bag, with the odor of lovemaking still on her
body, to sit on the floor watching the soaps — *von Amerika!*

On the last day, Dieter took her to see the ruins of Mendoza's citadel, reduced to shattered walls and pitted stone, its *trace italienne* bastions covered with grass. Four hundred years had passed since she'd sat here in a cell, waiting to be burned alive; to Kathe, it had been little more than a month. "I wanted you to see how deeply the past is buried," Dieter explained. "Going back will be far more dangerous. When I saw you in that cell, I already knew Tinka as an old woman. This time I am going into the pattern blind, or almost blind. I know the big events, but not our futures."

She stared out over the huge steel bridges that spanned the Waal, connecting Nijmegen to the "island" between the Waal and the Lower Rhine. A torrent of traffic roared in both directions. Without Dieter, nothing seemed safe. "You cannot make me spread the cards."

"I can find a Gypsy woman to do it."

"Will she go with you? Will she make sure you get back?"

"Probably not. A Gypsy woman would have more sense."

"Then there is nothing more to say." She saw him weakening. Was he as addicted to her as she was to him? Kathe was determined not to end up like Tinka, waiting out the years until Dieter came waltzing back into her life as though hardly a day had gone by.

"Enough!" he threw up both hands. "You begin to sound like Draga! Promise me this one thing."

"What is that?"

"Do you swear that you will leave me the instant you are no longer in love?"

She looked shocked. "I suppose I would."

"No, no supposing," he insisted. "Swear to leave if you no longer love me."

"I swear it. But it is a silly oath."

"All marriage vows are silly. And I swear to leave *you* the moment I am no longer in love. Today, tomorrow, or centuries from now." He took out a clasp knife and the last of Mendoza's coins. Handing her the coin, he opened the knife.

She hefted the heavy gold escudo. "What is this for?"

"Your bride-price. Draga would howl at me for getting a woman so cheaply." There were no Gypsy women about to make sure he paid in full.

"You don't have to buy me," she laughed.

He nicked his left wrist with the knife. "Shush. This is a Gypsy wedding. The only one you are likely to get." He pressed the knife into her wrist until the blade drew blood. Then he tied their wrists together with a handkerchief. "Now we are one blood. Man and wife. Sister and brother. No matter what happens, we will always belong to one another so long as we are in love."

On their way down from the grassy ramparts, they met a boy from Guido's block. He asked if they had been visiting the old fort. They smiled, saying that they had. Their hands were still clasped, bound loosely by the bloody handkerchief.

"Look what I dug up here." Reaching into his T-shirt, he pulled out a shell casing threaded on a string.

Dieter examined the shell. "German, 9mm," he decided. "It probably came from an MP40 — a submachine gun."

The boy grinned, bowing his buzz-cut head in embarrassment. "It is nothing, you find a lot of them. From the war. When Nijmegen was occupied by the Nazis."

They returned to the field at night, with the paintings in their canvas case. Dieter put on his SS uniform. He had told Kathe to wear the peasant dress. "We are headed for a party — people will take it for a costume." He made her practice two patterns. One to get them there, the other to get them back. The first pattern was so demonic it scared her to spread it — filled with swords, built around Death, the Devil, and a bursting tower. "It was not just Gypsy talk when I said we were headed for dangerous times," he said as he buckled the Walther about his waist. "If we are separated, you must use the second pattern to return here at once. Understand?" Mutely, she nodded.

They stepped into the pattern, and the second half of the twentieth century vanished.

For the first time, Kathe came out at night, emerging into chill dark air. It felt like early fall, after the summer stubble is burned away. Dieter led her across deep furrows to the dyke road.

White headlights careened out of the darkness, and Dieter flagged down the vehicle, a tall four-wheeled truck. A startled Luftwaffe driver stuck his head out the window. In his most abrupt German, Dieter demanded the man's name, unit, and destination. Surprised to find a Waffen SS Lieutenant-Colonel and a woman in a Dutch peasant dress standing in the dark atop the dyke, the driver replied that he was from a base defense unit, just assigned to the newly created First Parachute Army. He was headed for Eindhoven. . . .

Dieter cut off the man's explanation. "My car has broken down, and I am on my way to meet with your commander, Colonel-General Student — carrying valuable articles meant for the Reichsmarshall." Since the driver was in a Luftwaffe uniform, mentioning Göring could not hurt. Dieter ordered the relief driver out of the passenger seat, handing him the canvas case full of paintings. "Get in the back and guard this." The man scrambled into the back, taking a seat atop boxes of 88mm flak ammunition. Dieter hopped up beside the driver, reaching down to help Kathe in.

She hesitated, having learned to dodge autos in the streets of Nijmegen, but never having ridden in one.

"Don't worry," Dieter patted the dash. "Just a truck." He glanced at the make—a Ford G 997T, three-ton. "An *American* truck, but safe in German hands." The driver dutifully laughed at the colonel's joke. It was a sign of the sheer chaos reigning in Europe that the man was driving an American truck over Dutch roads for a German Army unit, while wearing an Air Force uniform. He did not even blink at being ordered about by an SS colonel. The First Parachute Army included invalids, sailors, coastal troops, flight mechanics, SS Panzers, untrained boys, and grounded jump instructors—everything but parachutes.

Kathe climbed aboard. The driver gunned the engine, jammed the Ford into gear, and they bounced off down the dyke—he must have wanted to be gone before Reichsmarshall Göring himself stepped out of the shadows, demanding to be driven to Portugal. Kathe found her first ride sufficiently terrifying. Dieter shouted directions as dark empty space rushed by the open windows. Without warning, the narrow dyke disappeared. The driver braked, shifted, spun the wheel. Then they tore off again, rattling over the cobbles of Groesbeek, climbing the heights beyond.

Dieter had told her something of what to expect—the gala they were going to was in the same *Schloss* where he had met del Río. But nothing prepared Kathe for seeing the witch-hunter's tiny castle done over for a twentieth-century victory bash. Light flooded from towering windows and French doors. Big Mercedes staff cars crouched on the gravel drive, and a battery of quad-40mm flak guns was dug into the lawn—multiple black barrels aimed at the night sky. A band played Wagner.

As they approached the music, Dieter explained that he was not really meeting with Colonel-General Student, "Merely a hard-working field commander. I mean to meet with Herr Direktor Posen of the Kaiser Friedrich Museum, a buyer for Reichsmarshall Göring. If Posen passes on these paintings, we will go on to Karinhall, Göring's estate in Germany. This Reichsmarshall is mad for artwork—he has huge Renaissance desks, silver candelabras, even thrones. You won't believe it—the walls of Karinhall are papered with paintings, hung one above the other, four tiers high—I have done a happy business with this Reichsmarshall. But

if we are caught, you know nothing. You are a peasant girl from Trier, I invited you to a party. And use the cards."

Inside, high-ranking Nazis were talking, drinking, making speeches, and pinning medals on Dutch collaborators. Tough, tall Dutch women in trailing evening gowns were having their cigarettes lit by heel-clicking SS officers — making the most of being occupied. Dieter guided her into the whirl of wine and faces. "Come, we will blend perfectly."

A fat genial Nazi introduced himself as the Gauleiter of Cologne, offering Kathe caviar, pouring her champagne. "You have to help us carry out the scorched-earth order." Seeing that she did not understand, the Gauleiter quoted from a recent directive, "Leave nothing for the enemy. Not a stalk of wheat, not a slice of meat . . ."

". . . not a glass of champagne." Dieter poured for himself.

"Exactly!" The Gauleiter grinned.

"Have you seen Herr Direktor Posen of the Karl Fried . . ."

A drumroll cut Dieter off. Drunk happy faces turned toward the windows at the back of the dining hall. A bright spark appeared on the dark forested slope outside, followed by a rumble, then a roar. Windows shook. A four-story metal rocket lifted from among the trees, climbing on a jet of fire, blasting upward, defying gravity to fling itself at an unseen target. Nazis cheered. The band played the "Ride of the Valkyries" from *Die Walküre.*

"Next stop London?" Dieter inquired.

"No, Antwerp," the Gauleiter sighed. "A fine little city. Entrusted to me by the Führer himself — until the British took it." He shook his head.

"To Antwerp." Dieter lifted his glass.

"To Antwerp!" the Gauleiter said, recovering his smile.

Other missiles followed the first — rising like giant candles, one by one, from hidden launchers. Somewhere in the surrounding forest, a V-2 battalion was hard at work. Each time there was a drumroll warning. Then the launching. Then a cheer. And they would toast another city, and another thousand kilos of high explosive. Brussels. Liège. Paris.

Conversation would then resume. "Speer is coming to Aachen next week. You can tell him your . . ."

"Those cowardly bastard Finns have thrown it in . . ."

It reminded Kathe of *Walpurgisnacht,* or Guido's Randy Newman LP *Sail Away,* the cut called "Political Science" — all about bombing London and Paree.

Nazis began pinning medals on each other. Dieter located the museum director and rescued Kathe from the Gauleiter, guiding

her past stained-glass windows and heavy velvet hangings—
toward a small annex room. But as soon as he opened the door,
she saw Dieter's face fall. Waiting with the nervous gray-haired
Herr Direktor were six agitated Gestapo agents, who informed
"Lieutenant-Colonel Harzer" that he was under arrest. The little
Herr Direktor Posen seemed about to die of fright. Only Dieter
took it all calmly, turning to Kathe with a concerned look,
mouthing the words, "Use the cards." Kathe did not understand
how horribly wrong things had gone until they forcefully
separated her from Dieter. Suddenly she was alone with a pair of
Gestapo men who would not let her go after Dieter, or even leave
the room.

## GABELSCHWANZ TEUFEL

*German Gypsies sang and danced, because they knew their
days were short.*                              —KONRAD BERCOVICI

Kathe's formal interrogation took place in that plush annex room.
The Gestapo men turned two chairs to face each other, both
decorated with the same cheerful Belgian upholstery. Kathe was
given one chair; the two men shared the other, one sitting while
the other paced and questioned her. A Gestapo stenographer and
two officers—one in an SS uniform, the other from the Wehrmacht—sat together on an ottoman.

Kathe quickly made it plain that they would get no militarily
useful information out of her. Yes, she knew there was a war on,
but she had only vague notions of whom Germany was fighting.
Thinking of the missiles aimed at Antwerp and Brussels, she suggested, "The Spanish?"

The SS officer frowned, asking who Germany's allies were.
She remembered the Ford truck and that President Reagan was
a Nazi. "*Amerika!*" she answered brightly, glad she had the name
ready. The Wehrmacht man grimaced.

She told them that she was from Trier, an orphan with no
papers. She knew the year was 1944—Dieter had told her that
much—but she knew nothing about the principles of National
Socialism. She had never heard of Chancellor Hitler. No matter
how her answers astonished the men, she persisted in being
friendly and forthcoming. Convinced that her sole hope was to be
utterly open and innocent, she looked them in the eyes, smiling
as she answered, showing none of the fear or anxiety they were

accustomed to seeing. It was hard not to believe her, harder still
to believe that she knew what was happening.

The Gestapo interrogator concluded that she was mentally
defective. "A simple backward girl from some Rhineland village."

"Or a very clever liar," suggested his partner.

"Or a foreigner posing as German." The SS officer shook his
head. "She sounds like she learned her German from a Schiller
play."

"Does it matter?" The Wehrmacht man lifted an eyebrow.

The Gestapo interrogator shrugged. The stenographer closed
his notebook. All such crimes carried the same sentence.
Simpleton, foreigner, or spy, Kathe was headed for a concentration camp. Having decided on almost certain death for her, the
men became more relaxed, even friendly. Her interrogators offered Kathe a cigarette, genuinely hoping to put her at ease while
waiting for the car that would take her away.

The cigarette was as harsh as Guido's hash, but not as stimulating. She recognized this guilty good-humor — guards had been
similarly kind to her family before they'd burned them to death.
Mendoza had been unfailingly polite with her. But inside she was
joyous, supremely confident, because *they had not taken her cards*.
They had not even asked her about them. A minute alone, and
she could be back with the Krakers in Nijmegen.

She could escape anytime she wanted to — but she was determined to bring Dieter back with her. Kathe could tell that that
would be harder. Yet somehow, sometime, she was sure that they
would bring her and Dieter back together. For further interrogation perhaps, or possibly a trial — she still had much to learn about
the exact workings of Nazi justice.

Once she and Dieter were back together, she would spin some
tale; she would promise these men anything, offer whatever it
took to get that minute alone with Dieter, or just lay out a harmless game of cards.

The car came. Kathe was disappointed to discover that Dieter
was not going with her, but she got in, hoping that wherever she
was headed Dieter would be there too. The ride was not too
terrifying — the driver was a wizard at night work — and sitting in
the backseat of a great purring Mercedes, jammed between two
Gestapo interrogators, was not nearly as frightening as jolting
along in the front of a Ford truck filled with artillery shells.

Nijmegen Station was blacked out. Stepping from the Mercedes, Kathe found the darkness full of noise and movement. Box-
cars were disgorging hordes of very young-looking Germans in
uniform. They were being given rifles and *Panzerfausts* right there

in the station, to fill out Colonel-General Student's First Parachute Army with live bodies. Flatcars supported the shadowy bulk
of *Panzerjäger* assault guns—their long iron snouts sticking out
from under canvas. Nijmegen was sixty miles from the front, well
within the range of Allied tactical aircraft. Every second of darkness was precious to the Third Reich. Directed toward a square
black cargo door, Kathe pulled herself up onto the cold floor of
a boxcar. A man warned her to mind her legs. She pulled her feet
inside, and the door rumbled shut. A lock clicked.

She was in a black metal box. But not alone. Kathe heard
voices in the darkness, women's voices, and children's—speaking
Dutch. She could tell by the tones it was a family talking quietly
among themselves. This was a real improvement. She was in with
women, children even, and would not have to worry about closing
her eyes among men.

The train jolted into motion. Startled, Kathe felt frantically for
her cards—they were still tucked in the bodice of her peasant
dress. She relaxed. The first frightening jerks were replaced by the
steady swaying beat of iron wheels on steel rails. Immensely tired,
Kathe searched the darkness for a place to lie down. Her hands
found a mattress, still warm, having taken some young soldier out
of Germany into Holland. Kathe did not mind the sharp male
odor—it reminded her of the sweaty sleeping bag in Guido's basement. She stretched out, lulled by the rhythm of the wheels, half-
dreaming of Dieter.

Dawn light entered the car through small chinks near the roof.
Kathe sat up. There were several families in with her, although
not whole families—she saw no men or grown boys. On the mattress nearest hers, a mother and teenage daughter were caring for
several quarrelsome youngsters, two small boys and a toddler.
Kathe watched them parcel out breakfast—apples and cheese.

The teenager was a thin active girl with black hair, large dark
eyes, and luminous white skin, almost translucent. Kathe guessed
it would be silky to the touch. The girl smiled at her, asking in
Dutch, "*Wat wil je eten?*"

"*Eten?*" Kathe looked hungrily at the apples, having eaten
nothing in 1944 besides cheap champagne and plundered caviar.

"*Ja, eten.*" The teenager made eating motions, adding that her
name was Ruth.

Ruth's mother smiled and pushed half an apple into Kathe's
hand. The mother's name was Miriam; she had wiry hair, Semitic
features, and piercing blue Dutch eyes. Beneath the cheerful
generosity, Kathe sensed a powerful sadness—as if Miriam knew
it was hopeless to hoard food for her children. Their lives were

already out of her hands. Kathe could tell that Ruth and Miriam were Jews, and that they thought that she too was a Jew, despite her blonde hair and Aryan features. She said nothing to dissuade them.

"*Nederlander?*" they asked.

"*Nein.*" She shook her head, saying that she was German.

They seemed taken aback, but did not question her further. The day grew long. There was no toilet, just a bucket in the back of the car. Worse, there was no water. Champagne had dried out Kathe's head. Her tongue tasted like leather. She found herself staring at the door, sucking on an apple core, hoping that when the train stopped and the door opened, there would be water.

Without warning, the car slowed, swayed, and jolted to a stop. But the door did not open. Kathe pressed her ear against the cold metal. She heard an eerie high-pitched wailing, which grew louder, more frantic, until it filled the boxcar, blotting out every other sound.

The walls of the car were fitted with bunks three tiers high. Kathe scrambled onto an upper bunk to look out through one of the chinks near the roof. At first, she saw only a patch of sky. Then she saw bright specks. More low-flying angels.

Ruth climbed up to be beside her, shouting in her ear, "*Vliegtuigen!*"

By now Kathe knew what airplanes were. In America, J.R. owned a whole fleet of them. She watched them crawl across the blue, dragging thin white contrails behind them. Black puffs appeared ahead on the silver specks. Beneath the wailing, Kathe heard the cough of cannon—someone was shooting at the airplanes. By the time the specks were directly overhead, the heavens boiled with shell bursts.

Suddenly the whole boxcar shook, slapped by a giant hand. She saw smoke and debris shoot upward. Blows rattled the metal box, drowning out the wailing. Kathe braced herself between the high bunk and the roof, with Ruth's arms about her middle. The girl's head was pressed into her stomach.

The explosions ceased. The bunk stopped bounding beneath her. The terrible wailing returned. All Kathe could see through the metal slit was a blue square of sky, dirtied by flak and crossed by white contrails.

The car door slammed open. Dazzling sunlight burst in. Men outside shouted, "*Juden. Raus!*"

She helped Ruth scramble back down. Miriam loaded her daughter with parcels, and Kathe took the two boys' hands. They tumbled out of the boxcar. As soon as she hit the ground, Kathe turned to help Miriam with the toddler. Soldiers kept screaming, "*Raus! Raus!*" and waving submachine guns. MP40s. The men behind the guns acted as though there were some great danger that the women and children would run, resist, or refuse to leave the boxcar.

Holding tight to the littler boy, Kathe glanced about. The boxcar stood on the wreck of a railway station, ripped by rubble and bomb craters. Thirty paces up the track, a boxcar had been smashed to splinters. Bodies lay in the wreckage.

Soldiers herded the women and children together, then marched them through the smoking remains of the rail yard. The wailing faded. Kathe saw forged steel rails twisted like fine wire. Reinforced concrete was cracked into chunks and heaved up at odd angles. Shattered glass crunched underfoot.

A locomotive wrecked in a previous attack lay upended, red with rust. Women in baggy coveralls were cutting off pieces of it with welding torches.

She passed the station house, cratered by a double row of direct hits, as though some wandering titan had trudged through the structure, too distracted to go around. The empty waiting-room had two walls sheared away. A table holding up a pot of flowers sat in one corner, miraculously intact. A second-floor door hung on its hinges, opening into empty air.

Beyond the station was a line of trucks—Fords, Opels, a couple of captured Chevys—waiting on the cratered roadway. Homes across the street had suffered as much as the station. Every window was boarded up or broken, and there were huge gaps in the line of row houses, blank spaces floored with rubble and twisted iron. Neat piles of relics dotted the pavement. A tea service. Two overshoes. A blue-eyed china doll.

Women and old men picked through the debris, pausing to shout insults at the Jews being loaded into the trucks, holding Ruth and Miriam responsible for the damage. Kathe could not fathom why. She climbed into the back of another Ford, along with Ruth, Miriam, the younger children, and several other families.

Two soldiers in field-gray uniforms hopped up beside Kathe, to sit at the tailgate. The line of trucks lurched into motion, weaving between the bomb craters as if they were oversized potholes. Over the rumble of the wheels, the younger soldier introduced himself as Kurt, offering Kathe the inevitable cigarette. Kathe pointed instead at his canteen. Kurt whipped the top off.

As she drank, Kurt looked her over. "*Juden?*"

She shook her head. "*Deutsche.*"

Kurt shot a surprised look at his companion. The older man scowled. "Communist?"

Kathe gave him a blank look.

"She's too pretty to be a Red," Kurt replied for her. "A criminal, maybe?"

Kathe nodded. She supposed she was, though she could not have named her crime. That satisfied Kurt. They talked about home, and what it was like to be a soldier. Very bad, but not so bad here as in the East. Kurt was from East Prussia, and he never expected to see home again. Whenever Kathe asked where they were headed now, Kurt would veer off onto another subject.

Without warning, the truck swerved, half-colliding with the Opel in front of it. Kathe heard shouts and curses. Before the truck came to rest, Kurt had grabbed her about the waist, lifting her over the tailgate. He leaped, taking her with him, side by side into a ditch. His companion came down on top of them. Ruth and Miriam were still in the truck. But when Kathe lifted her head to look up, Kurt shoved her face back down into the mud.

Lying between the two soldiers, she heard the mad stutter of heavy machine-guns and the rattle of cannon shells, like rocks raining on a tin roof. Shaking off Kurt's grip, Kathe looked up. Fragments flew off the truck. Metal zipped by her head, kicking up tiny fountains of mud.

A huge silver aircraft with stars on its wings shot down the line of trucks, guns clattering. Kathe was buffeted by prop wash and the high-pitched blast of twin Allison engines. Then the plane was gone.

"Der Gabelschwanz Teufel!" The fork-tailed devil. Kurt's companion spat out the Afrika Korps nickname for the Lockheed P-38. "Amerikaner."

"Americans?" Kathe was aghast. "Why are they shooting at us?"

The older man stared at her. Kurt answered evenly, "That is what every soldier wants to know — I suppose it is because we are shooting at them."

The plane did not return. Kathe lay in the mud, listening to screams coming from the back of the truck. As soon as Kurt relaxed his grip, she vaulted out of the ditch and scrambled up the tailgate. The back of the Ford was riddled. A woman was rolling about, clutching her shattered leg, howling in pain. Another was holding a limp child splattered with blood.

Kathe found Miriam, Ruth, and the younger children in a heap near the cab, unhurt but shaken. Kathe tried to calm them while she tore strips from her dress apron, using them to bandage the wounded woman's leg.

Kurt climbed over the tailgate, took one look, and sat down. "You need not bother."

Kathe looked at him. "How can you not help?"

The two soldiers said nothing. Kathe went over to see what she could do for the mother with her bloody child, but the baby was already dead.

Men rolled wrecked trucks into the ditch, and the convoy got moving again. The remainder of the trip was frightful. Children sobbed. The woman with the shattered leg would not stop moaning. The bereaved mother carried on a half-hysterical conversation with her dead baby—until Kurt threatened to throw the little body from the truck.

Kathe sat next to Ruth, hugging her the whole time. She could no longer wait for Dieter. This was too horrible. She had to use the cards, taking Ruth, Miriam, and the children with her—then somehow she would come back for Dieter. Only her fear of moving vehicles kept Kathe from spreading the tarot there in the truck. Instead she sat in a spiritual coma, holding on to Ruth. They had to stop the truck sometime. Prisoners had to be fed. Or at least locked up for the night. Otherwise, what would keep someone from leaping out in the darkness?

Finally the truck stopped. Kathe saw another, smaller rail station, surrounded by beech trees and piles of oiled wooden ties. A station without trains. The train that was supposed to be bringing them had been bombed to smithereens that morning. Guards with MP40s ran up, forming a tight circle around the trucks. Standing at the tailgate, Kathe could see a camp lager beyond the beech trees, barracks rooftops ringed with double rows of barbed wire and high guard towers.

A handsome officer with soft golden hair walked down the line of trucks, carrying a clipboard and a thin, wicked-looking whip. He paused at each truck, ordering women out. Not all the women—just a handful from each truck. The whip scared Kathe, but she took his swastika armband as a sign of good luck, touching the cards hidden in her dress. Soon she would be on solid ground.

The officer stopped at their truck, calling up to Kurt. "How many?"

"Twenty-six."

His blue eyes fixed on Kathe. "You." He motioned with the clipboard. "Out of the truck."

She leaped lightly down. He ordered two more women out. Kathe felt a sick misgiving. The women being selected were all young and good-looking. The mothers with children, the older women, the plain women, were being left in the trucks. She shrank back against a fender, not wanting to be singled out, separated from Miriam and the children. She could imagine only one reason why these men wanted pretty young women.

The man motioned for Ruth. Miriam shook her head, drawing her daughter to her. The officer scowled, staring at Miriam and her children as though they were inert obstructions. His whip tapped against the top of his jackboot. The guard behind him raised the barrel of his MP40.

Kathe stepped quickly forward, putting herself between Miriam and the gun. She reached up and took Ruth's hand, saying, "I will see that she is safe." She spoke in German, but her touch, her smile, her calm assurance, said everything. She had the cards—Ruth was safe, even among these men.

Frantically, Miriam divided her small stock of food, thrusting some sausage and a jar of marmalade into Ruth's arms. The girl descended, clutching her food, holding hard to Kathe's hand. Kathe turned and smiled at the officer, showing him that they would not make trouble.

Their eyes met. In that instant of contact, Kathe realized horrid things were about to happen. The man was not angry. For a moment he seemed to see Kathe as a person, an attractive smiling young woman, risking punishment to please him, to make his task easier. But she saw no feeling in his gaze, no compassion, not even desire—only a mild sort of surprise, instantly replaced by a vast indifference.

The blond officer turned briskly, made marks on his clipboard, and walked on to the next truck. The guard lowered his gun.

Selection done, the trucks rumbled off, trailing clouds of yellow dust, leaving the small knot of young women ringed by guards. Miriam stood at the receding tailgate, tears in her eyes, children clinging to her dress. She shouted thanks to Kathe. She blew a kiss to Ruth. Then they were gone.

# THE ART OF CONVERSATION

*No Gypsy ever voluntarily died for a principle.*
—KONRAD BERCOVICI

Sitting in front of a plain wooden desk in a windowless Dutch cellar, Dieter faced two Gestapo interrogators and an SS light colonel. He talked volumes, trying to be polite but firm with his captors, pretending he still had bargaining power. Dieter gladly confessed to fraud, impersonation, misappropriation of Reich property, and consorting with Gypsies — but he insisted, "My sole desire is to trade valuable paintings for people currently being held for no good reason by the Reich. Göring was willing." The Reichsmarshall might parade about in dressing gowns, makeup, and pinky rings — but he damn well had the right priorities. "If Eichmann is set to trade Jews for trucks — why not accept precious artwork for Gypsies?"

The two Gestapo men glanced at each other, then at the SS man leaning against the unpainted concrete wall — no one was supposed to know that the head of the Jewish Section hoped to trade Jews for more Ford trucks. And Dieter had managed to veer far off the subject. The chief interrogator put his fists down on the desk, leaning forward. "We know for a fact these paintings are forgeries."

"Rubbish." Dieter shook his head. "They are authentic works by Rubens, Hals, and Vermeer. The woodcut is a Dürer."

They dragged in the terrified Herr Direktor Posen to testify about the paintings, sitting him in a stiff-backed chair across from Dieter. "The landscapes are only poor imitations of Rubens . . ."

Dieter interrupted, "They are student works."

Posen looked from him to the Gestapo men, then went on. "But the portrait and the two so-called Vermeers are something totally different. I am really surprised to find them alongside such crude forgeries — since Rubens is much easier to fake." Posen adjusted his spectacles and warmed to his subject. "As you know, Hals and Vermeer are very different artists — but each was a genius, with a delicacy of detail almost impossible to copy. Hals's brushwork and Vermeer's use of light are unsurpassed, the height of the Dutch School. Such amazing falsifications are worthy of the originals."

"They are amazing because they *are* original," Dieter insisted. He spoke to the Gestapo men. "He has passed on the other paintings I delivered. Are the ones hanging in Karinhall fakes as well?" Once more Dieter had managed to drag Göring into the discussion.

The chief interrogator glared at Posen. "How do you know these paintings are forgeries?" Dieter had managed to turn the questioning around. Posen had to back down or admit to being fooled before.

"For one, they are not cataloged in any known collection. . . ."

"Neither were the Rembrandts I got for you," Dieter reminded him.

Posen squirmed in his chair. "The materials prove that these paintings are fakes — very good ones, to be sure. The forger was careful to use paint and canvas identical to sixteenth- and seventeenth-century originals. But paintings age—over time, colors darken, canvas deteriorates. The Vermeers in particular are very freshly painted. Within the last year. The Hals portrait is somewhat older—but not by five hundred years."

"And the Dürer? Is that a forgery? Did you submit it to the same tests?" Dieter smiled, seeing Posen squirm again.

"The Dürer is a problem," Posen admitted.

"How so?" Both Gestapo men and the SS officer were staring at poor Posen, who tried to hide behind his spectacles.

"It too is recent. Done in this century, but . . ." He did not want to finish.

"But you matched it microscopically against another copy of the print, the one in Berlin?"

Posen nodded miserably. "Line by line, they were identical."

"So, what is your explanation?" Dieter seized the upper hand. "Two identical woodcuts—printed five hundred years apart? Ridiculous, eh, Herr Direktor?"

The head interrogator made an icy interruption, to get the session back under Gestapo control. "Perhaps you would explain the paradox?"

Dieter grinned. "Delighted, but . . ." He nodded toward Posen. "The explanation involves vital military secrets, of little interest to the Kaiser Friedrich Museum."

Posen was gratefully dismissed, replaced by two officers—one from the Waffen SS, the other from the regular Wehrmacht. Dieter saw his interrogation progressing splendidly. Posen was disposed of. Now, if need be, he could play the military off against the Gestapo. Eyebrows went up as he plunged into a basic description of time travel.

"Absurd!" the Wehrmacht officer snorted. "Common sense and simple physics prevent it."

Dieter sneered. "Einstein's physics? *Jewish* physics? We Gypsies have discovered a way around it. How else would I have gotten freshly painted Vermeers? Portraits by Hals? Woodcuts by Dürer less than a century old?" Now that Posen was no longer there to object, Dieter presented the paintings as proof.

"How could Gypsies have solved such a monumental problem?" The Waffen SS was skeptical, but interested.

Dieter smiled. "We stole it. Physics in the far future—*German* physics, not Jewish physics—solved the problem of time travel. We Gypsies stole the secret. I can prove what I am saying. What is the date today?" Dieter had been underground too long to be sure.

"September tenth."

Dieter closed his eyes, pausing for dramatic effect like Draga before her crystal ball. "Tomorrow, September eleventh—U.S. troops will enter Luxembourg. The next day they will be in Reich territory. In two days, on September thirteenth, Romania will sign an armistice with the enemy. September fourteenth, the Americans will enter Maastricht. By September fifteenth, Field Marshal Model will move Army Group B headquarters to Oosterbeek." Prediction was no problem, since Dieter had memorized every major military event for the month of September.

"Why should we believe you?"

"You do not have to. Wait four days, and it will all come true. But do not wait too long. The next time gate will open at thirteen hundred hours on September seventeenth. Then I can give you a full demonstration—but I must have the Gypsies on that list. And the woman who was taken with me."

"Why?"

"The Gypsies are to show your faith in me, and that woman alone has the power to unlock the time gate." Despite his warnings, Dieter was positive Kathe had not used the cards. He knew her too well. She would have waited, trying to free him. Senseless, stupid, but just what he must do for her—they would get out together, or not at all.

"I will make one more prediction." He could see them wavering. "Fifty years from now, Germany will have shrugged off the effects of this foolish war—the Reich will rise again, united and stronger than ever. The new Germany will have supersonic jets, T-72 tanks, and nuclear weapons on its soil—some all too loosely guarded. There will also be Germans glad to help you smuggle weapons back here—perhaps enough to change history. Frankly, this is your one chance. Without such aid, Germany will lose the war in less than a year. But you do not need a Gypsy to tell you that!"

The interview dragged on. Dieter repeated himself ad nauseam until it was clear that he would not change his story. The two SS men kept giving him interested looks. The Gestapo left in a huff, hinting they would bring a torture expert from Berlin. Dieter blandly replied that torturing him would hardly beat the Americans.

Days passed underground. Dieter noticed changes in his jailor's attitude. More food. Better food. Cigarettes. Hints of friendliness. All sure signs that his predictions were coming true. His next interrogation was SS only. Wehrmacht and Gestapo had been squeezed out. Dieter had wanted something like this—whoever most needed to believe him would put themselves in charge. He wondered what these SS men had done to make them especially fear defeat.

The session opened with jovial introductions. The head inter-
rogator introduced himself as Obersturmbannführer Friedrich
Wolfard, sitting on one corner of the desk, swinging a polished
jackboot. Dieter casually asked how they had found him out at the
*Schloss*. He wanted to feed the man's smug superiority, letting the
SS think that they were in command.

Wolfard laughed, "The *real* Colonel Harzer has a saber scar."
He traced the line on Dieter's unmarked cheek. "He is with his
division north of Arnhem—perhaps we could arrange an introduction?"

Dieter smiled ruefully. "You might warn him that the Dutch
underground will try to blow the viaduct at Schaapsdrift—on the
night of the fifteenth."

"Another prediction?"

"As true as the ones before."

Wolfard eyed him warily. "You have been astoundingly correct. The part about Marshal Model's headquarters was most convincing. Model did not begin to look for a new command post
until the next morning. Tonight he sleeps in Oosterbeek."

Dieter shrugged. "I could lay out the whole rest of the war for
you, but you would find it depressing."

"Perhaps. First tell us why your demonstration must take place
at thirteen hundred on the seventeenth."

Dieter gave Wolfard his best Gypsy smile. "We use the time
gates, but we did not make them. I can only promise that there
will be an opening at that time. One step and you will be in postwar Germany—a strong and united Germany, where you will find
friends. Perhaps even the weapons to change history." Dieter did
not say it, but Wolfard was wise enough to know that whoever
stepped through need not come back. Why wait around to see
what the Allies' postwar plans were for SS officers? Wolfard at
least could start over in a new Germany. Dieter let him think on
that. Then he added, "But I must have the woman I was with;
without her, the gate will not open."

"Why so?" Wolfard was politely suspicious.

Dieter shrugged again. "Something to do with how time gates
work." He was veering ever further from the truth, but the Nazis'
saving virtue was their grasping stupidity. "That woman has the
talent for opening the gates—otherwise she would not have been
with me."

"I cannot promise anything—she has been sent to a concentration camp."

Dieter had feared that. "If she is dead, the gate will not open.
Then there is no hope of getting to the new Germany."

"And if you are lying, there is little hope for you."

"But of course!" Dieter smiled cheerfully—when a Nazi started to threaten, you knew that you were getting through to him. "Just get the woman, or we are *all* doomed men."

# DER HEXENKESSEL*

*Why was Christ crucified with three nails?*
*Because Gypsies stole the fourth.*
—Gypsy Proverb

Kathe swayed on her feet. Around her were lines of young women—more than ten thousand. They had all been standing since before dawn, being counted. By now the sun was high up, and she shivered with sweat—her head shaved, wearing nothing but a striped prison shirt and stiff Soviet trousers. Ruth stood beside her, slumped and miserable.

"Keep standing," Kathe whispered.

SS women, big-hipped, with hard faces and black boots, walked between the lanes of young women, looking for those who fell, for the weak, the sick, the insolent, or the dispirited. "Keep standing," Kathe repeated. "Here they come."

Ruth straightened up, tightened her lips, and looked forward.

A heaving struggling circle of women shuffled past, herded by a ring of camp guards. The doomed women groaned and sobbed, some cried out. To be tossed into that ring meant death. It meant being stripped, led to an open trench, then machine-gunned or shot in the head by an SS officer.

But this was not a bad selection—only a hundred or so would die this morning. Ten thousand women watched them being dragged away. Kathe stood, eyes front, looking beyond the lanes of women, beyond the terrified circle, beyond the wire and watchtowers, beyond the guards and machine guns. She saw clouds above, and birds soaring easily over the wire.

After roll call, she and Ruth gulped down cold coffee in the barracks, sitting on a hard unpainted bunk. She put an arm around the girl, sharing her coffee and resolve. It had not taken Kathe long to see how the camp worked. "We have to hoard our strength and will. It's the only way to survive."

Ruth gave a shudder. "How can we hope to survive?"

"Look at the Block Elder. She's survived six years, through five camps."

---

* The Witch's Caldron

"I can't take even one year."

"The war will be over in less than a year."

"How do you know?"

"Dieter told me." By May, the war would be done with, though Kathe had no idea who was winning. She kept on talking, half in German, half in Dutch, half to Ruth, half to herself. "When I was your age—years and years ago—I lived through worse than this. I saw my family burned, my village destroyed. I alone survived. In Nijmegen, when the Spaniard had me, they meant to burn me, but I saw Dieter. I told him with my eyes, 'Take me. Take me too.' Again I survived."

She looked out the open barracks door, into the camp compound. Blackened bodies hung from the punishment gallows. Two towheaded girls with unshaved heads played in the dirt by the door. Miriam's little ones had been murdered on the first day, along with their mother. This pair had somehow slipped through—perhaps they were too Aryan to be killed. Kathe sensed an awful arbitrariness about camp survival.

If she had meant to die of despair, she would have done it promptly, on that first day. Guards had hurried her and Ruth into the camp lager, past high fences, barbed wire, and barking dogs. Just inside the wire, they were told to pile their belongings. Suitcases, parcels, blankets, handbags, and loaves of bread landed in a heap. Ruth gave up her sausage and marmalade. The last real food they had touched.

Kathe kept the cards hidden in her dress.

At the next shed, they were told to strip. "Come, come, you must be disinfected. You cannot go into the showers with your clothes on." Women timidly took off their clothes. Dresses, blouses, coats, shoes, and underwear, landed in another heap. Men laughed at such modesty. "*Macht schnell*, into the showers." The bathhouse was cold and dank. There were no stalls. She huddled with Ruth under a showerhead, thinking only of her cards in the pile outside. The outer door clanged shut. Icy water cascaded over them, making her wince. Showering was not the wonder of the century here, the way it had been with Dieter.

There were no clothes waiting for them, just barbers who shaved their heads. Her long golden hair fell to the floor. When they were given clothes, they were not her clothes. Not even women's clothes. Kathe stared dumbly at a pair of men's trousers, reeking of disinfectant. Someone hit her on her naked back. "Stupid Jewess, get dressed! You must have seen how a man puts on his pants."

Inside the barracks, she asked the Block Elder, "Where are my clothes? They said we would get them back."

Five camps ago, the Block Elder had been young herself—now she was drawn and gray. She glared at Kathe. "They lied. Do you think people who would kill truckloads of women and children care about truth?" The Block Elder raised her voice so the whole barracks could hear. "I will tell you once and for all: Your clothes and your possessions are gone. Your families and friends are dead. Your mothers. Your fathers. Your brothers. Your little sisters. They are all dead. Their bodies are being burned. Outside you can see the smoke." An oily pall hung over the camp, all that remained of Miriam and the children. And Kathe's cards. If Kathe had meant to die of despair, it would have been then.

Ruth looked up from her coffee. "Kathe, how old are you?"

Kathe smiled. "Four hundred years. Five hundred. Does it matter? It only matters that I am alive. And as long as I am, I will not let you die."

"And you are not even Jewish."

She shook her head. "I am German—and maybe a little Gypsy." She thought of the time in Vermeer's studio when the painter had shown her his camera obscura, picturing her image on the white canvas. Kathe felt like that image, half-alive, able to move, but turned-about and insubstantial. And she could vanish in an instant if someone blew out the light.

Two shadows blocked the bright doorway. Kathe recognized the short square Block Elder—with her was a man in a peaked cap and jackboots. Dieter? When he stepped into the dim barracks, Kathe saw he was just another SS officer—not a Gypsy in disguise. The Block Elder introduced him respectfully. "This is Obersturmbannführer Wolfard. He has come for you, Kathe."

Kathe reached over and took Ruth's hand, twining their fingers together. She studied the Block Elder's bland face. The woman had repeatedly warned them, "Stick to the barracks. Don't try to escape. Don't ask to go to the hospital. Don't go with men and get pregnant. You will be killed for it." Every so often, SS women came through the barracks, looking for the sick, the listless, looking for anyone lost enough to go with them. Those who did, never came back.

But to disobey, that too was death. She searched for some warning in the Block Elder's face. No warning. Nothing. Just a slight nod, a hint of encouragement that said, "This is something you must do." So she stood up, still holding Ruth's hand. The Block Elder stepped forward to separate them. Kathe pulled the teenager tightly to her, looking straight at the SS man. "This is my sister. We go together."

Standing there in shapeless outfits, heads shaved—they might have been sisters. Kathe smiled broadly, to show that she was not defiant, but that she was determined. They would not be separated except by force. She had let herself be separated from Dieter, from Miriam, from her own family. She would not give up Ruth. If this meant death, they would die together.

Wolfard was annoyed and taken aback. But he was not camp SS. For him, Ruth hardly existed. Half the names on Dieter's list were now dead. Dieter wanted Gypsies—this girl was a Jew. So what? One woman, more or less, what did it matter? "Come," he commanded. Dieter would have to make do with a Jew.

Kathe followed him into the blinking sun, leading Ruth. Women watched them walk across the compound to the camp gate. On the far side of the dogs and wire, a Mercedes staff car waited.

At the car door, Kathe stopped. This man clearly did not mean to kill her. He could have done that in the camp yard, with the pistol in his belt. He needed her for something. Well, she had needs too—so she smiled again. "We are missing dinner. We need food." Dinner was coarse bread spread with greasy margarine—but she made it sound like a meal to be missed.

Wolfard gave an order to his driver. The man produced bread and sausage—fine wheat bread soft as cake, and dark smoked sausage with big flakes of fat and garlic in it. She and Ruth sat in the back of the staff car, tearing happily at the bread and sausage. Wolfard watched, quietly amazed.

The Mercedes took them to a tiny airfield, camouflaged to keep it from being bombed. There they were locked in a shed, with a number of starved and sullen Gypsies—dirty ragged men and women, comforting gaunt hollow-eyed children. Kathe gave them all broad smiles. Gypsies meant Dieter.

Wolfard's driver brought them two cotton dresses with gay summer prints. Kathe and Ruth changed right in front of the driver, shocking the Gypsies—but after the camp, it was nothing to strip in front of strange men. At dusk, they were hustled into a gaunt angular Junkers transport with corrugated-iron skin and three oily BMW engines. It smelled of gasoline and cold metal—but Kathe did not care; finally she had found a machine that would take her to Dieter. Her only regret was that she did not have the cards. The chance to rescue both of them was gone.

The Junkers rumbled out onto the field. Through a window, Kathe could see the dim bulk of a wing and blue exhaust flaring from an engine slung underneath. Gathering speed, the trimotor bounced and rattled as if it meant to fall apart before it could get airborne. Abruptly, the bouncing stopped. Runway lights fell away. They were flying.

Kathe could see nothing of where they were going, but she

sensed vast, endless depths of night beyond the blue exhaust flames. Once they passed an Allied bomber stream—an unforgettable sight. "Christmas tree" flares and flak bursts turned the bomber column into a river of fire. Searchlight beams waved from atop jewel-like flak towers, catching the aircraft in cones of light—a stricken bomber flamed in a dazzling arc, then vanished. Far off, a city was burning. Ghostly orange flames lit up a patch of the darkness. Bombers streamed toward the holocaust, to stoke the fires. It dawned on Kathe that Germany was not just fighting, but losing, losing badly. Night and day death rained down, and nothing seemed able to stop it.

By morning, they were on the ground, riding through Arnhem in a truck. Kathe recognized the old buildings—main streets were wider now, with double lanes for cars. Then they were on the island, the flat expanse of polder between the river forks, whipping past Dreil and Elst. They rumbled over the Waal bridge, through Nijmegen, and up the Groesbeek heights. Bombs kept falling, but by now she expected them.

As Dieter drew closer, Kathe's main concern was that she was coming to him empty-handed, with no hope of saving him or her, or Ruth. The truck took them straight to the field, where they shared a noon meal with the crew of a flak battery sited at the edge of the Reichswald—the men bragged that combat troops got the best food, happy to chat with women, even sickly looking prisoners with shaved heads.

Staff cars arrived. Wolfard was in the first one, wearing civilian clothes. With him was Dieter. Kathe stood up so that he could see her. Dieter said something to Wolfard. The SS man nodded, and Dieter strode over the field toward her, steps lengthening into a run. Kathe could not wait. She set off toward him, with Ruth bounding after her. They met in midfield, hugging, kissing, exchanging greetings.

"You look smashing," he laughed, stroking her starved body through the thin dress.

"I look a mess." She almost cried. "And I lost the cards!"

He shook his head. "A smashing, wonderful mess. Don't worry about the cards."

"But if I had them now, we could be free."

"We will be free. Now who is this?" He nodded to Ruth. Kathe reached out and drew Ruth over to them, telling Dieter who she was.

Wolfard came up. "It's thirteen hundred hours, the seventeenth of September. Where is your time gate?" The field looked empty as ever.

Dieter shot him a smile. "Your watch is fast. Don't worry. You got her here—that is all that matters. Is your team ready?"

Wolfard indicated his group of SS men, dressed like Dieter in nondescript civilian clothes, carrying heavy unmarked attaché cases. Gypsy eyes could tell from the way that the attaché cases were carried that they contained gold bars, twenty-four carat, 99 percent fine. "We have passports made to your specifications." Wolfard handed Dieter one of the little books.

Dieter leafed through it. "Excellent job. Couldn't have done better myself. I hope you have not loaded yourself down with weapons. Where we are going, they will just get you into trouble."

Wolfard shrugged. "A pistol or two. We cannot trust you completely."

"Naturally." Dieter nodded, smiling broadly. "I hardly trust myself half the time. In a few minutes, the time gate will open."

Kathe looked at him, not understanding this nonsense about time gates. Without the cards, they were stranded. He had told her so many times. She had thrown away their only chance.

Suddenly the flak battery opened up. An SS man shouted, "Bombers!" The air throbbed with engines, and Kathe saw a great stream of aircraft appear over the Groesbeek, coming in low from the south, shells bursting around them. Everyone threw themselves down in the furrows. She lay flat between Dieter and Ruth. Wolfard and his men sprawled a few paces off, hugging the earth, waiting for the stream to pass. Staff cars took off, bouncing over the plowed ground, heading for the safety of the Reichswald.

An angry buzz bore down on them. Kathe looked up. A fighter-bomber was making a firing pass over the field. Dieter shouted, "Heads down! It's a Mustang."

Side-slipping, sun at its back, the P-51 dived straight for the flak battery where Kathe had eaten lunch, six .50-caliber guns going. The 40mm flak guns hammered back. Kathe lay terrified, watching the battle between the plane and battery—a head-to-head duel in the afternoon between the Mustang and the guns. Higher overhead, the great river of aircraft filled the Dutch skies. White parachutes were opening in midair. Soldiers were leaping out of the oncoming aircraft, descending through the flak and fighters.

"God in heaven!" moaned an SS man.

The Gypsy families stopped stuffing themselves on German rations and disappeared into the Reichswald. One of them waved jauntily to Dieter as they lost themselves among the trees. Dieter reached out and touched Kathe, squeezing her hand.

"What's happening?" she asked.

He explained that the 505th and 508th regiments of the "All American" 82nd airborne division were landing around them. Behind them, in gliders, was the headquarters of the British First Airborne Corps. Like Maurice of Nassau, they wanted the Waal bridge. The Battle of Nijmegen had begun again.

The drop had come without warning, without pathfinders or advance preparation. Paratroopers landed, discarding their chutes, drawing their guns. SS men scrambled to their feet, hands raised in surrender. Hundreds of Allied soldiers milled about them, thousands more were leaping out of the torrent of aircraft. Kathe saw great long chains of fighters, transports, and towed gliders — from Eindhoven to Arnhem, twenty thousand men, four hundred vehicles, and more than three hundred cannon were descending on Holland by air.

As usual, Dieter alone did not seem surprised. He got up, drawing Kathe and Ruth up with him, dusting their summer dresses. "I'm so sorry. I wish I could have told you, but . . ." He tilted his head toward the SS men. Wolfard saw the nod and shot Dieter a dirty look. "That's why it didn't matter about the cards. There are always more cards. We will find a Gypsy caravan, and be back in business."

An American captain walked up, an unlit cigar clamped in his teeth, a huge crude .45 automatic in one hand. He seemed surprised to find Dieter holding two joyous young women with shaved heads in bright summer dresses. Speaking around his cigar, he asked, "Dutch or German?"

"Oh, no," laughed Dieter. "We are Gypsies!"

The captain looked pleased to hear English spoken so promptly in a Dutch field. "What about them?" He waved his .45 at Wolfard and the others — the American had barely arrived in Holland, but Kathe could see him taking charge. Just as J.R. would do.

"SS officers," Dieter replied. "Out of uniform, carrying false papers and concealed pistols."

"Ya don't say?" The captain grinned and reached into his pocket. "Well, have a goddamn cigar, Mr. Gypsy! You've just been liberated!"

# Four kings and an ace

## THE GOLDEN GATE

*They are a harmless race when white men leave them alone or treat them no worse than dogs. . . . A disorderly Chinaman is rare, and a lazy one does not exist.*
—MARK TWAIN

Eighty days out of Hong Kong, carrying coolies and opium, the clipper *City of Canton* sailed through the Golden Gate. Leaning hard against the starboard rail, Boy Toy saw yellow Marin hills part onto a great blue bay. Her black hair framed a pure, youthful face, full of joy at seeing her new homeland after waiting so long and coming so far. Boy Toy's happiness had an appealing innocence, not a child's innocence—though she was barely fifteen— but the studious, educated innocence of a girl who knew nothing of men, of money, or of the world, nothing but what she had read in books. It was the innocence of a young woman who knew only the love of the parents she had lost in Old China.

Standing at the starboard rail, she could see the city on the hill, the city that the coolies belowdecks called Gum San Ta Fow—Big City in the Land of the Golden Hills. Boy Toy knew its true name, San Francisco, California—a strange name, neither Cantonese nor English. To her, San Francisco looked like a city half finished, sprawling over the hills, fraying at the edges into tents and shantytowns, not standing foursquare with the world the way a Chinese city would. Sandlots and barren hillsides gaped between rows of rooftops, as though huge hands had flattened buildings to make room for more construction. This strangeness did not bother Boy Toy because she knew the city was built by free men. Just to feel free pavement beneath her silken slippers would be a miracle.

Whistles cut the air. Bare feet thundered over oak planking, and Boy Toy watched sunburned bodies swarm into the rigging, filling the yards with men. She marveled that the men stood motionless, making no attempt to slow the hurtling ship. Black arched bow foaming straight for the shore, the *City of Canton* careened under a mountain of white canvas toward an anchorage dotted with square riggers, coastal steamers, and fishing smacks.

Boy Toy heard the stern anchor drop, dragging its rattling chain. She stood on tiptoes, seeing the crew madly pull in sail. By the time she heard the bow anchor splash into the bay, every spar was bare, every sail was furled from spanker to flying jib. The crew had taken in almost an acre of canvas before the speeding ship ran the length of her stern chain. Few crews could come flying into harbor like the *City of Canton* could. Few clippers could claim twenty years on the China run.

To Boy Toy, the crew's easy competence was merely another wonder. Seeing free white men leaping about like monkeys, answering shouts and whistles, assured her she was really coming to America. In Old China no one worked like that. Straw-hatted peasants tilled the soil and coolies sweated in the ditches, but white men and Mandarins rode in rickshaws and palankeens, cursing the half-naked laborers clogging their path. The wind that carried Boy Toy across the Pacific had changed all that.

Before Boy Toy could walk the streets of Gum San Ta Fow, she had to crowd into the customshouse with the coolies off the *City of Canton*. She was impressed and pleased that such an important building should be a shabby clapboard structure, with no formal garden, no walled antecourt, not even a simple spirit screen. Young men speaking country Cantonese stood in long lines with tired pale faces, pigtail queues, and dirty blue blouses — strong backs with overwilling hands, smelling of sweat, opium, and bilgewater. Boy Toy was delighted, smelling democracy in the coolies' fish-oil breath, seeing justice in the simple architecture of the hall and in the lines moving slowly toward wooden desks. Crude honesty was everywhere. No Manchu court or customs hall would look so poor, nor proceed without formal kowtowing and favoritism. In Old China every pompous court official demanded his due, and nothing got done.

She waited until the end to take her turn. Be pleasant, be

polite, she thought, these are my people now. Nothing stood between Boy Toy and freedom but a lean man sitting at a big desk and wearing a blue frock coat, opened at the throat to show off his dirty shirt and sweaty chest. Though he had an important post, he seemed not to have bathed or shaved so far this week. He asked for her papers in pathetic Cantonese.

Trembling with pleasure, she replied in gentle and precise English. "Dear sir, here is my letter of introduction from the American Missionary Society." She used English to save this funny sweating man from trying to conduct his business in Cantonese, which he clearly could not speak.

"Damn." The man sat up in his seat as though the post beside him had spoken. "I never heard a singsong girl speak such good American." Bloodshot eyes looked her over, lingering on the slit in her white *chengosams*.

"I was taught by my foster parents, Minister and Mrs. Jonathan Clay. It is all in the letter." She pointed to the document, politely directing his gaze away from her hips.

He glared, as if a talking China Girl was not all to the good. "The *City of Canton* was not supposed to be carrying joy girls, not even talking ones."

"Joyful girls?" She smiled at the funny man. How could she be anything but joyful, now that she was in America?

"Sure, joy girls—singsong girls, pay-per-day girls—appears your English is not as good as you say." He looked down at the paper. "Are you really fifteen?"

Boy Toy nodded. The feeling of adventure faded; she felt less like talking, more like getting past this big sweaty obstacle. He pushed her letter back across the desk. "Says here the Clays are conveniently dead."

It felt like the fool in a frock coat had leaned forward and slapped her. Her parents had been dead less than a year, and she wore only the pure white of mourning. The man settled back, enjoying her discomfort. "You could hardly fool me. I have seen every sort of false paper and forgery used to get China Girls into the country, but this has to be the thinnest. With your English, you could just claim reentry."

Boy Toy stared at him, wondering why he looked for lies, why he preferred falsehood from her. "No need to look surly," he added. "I am letting you in. Hell, I enjoy a quick and clever China Girl as much as any man might. Just don't think you are tricking me, and remember what I have done for you if we meet in a *bagnio*." He said this with bored hopefulness, as if he knew not to look for gratitude from girls like her.

Humiliated, Boy Toy hurried through the door he indicated.

Her heart fell when it did not lead to the street. Instead she found herself in a small cubicle containing a grinning older man, who claimed to be a doctor and did an inane pantomime to indicate she should undress. "Doctor, doctor," he thumped his chest like an asthmatic having an attack. "You takee clothes off, pleez."

Boy Toy wanted to flee, but the door behind her led back into the customs hall. She started to speak, then thought better. Do not anger him; this man has the power to keep you out of the Land of the Golden Hills. Trapped and crushed, she undid her *chengosams.*

The old fellow grinned and bobbed his head, absurdly happy to be understood. Staring at the wooden planks between her feet, she neatly folded her silk *chengosams.* Blouse and pants followed. She looked past her bare belly at her nude legs and splayed toes while the man poked and felt her, enjoying his job, saying crude things about her private parts as if she could not hear him.

Then he stuck her with a needle, saying this would cost her "ten-dolla," rubbing the red spot he made on her smooth thigh. "Can savee money," he said. "Just bend down and makee me happy man." Spraying spittle as he spoke, the doctor pantomimed pulling down his pants. Hiding behind her newfound ignorance, Boy Toy pretended not to understand. He gave up and let her dress, taking her money instead.

Dulled with shame, passed from scum to scum, Boy Toy stepped out onto the free streets of San Francisco. Sunlight spilled over the Embarcadero. Blinking back tears, she saw the waterfront was crowded with yelling men. Coolies cowered under the eaves of the customshouse, holding up their hands to protect their heads, while a knot of white men in a nearby sandlot threw stones and garbage at the Chinese. They hurled insults too, but not in clear or correct English. Boy Toy could barely make out the shouts of "Ho-war, Ho-war," directed at her.

America was not what she had expected. Old China had been bad, even evil sometimes, but at least it made sense. San Francisco was a madhouse, a big barbarian asylum with the inmates running wild. A stone grazed her cheek. Clods splattered her white silks.

Four men pushed forward, appearing from nowhere, putting themselves between her and the mob. It was like in an old story when four guardians step straight down from heaven. Boy Toy did not know who they were, but they moved light and quick, like Boxers, wearing plain blue pants and padded jackets. She just felt grateful to be shielded. Their leader was a moonfaced fellow with big hands and a broken nose. He said something in country Cantonese, and the living box started up the street, away from the docks and customshouse. Boy Toy moved quickly to keep up with the magic box.

A big man with sunburned arms and a brick in his hand tried to block their way, squinting and shifting from side to side, glancing to see if his cronies would back his play. The lead Boxer walked right up to him, folded his hands into his padded sleeves and bowed, saying in polite but common Cantonese, "Please step aside, Stupid White Devil."

The big man hefted his brick and looked over his shoulder. None of his fellow heroes were stepping forward. The barbarian towered over Boy Toy's protector, but she could see he was afraid. Stammering a curse, the man stepped aside, letting the moving box march past. Boy Toy could barely believe it. The broken-nosed Boxer had spoken like a clod with dung between his toes, insulting a white man, but the white man backed down as easily as a coolie being ordered about. She had seen stark fear in the red-faced devil's watery eyes.

She studied the Boxer's flat basic features. His only hint of refinement was in his walk, which had the balanced effortless grace of a man schooled in the martial arts. She had seen such men in China, unstoppable assassins who walked up walls and across water, able to kill with a stick, a length of chain, or the flat of the hand. No wonder the barbarian with a brick had backed down. She hesitated, then asked, "Are you Triads?"

The Boxer's hard face softened. He smiled and nodded to her. "We are Hip Yee Tong. Your speech is like music."

Boy Toy lowered her eyes, modestly ending their conversation. Hip Yee Tong meant Hall of United Justice. These were Triads, from the secret Society of Heaven and Earth, enemies of the Manchus, warriors from the New China. She could hardly be in better hands.

Straight and proud they marched into a dirty, smelly city swarming with people, mostly men, of all colors and races: brown *Californios*, red-shirted miners, blanketed Indians, and hard-looking sharpies wearing silk hats and Colt revolvers. Spanish ladies in creamy lace shared the sidewalks with tobacco-spitting bullwhackers carrying black coiled whips. Buildings opened straight onto the street, and only the red-roofed adobes were turned inward the way a proper house should be. Passing a green park, they climbed a hill where she could see the full sweep of the city and the glittering blue bay. Cable cars clattered and swayed, moving uphill by some mysterious means. A strange new world indeed.

Turning off Clay Street onto Dupont Gai, they plunged into another city, one more familiar to Boy Toy. Here the very air was different, denser, smelling of fish, incense, opium, heavy spices, and open privies. The men thronging around her were Chinese, wearing blue blouses, baggy pants, and black braided queues. Dupont Gai, old Dupont Street, ran right through a truly Chinese city, with people piled on top of people and not a hand's span of space wasted. All along the east side of the street, banners and wall posters proclaimed in bold characters TEMPLE OF LUCK AND PROSPERITY or PIPES AND LAMPS ALWAYS LIT.

Despite the privies and opium dens, despite the Temples of Luck, Boy Toy did not doubt that this was the New China, without Manchus or Mandarins. Here the secret brotherhoods operated in the open, protecting the weak, fearing not even white villains in a white city. She saw no hordes of beggars, just men working—men's voices, men's faces. Where were the women in the New China?

They turned, descending stone steps and entering a dark tunnel through a doorway framed with heavy timbers. Light dimmed, and for a moment Boy Toy was blinded, but ahead she heard women's voices. She followed that sound, rounding a carved spirit screen and entering a cavernous underground room lit by paper lanterns. The closed-in air was sweetened with incense. Walls were windowless, painted in bright colors, half hidden by lacquered paneling. Young women sat on graying redwood benches, facing a bird-thin old woman who was holding up a small coin.

"Two bits," the young women said in unison.

Boy Toy stood watching without speaking. The crone held up two coins together. "Fifty cents," said the young women.

She held up a greenback bill.

"One dollar."

Useful information no doubt, but Boy Toy was already familiar with the Almighty Dollar. She grew bored and looked about. Her four protectors had vanished, going like ghosts, but she seemed safe enough; the heavy door behind her was barred, and she was surrounded by solid cement walls. Besides the crone and her pupils, Boy Toy saw only a rouged white woman with puffy eyes, sitting in a corner.

The crone held up two bills.

"One lay," said the women.

Boy Toy's head snapped around. She stared at the lesson. Seeming pleased by the answers, the crone put down the money and said in passable Cantonese, "Come, you must learn too."

"I do not need lessons." Boy Toy rattled off, "Two bits, twenty-five cents; four bits, fifty cents; one dollar, a hundred cents." She ignored the last part of the lesson, which had sounded vulgar and unchristian.

The flood of flawless English startled everyone. Pupils giggled over the old lady's surprise. The lone white woman in the corner got up and came over to Boy Toy. "Who are you?" Boy Toy saw lively curiosity in the woman's puffy eyes.

"My name is Boy Toy."

"How come I never heard of you?"

Boy Toy said she had been in San Francisco less than an hour and was not at all famous. Every word out of her lips amazed the white woman even more. She turned to the crone, "Hell, do the Hip Yees know what they got here?"

The birdlike woman rocked her head, suspicious that her routine might be broken. "Listen to her talk," insisted the white woman. "If she don't bring three thousand dollars, then screw me with a goddamned egg roll."

Nothing made sense to Boy Toy. "Three thousand dollars for what?"

"For you," said the white woman, "for a pretty young singsong girl who speaks so well."

"No," said Boy Toy, "I did not come to San Francisco to sing. I came to learn missionary work."

The crone seized on a word she understood. "Missionaries are devils. They beat girls and do not let them see men, making them learn the Lord's Prayer instead." The white woman waved the crone off, sitting Boy Toy down on a bench, saying in a motherly way, "My name is Mollie Maguire. You must tell me where you learned to talk like that."

Boy Toy told her, relieved to meet someone not just amazed by her words, but actually willing to listen. "I was raised by Mr. and Mrs. Jonathan Clay, American missionaries. As a child, I never thought of them as anything but mother and father, never thought of myself as anything but American; only slowly did I discover that I was Chinese too. My Chinese family must have been murdered by Manchu troops, so many villages were destroyed that way. My American parents died last year, and I was doubly an orphan, without parents and without a homeland. Missionaries in Canton raised enough money to pay my passage home." Boy Toy did not describe the horrible treatment at the customshouse. Why burden this nice woman with that ugly story? Instead she asked, "Where am I now?"

"This is called the Queen's Room. Every China Girl who comes to San Francisco comes here." Mollie moved closer and took her hand. "I know what you are feeling. Long, long ago I came to America with my head full of foolish notions."

"You came to be a missionary." Boy Toy brightened.

"Well, no," Mollie shook her head. "I wanted to be a Fenian, to fight the British, burn the bastards out of Canada, but that's a lot like being a missionary."

Boy Toy said nothing, but to her the two ambitions sounded very different. Mollie gave her a sorry smile. "There are a lot of things you cannot understand, having never been to County Cork. That's not important now. Look, you are not going to be a missionary. The only missionary work you are going to learn is how to screw on your back with your legs spread and eyes fixed on heaven."

Boy Toy looked aghast. "What you say is obscene. The Triads will protect me."

"The Triads?"

"The men who brought me here."

"Those were highbinders," said Mollie.

"Highbinders?"

"Yes, hoodlums, *boo how doy*, Hip Yee hatchet men. They go down to the boats to get girls."

"Not so, the secret brotherhood in China teach men to drink pure and clear water, not the wine of brothels."

"Well, that may be the way it is in China, but here in San Francisco the Hip Yees drink like salmon and screw like the Irish. You will get no help from them."

Boy Toy sat down, feeling the solid strength of the windowless walls and barred door. "This is not possible. Here in America we have democracy."

"Hell, honey," said the Irish woman, "this ain't America, this is San Francisco. Sure, they close the bars on election day and let Bog Irish vote, but there is no democracy for China Girls. The only democracy working girls see is in the *bagnios*, since men are pretty near equal with their pants down—not more than a few inches difference anyways."

Boy Toy closed her mouth tight, no longer liking to speak English when the conversation was becoming so unchristian. Mollie tried to explain that this was the wrong attitude. "Look, you have an appealing innocence, which makes a man want to protect you. Makes him want to take you somewhere private and screw you good and solid, but treat you right afterward. You need to use that innocence."

Boy Toy would not speak. She sat silently winding up her will. She would be neither a whore nor a concubine; she would not be used in an unchristian way. They could not make her. They could lock her underground, they could starve her and beat her, but in the end they would have to kill her. She would join her parents as pure as the white silk *chengosams* she was wearing. She sat wishing she had never left Canton, where the silver mist off the Pearl River rises over a landscape shimmering in seven shades of green. Why had she believed her father's fables about America?

Mollie gave up and left, grumbling that it was impossible to help the Chinese.

Boy Toy sat alone, dully listening to the crone's lessons. She heard the girls repeat handy phrases like "pleez-pey-furst" and "no-brass-nuggets," while the crone described all manner of unmentionable ways to "pleez" a man. Cackling with delight, she explored every possible penetration of female orifices by the aroused male member. Between each gross anatomy lesson, she sprinkled bits of wisdom: "Look for the ugly ones. Ugly men are good as gold. They only want to feel handsome by putting their turtle heads into a woman. Handsome men look good, but want more. They want what their wives and sweethearts will not give them."

Boy Toy felt herself going crazy with fear. She tried to think of the strength of women, the strength of nature that is mother to us all. She prayed for the yielding consistency of a stream that wears down the largest boulder into a tiny pebble, for the strength of water that bursts concrete walls. Her mother had told her a Chinese story that was very Christian. Kwan Yin, the Earth Mother, had taken the form of a young girl. Because she would not give herself, Kwan Yin was executed, her body tied to a tiger, and her pure spirit descended to the Land of the Dead. Like Boy Toy she was locked underground, threatened with shame and torment, but Kwan Yin did not give in. When the King of the Dead could no longer stomach her purity, he cast her back among the living. So it will be with me, she decided. I will stay pure, even if I am dragged down to the Land of the Dead.

The *barracoon* began to fill with men in silk jackets and black caps; fat happy men, their shining faces studying the women with professional disinterest. Other girls dropped their gaze, but Boy Toy looked boldly back at them, saying with her eyes that they could not break her.

She saw Mollie push through the crowd, with two white men behind her. One was tall and thin with a high forehead, long straight nose, and small black mustache. He wore a silk waistcoat and carried a silver-knobbed ebony cane. His companion was small and shabby, bald-headed, wearing a gray suit and official-looking badge.

Mollie knelt beside Boy Toy. "Look, I have come to help you, honey. Show these men your letter. Tell them your story."

The tall man looked dignified, and the shabby man was some sort of official, but Boy Toy trusted no one now; least of all Mollie, who wanted her to become a prostitute. She said nothing, meeting their gaze with silent resistance. Mollie begged her, pointing to the other men in silk robes and happy coats. "These are buyers for the *bagnios*: Yat Sing from Yreka, Yep Shung from Rough and Ready, Hing Yo from down south. If you clam up and play dumb, some fool will buy you for a few hundred bucks. He'll stick you in a closet-sized crib, letting men screw you for a couple of dollars apiece, dollar-fifty a prick for parties. I will tell you that girls die from that." She pointed out a man with a pockmarked face. "That is the doctor who checks girls for disease. You get too sick to work, and he will turn you out to starve or strangle you with that cord around his waist."

Boy Toy looked at the pockmarked man, with his red silk cord and cold uncaring eyes, like fish eyes. She reached into her sleeve and pulled out her letter of introduction, handing it to the tall stranger. "My name is Boy Toy. I am the adopted daughter of Mr. and Mrs. Jonathan Clay, of Akron, Ohio, American missionaries to China."

Mollie beamed at the men. "Didn't I tell you the girl could talk?"

The tall thin man took her letter and looked it over. "Indeed she can. I am pleased to meet you, Miss Boy Toy. My name is Stanley Lealand." He turned to the stubby little man. "Ned, this is an amazing story. Did you ever hear the like?"

Ned shook his head and said nothing. His jaws were working, but he appeared to be chewing a cud. Lealand apologized for his friend's silence. "Ned here is struck speechless. Ned Bailey is with the Chinatown Police, and he surely never saw a China Girl who held her head so high." Lealand's eyes twinkled. "I bet you even show your teeth when you smile."

Boy Toy smiled, shaking with relief.

Lealand turned back to Ned. "Buy her," he said, "no matter what she costs."

Stunned, she watched Lealand spin about and stride off, taking her letter with him. Mollie's arm was around her middle. "See how easy that was? No *bagnio* crib for you, Boy Toy. Mr. Lealand owns the best sporting house on the coast; got a grand piano, feather beds, Italian paintings, silk sheets, and satin swings. Can't ask for better coming right off the boat."

"He has my letter." Boy Toy struggled to her feet.

Ned spit a big wad of tobacco onto the spotless floor. "He will have more of you than that, or I miss my guess." He called to the crone, "Get the bidding going. Mr. Lealand has made his choice."

Everyone crowded around to see what the white men were bidding on. The crone commanded Boy Toy to be silent, threatening her in Cantonese with dire and shameful punishments. The other buyers wanted her stripped. A rich fool might bid on a sealed package, but they were men of business.

"No," said Boy Toy. Mollie took her hand. "Look, in this business you have to get used to taking your clothes off; it's like getting dressed for work." The crone told her that her clothes would be ripped off, and she would get a beating on the soles of her feet where it would not show. She added she had never seen a girl so ungrateful.

Completely betrayed, Boy Toy undressed to save her *chengosams*. Again she stood shamed and naked, though what had happened in the customshouse was a pleasantry compared to standing naked in this circle of men, knowing worse was coming. She hated their fishlike faces and gaping mouths, and wanted to drive her nails into their glassy eyes. Yep Shung from Rough and Ready began the bidding at $1,000.

The policeman called Ned's bid, "Fifteen-hundred dollars. What do you want her for, Yep Shung? Up in the Sierras they will screw anything prettier than a she-mule." Yep Shung bowed politely, dropping out when the bidding passed $2,000.

Naked and alone, thinking of the water and the rock, Boy Toy listened to the bids mount. In the end there was only Ned Bailey and a man from Los Angeles named Hing Yo. She thought about what the crone had said. For a white man Stanley Lealand was handsome, and she feared what he would do to her to get his money's worth. Already he seemed like the King of the Dead.

Ned outbid Hing Yo, and Boy Toy was bought for $3,700. Ned said in a good-natured way that white men had been cheated again. "You Celestial bastards always overbid to drive the price up. Draw up her contract and deliver her to Mr. Lealand." The crone replied that her price honored everyone; Boy Toy, the Hip Yee Tong, and Mr. Lealand most of all. Ned gave them a last look at Lealand's purchase, then let her dress.

Mollie and the crone led Boy Toy to a little room, thick with joss smoke. The crone fingered Boy Toy's *chengosams*, saying, "So gloomy. Men do not like to see so much white." She handed Boy Toy a black jacket. "Here, wear something cheery." Boy Toy pulled on the oversized jacket, huddling inside its padding. The crone slipped a paper covered with characters into the jacket pocket. "This is your contract."

Boy Toy did not even glance at the document. Stanley Lealand wanted $3,700 worth of use from her, and she did not want to know how he would get his money's worth.

The Boxers who brought her came to take her away. Back in the moving box, she felt trapped, knowing they were taking her not to the New China, but to the King of the Dead. Already her life felt finished. She was surprised to see that it was night outside. She had spent almost the whole day underground. Dragon-tail banners hung limp over wet dark streets shrouded in fog and woodsmoke. Paper lanterns lit bits of pavement, splashing brick walls with yellow pools of light. Passing curtained windows, Boy Toy could feel the warmth of taverns, joss houses, and gambling dens, all smelling of incense or opium.

She studied the Boxer who was leading them, since he seemed her only hope. Speaking slowly and softly she said, "You must not do this."

The man's head snapped about, but he did not stop walking. She attempted to stop, and the moving box jostled her along from one lantern pool to the next. "You know this is not honorable. You must not make me go. There is no place for slavery in the New China."

"You must be silent," said the Boxer. "We must accept. It is not for us to judge." His voice was not harsh, just firm. Boy Toy could see the sort of man he was, a bright unsheathed blade that cut without questioning.

From up the street Boy Toy heard a tapping, a gentle rapping that grew louder as they advanced, like hardwood hitting the pavement. The Boxer stopped speaking. Boy Toy saw his walk slow, his body loosen, and his hands slip into his sleeves.

In the next circle of light stood a man and a woman. The man was not Chinese, and built like a busted barrel with his belly hanging over his belt. He wore a baggy white suit and a frayed strawhat tipped back over a pitted, craggy face. A skinny little cigar was clamped between his teeth. One elbow rested on an upturned suitcase, and the other hand held an ax handle. He was absently tapping the ax handle against the brick pavement.

The woman beside him was even stranger still. She was older than the man and had black skin, a black dress, and a black kerchief binding her hair. Her eyes had large whites, deep-set and staring. A feeling of casual power hung over both of them.

The moving box halted. The stranger brought his ax handle up, holding tight to the slim curved wood, resting the business end lightly on his palm. He wore tiny glass spectacles, and Boy Toy watched them turn from her to the lead Boxer. "Hello, Mau Yee." He spoke in the flat, benign voice of a country preacher on a social call. "Yer gonna have to give up the girl."

The Hip Yee Boxer did not speak, but shook his head, keeping his hands in his sleeves.

"Mau Yee," the man drew the name out, "I admire a man who works hard for his bowl of rice, but you are going to have to give her up. There is no way around it."

The Hip Yee's hand came flying out of his sleeve. His whole body extended, sending something bright and metallic spinning through the lamplight toward the stranger, whirring as it went.

The fat man's ax handle came up, protecting his face. He pivoted from the hips, swinging the big bat as though the wood were an extension of his hands. The whirling object hit the ax handle, wrapping around it, clawing the air like a living thing. Boy Toy could see it was three lengths of chain weighted with spiked balls, forming a wicked steel bolo. Grasping the thick end of the ax handle, the big man flicked it free of the chain, sending Mau Yee's glittering weapon spinning off into the darkness to clatter against a wall.

The black woman stepped forward. Keening in a strange tongue, she raised an object over her head and shattered it on the pavement at their feet. Yellow smoke billowed in the lamplight, spreading slowly outward, carrying a heady overpowering odor. The air tingled and Boy Toy's head swam. As the smoke continued to spread, the black woman seemed to dissolve into it. There was a screech like a hundred cats mating, and a black cat the size of a horse sprang out of the choking smoke. The huge apparition had eyes like yellow fire and snarled as it stalked toward them, moving with the smoke.

Boy Toy stood rooted, not daring to look away. At either hand, she heard the fast scuffle of retreating feet as three of the Tongs turned and ran. Only Mau Yee stood his ground. Reaching into his jacket, he drew out a steel hatchet with a stubby handle.

The fat man and the cat advanced together. Mau Yee sprang, holding his hatchet sideways, blade forward. The white man took a swipe at him with his ax handle. Turning sideways in midair, the Boxer let the ax handle slide by him, then he brought his feet down sharply, catching the wood against the pavement. With a sharp report the ax handle shattered.

The big cat snarled, tensing as if to spring. Smoke streamed from the beast, making her seem afire. Mau Yee turned again, trying to keep between the feline monster and Boy Toy.

The white man tossed away his broken weapon. His hand went inside his coat and came out holding a sawed-off shotgun. Two gaping barrels less than a foot long pointed right at the Boxer's middle. "Mau Yee," he said slowly. "We are making this fight more serious than it needs to be. You cannot get her away without killing me. We know what will happen if you kill a white man in front of witnesses. The whole Hip Yee Tong will suffer. The Irish will come in and bust up your joss houses, burn down your Jackson Street restaurant. Maybe hang a few Hip Yees. It won't matter to them who's right, or that you were just doing business."

The cat started to circle. As the panther edged behind him, Mau Yee had to move sideways to see both ways at once. The stifling yellow smoke filled the whole street. Stepping toward Boy Toy, the white man with the shotgun clamped his free hand about her wrist. "I hear you speak English."

Scared by the ghost cat and the man's gun, Boy Toy merely nodded.

"Well, thank goodness for that," said the fat man. "So come with me, unless you want to see a Hip Yee blown in half. That is not a pretty sight, even in poor light."

Boy Toy said she would go. What could be worse than being taken to the King of the Dead? Backing away from Mau Yee, the white man shouldered his suitcase and propelled Boy Toy up the empty street. She ran, and he pushed, with the yellow-eyed panther padding after them. As the man steered her around a corner into a narrow alley, the highbinder's hatchet whizzed between them, cartwheeling through the night and fog.

# THE MONTEREY SPUR

*The Chinaman is a great convenience to everybody—even to the worst class of white men, for he bears the most of their sins, suffering fines for their petty thefts, imprisonment for their robberies, and death for their murders.*

*—MARK TWAIN*

The big man and the huge black cat sped Boy Toy down the dark alley, then up a flight of rickety wooden stairs and onto a flat roof. There she could make out the lights of Dupont Gai threading through the fog of Chinatown. Crossing the rooftop, they came to a second building, flush against the first, but half a story higher. The cat leaped to the second rooftop in a single fluid motion. Boy Toy felt the man grasp her waist and hoist her overhead. There was no time to feel alarmed. His gnarled hands were strong and steady, and his fat body felt as solid as a sack of iron. His suitcase landed on the roof beside her, and a moment later he was there too, shouldering the suitcase and telling her to hustle.

Scrambling through the night, she followed the cat as best she could. A black crevasse separated this roof from the next. The cat leaped lightly over the yawning gap, and the man herded Boy Toy across a narrow plank. On the other side he turned to dispose of the bridge. Boy Toy paused, watching him tuck the plank behind an abutment. Without looking, the man growled, "Get going, girl. Got bound feet, or something?"

She hurried after the cat. Crossing to another building, they descended a fire stair on the far side. The cat ducked into a dark curtained window, and here Boy Toy balked. The room within was a black pit. Below she could see Stockton Street and the lights of the American city beyond. Dupont Gai was blocks away. They had crossed half of Chinatown without once touching the ground.

The man came down the fire stair behind Boy Toy, chiding her and helping her through the window. He came in after her, his big form blotting out the streetlights. Boy Toy felt the man's suitcase thump down beside her, and she heard his labored breathing in the dark. Fumbling, he muttered something about "Damned Locofocos," and struck a light. Blinded by the flaring match, Boy Toy could see nothing until the man managed to light an oil lamp and set it on an upturned crate. She was in a small spare room, with a single door opposite the window and no furniture except for a few packing crates and a small cast-iron stove. There was no sign of the giant cat. Slumped in one corner was a gaunt dark-skinned man with a mass of kinked hair falling in great tangled curls to his shoulders. He wore a torn shirt and canvas pants, and sat on a frayed Navaho blanket. Another Navaho blanket was wrapped around his skinny shoulders.

By the light of the lamp the fat man looked more than ever like he had fallen in a ditch and let his suit dry on him. Without looking at Boy Toy he said, "My name is Aaron Maria Spinoza. The fellow who was sitting in the dark is King Ahab. King Ahab, this is Boy Toy."

"Was not sitting in the dark," said the man in the corner. "King Ahab was sleeping until Mama Love came banging through the window. You wasn't too quiet, neither."

"Where is the cat?" The big cat was the only thing Boy Toy could think about. It was the most astonishing thing she had ever seen; frightening yet protective, very otherworldly. "I saw it come in the window."

"King Ahab, you see a cat?" The man who called himself Aaron Maria knelt down, flicking the latches on his suitcase.

"Me see only Mama Love." King Ahab adjusted his blankets.

Boy Toy was too drained to argue. She had seen the cat, so had the three highbinders who took to their heels. She watched the fat man pull a long gun out of his suitcase. "What is that for?"

"Distance work." Aaron broke open the trapdoor breech and inserted a shell. "Springfield .45-55 carbine, the best rifle for under five hundred yards." He snapped the breech shut. "Some swear by magazine rifles, more shots and all, but I never seen a magazine gun good at any distance. Hit the first time and you don't need extra shots." He laid the Springfield down on the floor next to his sawed-off shotgun, a 10-gauge Whitney. "A Springfield will jam on you, but if you stick to the 55-grain factory loads, you'll have no problem with a cold piece."

Boy Toy could see a Colt Lightning revolver and a two-foot Bowie knife strapped to the interior of the battered suitcase, which contained a shoulder holster and numerous boxes of cartridges. "Do you always go around armed like this?"

"Only when I am working, ma'am." He removed the stubby revolver from the suitcase, pushed it through his belt, then leaned back against the packing crate that supported the lamp.

"Who are you working for?" Boy Toy stared at the small arsenal Aaron was keeping in reach.

"I am a Range Detective and an authorized agent of the Carmel Valley–Watsonville Grange. In San Francisco on business, more or less legitimate, so you need not worry."

She sighed and sat down. By now so much had happened that Boy Toy was beyond worrying.

Aaron took some oily paper out of his pocket. Wrapped inside were a dozen cold corn tortillas. He bit into one and gave another to Boy Toy. "So tell me about your day. We have most of the night to talk."

Dazed and hungry, she bit into the tortilla and started to describe her day, beginning with the crowd of strangers at the dock who threw garbage on her, skipping over the degrading "medical" examination.

"Bog Irish," said Aaron, taking a light view of her troubles. "Shouldn't let them bother you. They just ain't got the sense to see where their interests are. They are afraid that coolies are going to take their jobs away. If they stopped to consider, half of them would discover they did not have jobs. Besides, can you picture an Irishman doing laundry? Who would bring their cleaning to a man who never washed his shirt?"

She told him about the Triads who took her to the Queen's Room.

"Hip Yees," he said. "They meet every boat to grab girls and sell them as prostitutes. I cannot say I like it, but it is their rice bowl."

King Ahab asked, "Do you have any paper?"

Aaron stuck one paw into his pocket and pulled out two thin pieces of paper covered with characters. He gave them a puzzled glance peering over his glasses, then turned to Boy Toy. "Do you read, girl?"

"Only English, French, and Chinese."

"Here, take these." He handed her the papers. "One is yours. The other is the laundry ticket for my suit. Give the ticket to King Ahab."

Boy Toy separated the papers and passed the laundry ticket to King Ahab, staring at the other document. "This is my contract. How did you get it?"

"Took it out of your jacket when I lifted you up to that roof. Thought it might be important, and in the dark I did not know it was Chinese."

King Ahab sprinkled the laundry ticket with some crushed leaves, shaking his head. "She reads chicken scratches?"

"Didn't you hear the lady? She knows American, French, and Chinese. She is a goddamn China Girl genius." Reaching into his pocket, he took out a five-tael tin of opium and passed it to King Ahab. "Sprinkle some of this in the mix, makes the hemp burn sweeter."

"This is horrible," said Boy Toy softly, reading through her contract. It did not seem as dangerous now, but it was coldly nauseating to see her name in a viper's pit of lies. "It says I was paid thirty-seven hundred dollars. And I must work twelve years to pay it back. For every week I am sick they add a month. Can this possibly be enforceable in court?" It seemed that everything her father had said about America was a carefully constructed falsehood.

Aaron was watching King Ahab roll the hemp and opium into the rice-paper laundry ticket. "Nothing in Chinese is enforceable in American courts. The Hip Yees have their own courts, and you may bet they mean to enforce that contract. If they find out where you are, they will come after you with hatchets, highbinders, and writs of habeas corpus. Maybe some spooks too. Hip Yee are not above using Hoodoo and the law to have their way."

"Spooks?"

"Ghosts, ghoulies, and things that go bump in the night." He said it so blandly that Boy Toy could not tell if he were serious. It could have been anything from a dire warning to a sour joke. She kept staring back at her contract. "Such slavery must be illegal?"

"So it is," said Aaron. "As is stockjobbing, rate fixing, and railway fraud; but you won't see anybody sitting in jail for it." He turned to King Ahab. "Here, let me ignite that." King Ahab handed him the rolled-up laundry ticket, packed with hemp and opium, making a lumpy cigarette the size of a candle. Aaron reached over his head without looking, lighting it off the lamp. The paper sputtered and sparked, then began to burn. Aaron put the unlit end to his lips and took a deep drag. Holding his breath, he handed the lit ticket back to King Ahab.

Exhaling a cloud of smoke he said, "Not bad," looking at Boy Toy. "Wild hemp, *Cannabis sativa*, a harsh smoke, but it has a fair kick and is a boon to those who cannot afford tobacco. The Holy Fathers brought hemp with them; now it grows in the ditches. The Lord works in mysterious ways."

"Blessed be the name of the Lord," said King Ahab as he inhaled. Adding, "Not bad for Babylon, but cannot compare to Jamaican."

"Sure," sighed Aaron, "everything better in Jamaica; the hemp, the rum, the women . . ."

". . . the boys, the music, the sunshine," said King Ahab.

"As well as being a pagan, King Ahab is a sodomite," said Aaron.

"No pagan," said King Ahab, passing back the cigarette. "Just a tender loving child of Ja."

Aaron offered Boy Toy the ticket, but she shook her head politely. "There will be no opium in the New China."

"This New China sounds as jolly as a Presbyterian funeral," said Aaron, drawing the smoke into his lungs.

She shook her head over the contract. Lies put so boldy in writing were as unbelievable as that giant cat. "But I never even saw any money."

"You would be hard put proving that. The Hip Yees will have a written contract and twelve highbinders to swear you saw the money, and took it."

"If the Hip Yees are so powerful, why did you rescue me?"

"We did not take you from the Hip Yees." He held the smoke in, speaking through his teeth. "If you read the fine chicken scratching on that contract, I'm sure you'll see you belong to Golden Gate Trust and Savings. Golden Gate Trust and Savings belongs to a Nevada senator, name of Stanley Lealand, who you met earlier this evening. The Hip Yees are not pimps, merely middlemen between the *bahngar* who import girls and the brothel owners like Lealand. As I said, that is their rice bowl." He handed the cigarette back to King Ahab.

Boy Toy shook her head. "Yes, I remember Mr. Lealand. I thought he would help me. . . ."

"But he ended up owning you? I have had similar experiences with Stanley Lealand. He is a Nevada senator, a pimp, and a railroad lawyer; all three professions having much the same qualifications. He is also a saloonkeeper, but no man in Nevada is anything unless he is also a saloonkeeper."

"Nevada." Boy Toy rolled the name around. "That is another state. We are in California."

"Nevada is not a state, but a big sandlot inhabited by prickly pear cactus and poison-belly lizards, and infested with the lowest sort of rowdies in the employ of the Central Pacific. Not even the Mormons want it. Senator Lealand prefers to represent his constituents in the poker parlors and knocking shops of San Francisco. So would I, if I had the money or the drink to buy their votes."

King Ahab cocked his head, listening, then handed the smoking remains of the laundry ticket to Aaron. Reaching behind himself, he drew out a set of hardwood sticks and a box drum. Taking the sticks, he began to tap the slotted box lightly, rapping out a simple beat, both soothing and stirring:

*Tinka, tinka, tink*
*Tinka, tonk*
*Tinka, tonk*

Boy Toy pictured the dapper man who had betrayed her. "He took my letter, my proof of adoption." She felt robbed of her family, her hopes for a home.

"Senator Lealand has been the undoing of many young ladies," said Aaron. "He has two notable weaknesses. One is poker, and the other is buying Chinese girls straight off the boats, young ones with little tits and big almond eyes. Seems like a harmless hobby, but it gave me the notion you might be useful when Mama Love saw you in her crystal ball."

"Useful?" The word had a chilling effect. Boy Toy was mortally tired of men finding novel uses for her.

"Yes, I mean to do business with Senator Lealand, and he does not wish to do business with me. Senator Lealand owns women, saloons, real estate, and a railroad called the Monterey Spur. It is a small railroad, but it is strangling the life out of the fairest valley in California. I represent a group of landowners—from Spanish grandees to peons and sodbusters—who wish to buy it from him."

"If it is Mr. Lealand's railroad, he does not have to sell." Boy Toy still believed that much of her father's lectures on U.S. political economy.

"Grangers do not see it that way. Mr. Lealand came to our valley preaching the railroad, organizing a syndicate, buying up rights-of-way, all the while dangling government money in our faces. We all bought shares and signed right-of-way agreements, but by the time the railroad was built it was bankrupt; then Mr. Lealand foreclosed on us."

The laundry ticket had burned down to a stub. Taking it in two fingers, Aaron drew the last bit of smoke from it, then tossed it aside. "In our innocence it never occurred to us that a railroad could go bankrupt while the money syndicate that backed it turned a handsome profit. We offered to buy our railroad, on time, but Lealand prefers to bleed us with usurious freight rates so that he may one day own the valley as well as the railroad. I intend to get Senator Lealand to take back his useless stock and give me the Monterey Spur."

"How?" asked Boy Toy bitterly. "By trading me for the railroad?"

"Now there is a thought." A smile split Aaron's craggy face, and he looked her over. "You are a mite thin and underdeveloped, but what man could resist a girl who values herself so highly. At thirty-seven hundred dollars, I am sure the Hip Yees thought they were well paid, but now it appears you are worth a railroad as well."

Boy Toy studied the man, wondering what he would say next. King Ahab's drum solo grew louder and deeper.

*Tonka, tonka, tonk*
*Tinka, tonk*
*Tinka, tonk*

"I have been a number of things in my life," said Aaron, "a farmer, cardplayer, carnival wrestler, a Mason, and now a Range Detective; but I have never yet been in the business of trading in women. It appears to be a chancy occupation; more uncertain even than trading in mules. Besides, Mr. Lealand has turned down an offer of a hundred thousand dollars for the Monterey Spur. What makes you think he will trade the railroad for a talking China Girl?"

"I hope he won't." Boy Toy remembered Lealand saying to Ned Bailey, "Buy her, no matter what she costs." She shook herself. "I only want to know what use you plan to make of me."

"I am not totally sure," said Aaron. "It is enough now that Stanley Lealand wants you, and we have you."

"We?" She looked from Aaron to King Ahab.

*Tonka, tonk*
*Tonka, tonk*
*Tonka, tonk*

Before Aaron could answer, King Ahab ceased his drumming. "Mama Love is calling," he said softly. Aaron lifted an eyebrow. Boy Toy could hear nothing. King Ahab tilted his head toward the closed door. "Yes indeed. Appears Mama Love wants both of you right now."

Aaron looked vexed. "How come, King Ahab, you are all the time hearing Mama Love when no one else can?"

"It's Ja, man, just Ja." He began to beat again.

"Ja." Aaron pushed his bulk upright and offered Boy Toy a huge hand, opening the door. "We should not keep Mama Love waiting."

Boy Toy stood up, hesitating. The big cat had come in through the window ahead of her and could only have gone out through that door. She was more than a bit frightened, but also curious about the cat. Better to know what was happening, and how she might protect herself in mad, mad America. Besides, it was not her ambition to spend the rest of her life in that room. So she entered the dark doorway in the wake of Aaron Maria Spinoza.

The room beyond was close and dimly lit, smelling of joss smoke, burned spices, sweet opium, and orange blossoms. Before them was a tall carved spirit screen, hiding the rest of the room. Curtains, a thick carpet, and the closed door muffled the drumbeat, making King Ahab's music sound far off and otherworldly, like a rap-rapping on your coffin lid.

Stepping out from behind the spirit screen, Boy Toy saw no sign of the cat. The only illumination came from a tall candle. Two women were seated facing each other; between them was a clear spherical crystal the size of Boy Toy's head, resting on a small table draped with black silk. Sitting cross-legged on a dark cushion was the black woman she had seen earlier, still wearing the black dress and kerchief. In the dimness her eyes shone like hardened gems, their hypnotic gaze filling the small room, looking nowhere and everywhere.

The other woman was white, young and pretty with her hair in short gold ringlets. She had on an elaborate flowered dress and a high stiff cameo necklace. A lace handkerchief and a small package tied with string lay in her lap. She was staring into the crystal, brows knit, concentrating. Her cupid's-bow lips parted, and she whispered hoarsely, "It looks like him, but Mama Love, how may I know?"

Boy Toy stared into the crystal too. The whole room with its curtains, heady incense, and smoke illumination seemed to focus attention on the sphere. In its depths, she could see sensuous movement, bare flowing contours, twining into each other, releasing and twining again with the suggestion of fevered embrace. She was not sure how much she wanted to see.

The young white woman brought the lace handkerchief up to

her lips, muttering that she could not be sure.

"Then perhaps, child, you should ask them." Mama Love lifted her arm, pointing toward Boy Toy. The drumming rose, as though Mama Love could control the tempo.

The white woman turned, and nearly leaped out of her flowered gown. To her, it must have seemed that Boy Toy and Aaron had come from nowhere.

"Do not fear, child," said Mama Love. "This is our associate, Mr. Aaron Maria Spinoza, and Miss Boy Toy, a girl that has come under our protection." Mama Love's soft commanding voice seemed to tug at your soul. Hearing her own name, Boy Toy felt like she was being given an identity.

The blonde woman's eyes were opened unnaturally wide, staring as though she could no more speak than spit.

"I have shown Mrs. Lealand the crystal," said Mama Love, "and her husband's infidelities, but the poor child barely believes what she sees."

Aaron Spinoza leaned forward, adjusting his glasses and studying the depths of the crystal with lively interest. "It appears to be Senator Lealand—though I never saw him bounding about in bed before—but with his britches down and his flag up, his wife should know him better than most." He peered deeper into the crystal. "Neither of the women looks familiar, though the white one has an engaging bottom and a buxom enthusiasm that I would be likely to remember."

The blonde woman blushed, glancing quickly at the crystal. "Oh, it is him. It is just, well, perhaps. . . ."

"Afraid you are seeing through the power of suggestion?" asked Aaron. The young woman nodded gravely, not daring to look at Mama Love.

"Well, you are," Aaron answered his own question cheerfully. "But just because this is an illusion doesn't mean it is a lie, Mrs. Lealand. My investigations of your husband have turned up convincing proof of every form of adultery and fornication a civilized person could aspire to, and a few that would come as a surprise to most folks."

The white woman twisted her handkerchief. "But have you anything that would stand up in court?"

"Alas," said Aaron, "our most reliable witnesses are Chinese." The woman's eyes turned to Boy Toy, giving her a look of anguished curiosity, touched with scorn.

Aaron went on in his dry way. "Mrs. Stanley Lealand, I would like to introduce Boy Toy, a pious virgin, twice orphaned and raised by American missionaries. During my investigations I had the good fortune to pluck her from the hands of the Hip Yee

Tong, who were acting for your husband. Had we not been prompt, and lucky, you would probably be seeing her now in that crystal ball."

The woman's scorn turned to embarrassed confusion. Like most of San Francisco, she had expected Boy Toy to be a prostitute.

In quiet terms, Boy Toy told her whole story; how she had been scooped up at the docks, taken to the Queen's Room, and what had happened there. She explained how she had appealed to Senator Lealand for help, and he had instead stolen her letter and made arrangements to purchase her. It amazed her that she could recount the events so simply and forcefully, but she realized that for the first time she was telling them to a woman who might understand. They had both been wronged by the same man.

Once it became clear that Boy Toy had not actually been to bed with Senator Lealand, his wife brimmed with sympathy. The blonde woman told Boy Toy she felt mortified by what her husband had done, or had almost done. She took a moment to thank God on the spot for seeing Boy Toy to safety.

Aaron murmured an amen.

Twisting her handkerchief harder, Mrs. Lealand admitted that she had questioned her husband's fidelity, especially since finding out he had purchased a bordello.

Aaron agreed that buying a knocking stop tried a wife's trust.

"But he claimed it was a business venture."

Aaron gently pointed out that it would not be the first time that a husband's passion for business tempted him to neglect his wife. "The biggest proof of our bona fides is we are not asking for money," Aaron reminded her. "In fact, we intend to make you a rich and free woman."

Boy Toy saw Mrs. Lealand dry her tears, listening more sharply.

"You could try to divorce your husband," said Aaron, "but you would have to search hard in San Francisco to find twelve men, white and true, who would convict another white man of adultery just for screwing a few dozen Irish whores and China Girls. If you find twelve men so inclined, Senator Lealand would see that not one of these saints ever sat in a jury box."

The senator's wife admitted that she had dined and entertained the cream of California's legal profession, and what Aaron said was probably correct.

"Or you could stay married to Senator Lealand, sharing his marriage bed when he gets an itch for something different. Or you could do as Mama Love says."

Everyone turned toward Mama Love. Boy Toy saw the old

black woman was smiling, looking as benign as she was powerful, showing no trace of menace. Her eyes shone with kindness and understanding. "Honey, we aren't asking for your money, or to harm you. We are offering help. Your husband has betrayed your trust, just as he robbed Mr. Aaron Spinoza and shamed Miss Boy Toy."

Boy Toy saw Mrs. Lealand leaning forward, lips parted, eyes moist, clutching her package and handkerchief.

Mama Love's words were like soft lulling strokes. "Mrs. Lealand, I mean to free you from a loveless marriage; not the freedom that comes from a divorce that leaves you in the streets, but the freedom that comes from having some of what your husband has, what he wants to keep selfishly for himself."

Mrs. Lealand looked torn. She blinked and stared down at her package, but Boy Toy could see she was not blinking back tears. Mrs. Lealand's demeanor was more calculating. She asked in a weak voice, "How much?"

Without looking, Boy Toy could hear the smile in Mama Love's voice. "Enough, child. Enough so you can live in comfort. And Miss Boy Toy can have her freedom. And Mr. Spinoza can have his railroad." She marveled that the black woman had so casually included her name, and that the woman never said what Mama Love was going to get. Boy Toy saw Mrs. Lealand hesitate, make intention movements, then hand the package to Mama Love.

The black woman chuckled, and in return gave Mrs. Lealand a slip of paper with characters on it, looking just like the laundry ticket Aaron and King Ahab had rolled and smoked. Boy Toy watched Mrs. Lealand fold the ticket, like a woman accustomed to sending out her laundry.

Mama Love slit the string on the package with a long sharp fingernail. Inside was a man's silk shirt, somewhat the worse for wear. It was natural to get a dirty shirt in exchange for a laundry ticket, but Boy Toy could not imagine what the trade was about. Mama Love appeared to be going to tremendous trouble just to take in laundry.

Mrs. Lealand stood up, still looking nervous and unsure. Aaron offered to escort her to her hackney. "Since this neighborhood is not the best." He fetched his sawed-off Whitney, then led Mrs. Lealand out through the door concealed in the curtains. Boy Toy was alone with Mama Love.

She was no longer in the least afraid of the black woman, but she was almighty curious. Mama Love seemed to know this right away, and asked, "Are you wondering why I am doing all this?"

Boy Toy nodded gravely.

"Child, I am much older than you, but in our hearts we are not so different. Tell me why you came to America."

Boy Toy explained her ambition to become a missionary, to help build the New China. She felt transported by Mama Love's good faith and affection, and for the first time that day she was at home in this strange land. At the same time she was able to remember how it had been in Old China, how she had been shielded by her own mother's love, but brought up to believe that there was more to life than being sheltered and privileged, brought up to believe in the New China where love and brotherhood would replace the rule of the Manchu.

The black woman smiled. "Well, in her own way, Mama Love is a missionary. Only I am not building the New China, maybe I am building the New America. Believe me, Mama Love knows what it is like to be enslaved, to be shamed, and to be robbed of the fruits of her labor by men holding the public's trust. So when Mr. Spinoza came to me, I agreed to help him."

"But how will you help?"

She saw Mama Love run wrinkled hands over the shirt, smoothing out the silk. "This shirt belonged to a bad man; well, maybe not *bad*, but certainly thoughtless, selfish, and cruel. There is a good deal of him still in the shirt. Mama Love is going to turn his thoughtless selfishness to good ends."

"How?"

Instead of answering, Mama Love cocked her head. Her attention was suddenly elsewhere. Boy Toy realized that King Ahab's drumming had stopped. She looked toward the spirit screen and saw the Jamaican step around it.

Mama Love spoke in a low voice. "King Ahab, you had better fetch Mr. Aaron Spinoza. A man is coming down from the roof."

King Ahab glanced toward Boy Toy, clearly worried. "Don't fret for this child," said Mama Love. "I will see she is safe." Without a word, King Ahab slipped out the door that Aaron and Mrs. Lealand had used.

Chilled, Boy Toy moved closer to Mama Love. "Who's coming?"

"Don't fret, child, Mama Love has you." The old woman put her arm around Boy Toy's shoulder. There was a faint scraping, like a latch being pulled back, and Mau Yee stepped around the spirit screen, hatchet in hand.

# EL DORADO

*No California* gentleman *or* lady *ever abuses or oppresses a Chinaman. . . . Only the scum of the population do it, and likewise the policemen and politicians, for these are dust-licking pimps and slaves to that scum, here as well as elsewhere in America.* —MARK TWAIN

Boy Toy could see that Mau Yee was dangerously agitated, no longer the composed and confident Boxer he had been at the docks. His gaze kept darting from her to Mama Love, as if the hatchet man expected the old woman to spring at his throat with fang and claw. His lips moved slowly. "You, Boy Toy, must come with me."

"No, Mau Yee, I will not go." She drew strength from Mama Love. Mau Yee lifted his hatchet. Boy Toy stood up straight on trembling legs. "Mau Yee, you may kill me, but you may not take me away." Exhaustion and desperation made her reckless. As long as she was in this room, she was not alone. She would not be dragged back into the heartless city.

Mama Love spoke in an even, soothing manner. If Mau Yee did not catch all the words, he would feel the tone. "Tell him, if he harms you, child, no one will protect him, not Mr. Lealand who wants you alive, and not the Hip Yee who will be out thirty-seven hundred dollars. Mr. Aaron will track him down, and my spirit will pursue his ghost beyond the grave."

Boy Toy translated. "You know what you do is wrong. Why does a Triad risk death and damnation in an ignoble cause?"

Mau Yee looked directly at her, still not lowering his hatchet. "Even a gangster has his honor. Without the brotherhood of the Hip Yee, I am nothing."

"You are still a man, Mau Yee." As silent as death Aaron Spinoza stepped around the spirit screen, aiming his sawed-off Whitney at the small of Mau Yee's back.

Boy Toy said, "Be a man, Mau Yee, and live, do not serve the King of the Dead."

Aaron's gravelly voice added, "I hope you are telling this high-binder to drop his hatchet, before I am forced to scatter his guts out onto the Bay."

She saw Mau Yee stiffen, then relax. He did not scare easy. Instead of dropping his hatchet, he returned it to his coat, rotating slowly so he could see both Aaron and Mama Love.

"You have made the right choice, Mau Yee." Boy Toy smiled with unfeigned delight, having been too close to death herself.

"Let's go back in the other room," said Aaron. "Mama Love is going to have to make Medicine here, and I hate to get blood on her carpets."

Boy Toy stepped up to the highbinder, inviting him to lead her into the little bare room beyond the spirit screen. As she entered, she saw King Ahab sitting in the corner with the Springfield carbine across his lap. Aaron set his Whitney down within reach, but kept the Colt Lightning in his belt, saying, "You may tell Mau Yee he is one mean highbinder. I whipped a half-dozen Irish plug-uglies with the ax handle he snapped like a cheap pine board."

Boy Toy translated, and Mau Yee replied, "Someday I will show him how to fight without his barking dogs," by which he meant guns.

Aaron added, "While we are getting so chummy, ask him if he has a honey." Boy Toy stiffened, but Aaron insisted. "Ask him. All these highbinders have a little whore that they have gone soft on."

She spoke with Mau Yee, listened intently, then said, "It is so very sad. He does have a sweetheart. Her name is Ah Ho, and she is kept in a house off Spofford Alley." She guessed that right now Ah Ho was hard at work, "pleezing" any man that came along.

"Ask him the price of her contract, and if he wants to buy her free."

Boy Toy asked. Mau Yee looked miserable, saying, "Seven hundred dollars. I am saving, but maybe Ah Ho does not even love me, and just wants to whore."

Aaron snorted when he heard the answer. "You tell him, Boy Toy. There is not a goddamned woman in all Chinatown who just wants to whore. If there were, I would marry her myself and live off her earnings. As it is, I have nothing saved for my old age." He reached into his coat and withdrew a wad of bills big enough to plug a pipe drain. "This is a thousand dollars. Mau Yee can have it this time tomorrow, if he helps me. He can buy Ah Ho's freedom and run from the Hip Yees, to L.A., or to Canton, for all I care."

Boy Toy explained about the money. Mau Yee smiled, "Who does he want dead?"

Aaron said he did not have to kill anyone. "I want you to get word to Stanley Lealand that the China Girl he wants will be at the El Dorado tomorrow night. If Lealand shows, Mau Yee's got his money." Aaron peeled off a hundred-dollar bill and tossed it to Mau Yee.

Boy Toy translated, then said, "It is a strange thing you ask of him." She thought it was pretty peculiar too. "He adds that you have no reason to treat him so well."

"I have my reasons," said Aaron. "Ask him if I may borrow his hatchet." Mau Yee handed over the hatchet, looking suspicious, but Aaron merely used it to bust up a crate. He fed the wood into the iron stove and lit it with a Locofoco match.

When he got his hatchet back, Mau Yee said, "Since we are being friends, tell him the Hip Yee will be sending more than me tonight."

Aaron produced a pack of cards, shuffling while Boy Toy translated. "You may tell Mau Yee he's the only Hip Yee who fretted me."

"He says they are sending ghosts." When Aaron made no comment, she asked, "What are these spooks?"

"It's the Hoodoo," said Aaron, continuing to shuffle, "like the cat you said you saw."

"I did see a cat."

"You thought you saw a cat. That is how Hoodoo works. Here, watch my hands." As he spoke, he flicked five cards off the deck onto the bare boards in front of him.

Boy Toy said she knew nothing about playing cards. Aaron said that did not matter, spreading the cards out. "These four are kings, and that one's an ace. In plain poker, not playing straight flushes nor wild cards, four kings and an ace is an unbeatable hand; because only four aces can beat four kings, and you have one ace in hand." He tapped the ace. "In fact, it is the rarest unbeatable hand; there are only four ways you can make it out of two and a half million possible hands."

He scooped up the cards, put them onto the deck, and did an elaborate overhanded shuffle. "Now you see me mixing the cards. Right?" He set the deck down. "Now cut."

Boy Toy did not know what he meant, but Mau Yee reached over and divided the deck into two almost even piles. Aaron scooped up the two halves, first the bottom, then the top. He held the deck high with one hand. "Completely mixed, and you saw me do it." Then he flipped over the top five cards. Four kings and an ace lay on the floorboards. "Same cards," he said. "The odds against that happening are better than two million to one."

"Now watch while I do it again." Boy Toy watched. She could see the cards mixing, and this time she cut. Aaron even had her turn over the top five cards. They were the same.

"I could have an unbeatable hand every time I dealt," said Aaron, "which would surely get me shot."

"How do you do it?" Boy Toy did not know four kings from a pair of deuces, but she could tell these were the same cards as before.

Aaron picked up the cards and started to shuffle. "I did it the simplest way there is. I never mixed those kings in. Right now it looks like I am mixing the cards, but I am keeping those four kings and that ace out of the shuffle. Your eyes see the cards moving, your mind tells you they are being shuffled, but the mind and eye are fooled."

King Ahab gasped, pointing the Springfield carbine at the wall behind Boy Toy. She swung about. Emerging from the wall was a nightmare figure, a huge Manchu warrior, an Imperial Bannerman in black lacquered armor, shining like a giant grotesque beetle. Peacock-tail banners fluttered behind his back, and a green grinning face leered from behind the bars on his huge pagoda helmet. He was stepping straight out of the wall, flourishing a sword as big as Boy Toy.

Out of a corner of her eye she saw Aaron slap down the cards and scoop up his Whitney. With a deafening roar, flame jumped from one barrel of the shotgun, filling the room with smoke and making the window curtains leap. The Bannerman vanished as the wall behind him exploded, leaving a gaping hole surrounded by pockmarks where the Bannerman had been.

Aaron broke open the shotgun, popping in a fresh 10-gauge shell. "Bet you saw something really bad," he said. Boy Toy's ears were still ringing and she did not answer. He snapped the shotgun shut. "Well, what you saw was a spook."

"How could you shoot a ghost?" Boy Toy stared at the ragged hole.

"I did not shoot him," said Aaron, "because he was not there, but my shotgun sure took your mind off whatever you were seeing. Chinese use the same principle when they chase off demons with firecrackers. The Hip Yee have put their Hoodoo on us, trying to spook us, maybe scare us into giving you up. But with Mama Love making Medicine for us, their Hoodoo will be weak, and we can wait it out."

He passed the cards back to her, inviting her to cut. With shaking hands she divided the deck. Again Aaron seemed to take the bottom half and place it on top, but when he dealt, the top hand was still four kings and an ace.

Watching intently, Mau Yee asked, "Can he show me how to win at fan-tan?" Boy Toy translated. She knew fan-tan as a popular guessing game where each player tried to predict the number of coins remaining under an overturned bowl, after they had been divided by four.

"Fan-tan?" Aaron looked disgusted. "No one but the house wins at fornicating fan-tan. There is no edge to the game. Only a Chinese would gamble when everyone's chances are even. It is in the Chinese character to expect order and justice. Look, Mau Yee, do you want to die rich?"

Mau Yee said he wanted to die in China.

"Well, if you want to die rich in China, you have to learn poker or blackjack."

A raging piebald bull burst through the window, parting the curtains like an express train charging out of a tunnel. Boy Toy could see the bull's great bloodshot eyes, and his huge nostrils snorting smoke and flames. This time Aaron drew his belt gun, firing a double-action Colt Lightning as fast as he could pull the trigger. The bull vanished, and Aaron's bullets went whizzing off into the night, over the rooftops of San Francisco. Fortunately Chinatown was high on a hill.

He broke open the Colt and fished in his pocket for more .38 cartridges. "There are two secrets to gambling: the secret of winning and the secret of losing. The secret of winning is to know the odds. Watch the cards, and bet when the odds are with you, and fold when they are against you, then you will win—not every hand, but over the long run. Since the odds in fan-tan are always the same, the only way to get rich is to open a parlor, charge for the use of the tables, and let other fools play fan-tan."

"You make it sound too simple," said King Ahab.

"All truths are simple," insisted Aaron. "But winning is not enough. You must also convince someone to lose. There are a million ways to win; you can play the odds, trim aces, mark cards, carry a cold deck or aces up your sleeve—you can even use the Hoodoo—but none of these will avail if no one wants to lose to you. Gambling houses hate a winner. Go into a gambling den and beat them every day, and soon they won't let you play; it's plain bad for business—*and they won't care how you are winning.*"

A grinning skeletal ghoul, with his fangs dripping gore, slowly materialized in their midst. Mau Yee threw his hatchet through the monster while King Ahab fired off the .45 carbine. The ghoul faded away with a distressed look on its face.

"Gambling houses stay in business by making it pleasant, even exciting, to lose," said Aaron. "They treat the loser like a king, providing him with food and drink in a luxurious setting, allowing women of easy virtue to rub up against him. They will ply the loser with every pleasure known to men so he may give up his money and come back when he has more. Most gamblers lose. Not one in twenty has a bank account. Some will play poker like assassins, then throw their winnings away on the ponies. Winning takes hard work and strict accounting. Losing is open to all. That is the secret of losing."

"What good is this to us?" Boy Toy was bewildered by the torrent of words, and the thunderous interruptions.

"We need to draw Stanley Lealand into a game," said Aaron, "and convince him to bet everything, even the Monterey Spur, on a losing hand."

She remembered the senator's cool confidence. "That hardly seems possible."

"Unless I miss my guess," said Aaron, "it will happen tomorrow night."

Boy Toy gave in before the Hip Yee Tong. She dozed off as ghosts continued to appear: a great green ape, a silver-gold dragon, a headless fiend, a half-man/half-tiger. All were dispatched with wild volleys and raucous laughter from the men. Between apparitions, Aaron Spinoza introduced Mau Yee to blackjack, Poor Man's Baccarat, showing him a betting system that required counting the number of tens and court cards that had been played.

Soon Aaron had mastered enough pidgin Cantonese—words like *bet* and *stand*—that he no longer needed Boy Toy to translate. She was exceedingly grateful, for she had not slept since coming ashore; having been by turns too excited, too horrified, and too tense to shut her eyes. Slipping into an exhausted stupor, she curled up against Aaron's suitcase, jerked awake every so often by the roar of gunfire.

Awaking to her first morning in America, she saw the room a shambles; three walls were riddled with bullets, and the curtains were shredded by gunshots. Only the door and wall adjoining Mama Love's room were untouched; no "spooks" had come from that direction. Aaron and Mau Yee were gone, which made her nervous. They were dangerous and violent men, but comforting to have within call. King Ahab was still sitting in the corner with the carbine across his lap, rolling his morning cigarette, a huge tube packed with hemp leaves. He smiled at her and said goodday.

A moment later the door swung open and Mama Love appeared. In daylight she seemed even older to Boy Toy, with wisps of steel-gray hair straying from under her black kerchief. Her face looked haggard, as though she too had passed a hard night, but she gave Boy Toy a warm smile, rolling her big eyes, surveying the wreckage. "My, my, but them men made a mess of things."

Boy Toy felt very much a mess herself. Her *chengosams* were a mass of wrinkles, no longer pure white but dirty from being dragged over roofs and spattered with garbage. Like everything else in the room, they smelled of gunsmoke and were covered with a grimy powder residue. She was also famished, having eaten nothing but cold tortillas since coming to America.

Mama Love settled down beside her, patting her, calling her "poor child," and promising that things would soon be better.

"All of us have too much to do today, and when Mr. Aaron Spinoza gets back, Mama Love will have to leave. Tonight will be as difficult as last night, different but every bit as difficult." Boy Toy could see the woman was holding tight to the shirt that Mrs. Lealand had given her. Mama Love leaned over and kissed Boy Toy on the forehead.

Aaron arrived, whistling through his teeth and looking not in the least affected by the night's ordeal. He was wearing a starched white suit that appeared brand new, and a crisp strawhat with a scarlet band. Parcels of various sizes were tucked under his arms, and a rope bucket hung from one hand. He began tossing the parcels about like a white-suited Santa. "This is what you ordered, Mama Love. Luckily we are in Chinatown; it's hard to get ground goat's hooves and unicorn horn anywhere else in town. King Ahab, here's your monkey suit." He set the bucket down in their midst. "This tub of tamales is for everyone."

The tamales turned out to be corn husks wrapped around warm cornmeal filled with shredded meat. Boy Toy found them gross and spicy, but delicious in her starved condition. As she ate, Aaron opened her parcel personally. His worn face beaming, he presented her with a shimmering high-collared silk gown, trimmed with tiny peach roses and jade buttons. King Ahab's package contained a ruffled silk shirt, stovepipe pants, and a red velvet coat with tails. Aaron said they had to step out into the street "in style" because, "We're already registered at the Palace Hotel, and we have to look sharp to claim our suite."

Mama Love took Boy Toy to her room, fussing over her and the dress, fixing up her hair with pearl-studded combs. When she was done, she pulled back a curtain to reveal a full-length mirror. Boy Toy found her transformation stunning. Only her red silk slippers remained the same. She looked older, more dignified, with pearls twined in her dark hair, and jade teardrops on her white gown. Mama Love said, "Magnificent." She held Boy Toy's shoulders hard, adding, "No matter what happens tonight, remember, child, Mama Love will be with you in spirit." She kissed her again, and turned her over to Aaron and King Ahab.

By the time Boy Toy was out on the street, she was already missing Mama Love. A terrifying crowd of men thronged along Stockton Street: swearing stevedores, sailors fresh off the boats, big Irishmen with guns and badges, and bumarees with carpetbags and crushed hats. An open coach sat waiting to take her to the Palace Hotel, with Mau Yee sitting on the high seat behind the horses, dressed in a black silk suit and looking like a Manchu butler.

As King Ahab helped her into the carriage, Aaron leaned over and ripped down a fresh wall poster. He tossed it into her lap, saying, "Can you read this? It has the Hip Yee chop on it."

Boy Toy gasped. "This says the Hip Yee Tong will reward any man who kills you. It gives your name and description." She was amazed to see a solicitation for murder hanging in plain sight. Several more were plastered to nearby buildings.

Aaron seated himself beside her. "What sort of money are they offering?"

"Five hundred dollars." It slowly occurred to her that there was probably not a single policeman in San Francisco who could read Chinese.

"That is no reward, that is an insult." Aaron waved for King Ahab to start the horses. "Your meanest, most hopeless hophead would spit at five hundred dollars for killing a white man. Five thousand would be nearer the mark. The Hip Yees are playing with us. They should know such antics only bring them down."

Five hundred was enough to give Boy Toy the shivers. Riding through the streets, she saw dozens of armed men, and she braced herself to leap overboard if anyone sprayed the carriage with bullets.

The Palace Hotel was imposing with its wide lobby, crystal chandeliers, plush velvet, and flower vases of cut bohemian glass. "Beware," said Aaron, "small dogs have been known to lose themselves in the nap of these carpets." Smart young men in tight pants and pillbox hats carried their bags upstairs. As they ascended, she felt that every man's eye was on her. Safe in their paneled suite, she collapsed into a deep sofa, saying, "I thought they were all looking at me."

"Well, I should hope so," said Aaron, opening a carpetbag and removing an opium lamp and a long-stemmed pipe. "You are far safer being a spectacle. No one grabs paying guests out of Palace suites."

"I must stay here to be safe?" She surveyed the high draped windows, with a view of the Bay. Each one had an elegant little window seat. A ribboned basket of fruit sat on a table trimmed with French lace.

"There are worse fates," Aaron assured her, "but we cannot afford the rates." He lit the lamp and dug a small lump of opium out of his five-tael tin, plastering it like putty into the pipe bowl. "I advise you to settle back and have a smoke, does wonders for your digestion."

"No, I must not." She looked nervously at the pipe. The calm it offered was inviting.

"Here, have some," he said. "You are shaky as a cat licking coffee. We are here to rest and to advertise ourselves. Before we get to the El Dorado, I want the rumor going ahead of us that a Chinese princess has checked into the Palace."

"Who would believe a Manchu princess speaks English and stays in American hotels?"

"They'll believe it because they are a bunch of dumb, round-eyed barbarians, and because the Hoodoo will be with you. They will be worked up and ready to see a princess. When you start winning, it will make you even more special."

"But I cannot do it," said Boy Toy miserably, wishing Mama Love were there. Her carefully hoarded confidence had evaporated. "I cannot play cards. It is unchristian. The New China will not have gambling halls or gaming parlors."

"You don't have to play. A princess does not need to touch money, nor handle cards. Her servants do that. Cards may be unchristian, but my mama was a jack-Mormon, and my daddy was a Jew turned Mason, which makes me as much a heathen as Mau Yee over there." He indicated the highbinder, sitting calmly in his new black silks.

He offered her the opium again. "I can see the New China will be a splendid place, full of psalm singing and pious spinsters flailing away on the harpsichord, but this is Old San Francisco. I need you, Boy Toy, but you are not my slave. If you wish, I will turn you over to the Christians at the Presbyterian Mission, but I warn you they will offer little protection. They can only hide you in a room poorer than this one. You dare not go to the police, for they are a bunch of Ned Baileys in the employ of men like Senator Lealand. If you have not the money to purchase a lawyer, the police will hand you cheerfully over to the Hip Yees."

He cocked his head over toward Mau Yee. "Or you may appeal to the Six Companies that run Chinatown."

She asked Mau Yee who the Six Companies were and what protection they could offer. The hatchet man laughed. "The Six Companies are useless rice ladles." He assured her that the Chinese companies could not stand up to the salaried soldiers of the Hip Yee Tong.

"So you see," said Aaron, spreading his hands, "this is not the New China. Here in the Old U.S.A. we are all slaves to money. Tonight you are going to make us a lot of money. If a busted old duffer like me beat the El Dorado, it would not create a spectacle, nor entice Senator Lealand into a game. They would call me a cheat, or slip in a House mechanic with a loaded pistol and a rigged deck. With you it will be different. Losing to a princess will seem like a privilege, a story the El Dorado can bank on for years to come."

He pressed the pipe into her hands. "I need you to go into that casino fully rested, talking and smiling, making those men think you are something special."

She looked down at the pipe in her hands. Aaron touched the bowl to the lamp and steered the stem to her lips. The opium sizzled, gurgled, and began to burn. She breathed in the hot, sweet smoke, and presently drifted into a dreamy sleep.

She dreamed of Mama Love, holding her and enfolding her, and replacing the mother she had lost. Between Mama Love and the opium, she awoke in a fine trim, relaxed and dreamy, ready to sit down to a sumptuous candlelit dinner. King Ahab had ordered boiled crayfish, steamed crab, and Cajun baked blackfish brought up to the room, where it was all served on willowware china and white tablecloths. Ahab swore none of it touched Jamaica, but in Babylon you had to make do.

While they ate, Aaron went over the betting. "I have a ten-thousand-dollar stake. This money is the blood, sweat, and tears of hundreds of families. We must win, or they will have nothing. I will handle the blackjack bets, but when Lealand sits down, it will be up to you. We will have at best one hand of poker with Lealand, and you must push the bet no matter what, getting him to put up the Monterey Spur." Such responsibility should have horrified her, but Boy Toy found herself brimming with confidence, as though Mama Love were at her side.

He finished by presenting her with a set of black lacquered false fingernails. She giggled and said that was going a bit far, but Aaron insisted, saying, "I can win at blackjack without touching the cards, but when we get down to poker, I need a pat excuse to shuffle and deal for you."

She played with her new fingernails while Aaron buckled his shoulder holster under his coat and slipped the Lightning inside. His suitcase was staying in the hotel. Buoyed by her nap and meal, and by the opium, she floated down to the lobby and off to the El Dorado. She was no longer alarmed by the wild sea of big men, with their great black beards, round eyes, hooked noses, and white, brown, and black skins. When they reached Portsmouth Square, where the central plaza of Spanish San Francisco had been, half the men in town seemed to be there, drunk, waving, yelling jokes, the more foolish ones firing off their pistols.

Stepping out of the carriage, she saw every man's face turned to look at her. Why shouldn't they stare, she thought; I must look as strange to them as they are to me. So she gave each man a broad and earnest Christian smile, drawing encouragement from the happy looks she got in return. She noted that they crowded after her.

Americans had turned the old Spanish plaza into a park, knocking down adobes and putting up gambling halls. The Bella Union, Veranda, and the El Dorado stood at one corner of the square. Within walking distance were the Parker House, Empire, Alhambra, and a half-dozen other gaming dens. Sinful as it was, she liked the look of the El Dorado. It was taller, set back from the street with trees in front, lit by gas lamps. She walked in with her head held high, aware she was trailed by a crowd of curious men. The inside was not nearly as rich as the Palace, but ten times as gaudy with gilt walls, tall mirrors, and fresco copies of Titian nudes. Veiled lamps and cigar smoke gave the air a golden glow.

She heard the click of dice, slap of cards, and clink of money subside as heads turned her way. "Who is she?" went round the tables. "Some sort of fancy whore," said a hopeful voice. "Nah, it's the princess from the Palace."

Men leaped up to offer her their seats, but Aaron steered her toward a particular blackjack table and a particular dealer. King Ahab seated her, ordering tea. Aaron and Mau Yee were on her right and left, keeping the crowd back, while King Ahab gripped her chair, covering her cards. Beyond them stood the crowd: high rollers with cigars and top hats, *Californios* wrapped in blankets and smoking *cigaritas*, prospectors down from the Sierras in greasy fringed leather and ratty leggings.

Aaron leaned over toward the dealer, who looked young and a little amazed. Softly the big man said things like, "Her Highness will play *vingt-et-un*. Her Highness will purchase chips worth three hundred ounces in gold."

Giving the gangling dealer a solicitous look, she added, "If you please, sir."

A shocked ripple ran around the table. "By God, she does talk."

The dealer deftly measured out thirty blood-red ten-ounce chips, and Aaron paid with a bank draft, stacking the chips before Boy Toy, leaving one out as an opening bet. Someone behind her asked where the whore got so much gold, but the men on either side shut him up, saying he was a bad-mouthed drunken bastard, apologizing to the princess.

Boy Toy thanked them, ignoring the cards that came slithering across the green felt table. Knowing next to nothing about blackjack, she could concentrate on the men, giving each one a smile of greeting. Aaron tipped up the corners of the cards, whispering their value into her ear—a five and eight, making thirteen. The dealer was showing a red seven, with his hole card hidden. She chattered to Aaron in Cantonese, pretending to give instructions.

"Her Highness," he said, "will have another card." The dealer flipped them a nine to make twenty-two, a bust. He turned over his hole card, a three, and took their chip. Aaron put out two chips to replace the lost one.

With Aaron minding the cards, Boy Toy felt free to enjoy herself. For the first time since coming to San Francisco, she was able to meet the men on equal terms, talking, laughing, and asking questions, telling them how happy she was to be here in America. She was delighted to discover that they were polite and well mannered, tickled to talk to her. She deflected all questions about her history, insisting she wanted to hear about their country. And they were happy to describe their native land, with its grand spaces and great people—give or take a few micks, spicks, and Injuns—why, she was one lucky princess to come to California.

She also refused to discuss her play, though she could see Aaron was raising the bets, betting ten or a dozen red chips at a time. A princess did not care if she won or lost. She noted that sometimes Aaron would cut back his bets, which meant the deck had only the low cards that favored the house. Then he would say Her Highness wanted a shuffle, "Just for luck." Men pressed her about wild swings in the betting, but she laughed and said she bet on whim, waiting for the God of Luck to speak to her. Word went around the casino that she was using some sort of Chinese magic.

After hours of playing and chatting, Aaron asked for the blue hundred-ounce chips, and she knew they were far ahead. She felt sorry for the sweating dealer as the El Dorado's money slipped through his fingers. Aaron would switch back and forth, putting out red chips when the odds favored the house, bringing out the blue ones when the deck was rich with high cards, all the time pretending to consult Boy Toy.

By watching, she picked up the rhythm of blackjack, and some of Aaron's system. When the dealer slid a pair of queens across the table, she knew now that was twenty points, just one short of a winning twenty-one. The dealer dealt himself a six, and a face-down hole card. Aaron whispered, "Split the queens. There are no low cards left and he's bound to bust." Using a lacquered fingernail, Boy Toy flicked the two red queens faceup, telling the dealer she wanted to play two hands. To the circle of men she explained, "Queens are very lucky for me." Aaron doubled the bet, so each queen had two blue chips covering her, $3,000 riding on each hand.

The dealer nodded grimly, dealing her a seven and a queen of spades. Without waiting for Aaron, Boy Toy split her queens again. That must have been right because Aaron plunked down $3,000 more on the queen of spades. The shaking dealer gave her two more cards, a red ten and the queen of clubs. Poor man, thought Boy Toy, he is about to faint. She pushed the queen of clubs to one side, and Aaron put a pair of chips on it. Before taking her hand away she tapped the queen and two blue chips with a black fingernail, smiling graciously to the dealer. "This bet is for you. If my queen wins, the money is yours."

Men pressed closer, craning their necks. The dealer licked his lips, staring at the black queen and two blue chips, dealing a nine and a jack of clubs to match the queen. Now there were four hands in front of Boy Toy totaling seventeen, twenty, nineteen, and twenty. The dealer flipped over his hole card, another jack, giving him sixteen. He had to take another card.

Everyone but Boy Toy eyed the dealer's sweaty fingers as he slid the top card off the deck. Boy Toy looked straight into the man's eyes, giving him an encouraging grin. If this last card was a five, the El Dorado would win all four hands, but the dealer himself would be out the $3,000 that Boy Toy was offering him. His trembling fingers turned over a seven, giving him twenty-three, a bust.

Pandemonium swept through the El Dorado. "The princess" had won $12,000 on the turn of a card, and given $3,000 of it away. The dealer struggled to his feet, pocketing the two blue chips, and saying he would not play any longer. If the El Dorado wanted to keep losing, they had to find someone else to deal the cards.

A dirty-shirted miner in canvas pants wanted to know why she had given away 200 ounces of gold. Boy Toy asked blandly, "Is that very much? I thought these were Chinese dollars." They yelled, laughed, and slapped the table, saying the princess was a real card. "Goddamn, these are genuine American dollars, not those cheap Mexican dollars you got in China."

As the laughter died, the smoky sea of men parted, and Stanley Lealand stepped up to the chair where the dealer had been sitting. He stood there, staring hard at Boy Toy, his silk ruffles reminding her of the shirt she had seen in Mama Love's hands. Ned Bailey was behind him, along with another policeman. Seeing Lealand blew away her giddy confidence. She felt both awe and revulsion, but she told herself to be pleasant and polite, not to antagonize. "Mr. Lealand, we meet again. Please be seated."

Lealand looked down at the chair, as if he had never seen one before. Other men's hands pulled the chair back, and the crowd hustled him into his seat. Eager and expectant, they pressed around the table, hemming him in. Boy Toy saw Aaron take a blue chip off the stacks and hand it to Mau Yee. She nodded to the highbinder, saying in Cantonese, "Whatever happens now, that is yours." Then she turned back to face the man across the table.

"Are you the girl I talked to in the Queen's Room?" The senator had a troubled look on his face, as if he were not sure why he was there. Like the Crows said, he was a breath feather, blown there whether he willed it or not.

Boy Toy did not answer directly; instead she said, "This House will no longer deal blackjack to me. I was hoping you would play poker." She knew that poker was the name of the game that Aaron wanted to play.

Men cheered, slapping Lealand on the back, saying he didn't dare play. "This cute little princess had just plucked the El Dorado. Now her eyes are on your wallet." Advice like that made it harder for Lealand to say no, not without being remembered as the senator who slunk out of the El Dorado rather than risk a hand with a China Girl. Lealand looked hard at her, asking evenly, "What stakes?"

She casually indicated the chips on the table. "We can play for these. It is not my money." Men laughed even more.

Glancing at the piles of red-and-blue chips, Lealand asked the nearest dealer to give him the same amount and charge it to his account. Everyone watched while the chips were counted, and Boy Toy was startled to hear there was $70,000 on the table. "Them's real American dollars, Princess," the dealer assured her.

Was she risking too much? Standing behind her, Aaron said nothing. She could only plunge ahead.

The El Dorado dealer supplied a deck, placing it between the two players. Lealand said, "A lady deals first."

She thanked him and tapped the deck with her nail. Aaron bent down and spread out the cards to see the deck was full and fair, then began to shuffle. It was the first time that night that he had a deck in his hands. Lealand looked from Aaron's hands to hers. "You did not have long nails last night."

She studied her nails. "False vanity, Mr. Lealand. Many things have changed since last night."

Aaron thumped the deck down in front of Lealand. The senator cut, and Aaron scooped up the deck. To Boy Toy it looked like he placed the bottom on top, but she knew now not to trust her eyes. "Her Highness plays only straight poker," said Aaron. "No wild cards or straight flushes." These were his first words since the senator sat down.

"Her Highness?" Lealand raised an eyebrow. "If it's straight poker the lady wants, straight poker's what we play."

Boy Toy did not know a straight flush from a crooked flue, so she just tried to seem at ease while Aaron dealt out the cards, five to her and five to Lealand. This time he did not tip up the corners or whisper in her ear. He seemed to be doing as much as he could to distance himself from the play.

For form's sake, she peeked at her cards. There was only one face card, and the whole hand did not equal twenty-one. It would have been a perfect blackjack hand, but this was poker, a game she knew nothing about. Lealand looked very pleased with his cards, tossing in four blue chips, $6,000. All Boy Toy could do was force the bet the way Aaron had said at dinner. Carefully lifting four chips off her stack, she met Lealand's bet, then added four more to raise him $6,000. Lealand met her $6,000 and raised a like amount.

So it went back and forth. The El Dorado had never seen such furious betting. As the chips piled up in the center of the table, men called for their buddies to come see the senator and the princess trying to buy the pot before there was even a draw. Boy Toy saw men scrambling up on the tables and sitting on the bar to get a better view. She hoped Mama Love was with her, because now the opium had soured. Her hands were sweaty and her mouth was dry. Lealand at least knew what he was doing.

Suddenly she was out of chips. An amused Lealand matched her last bet with his last chips. "Well," he said, "I guess we had better call." He seemed totally confident.

Aaron said softly to Lealand, "Do you want a card?"

Lealand shook his head. "I couldn't be happier with this hand."

Since Lealand did not ask for a card, Boy Toy did not ask for one, either. "Hot damn," said the mountain man, "both them coons got pat hands." A sharpie in a silk hat started booking side bets, and men put money on the hands, sight unseen. "Five hundred on the senator's cards. A thousand on the princess to win."

Lealand grinned at her across the huge pile of chips. "Since we have nothing left to bet, I guess we should show."

"No." She did not want to show. Aaron had said she must keep forcing the bet. Boy Toy reached inside her gown, took out a folded sheet of paper covered with Chinese characters, hesitated, then laid it alongside the chips.

"What's that?" muttered Ned Bailey. "A goddamn Chinese bank draft?" The senator's backers yelled, "Hey, honey, you gottee use American money." Lealand gave the document a puzzled look. "You said we were playing for table stakes. You cannot add to your chips now."

She looked coldly at Lealand, tapping the piece of paper. "This is a contract to work for twelve years as a prostitute. It is worth thirty-seven hundred dollars. That is the price that you put on me." She straightened up. "I am here at the table."

As word went back through the crowd, men began to argue. Lealand's backers said the princess was trying to buy the pot. Men with money on her said Lealand was raised out. "Appears the senator will have to offer himself."

"That's silly, who would pay to screw a senator?"

"Lots of folks would."

"Back in Washington they rent out by the hour."

Boy Toy forced herself to be firm. This man had shamed her. "I do not want his body. I want his railroad. He may match my contract with the Monterey Spur."

Lealand laughed, looking again at his cards, which seemed to make him supremely confident. "The Monterey Spur is worth much more than thirty-seven hundred dollars."

"That is strange," she said, "I understood it was bankrupt." Now she heard Lealand's backers arguing among themselves. Some said she was still being unfair. Others did not care. "Put up the Spur." It wasn't their railroad, and they just wanted to see the cards. Everyone wanted to see the cards.

"Now what would you do with a railroad?" Lealand sounded patronizing, as though she were already his to play with.

"Oh," she tried to sound offhand, "we have so few of them in China."

That brought down the house. "The princess thinks she can take a train home on a clipper." A drunken miner with his money on Lealand yelled, "The senator will show you all about railroading when he gets his paws on your caboose."

Taking a last look at his cards, Lealand dashed off a note agreeing to sign over the railroad, tossing the paper on top of the contract. "There, no more bets. I'm calling you, because it does not matter. You cannot beat four kings and an ace." He started to lay his hand down faceup.

"The lucky coon has four kings and an ace." Men licked their lips, wondering what it was like to win $140,000 and a real Chinese princess for your bed.

Four kings and an ace. Boy Toy remembered Aaron saying that was an unbeatable hand in straight poker. Why had he dealt it to Lealand? Fear blew the last of the opium from her brain, leaving her sober and scared. Feeling she had done something horribly wrong, she flipped her cards over one at a time with a lacquered nail.

Faces peered over her shoulder to look at the losing hand.

"Holy Christ, the princess has got four aces." Boy Toy saw the four small cards in her hand were indeed all the same. Men fought their way forward to see two unbeatable hands. To see if there really were five aces in an El Dorado deck.

Lealand stared openmouthed at her cards, then back at his. Four kings stared up at him, but the fifth card was suddenly different.

"Ain't an ace, it's a four." The four of hearts lay next to his kings, a card whose corner looks so much like an ace.

Aaron leaned forward. "Seen several men make that mistake," he said as his big hands raked in the $140,000 in chips, Boy Toy's contract, and Lealand's railroad.

For the rest of his days, Stanley Lealand swore he had seen an ace in his hand. Behind his back even his friends said, sure he had *seen* an ace, but when a man wants to win badly enough he will see things that just aren't there.

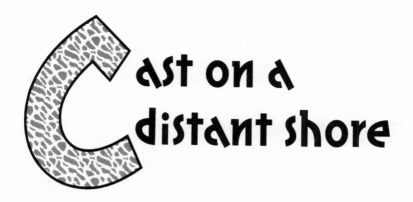

# Cast on a distant shore

## WINDWARD MAT

Floating facedown in the blood-warm water, Kafirr watched the sea creature become a carnivore. A heartbeat before, it had been a harmless root scavenger, but now its body sucked in salt water, expanding and elongating. Its tail flattened into a single stiff blade, and its jaws drew back, revealing a predator's evil grin. Dark shadows crept over the creature's upper surfaces while the belly turned corpse white. This coloring mimicked the two-tone camouflage favored by deepwater hunters. Pseudolimbs beat faster, and the scavenger's tentative movements turned to swift, decisive lunges. Tiny grim teeth prepared to rip apart anything in its path.

The first time Kafirr had seen a copyfish go through this act, it had scared him right out of the water. He had stayed out for over a hundred hours, and only hunger had driven him back in. Grown children who did not dive did not eat. Now, after thousands of hours in the water, he found the sudden transformation comforting. Copyfish were harmless; they mimicked a dozen different carnivores to disguise themselves and scare off smaller predators. By keeping watch on the copyfish, Kafirr could tell what real predators were hunting through the root grottoes. Neither the copyfish nor the carnivores it mimicked were true fishes. They were crafty, warm-blooded sea creatures, swimming

with the aid of paddlelike pseudolimbs. Kafirr did not know the
names he used were wrong; he was not an ichthyologist, just a
child of Earth cast on a distant shore, using the words of a world
that he had never seen.

Every odor, every vibration, triggered a change in the copyfish.
This one had heard or smelled a deepdevil coming up from below.
Since deepdevils never ate their own, a good disguise was effec-
tive defense.

Kafirr had no defense and no disguise, but the boy had been
warned. He had to dive fast and be done before the real deepdevil
arrived. Kicking down from the surface with his foot paddles, he
edged toward the nearest grotto. This hole in the sea was a shaggy
opening between the roots, filled with sinister shadows. Working
fast did not mean working foolishly. Worse things than deepdevils
clung to the roots all around him. Puffballs crowded the grotto,
warning predators away with speckled red-orange and yellow
spines. Nothing fed on puffs, or at least not for long. Kafirr had
once seen a diver brush a puffball and die before he broke the surface. The victim's muscles had contracted so violently that his
back was broken and intestines protruded through his gaping
mouth. The only nice thing said about puffs was that they were
quick. Stingworm venom took over a hundred painful hours to
kill, giving their victims plenty of time to regret the mistake.

Kafirr pulled on his safety line for slack, then swam into the
grotto. Large roots and boles were all about him, forming a twisting shadowy tube barely three meters wide. Kafirr doubted that
the deepdevil would follow him here. In a grotto the slightest
mistake brought hunter or hunted into fatal contact with a venomous root dweller. Deepdevils preferred the root fringes where
meals were scarcer but safer. Kafirr had to work down here, swimming naked among the multicolored puffs and the blue-banded
stingworms, because the root fringes were plucked clean of seastones.

For as long as his lungs would allow, Kafirr used his pry bar to
pick seastones off the roots. When the need to breathe was over-
whelming, he stopped filling his stuffsack and turned back on his
safety line, kicking toward the surface.

Waiting at the entrance to the grotto was the real deepdevil.
It took only a glance for Kafirr to tell that this was the true carnivore: two hundred kilos of hungry flesh feeder wearing the same
wicked grin that he had seen on the copyfish. The long white
knives behind the grin were a part of this predator that even a
copyfish could not mimic. Deepdevils were as cunning as they
were cruel. Kafirr had once seen a deepdevil feeding on a sea-

snake calf several times its size. The deepdevil had ripped slice after slice out of the screaming calf, keeping its meal warm by avoiding a deathblow.

This deepdevil had seen Kafirr's line going into the grotto and was waiting for a meal to come out. For a moment, Kafirr hung like a hooked fish, tethered to a surface line with death at the other end. Then the boy exhaled and slipped off his loincloth, leaving weight belt and stuffsack attached to the safety line. Wearing only his foot paddles, he dived deeper into the dim grotto, searching for the passage that led to the surface. Pressure stabbed at his eardrums, and shadows closed in around him. His vision blurred as oxygen debt built up and his limbs turned leaden.

Seeing nothing but a pale circle of rosy light, Kafirr kicked upward. With lungs bursting, he broke the surface in a fountain of fine spray. Taking air in great gulps, Kafirr was too exhausted to do anything but tread water. Here on the fringes of Windward Mat, holes opened in the tangle of branches overhead. Kafirr could look up from the somber water and see rose-colored clouds above the dense vegetation. Thin streaks of lightning crackled across the pink cloud bottoms, connecting deep red chasms many kilometers tall.

Catching a branch, Kafirr heaved himself into the dense, wet air. Brine ran off his body, instantly replaced by beads of sweat. Kafirr preferred the feel of the water, which was several degrees cooler and did not tingle with static. Too bad the ocean's cool embrace included stingworms, puffballs, spinebacks, and hordes of large predators.

Supersaturated air tasted of ozone. Several seconds of rain swept by as the boy sat shaking, wishing that he never had to dive again. When his shivering stopped, he got up, threading his way through the catwalks to the dock where his line was tied. Green gillhoppers, slim humanoids with stunted fins and small, dry scales, jostled past him as though he were a moving obstruction. Gillhoppers ignored even the ocean that lapped around their mats; they could hardly be expected to notice adolescent humans. When he was growing up and learning to dive, Kafirr had wanted desperately to be a gillhopper. He had wished for green skin and scales; to never be hungry, to never go near the water. Now he was beyond such childish fantasies. He had been born a diver, and he expected to die a diver. His mother had dipped him newborn into the water, telling the sea to make her son a strong swimmer. Both Kafirr's parents had been divers; both had died in the water. The boy learned to ignore gillhoppers just as they ignored him.

Kafirr came to the end of the catwalks and stepped down onto the dock. Here the smell of the undrinkable, iridescent ocean was overpowering. Air and sea surface were pressed flat by many kilometers of atmosphere, and greenhouse effect kept the air hot and the water blood-warm. The *Systems Guide* said the air was breathable, but *bearable* would have been the better word. Excursionists took one whiff and went back to their landers for filters. Somewhere above the distant cloud tops was a feeble red sun that the boy had never seen. Dayside was always turned toward this invisible primary, so half the world was in red twilight, and half the world was a hot, dark oven. Kafirr had never been to Darkside; Dayside was bad enough.

A crowd had gathered around his slack safety lines. The outer ring was excursionists, not too secretly expecting tragedy. They were a typical tour group wearing nose filters and extravagant costumes—gossamer wings, shaved silver headdresses, chrome-yellow skindye with circular patches of purple fabric covering their private parts. Kafirr was no prude—he dived in only a loin-cloth—but the metal in the costumes bothered him. Some of these clanking off-world outfits had more metal than he could earn in a hundred hours of diving. Kafirr struggled to set aside his anger. Anger did a diver no good, and he had not seen enough of the universe to know that hating the hand that fed you was a common phenomenon.

As he slipped through the tour group, Kafirr saw divers down on their knees, sniffing for blood in the water and checking the copyfish. They leaped up, happy to see the boy and slapping him on the back. Kafirr reeled in his safety line, spilling his stuffsack on the dock. Seastones tumbled out. He selected a pure crimson for the diver who had stood watch over his line.

Making the best of his survival, the excursionists crowded closer to look at his stones. The ring of human and humanoid faces made the air even less breathable, wasting oxygen with inane noises. The immense atmosphere and planet-wide ocean kept a constant balance between $CO_2$ and oxygen, but it was not the balance that humans had evolved in. Only high atmospheric pressure made the air breathable, forcing relatively scarce oxygen into the blood. Divers bought whiffs of pure oxygen from vendors before each dive. It burned the back of Kafirr's throat and made his head spin, but pure high-pressure oxygen fueled long, deep dives.

This time the seastones that glittered on the dock were prime. Only a few were pales and buffs; the rest were crimsons, beryls, and indigos. Kafirr got good prices. Off-worlders always paid the best at dockside. Seastones were small metallic deposits produced by prolific colonies of microorganisms that clung to the mat roots. The stones themselves were common enough and no problem to manufacture off-planet. What tourists were really paying for was the danger. As he bargained, Kafirr described the venomous grotto, the copyfish, and the deepdevil. A harrowing story, told by a naked boy with a diver's whip-hard body, easily tripled the price. Insensitive souls could buy their stones much cheaper from waterfront shops, but those who wanted the real thing had to come to dockside, to touch the grim water, to buy from the diver who risked death to bring the stones up. Each curio came complete with an enthralling anecdote, and off-worlders had not crossed time and space just to get bits of metal and stone they could have bought at home.

Kafirr could see the rough justice in all this. If the waters of his world were not so deadly, off-worlders would pick their own seastones. Then he and the other divers would probably starve.

When the last stone was sold, the excursionists drifted away. Divers left to buy oxygen or lie down next to their lines, readying bodies for the next dive. Others sat gossiping in two or threes, or gambled for bits of metal and unsold stones. The water-shy ones moped alone or begged. A female diver strummed a crude-stringed dulcimer, and someone joined in with a pair of pipes, playing a tune brought from ancient Earth. As he struggled into his wet loincloth, Kafirr hummed what he thought were the words, though he hardly understood them:

*May the circle be unbroken by and by, yes, by and by;*
*There's a better world awaiting in the sky, yes, in the sky. . . .*

His humming stopped, and Kafirr searched about in shocked disbelief. His pry bar was missing. He must have dropped it in the grotto when he was escaping from the deepdevil. The metal tool was so valuable that Kafirr snapped on his safety line, getting ready to dive after it. One look at the solid gray water brought his senses back. By now the pry bar was drifting down into the smoky depths, past the deepdevils, to where the pressure was heavy enough to float metal and flatten an armorfish. It was approaching the planet's sunken crust, where thousands of vents and volcanoes spewed out the minerals that gave the ocean its metallic taste.

Kafirr sat stunned on the dock, weeping at the unfairness in the world, missing his mother and father. Masses of metal landed and departed for orbit every dozen hours. Moored nearby was a slick orbital yacht, a Fornax Skylark, with a bulb-shaped body and a needle-sharp nose. Next to it was a hydrofoil cruiser with a catamaran bow and smooth airfoils over the stern. Both of these vessels must have held over a hundred tons of metal. Airless worlds and lifeless asteroids had metal in abundance, but on this ocean each gram had to be brought down from orbit or screened from the mineral-rich water. Gillhoppers did not use metal at all, except for trace amounts their mats extracted through osmotic pumps. Only oceanography and excursionists brought in the hard credit needed to support metal import or production. By far the most common metal makers on the planet were the microorganisms that made seastones, but most of their harvest was carried away as curios by off-worlders. What metal remained was expensive. The pry bar was his most important inheritance from his parents, the one material thing they had passed on to him. The few kilos that went into that pry bar would cost Kafirr more hard credit than he had accumulated in thousands of hours of diving.

Life went on by the dock. Kafirr could hear the pipes and dulcimer playing, along with the groans and yells of the gamblers. It grated him to hear that other divers could be so happy while he had lost half his livelihood. But that was how it had to be; and music always played loudest after a diver was pulled dead from the water.

Kafirr kept looking at the hydrocruiser, and saw two xenos come down the gangway. The first was an Eridani Hound, a fairly common species in this reach of Eridanus Sector. Hounds adapted well to star travel and looked comfortably familiar to humans, resembling semi-upright hyenas or oversized baboons. This Hound was probably a pilot, since he wore a zero-g harness and had a comlink clipped to his left jaw. The Hound had a zestful good-living air, and addressed his larger companion as Q'Maax'-doux. This Q'Maax'doux was an aquatic xeno unlike any that Kafirr had ever seen, with webbed digits, strong legs, and the barrel chest of a swimmer. A blunt amphibian head sat directly on Q'Maax'doux's huge shoulders, topped with a webbed crest that blended into a dorsal fin running the full length of the spine. The creature had gill fringes under the forelimbs, and nostril flaps to keep liquid out of the lungs. Kafirr envied the webbing and powerful limbs, wishing nature had equipped him half so well for the water. The xeno had no clothes, no obvious sex, and was colored like a deepdevil, dark on top and light on the belly. The colors were shades of blue-gray that seemed somehow too drab and similar, as if the xeno's home star were whiter and brighter. The bulging muscles and rapid gait certainly suggested a home world with greater gravity, though local gravity was a tiring 1.6 g.

Q'Maax'doux spoke to the Hound through the standard tourist speakbox: "I have promised a school of silver rippers to the Institute of Zoological Morphology on Epsilon Eridani IV. In a few hundred hours, a high-boost institute ship will be here to take delivery."

"Silver rippers; sounds exciting and strenuous," said the Hound. "I would be right in the water beside you, but I have a rare allergy to ocean spray. The mere mention of deep water makes my skin creep uncontrollably."

"I am sorry to hear of your handicap." The bigger xeno set the speakbox to a correct mix of pity and contempt: "At the moment I am in the market for nothing more dangerous than a couple of creatures suitable for deepwater work."

"Do you have any particular type of creature in mind?" The Hound also had a speakbox, whose tone signified helpful disinterest.

Q'Maax'doux indicated the green gillhoppers tending their pods from catwalks. "This planet has an indigenous semi-intelligent species. They should know their own waters best."

The Hound reset his speakbox to indicate amusement: "Gillhoppers share my allergy and never go near the water."

Q'Maax'doux came to a surprised stop a few meters from Kafirr, with gill fringes flaring and dorsal spines erect. "This planet is entirely oceanic; how can any sensible species ignore that?"

"Are gillhoppers sensible?" said the Hound. "Since they ignore us completely, it is difficult to judge. No doubt they consider themselves prudent. They are related to several aquatic-prey species that inhabit the root fringes. Note that they still possess stunted fins and the rudimentary gills that give them their name."

Q'Maax'doux's neckless head could not nod; instead, the xeno set the speakbox for impatient assent. "All the more reason for them to be in the water."

The Hound grinned. He had learned from humans to express humor by exposing his fangs. "Eons ago, the ancestral gillhoppers learned to grow these great vegetable mats and harvest the mat pods. There are now hundreds of these mats totaling thousands of square kilometers, each inhabited by a different variety of gillhopper. Once they left the water, gillhoppers probably saw no good reason to go back. The waters of this world are not as safe as they should be."

Despite his troubles, Kafirr smiled at the Hound's grim humor. Heavy metals made the mat pods poisonous to humans. If Kafirr could have harvested pods like a gillhopper, nothing could have dragged him back into the water.

Q'Maax'doux found a rude noise in the speakbox's vocabulary. "Then what sort of creature shall I use for deepwater work?"

"That sort." The Eridani Hound turned his sharp snout toward Kafirr.

"Oh." Q'Maax'doux's speakbox transmitted profound disappointment. "I already have one of those, and frankly, I hoped to do better. These creatures were not bred for water work."

The Hound shrugged, another human gesture he had learned to imitate. "No doubt they do their best. Humans are what everyone here uses for water work. Their need for processed food and distilled water makes them tractable and tolerably anxious to please. Though, I would address him as 'man'; they are often slow in answering to 'creature.' "

Q'Maax'doux gave the Hound grudging thanks, and bid him farewell. Kafirr was already on his feet when Q'Maax'doux strode over to him. "Man," said the xeno, "are you suitable for deepwater work?"

Kafirr bobbed his head, nodding and grinning. "Yes, yes, more than suitable." He wanted to land the job before the big xeno attracted a crowd. The hint of steady work drew divers as fast as blood in the water drew copyfish.

"Have you done deepwater work before?" Q'Maax'doux was still casting about for some reason to reject the human.

"Yes, yes." Kafirr lied enthusiastically, amazed that a chance conversation between two xenos had turned his life around.

"Are you familiar with silver rippers?" Q'Maax'doux was still reluctant to reel in this easy catch.

"Of course, very familiar." Kafirr would have sworn he mated with them, if it would get him the job.

Q'Maax'doux grunted through the speakbox, then picked up Kafirr's safety line. Nothing had been said about payment, but then, Kafirr had never worked for a wage before. Anything was better than being a diver without a pry bar.

Leading Kafirr by the safety line, Q'Maax'doux boarded the hydrocruiser. Kafirr could not really accept his good fortune until the gangway retracted behind him, vanishing into the seamless hull. "I have another man in my employ," said the xeno. "He will tell you your duties." Q'Maax'doux started to walk away with the safety line, then dropped it on the deck. "Wait here until the other man comes for you."

Kafirr waited for the man to come, his bare toes caressing the cruiser's smooth deck. The cruiser's reactor and superstructure were slung between the two light hulls. He could feel the hum of power from the stern and saw the graceful double curve of the bow. Kafirr had watched boats come and go all his life, and this one was by far the largest. The hydrocruiser was over a hundred meters long and a dozen meters wide; but with superlight materials everywhere, Kafirr doubted that it massed a thousand tons.

He saw a large electroprojector forward and two smaller ones aft.
A matched pair of gigs rested on the fantail.

Still the man did not arrive. Kafirr studied the towering superstructure, topped by a silver hedge of antennas that he could not
identify. Kafirr was puzzling over a laser range-finder when a
voice behind him asked, "What are you doing here?"

Kafirr turned faster than a copyfish, but it was not the man he
had been expecting. Instead he saw a woman stepping down from
the gangway that led to the main deck. But for her sex, he might
have been looking into a mirror. She was a diver: her head was
shaved as close as his; her limbs were as thick, her belly as flat.
Like Kafirr, she wore only a loincloth; her breasts were small, with
large flat nipples. Her eyes were as wide and brown as his, but the
lines on her face were deeper. The woman was several score
kilohours older than Kafirr.

"I am waiting for a man," said the boy. "The xeno who owns
this boat—"

She cut him short with a curt shake of her head. "I am the man
you are waiting for. Quasimodo never learned how to sex humans."

"Quasimodo?" Kafirr missed the allusion; the nearest tape of
Victor Hugo's works was trillions of kilometers distant.

She cocked her head toward the main deck. "The xeno who
owns this boat. Our web-fingered master does not mind the name,
and just assumes that I cannot pronounce Q'Maax'doux. My own
name is Nila." She said it in a flat voice; not an introduction, just
information. "Q'Maax'doux hired me a couple of dozen hours ago,
which makes me senior to you." There was a hint of challenge in
how she said that. "The xeno said that we were getting something
suitable for deepwater work. Are you supposed to be that something?"

Kafirr nodded. Lying to these cold brown eyes was going to be
harder.

"And you misled him." Nila's words were easy and matter-of-
fact; no accusation, just more information.

He started to deny it, but she cut him short with another shake
of her head. "Look, there are not a dozen divers on Windward Mat
who have ever done deepwater work. You are too young to be one
of them. This xeno thinks that all humans are alike; you and I
know better."

Nila paused, swinging her hand about to indicate the hydrocruiser. "You like this boat?"

It was better than anything Kafirr had ever seen, but the boy
barely had time to say yes.

"Right," she went on. "If you want to stay aboard, never lie to me. I do not care if you lie to Q'Maax'doux. I do that myself. But if I catch you in a lie to me, I will tell Q'Maax'doux that you have never done deepwater work. This tenderhearted xeno will heave you into the water and get another diver. Like I said, we're all the same to the xeno."

Kafirr's yes was overready, anything to keep that smooth deck beneath his feet.

"Good." Nila made the word sound menacing. "You stay, and you do all the diving. I do not go into the water."

The boy hated the water—only fools or suicides welcomed it—but he still found Nila's adamance startling. He had seen water-shy divers before; those with bad omens, or who had lost any will to live. You could read the fear in their eyes, and they never lasted long. Fear can kill you quicker than a puffball. But Nila did not look afraid of anything; her gaze was as cold and hard as the waves in the wake of a storm.

Kafirr agreed again, since doing the diving was no more than he had expected. Nila relaxed and took him to the forecastle. From amidships aft, the hydrocruiser was almost all engine, but the forward hulls were filled with flotation foam and cross-bracing. There were several pockets in the foam large enough for spacious cabins. The hydrocruiser was human-built, but with more than humans in mind, and each cabin was big enough for a few Q'Maax'douxs.

"This is mine?" the boy asked.

"Ours," Nila replied. "The xeno thinks one cabin is more than enough for two humans." She deposited him and left without ever asking his name.

Kafirr put Nila out of his mind and poked about, finding an inner cubicle with an equally large basin and bath. There was also a spacious locker stocked with meals. Testing the food, he found it better than any he had ever eaten. Only the need to dive would keep him from getting fat. Kafirr sprawled on the huge sleeping mat, thinking that if he died on his first dive, he would have already lived as no one he knew had ever lived.

# DEEP WATER

Garrulous as a gargoyle, Q'Maax'doux did not head right for deep water. Instead the hydrocruiser steered along the leeward line of mats at four hundred kilometers per hour, rocking the great floating gardens with its wake. Huge airfoils extended out over the stern to keep the cruiser from porpoising or blowing over at high speed. Every millimeter of the hydrocruiser was computer-controlled and coded in Q'Maax'doux's language, a code harder to break than any human cipher. Nila taught Kafirr the few words she had learned, the ones that opened hatches and called down ladders. Otherwise, there was nothing the two humans could do to control the craft or affect their fate. Their only duties were to keep to themselves until their xeno needed them. Swift orders punctuated long silences.

Nila acted like a shadowy extension of Q'Maax'doux, transmitting orders and limiting conversation. Neither human stood watches, and no duties drew them together. Kafirr ate when he was hungry and slept when he was tired. Still, it shocked him the first time he entered the cabin and found Nila sleeping. She lay curled on one side of the mat: with trim feet tucked below her buttocks, one hand shielding two tender breasts, the other hand clinched in front of her face, thumb tip almost touching moist lips. Curved in sleep, her strong shoulders had no tension. Close-clipped hair ended in a soft tangle at the nape of her neck. With her eyes closed, Kafirr could now see that her lashes were long and silky, and she looked much younger.

For some time he sat on the mat, close enough to have touched her, watching her breath move in and out. Then he went up on the deck to lie down. Kafirr needed his sleep, and he would have gotten no rest lying beside Nila.

When they were both awake, Kafirr tried to create conversation. On deck he asked Nila why they were not headed straight for deep water. Instead they seemed to be on a high-speed tour of the mats that banded the planet's equator.

She shrugged, staring at the long jade mat that was whipping by, less than a kilometer to starboard. "Q'Maax'doux does not tell me. If our lord feels lonely, talking to humans is not the cure." Nila bent her wrist backward and twisted a finger against the solid substance of the cruiser. "The xeno thinks that talking to us is about the same as talking to the bulkheads. Maybe Quasimodo just wants to shake up the gillhoppers, startle them into showing how they run their mats."

That last comment was pure extravagance, a speculation that served no purpose except to converse with Kafirr. No one knew how gillhoppers controlled their mats. Gillhoppers treated the ocean the way humans sometimes treat sex. They pretended it did not exist, but privately knew every nuance of wind or current.

Noting how gillhoppers tended their pods was better than satellite forecasting if you wanted to know what the local weather would be like. Nor did their mats drift aimlessly. Instead they inscribed slow circles in the planet's equatorial regions, somehow alternating between the prevailing currents that ran in the opposite hemispheres. Any other course might carry them through the terminator, into Darkside, where pods would die and mats disintegrate. How they maneuvered their mats through these currents was a mystery, gillhoppers being as vocal on this subject as they were on any other.

Kafirr could have been sharing his cabin with a gillhopper, for all the attention he got out of Nila. Yet through it all he was enthralled. He was eating, sleeping, and not diving.

At the tip of the last archipelago, Q'Maax'doux made a wide turn that carried them out toward the terminator, then doubled back. The cruiser dropped its sea anchor off the most leeward line of mats. When he saw Nila coming to fetch him, Kafirr knew he was going into the water. She was cold and hard-eyed again, determined not to be drawn into conversation, as if contact with Kafirr could contaminate her. She merely handed him goggles, snorkel, and foot paddles.

Q'Maax'doux was waiting on the fantail, looking at the mats, now a few kilometers off. "I want you to swim," said the xeno.

"Where?" asked Kafirr.

Finding a patient tone in his speakbox, the xeno replied, "Swim to the root fringe, then turn around and swim back."

Swimming three or four kilometers in open water was not like diving for seastones. Out in the ocean there was no safety line, nor was there rest at the other end; the root fringes were loaded with puffs, and divers always worked from cleared docks. It was a long swim without a shred of protection, and Kafirr now knew how he would pay for all those hours of sleeping and eating.

Nila was ready by the oxygen line. Looking straight into his eyes, she helped him hold the oxygen mask. For a moment, Nila put a firm hand over his, then she took it away. Another pure extravagance.

Charged with oxygen, Kafirr swung over the stern rail and dived into the dull gray water. As he sank, Kafirr could feel that the sea was different here. He heard a strong sea surge in his ears, the pulsing of the planet-wide ocean. The water itself was vibrant and bottomless, divided into descending layers of light. Below, Kafirr could sense nothing but the limitless smoky deep.

Taking his direction from the cruiser's twin hulls, Kafirr kicked off toward the mat, senses alert for any sea changes. Almost at once a larger body broke the surface behind him. Kafirr spun about and saw Q'Maax'doux passing him. A few powerful kicks, and the xeno was well ahead, with a portable electroprojector trailing from a forelimb. Kafirr wondered why the xeno needed lumbering humans crowding the water when he could swim like that.

He struggled after the disappearing xeno. By now his oxygen was gone, and Kafirr had to rise, breathing through the snorkel. Q'Maax'doux's finned feet vanished in the murk ahead, and the emptiness closed in. Kafirr was alone again, hearing the sea surge and feeling the vast void of the ocean, stretching around the world and down to the sunken planet surface. Deep water even smelled different, more mineral, more metallic; it had not been swept and strained by the mats.

After an eternity of kicking in emptiness, Kafirr saw copyfish ahead. Now he was nearing the root fringe, though he had no idea how far out from the fringe these scavengers swam. The copyfish crowded around him, knowing he was harmless and making no attempt to match his alien outline. Kafirr felt the comfort that copyfish brought. Then they all turned in unison, alerted by an invisible signal. Without changing configuration, the copyfish dashed off in the direction of the mats.

Kafirr redoubled his efforts. That sudden flight meant that the copyfish had sensed a predator too big and horrible to be mimicked. For a full minute he fled from the unknown, then he saw immense inky shapes emerging from the murk. Big black shadows with slow-beating wings drew closer, growing larger and more distinct. Kafirr had never seen giant mantlewings before, but the configuration was unmistakable: thick black wings with a tired beat, followed by a long undulating tail. Kafirr could not see their mouths, but he had heard they were two meters across and shaped like air scoops.

Kafirr kicked harder. The gliding shadows were gaining on him, eating as they went, swimming in a staggered formation so each had a clear feeding path. Kafirr could hear soft, high-pitched, and penetrating calls, probing after him and echoing off the mat fringe. He had to reach the roots, where large predators did not dare follow; but his puny human effort would never be enough. The mantlewings did not even bother to increase their speed. One of the larger ones would scoop him up without breaking rhythm. Blind panic kept Kafirr pushing forward, straining to see the root fringe through the gloom. All he saw were visions of his parents, and how they had died.

First there was the flash of a sighting laser, followed by an electric crackle in the water. Q'Maax'doux kicked into view, the electroprojector already at rest and trailing from a forelimb. The lead mantlewing was collapsing, folding in on itself. The others broke formation and circled about, confused by conflicting signals from their stunned leader.

Q'Maax'doux signaled for Kafirr to surface. The boy obeyed, his lungs and legs aching. When his head broke water, Kafirr saw he was still a kilometer short of the nearest mat. If Q'Maax'doux had not come back, Kafirr would have been an easy meal. The mantlewings were milling about a few hundred meters off, flapping to the surface, then diving again. The hydrocruiser was charging over the waves toward its owner, obeying commands from Q'Maax'doux's comlink.

When the cruiser churned up, the soft black phantoms faded into more distant water. Kafirr called down a trailing ladder and hauled himself aboard. As he lay gasping on the fantail, Nila knelt beside him. In her lips and breasts, and in the cloud bottoms, Kafirr saw beauty that he had not remembered from before. All Nila said was, "You cannot study predators if you haven't any prey."

Q'Maax'doux was still in the water, directing the port crane to grapple and raise the paralyzed mantlewing. Kafirr lay limp and exhausted until he saw the mantlewing swing up over the rail. At once he rolled to his feet and retreated from the fantail to the main deck, before the monster could come down on top of him. Q'Maax'doux rode the mantlewing aboard, a conqueror lifted high on the back of the vanquished.

The xeno spent a happy hour or two butchering the living beast. Q'Maax'doux poked and peered, making measurements and stimulating internal organs with a variable-voltage prod, then cutting off bits for the bioscope and laser spectrograph. When the study was complete, Q'Maax'doux ordered the remains lowered into a hold. Then the xeno came bounding up the ladder, reeking of bile and preservatives.

As soon as Q'Maax'doux's speakbox was on-line, it began to fire questions at Kafirr: "How did that attack compare with attacks by other deepwater predators? Do they move that slowly in deeper water?" Q'Maax'doux returned to his special subject, the "silver ripper." It was known to be much smaller than the mantlewing, the xeno explained, but thought to be more active and even deadlier. How would Kafirr compare them?

Kafirr had nothing to compare the mantlewing with, and was too aghast to invent replies. The monster cut up and lying in the hold was twenty meters of wing supporting thirty meters of digestive tract. Something "more deadly" was not the sort of horror that Kafirr could just fabricate answers about. He had to admit that this piece of ocean was as far as he had ever been from a gill-hopper mat. Q'Maax'doux adjusted the speakbox, playing back the boy's reply. When the xeno was sure of the sense of it, Q'Maax'doux dismissed Kafirr and turned to Nila. "This one is unsuitable, and you failed to apprise me. I am ready to hunt again, so this time you will swim."

Nila's brown eyes narrowed. She shook her head, without taking her gaze off the xeno. "I do not go into the water. You selected this diver, and so far he has been adequate."

Q'Maax'doux lowered the tone of the speakbox until the words turned to a growl. "You are going into the water. There is no other option. You may go in as my employee, or you may leave my employment and swim to the nearest mat."

Nila snatched the goggles and snorkel from Kafirr, and sat for a moment on the stern rail, adjusting the lenses and pulling on the foot paddles. She kept her chin and head averted. Muscles rippled under soft skin, making each movement swift and sure. As soon as the foot paddles were secure, she rose up on the rail, balanced for an instant, then went into the water, leaving barely a ripple. Kafirr watched with professional interest, finding her form perfect. Q'Maax'doux splashed in behind her; as powerful as the xeno was in the water, Q'Maax'doux could not match Nila's grace in the air.

Once the waters had swallowed them, Kafirr returned to the cabin. He told the lights to dim, and relaxed on the sleeping mat. The terror of the swim had been cleansing, a frightening baptism in deep water, but he actually felt better for it. The worst had happened. Q'Maax'doux had discovered his lie, but had not thrown him overboard. Now Nila had nothing to hold over him. She was now the one in danger, but doing no more than he had done. Happy with the world, Kafirr went to sleep.

He awoke in hot darkness. Nila was standing over him, dripping wet, with her arms folded across her chest.

"So," said Kafirr, "you went in the water."

She glared past him, seeming to see nothing, not even the cabin bulkhead, and least of all the boy.

Kafirr did his best to coax her into a better mood. "Being bait for Q'Maax'doux is spooky, but it is much safer than working the root grottoes. No stingworms, no puffs, and Q'Maax'doux is an incredible swimmer. We are safer with the xeno than we would be alone, or with any dozen human divers."

Her eyes remained distant; her mouth moved slowly, trying to make her meaning clear. "You may find this difficult, but I do not want to be a happy slave: eating, sleeping, and relaxing on safe dives. I do not want some xeno making life-and-death decisions for me. Remember, Q'Maax'doux's ganglia are fixed on bringing in a school of silver rippers. Those are the carnivores little bigger than copyfish, but connoisseurs consider them the worst predators on the planet. Few have ever been captured, and live ones have never been taken off-planet. Ever wonder why? If he plans to use us as bait for silver rippers, it will not be a pleasant splash around the boat with a flock of mantlewings. Rippers hunt in huge packs that can strip a thousand-meter sea snake in a matter of minutes. They will use that electroprojector for a toothpick."

Kafirr was somewhat stunned. He had never heard Nila speak for so long on any single subject, but once she started talking, there seemed to be no stopping her. Nila sat down on the mat, with her moist skin only millimeters away. Kafirr could see tears in her eyes, and felt the way he had the first time he saw her sleeping. He wanted to hold this new Nila and tell her not to worry. "There are no rippers right now," said Kafirr. "We are safe and fed. Why worry about things that have not happened?"

Nila dried her eyes, then rested her hand on the mat next to his. She leaned forward, trying desperately to be understood, but her body had an intoxicating fragrance that kept Kafirr from concentrating on her words. "Don't you see? What I want is no more diving, no more hours in the water."

"How?" To the boy, that sounded insane. Diving was horrible, but how could you give up the one thing that put food in your mouth?

"Do you know that a River Lines packet accelerates at thirty pseudogravities, and can reach near light speed in a few hundred hours?"

"So?" Kafirr could see no connection between diving and the performance of a River Lines packet.

"A few hours after Q'Maax'doux docks, the packet *Jordan River* will lift off from orbit. When it does, I am going with it. This job will give me the last credit I need to cover my fare. I am not going to die only hours from freedom."

"You are going off-planet?" Kafirr had never seen a moon or star, never seen anything but the bottom of perpetual, impenetrable cloud cover.

"As far off-planet as a cheap ticket will take me. I was not born on this world," said Nila, "and nothing I have seen here encourages me to stay."

No wonder her head was always so high in the cloud cover, thought Kafirr. Nila was an off-worlder. To Kafirr, that explained a lot. Her distance and coldness were now natural, and he no longer wanted to touch her. Before, he had considered Nila aloof, arrogant, and uncaring, but he had never suspected she was a tourist. Kafirr got up and left, leaving her alone in the cabin.

# JORDAN RIVER

Q'Maax'doux set a course for deep water, skipping over the equatorial current, heading for the terminator. The hydrocruiser wove through floating forests spread over the sea. Long strands of gold-green vegetation lay in parallel rows, streaming with the current. The sea around the gillhopper mats had been free of such obstruction because the mats swept up stray vegetation, growing by a process that only the gillhoppers understood and controlled. Cyclonic storms blew out of the terminator, covering the sea-forests with sheets of warm rain. The hydrocruiser skipped between the typhoons, sonar and all-weather guidance finding lanes through the storms and vegetation.

The sea change that had come over Nila continued. No longer aloof, she found reasons to comment on everything: the speed of the cruiser, the clouds overhead, the sea around them. With little else to do, Kafirr listened. Then, in their dark, warm cabin, she told him her whole story. It was overloaded with off-world concepts, but Kafirr could follow most of it.

"My parents retired young," she said, "and took me on Tour, investing their savings in several corporations. That way their credit would accumulate for millions of hours while they were on Tour. They would have come back both young and wealthy. I saw half the worlds in Eridanus Sector while I was still growing up. The deal was a cheap package tour bought from Pisicum Freight and Ferry; but to me, it was wonderful. Even this planet was a delight seen from orbit, a clouded pearl resting on the black fabric of space. As we decelerated from light speed, communications returned, and people discovered that Pisicum Freight and Ferry had gone belly-up. It was the biggest bust in millions of hours; ships were stranded all over Eridanus Sector. A battalion of smart lawyers got a venue ruling that said all claims against Pisicum had to be adjudicated at the sector capital in Epsilon Eridani system. I watched my folks go crazy. It takes three hundred thousand hours to get a message through to Epsilon from here, and claims on Pisicum were selling at a mil on the credit in the local securities market. Pisicum Freight and Ferry had only one local asset, the ship that had dumped us here, which Paradise Development attached. Pisicum had left monumental debts to Paradise Development, and at one mil on the credit, our little claim was not even worth a ride into orbit."

She lay back on the mat, looking straight up at the deckhead above. A thin metal skin and layers of foam kept out the gray sea and gray rain. "We were washed up on a worthless world. Anyone who knew us or could help us was tens of thousands of hours off by ship or signal." Her gaze seemed to go through the deckhead, searching for the heavens that were hidden by pink cloud cover. "Our original complaints are still crawling to Epsilon at light speed. My dad died trying his hand at diving. My mom became a wharf rat, telling her story to tourists and living on handouts. Finally some mildly disgusting guy offered her a lift to Paradise system, just a single seat. He had no room for overgrown children, since I would not do for him what my mother did. I suppose if I had done it, he would have taken us both. He was pretty broad-minded in his own repulsive way. Mom said she would come back for me, but that was forty thousand hours ago."

She sat up, resting her chin on her hand and looking Kafirr over. "By then I was already a diver. You know what that is like. I spent long hours in the water, saving every bit of credit, eating any way I could. Quasimodo is warmth itself compared to some of the humans I worked for. At least this xeno never learned to sex humans, and does not expect us to spread for him after hard hours in the water." She paused, noting that he had said nothing. "This may not seem much of a tragedy to you, but I wasn't born here. Believe me, I know better."

"I am sorry for you anyway." Kafirr could think of nothing else to say. He did not know which Nila he liked better: the old Nila, who ignored him and whom he half hated; or this new Nila, who seemed determined to expand and complicate his world. He half wanted to tell her his story and talk about his family; but how could he expose his private pain to Nila? Nila could think of going off-planet, but leaving was plainly beyond him. Diving was a delayed death sentence, but it was all he had.

She flopped back on the bed. "You are probably dumb enough to be sorry for me. Take some off-world advice, start being sorry for yourself."

When Q'Maax'doux called them up on deck, the storms had evaporated, and the cloud cover was the gray-pink of decaying meat. In the wake of the rains, the clouds had come down to blend with the water, fusing into a single wet substance. At various distances into the murk, Kafirr could see long undulating lines that looked like standing waves in the sea. These lines slowly slid across each other, appearing ahead, disappearing behind.

"Sea snakes," said Q'Maax'doux.

Looking closer, the humans could see that the moving wave crests were really parts of immense creatures whose long bodies extended off into the fog. A dozen lay off either bow, thick black lines drawn on the sea mist. The cruiser was a slick little toy, rocking in the troughs between them, with three mites standing on its surface.

The triumph of the moment made Q'Maax'doux almost talkative. "This is the hunting ground," said the xeno as he spun the cruiser around. "Silver rippers are the only predators that feed on adult sea snakes." At low speeds, the cruiser had a tight radius, but even so, they nearly beached on the head of an oncoming snake. Wide gill fringes and thousands of feeding tentacles slid by the starboard hull. The huge head had no eyes: sea snakes steered by sonar and were stone-blind on the surface, ignoring any obstacle smaller than a gillhopper mat.

Weaving between the rows of snakes, Q'Maax'doux kept the cruiser on a reciprocal course until it shot out of the rear end of the herd. Then the cruiser leaped about, bouncing high on the chop left by hundreds of huge bodies. The bow electroprojector spun at Q'Maax'doux's command, taking aim at one of the rear snakes. When the projector flashed, the snake twisted in pain, howling out of its air holes, with a deep burn mark all along its back. Seismic waves spread over the surface as the wounded giant lashed the water.

Q'Maax'doux halted the cruiser, throwing out the sea anchor. The superstructure was swinging in a wild arc, falling and rising fifty meters with each wave. The catamaran hull was stable at any angle of inclination, but as springy as a raft in heavy seas. As the spasms slackened and the beast grew limp, scavengers assembled. Nila pointed out several varieties of deepwater copyfish.

The cruiser circled beside the dying snake until it stopped twitching. Then Q'Maax'doux hauled in the anchor and gunned the cruiser after the herd, slaughtering another snake in similar fashion. For hours the xeno continued to kill sea snakes, leaving an archipelago of long, dead islands rocking in the swell.

"This is senseless," said Kafirr. The sea snakes were so huge they hardly seemed to be living beings, but their screaming and thrashing would have gotten pity from a gillhopper.

"Silver rippers are not scavengers," Nila explained. "They come up for live meat. Only a wounded snake can get their attention. Do you want to go back to being bait?"

Many dead monsters later, the hydrocruiser's sonar signaled a large contact separating from a deep thermocline. Q'Maax'doux announced that a shoal of silver rippers was rising to feed. Soon the sea around the latest victim began to boil with silver bodies. The snake's struggles increased. Now it was not only dying, but also being eaten alive.

It seemed then that the whole ocean had gone mad. The water was alive with thousands of silver rippers. While they tore at a struggling sea beast many times larger than the cruiser, scavengers crowded close to share in the feast. Even Nila had nothing to say.

Q'Maax'doux gave a gleeful command to the cruiser, and the boat began to fling little dark packets in a broad pattern. These small black specks hung for a moment at the top of their arcs, then splashed into the sea. Where each one landed, the water was indented for a moment, then thrown up in a thick column. All around these pillars, the air and water surface shook with the muffled boom of deep explosions. For a full minute, the hydro-cruiser was hidden by a forest of splashes, then the last column collapsed and the sea subsided. The whole community of predators and scavengers that had been drawn by the dying snakes was knocked senseless, with most of its members dying. Q'Maax'-doux tossed Nila a net. "You will look for any silver rippers that might survive."

Fresh copyfish collected to feed on this new bounty. Working from the gigs, Kafirr and Nila moved over the dead sea, looking for living rippers. While Q'Maax'doux watched from the bridge, the humans dragged stunned carnivores into the hold, entering directly through an opening on the trailing edge of the starboard ram wing.

When they were done, they collapsed in the cabin. Kafirr said nothing; the killing had made him morose.

"I suppose you think this is a waste of time," said Nila. "Just wait; we may be doing all this for nothing. The rippers we got are so weak they may never reach Windward Mat, much less Epsilon Eridani."

Once the hold was full, Q'Maax'doux swung the hydrocruiser around. The xeno was in a silent frenzy to get his catch back to Windward Mat, where they could be loaded for the long voyage to Epsilon E. Many hours out of port, Nila returned from the hold with the news that the rippers were dying.

Q'Maax'doux adjusted his speakbox to indicate annoyed indig-nation. "It is your job to keep them alive."

"Listen, Quas," the woman replied. "Your collecting methods have shaken them up. Silver rippers are social, active carnivores. You cannot just knock them silly, keep them comatose, and then expect them to come out on their own. They need to be revived, exercised, even reintroduced to eating."

"Then you will do that." Q'Maax'doux spoke simply, as though explaining the world to children.

Nila folded her arms over her breasts and gave him a sidelong look. "Do I pipe dance and dinner music down into the hold?"

"No," said Q'Maax'doux. "That would be pointless. Your companion will exercise them."

"Exercise them?" Nila did not even bother to look at Kafirr, who was himself astonished.

"Yes, have him push them about," said Q'Maax'doux. "Use mild electric probes, and hand-feed living bait to any that show signs of hunger."

Kafirr was staggered at the thought of spending any extended time in that hold. It was as dark and stagnant as the deepest root grotto, filled with dead and dying hundred-kilo carnivores.

Before he could speak, Nila spoke for him. "Don't you think that is a bit dangerous? If he succeeds, the little dears will wake up hungry. The boy will be pinned in a dark hold with angry and ill-fed predators twice his size."

Q'Maax'doux's blunt head swiveled back in her direction, and the xeno selected a lecturing tone: "Risk is what he is paid for. He is only human and has no special skills. It is sensible that any danger should fall on the least essential creature available."

Nila's eyes narrowed. "Well, listen, neckless wonder, I am no more essential than he is. Let me exercise the rippers."

Kafirr was surprised, but Q'Maax'doux was not. The xeno merely said that one would do as well as another.

"But," she added, "before I go back in that hold, I want to be paid in advance; I want to hold the payment in my hand."

"That is a strange and primitive request." Now Q'Maax'doux did seem surprised.

"I am a primitive-type person," said Nila. "Now or later—what does it mean to you?"

"Nothing," said Q'Maax'doux, and he paid her.

Kafirr watched the xeno's broad back depart. "You did not have to do that."

"Didn't I?" Nila gave him a sour look.

"I would have gone in the hold," said the boy.

"That is just why I did it." She shook her head. "This is a job that must be done only one way. The first rippers to wake up would have had you for hors d'oeuvres. Then kindly Quasimodo would have sent me into water warm with your blood, or made me walk home."

"Why don't you just call me stupid?" Kafirr complained.

"Because that would be rude. Look, I know I sound hard," said Nila, "but this job is my ticket." Her fist tightened compulsively around the credit scrip. "I need to feel the payment in my hands, and to give Q'Maax'doux no reason to back out or complain to the Port Authorities. That makes my life very simple; I just have to stay alive until the *Jordan River* lifts for Paradise system."

For the entire trip back, Kafirr had nothing to do but watch Nila go in and out of the hold. Several times he offered to help, but she shrugged him off. He should have been pleased to be paid for nothing, but instead he felt slighted. The closer they got to Windward Mat, the more he felt the tension, thinking by now the rippers were bound to be more active. Nila was spending almost all her time in the hold, but Kafirr caught her getting up from a short rest in the cabin. "Look," he said, "this is crazy; you are bound to make a slip. Why are you taking all the danger onto yourself? There was a time when you did not care if I lived at all."

Nila sat up on the edge of the sleeping mat, looking up with weary eyes. "That was different. I was trying to keep myself separate from diving. I did not dare know you, or care for you. You were just a diver who was going to die in my place."

The boy sat down beside her. "But you have gone too far the other way. You will not even let me help."

She rubbed the sleep out of her eyes. "You cannot do what I am doing. You don't have the training for it." Seeing he was hurt, she reached out and took his hand. "It is just that you have spent your whole life taking horrible risks for next to nothing. What I am doing requires a keener sense of self-preservation. Are you mad at me?"

The boy shrugged. At that exact moment, he was not sure of his feelings.

She sighed. "I promise to apologize, if you promise to grab your ticket when it comes."

"My ticket?" Kafirr had never thought of anything as being reserved for him.

She looked hard at him. "If you get a chance to go off-planet, will you take it?"

"I guess." It seemed safe enough; no one had ever offered him even a ride around Windward Mat.

"Then I am sorry," she said. "You are not so stupid."

She paused and pressed his hand. "This farce is almost over. If anything happens to me, I want you to ask Q'Maax'doux for a ticket off-planet. Tell him that the Port Authorities will not let him lift off if there are any complications."

"What complications?"

"Just promise to use your brain. If anything happens to me, just press the xeno. Quas is not that smart. I have already beaten him. Having my ticket makes me free; even if I never come back from that hold, even if I die in the next hour, I have still won. I would feel better knowing you had a chance too." She leaned over and kissed him. Her warm body and soft lips took Kafirr by surprise. She left him sitting on the mat, watching her leave for the hold. Her strong back was beaded with sweat; buttock muscles bunched and released with each firm step.

Even when she was into the hold and out of sight, he sat there, thinking over what he would say when she came back. He turned the words over in his mind until he had them just right. But Nila never returned to the cabin.

When they docked at Windward Mat, Nila had still not come up from the hold. Kafirr was worried, but Q'Maax'doux showed no concern. The xeno was delighted to have docked, and made immediate plans for transferring the entire hold container from the hydrocruiser to the Skylark. Kafirr went at once to check the hold, before it was embedded in the orbital yacht and headed for Epsilon E.

Pausing at the hatch, he heard no noise from behind the panel. He said the alien word that opened the hold, and light streamed into the gloom, scattering on the water's surface and dancing off the bulkheads. Active silver shapes whipped back and forth amid the light. Eagerly, they collected near the hatch, jostling each other, displaying the feeding energy that distinguished the silver ripper. Once this frenzy was under way, nothing halted it until prey or appetites were exhausted. There was no sign of Nila, just a bed of bones at the bottom of the hold. Kafirr could not even see if they were human, but the lively shapes and the absence of Nila told him all he needed to know.

Both the hold and human cabin were in the starboard hull. Kafirr retraced his steps. He had seen Nila go into the hold. Since she had not come back out of the hatch, she must have gone into the water with those creatures. The only other hold exits were underwater ones.

When he got to the main deck, Kafirr told the xeno that Nila had gone into the hold and now was missing. He added that the creatures in the hold were very much alive and alert. Q'Maax'doux was happy to hear that all was well in the hold, and Kafirr had some trouble fixing the xeno's attention on what had happened to Nila. But this time the boy persisted, drawing on some of Nila's anger.

"Nila?" Q'Maax'doux's speakbox turned the name into a question.

"Yes, the other human."

"That man demanded—and received—payment in advance. His relationship with me has ended, and so should yours." With unsentimental efficiency, Q'Maax'doux proceeded to pay Kafirr off as well.

Kafirr looked down at the scrip in his hands; it was more than enough for a new pry bar, but he remembered how Nila had spoken to him a few hours before. "This is not nearly sufficient; a human is missing. I want the Port Authorities to inspect that hold, and examine the bones at the bottom."

"Impossible," explained Q'Maax'doux. "As you must know, I am working within a tight schedule. There is no time to remove the rippers. I must lift at once to make connections with a high-g institute ship headed outsystem. You may be certain that the content of this hold will be thoroughly studied by the Institute of Zoological Morphology when I reach Epsilon Eridani IV. A report will be made available to the public."

This promise of eventual publication did not meet immediate needs. "That is hundreds of thousands of hours in the future. Am I supposed to just sit here wondering what happened to Nila? What do I say if someone comes looking for her? You and all the evidence will be off-planet. I will be left to face all the complications and consequences."

Q'Maax'doux set his speakbox for patient reproof. "What consequences? One human more or less is no concern. Who would come looking for him?"

"Her," Kafirr corrected.

The xeno adjusted the speakbox: "Who would come looking for it?"

Kafirr was adamant, thinking of Nila's last words to him, because the last advice of a diver is always the most valued. "Then I am going direct to the Port Authorities. I will not be left holding the line; either we both answer their questions, or we both go off-planet."

The speakbox expressed surprise. "The specimen deck on the *Skylark* is full, and I no longer need your services. Taking you to Epsilon Eridani would be a pointless exercise."

"Fine," said Kafirr. "I will take a ticket to Paradise system instead; the *Jordan River* lifts within the hour."

More surprise came from the speakbox: "Such an expense exceeds all reasonable wages."

"Be unreasonable," Kafirr advised. "A human is missing, and

those creatures in the hold are material evidence. The Port Authorities might not want you to export them."

Q'Maax'doux took back the scrip, telling Kafirr that it was senseless to haggle with a human. The xeno then told the hydrocruiser's comlink to order a single-seat, one-way ticket to Paradise system.

In less than an hour, Kafirr was waiting for a shuttle to lift, thinking of Nila and watching magnetic cranes transfer the hold container from the hydrocruiser to the Skylark's belly. He was surrounded by a small wave of humanity. The last humans allowed to board the shuttle were pressed against the loading gate, carrying packages, bundles, bags, and possessions of every description. With their future slung on their backs or tucked under their arms, these lucky few were preparing to start life anew in Paradise system. The shuttle doors dilated, and people stumbled forward, sea creatures surging into the metal net.

The shuttle pilot was an Eridani Hound, cordial and aloof, whose firm commands showed he was used to herding humans about. He packed them as tight as he could, so the press of bodies and cargo would cushion any minor acceleration effects. When the Hound came to him, Kafirr studied the alien face and asked, "Do you remember me? You got me a job with Q'Maax'doux."

The xeno paused. There were so many humans; they all looked so alike. "The diver on the dock? Deep water must have been good to you, if it brought you here."

"It was a mixed experience," said Kafirr, "but I am grateful for it."

The Hound nodded; human gratitude was something the xeno had learned to take with good grace, though he had no particular use for it.

"I would also be grateful for a seat over there." The boy pointed out an open space beside a nearly nude young woman with a short pelt of brown hair.

"Of course," said the Hound, drawing his lips back in an imitation of a human grin. The Hound had learned to sex humans. He sat Kafirr down, pressing him against the female and telling them both to look up at the viewer. "Soon you will have your first look at the stars."

The woman turned to correct the xeno. She was about to say that she had seen the stars before, but seeing Kafirr made her forget the Hound. "You," she said, "I did not really expect to see."

It was the first time Kafirr could remember seeing Nila's brown eyes wide with surprise. He enjoyed the feel of her bare hip and shoulder pressed against his. "I knew you would be here, Nila. I knew it as soon as I saw what you had left in the hold."

"Yes," she said, hanging her head but keeping her smile. It was the sort of gesture the Hound might have made, to mimic human sorrow. "The silver rippers all went belly-up. Maybe I did not walk the little monsters well enough. Anyway, I did my best to break the tragedy gently; you know what a sensitive soul Quasimodo is."

The gasp went round the circle of faces as the shuttle burst through the cloud cover and they saw the stars spread overhead. The world they were leaving looked just as Nila had said it would, a white pearl hanging on the black ear of night. The people huddled in the shuttle began to sing:

*There's a better world awaiting, in the sky, yes, in the sky. . . .*

Nila took Kafirr's hand again, saying, "It could hardly be worse."

The Skylark lifted soon after, and matched with the high-boost ship bound for Epsilon E; but when Q'Maax'doux displayed his catch, the Institute of Zoological Morphology was not interested. They told him that the hold held nothing but copyfish, common scavengers that would enter any baited hold. The copyfish fed on the dead rippers while mimicking the dying ones. Q'Maax'doux took his speakbox off and cursed shiftless, thieving humans in an alien tongue.

# The moon maid

## THE LAUGHING STEPPE

On the first day of her twenty-second spring, a Moon Maid topped a low rise in the Laughing Steppe, riding her dark mare toward a nomad wagon lagger. She was dressed in animal skins, a fur-lined fleece jacket over stag-leather pants and calfskin boots; her hair hung in long black ringlets from a silver crescent-moon comb. Bow, quiver, and mirror case banged against her sheepskin saddlecloth. Grease and grime protected her face from the boreal wind. She was an only daughter, and her mother had named her Aganippe—"The Mare that Kills with Mercy."

Wailing drifted over the long grass from the Cimmerian camp. A cold wind in her face carried the odors of death—dried blood, burnt frankincense, anise, and lion scent—making her mare shy. Aganippe leaned down, stroking her mount's shaggy coat. "Easy, Melanippe. Ignore the smells and admire the stallions." Mollified, the black mare set out again, trampling wildflowers pushing up between patches of snow—anemones, irises, and wild tulips.

The Hetman in his sable cloak met her at the entrance to the lagger, backed by a mob of armed men with fierce tattooed faces. He was twice her age, with a forked beard, frost gray eyes, and a face as long as a saiga antelope's. In his right hand he held a bronze-tipped spear—his left was pierced by an arrow shaft, show-ing he mourned his son and heir. Tears streaked the grease on his cheeks.

Aganippe dismounted and gave her name, saying she was from the Lion Shrine. Men stiffened, staring sideways at her, making signs against witchcraft.

Grounding his spear, the Hetman spat in his right palm, then reached to shake her hand—showing he did not fear her magic. Next to blood, spittle is the most prized ingredient for fixing spells. "Come," he told her, "see what your lion has done."

Swallowing her anger, Aganippe shook the man's soggy palm. What did these nomads know about lions? They were Cimmerian battle-ax folk, kazakhs who called the gods by strange names, rais-ing temples to war and slaughter. Driven south by a bad winter, they had overstayed their welcome. With the grass well up, they should be following the frost line north. Instead they were making accusations—threatening to extend the visit.

The Hetman's son was laid out on a cart. He looked to be about sixteen summers; his body was slit up the middle and stuffed with straw, galingale, parsley-seed, and anise. Head and shoulders hung at an angle. Older wives were comforting the boy's mother and her young daughter-in-law, who were down in the dirt, faces furrowed by their own fingernails, shrieking at the heartless gods who let this happen.

Aganippe had hoped to see the slash marks of a leopard, but the throat and chest had been torn open by a single bite—otherwise the boy was barely touched. Just a claw mark on the thigh, where the beast braced a paw as it bit down. Only one cat killed that casually.

Staring into the face of a corpse is sure to make one question where life is headed. Aganippe felt a surge of pity for the child-widow, wondering what it would be like to cleave to one man, to raise his sons, to weave and spin instead of wearing skins and serv-ing the Lion Shrine. The girl had been pretty, with somber eyes and a wide sensitive mouth. Now she was bereft and terrified, clutching her remaining child, a baby daughter. Hers was cer-tainly a miserable lot, alone among pitiless strangers, with no son or husband to give her life.

Fortunately she would not suffer long. At the funeral a bow-string would be looped around the girl's neck, with a short stick thrust through it. After an appropriate prayer, the noose would be twisted tight so she might be buried beside her boy husband.

Aganippe told the Hetman, "Show me where this happened."

The nomad chief motioned with his spear. Boys took her

mare, and she followed the Hetman past where his yurt stood atop
a cutbank, closest to wood and water. Human scalps fluttered
from his tall standard-pole, and a hooded eagle preened herself on
a padded stand—a hunting bird big enough to bring down a young
gazelle.

Upstream from the yurt, Aganippe saw the deep broad pugmarks of a large lion. She knelt and felt the mud. It had hardened,
preserving prints laid down before last night's frost. Sticking her
nose in the nearest pugmark, she sniffed, then went on to the
next, and the next, until she had examined every print. When she
was done, she rested on her heels, listening to lowing cattle. A cold
feeling crept over her. "Did anyone see this happen?"

The Hetman shrugged. "Thralls watering cattle heard a
scream and loosed the dogs." No help there. The knots of cattle
by the bank were tended by blinded slaves.

Aganippe turned back to the tracks. Utterly illiterate, she had
seen enough kill sites to read the muddy bank like a Babylonian
scanning a clay tablet. "In late afternoon a young man with a spear
and a child with a water jar came down to the stream." There was
a rounded gouge and a circular mark, where the man had leaned
on his spear and the child had set down the jar.

The long-faced Hetman nodded. "My son took his daughter to
draw water."

Aganippe pointed out a matted bowl of wheat grass on the far
bank. "The lion had been waiting for some time, and leaped
straight onto the child. Your son dashed to his daughter's aid"—
she showed where the boy's strides lengthened to a run—"and the
lion turned to meet him, dropping the child." Aganippe traced out
the curving claw marks and the shallow imprint of a tiny body,
also the bigger body print where the lion brought the young father
down. Then the lion's prints turned again, vanishing across the
stream and into the tall grass, forepaws pressed deeper by the
dead weight of the child in its teeth.

The only distinctive feature of the pugmarks was the way the
left forepaw splayed outward, making the killer easier to track. A
good omen, she thought. A godsend, actually. Something needed
to be done soon to appease these Cimmerians.

The Hetman led her up to his yurt, sitting her down inside,
pouring wine with his own bloody hands. Aganippe thanked him.
The place stank even by nomad standards, reeking of sweat and
urine—but he was her host, and wine would brace her for what
had to follow.

"This is an *Oeorpata*," the Hetman told her, laying emphasis on
the last word, *mankiller*, which had a double meaning. It was also

a name for Amazons, like the Moon Maids of the Lion Shrine—
mankillers who obeyed no laws but their own.

"No," Aganippe corrected him, "this is a child-killer." The lion
had not turned on the father until the man attacked. That was
what scared her most. The beast passed up cattle and sightless
herdsmen, waiting patiently until the little girl appeared. And
after bringing down the Hetman's son it ignored the bigger meal,
turning back for the child.

This was a thinking beast who knew humans, a hunter that
picked just the prey it wanted, refusing to be swayed. Aganippe
had known a man-eating leopard that stepped over a sleeping
herdsman, and stood *atop* another, to get at a third. Like humans,
lions specialized. Some hunt antelope, others kill cattle. Prides in
Libya hunted elephants. But once cats tasted human flesh and
found it easy to take, they almost never forgot. If a lion dragged
its prey home, feeding it to the cubs, a whole pride became
infected.

Luckily none of the local prides had a large active lioness with
a splayed left forefoot—this looked to be a wandering male who
had learned his killing ways somewhere else.

The Hetman tugged at his forked beard. "When I sent word to
the Lion Shrine, my men protested. They claimed it would slight
us if an Amazon brought in the lion—though the younger ones
are eager enough to lie down in the long grass with any Moon
Maid who is willing."

She sipped from the Hetman's golden cup, carved from the
skull of a clan enemy. "And what do you think?"

His grief-scarred face softened. "When I was young, I too liked
to lie in the long grass with the Moon Maids—but I got only
daughters. You might even be one of them. You have the courage
for it, coming alone to an angry camp."

Aganippe took this as a compliment. Moon Maids naturally
fantasized about their fathers. As a girl, she imagined hers to be
a famous warrior, a vagabond prince, or some god's son—never a
nomad Hetman.

"But bravery is not enough." He tilted his head toward the
entrance flap, to indicate his warriors and kinsmen crowded outside. "They are brave. And could easily bring me a lion. I could
even kill one myself. But I want *you* to bring me *the* lion—the
beast that took my son and granddaughter."

Aganippe nodded. "That is what I mean to do." She was not
going to kill just any lion.

"Then swear to it." The Cimmerian brought out a great bowl,
beaten from a hundred bronze arrowheads. Filling it with wine,

he mixed in blood from his left hand. Lifting his spear, he told Aganippe, "Give me your arm."

A blood oath was totally unneeded, and none too pleasant — but to satisfy him Aganippe bared her arm, holding it over the bowl.

The Hetman pressed the razor-edged spear point against her flesh. The spear shaft was inlaid with seashells, but the point was a local copper-arsenic alloy. He bore down until it drew blood. Then he jabbed the weapon point first into the wine bowl. "This spear was mine, until I gave it to my son. Swear you will bring it back with his killer's blood on the blade."

Aganippe swore by the Hearth Maiden, by the Snake-tailed Mother, and by the Black-faced Mistress. Then they drank.

Wiping blood and wine from his lips, the Hetman added, "And do it soon. Or we will come looking for a lion."

Aganippe took up the spear and left. Outside the yurt she saw the Hetman's son sitting up in his painted cart, stuffed with straw and spices, wearing his best gold-embroidered jacket — all set to go calling. His child-wife sat at his side, dressed in silk and ermine, looking woefully pretty, her hair combed back from her scratched face, her spirit snapped like a broken spear shaft. For the next forty days wife and corpse would go around the yurts, feasting as if he were alive.

The scalps overhead snapped in the breeze. Aganippe knew that if she disappointed this Hetman, he had the means to make her wish *she* were sharing his son's couch in Hades. She held down another surge of anger.

Aganippe had lain with several young warriors, and on the whole rather enjoyed having a sturdy nomad thrusting inside her, galloping in the grass with her calves hooked behind his. But to say that if one of them died, then she should be throttled and buried beside him — that was absurd. If this was law, Aganippe was happy to be beyond it.

Leading her mare down to the water's edge, she went over the tracks until she could see the pugmarks in her sleep. Then she set out, looking for dark flecks on the grass tops of the Laughing Steppe. Soon the filthy sprawling camp and its huge bleating herds were swallowed by the great dun-green sea of grass.

Lions could be taken with a bow and spear. Pharaoh Amenhotep had brought down over a hundred that way. But he went out with a mob of beaters, a chariot to shoot from, and a double ring of spearmen to keep the beasts off him — outings so ostentatious they could hardly be called hunts. Aganippe had only herself and her mare, alone under a sky so vast the sun seemed to shrink into blue emptiness. She could only see a few paces into the tall grass — a distance that a charging lion could cover in half a heartbeat. A twitch in the grass tops might be her only warning. Nor was being mounted an advantage. Surprised and terrified horses were a staple of the lion diet.

Hearing was her best defense. That man-eating leopard had sprung at her without a sound, but a lion usually gives a low grunt to freeze its prey. Not always, though. Lions made silent charges just often enough to keep things interesting. She had managed to kill the leopard, but never a lion.

And this lion knew all about hunting people, having taken its prey from under the snotty suspicious noses of a thousand armed nomads. Aganippe would have to meet the beast on its own terms, or not at all.

Twice she spotted soft dents where the lion had set the child down, getting a better grip on its kill. By now the beast must have shaken the dogs. The feeding site would not be far off.

A little farther on she found it, a blood-spattered bowl of matted grass. Aganippe dismounted, holding tight to the spear. She found a hank of honey-brown hair and some chewed bone splinters. Saying a prayer to the Black-faced Mistress, she wrapped them in a square of leather, stuffing it into her jacket so the Hetman could bury what was left of his granddaughter.

Standing up, she stared about, seeing only swaying grass tops. Her best chance of finishing this quickly was fading. Lions liked to lie up after a meal, usually close to the feeding site, fearing almost nothing and perhaps anticipating a second helping. But this meal was pitifully small, and the lion had been attacked in the act of taking it. No reasons to linger. And now there would be no blood spoor to follow.

Seizing her mare's stiff upright mane, she swung onto her saddlecloth, making a slow circuit to pick up the trail. She found a depression where the lion might have lain up. Otherwise nothing. No claw prints. No pugmarks. Not so much as a scat.

She took her bearings from the sun, finding she was well to the west of the lagger. If this was a male on the move, he might keep heading that way. Aganippe followed the sinking sun on a zigzag course, casting about for sign. All she saw were humpbacked burial kurgans rising out of the dun-colored steppe.

Her search ended at the east bank of the Amazon, the broad gray flood cutting through the Sea of Grass between the Dnieper and the Volga, emptying into the Black Sea. Furs, gold, slaves, and amber all flowed down the Amazon, headed for sale in Sinope, Troy, and Tyre — maritime cities so far to the south that if you were to show a Cimmerian a ship's oar, he could not name it, or guess what it was for.

Lazy smoke rose from farmsteads along the river, where dutiful peat-eating peasants labored alongside their oxen. There was no reason for the lion to cross, but perhaps the beast got thirsty. The scent of the river carried for miles. She rode north, then south along the narrow bank, looking for lion sign. Finding nothing but a small cattle trail. The second time she crossed the cattle trail she noted fresh chariot marks in the wet sand. Between the wheel marks was a bare footprint twice the size of hers.

The spring sun sank on the far side of the Amazon. Even if she somehow found her child-killer now, she would be no match for a lion at night. Tomorrow she would try backtracking. Getting down, she walked her horse toward the Shrine. A warm black drizzle blew up from the south, melting the last of the snow. Wet grass tops whipped at her hips. Near to dawn she heard lions calling — a local pride hunting. She took it as a lucky omen.

The Lion Shrine's stockade and wooden tower stood tall and dark above the predawn steppe. Temple bells tinkled on the dawn wind. Walking her mare through the stockade gate, Aganippe found the rammed earth *maidan* nearly deserted — only those who cared the most had stayed up to see her safe.

Hippodameia, the horse tamer, fed a low dung fire, looking on as an Enaree fortune-teller twisted and untwisted strips of lime bark. A teenage novice named Eohippe played with a pair of orphaned cubs, watched over by Kali, an aged lioness with a crooked front foot. Kali was too crippled and toothless to be the child-killer, though Aganippe had once seen the grim old girl gum a hapless intruder half to death.

Both Eohippe and Horsetamer wore stag-skin pants and loose leather jackets — though Hippodameia was at the age when she should give up horse-taming, don a bell-shaped dress, and retire to the Inner Shrine. Only the Enaree wore full feminine attire, a tall headdress, dangling jade earrings, and a flounced skirt with a silk-embroidered bodice, padded to enhance the hips and bosom.

Young restless eyes saw her first. Setting down her cubs, Eohippe leaped to her feet, taking the mare's reins and greeting Aganippe with a shy smile, offering a massage — "If you wish."

Horsetamer called to the novice to feed and water the mare. "Give her a grass rubdown and a warm stall. I'll do the massage."

Throwing off her jacket, Aganippe sat down by the dung fire. Hippodameia settled in behind her, taking hold of her tight stiff shoulders. Horsetamer knew every aching fold by heart; as she kneaded, she called out instructions to Eohippe — how best to rub the mare, what sort of feed to give her, which stalls had fresh hay.

Horsetamer's hands worked their way down Aganippe's spine to the tops of her buttocks. In summers past she had given many such massages. Only then both of them had lain naked in Horsetamer's warm loft above the stables, lulled by sunshine and the drowsy smell of green hay and horse dung. Hippodameia would press hard with her haunches, her hands stroking Aganippe's nipples, thighs rubbing bare hips, lips nibbling at the nape of her neck, until the girl rolled over and gave herself completely. But that was summers ago. These days Horsetamer's hands stayed on her back.

"How did it go?" asked Horsetamer, her thumbs putting parallel pressure along the coccyx.

Aganippe gave a tired grunt. "Terrible."

"How terrible?"

"Someone has eaten a Hetman's granddaughter, and I lost the trail." Botching the track was going to bring no end of trouble, starting with a hard day of backtracking on the morrow.

The Enaree smirked, fingering a necklace of colored Egyptian glass. "What does a nomad call it when a cow pisses on his leg?"

Aganippe said nothing. Horsetamer answered for her, "What *does* a nomad call it when his cow pisses on him?"

"A bath."

Eohippe laughed, but Aganippe had heard it before. And she no longer found it funny—not after seeing the Cimmerian's rage. The Lion Shrine could suffer the same fate as Artemis's Tauric temple. Marauding Greeks fired the temple and made off with the virgin priestess, avenging some imagined insult. The Taurians had since found it prudent to placate the goddess by sacrificing any Greek landing among them.

Aganippe merely asked, "Where are the prides?"

"Brave Pride is at Lion's Rest," Horsetamer told her. "Tawny Pride has returned to the Shrine—they must have had a successful hunt. Dawn Pride is on the eastern steppe. Goddess Pride has not been spotted since three days ago at dusk. None were seen anywhere near the nomad camps."

Aganippe nodded. Very normal. Lions were surprisingly shy around people. There had not been a killing like this since she was a girl, and that one had followed a lion hunt. The Shrine had successfully kept the peace between men and lions.

"We should offer up a big dawn sacrifice," she decided, "to draw in the lions. Cyme and Phoebe can take the novices out and look for Goddess Pride." Cyme and Phoebe were the other Moon Maids dedicated to the Shrine. "I'll do the backtrack."

Having assigned herself the hardest task, Aganippe asked the Enaree, "What does the lime bark say?"

The fortune-teller kept twining the bark strips back and forth between long delicate fingers. The Enaree's painted lips parted, showing pearl-white teeth. "Pray to Apia."

Aganippe nodded her thanks, hiding a twinge of guilt. Since girlhood she had gladly served our Lady of the Beasts, the Hearth Maiden who presided over warfare, childhood, and the hunt. Apia, the Snake-tailed Earth Mother, was an uncomfortable reminder that maidenhood did not last forever—just as the Black-faced Mistress reminded mortals of death. But to Aganippe, losing the freedom of maidenhood always seemed like a little death. She would rather have called on the Black-faced One.

Eohippe came trotting back from the stables, offering to take over the massage—irreparably cute and aching to be taken seriously. Horsetamer said nothing, her thumbs digging under Aganippe's shoulder blades. The Enaree's red grin grew into a broad smile, accompanied by an exaggerated wink.

How like a man, thought Aganippe.

No intact male could serve the Shrine. The Enaree put on kohl, rouge, and a padded blouse, and had hacked off his privates to please the goddess. But sex was in the head, not in testicles or face paint—and the Enaree saw Eohippe as pathetically available. Aganippe had only to nod and the novice would be out in the long grass, kneeling naked between the Moon Maid's knees. The Enaree could not understand her passing that up.

But when Aganippe looked at Eohippe, she saw herself, six summers ago, hopelessly in love with Horsetamer. And that had ended ill. She was not a calf-stealer. Standing up, she thanked Hippodameia for the back rub, saying it was time to visit the Inner Shrine.

The Inner Shrine was like a burial kurgan, dug into the base of the watchtower—flanked by the horse stalls and sweat lodge. She entered through a narrow sloping tunnel paneled with cedar and floored with river stones, smelling of damp earth. Accustomed to flat open steppe and towering sky, Aganippe always associated going underground with death and burial.

Her mother was the Crone doing dawn duty by the altar lamps, wearing her sable robe, serpent belt, and cap of priceless sea pearls. She greeted Aganippe with a cold glare. A holy silence lay between them, but Mother had seen the massage in the courtyard.

Enough, thought Aganippe. What was the harm in a back rub? With Mother, everything was suspect. Aganippe was an only daughter. Mother had borne four sons, giving them up to their fathers. Beyond childbearing, she now yearned for granddaughters — which Horsetamer could hardly give her. Past reproaches echoed unsummoned in Aganippe's head. "Do you want to end up like Horsetamer? Chasing young girls, with only aging friends and ex-lovers for company?"

Mother did not know the half of it. At Eohippe's age, Aganippe wanted desperately to *be* Horsetamer — competent, independent, owing nothing to anyone. She had given herself gratefully to the older woman. Now she was not sure what she wanted.

All she said was, "I must sleep the Dream Sleep."

Mother nodded. As Dawn Crone she presided over that small death. "Who will you pray to?"

"To Mother Apia." Aganippe thought she detected a thin smile of triumph, though her mother tried never to let personal feelings intrude on ritual.

The Mother on duty woke her maiden daughter, a sleepy girl of seven. Fortunately for the girl, the Maiden's part was minor, but Maiden-Mother-Crone — the three ages of women — had to be there for the magic to hold. To insure the Goddess was constantly served, three Maidens, three Mothers, and three Crones were always in residence at the Shrine, plus the Moon Maids, and a dozen or so girls, novices, and attendants — making a score of women overall. They lived off the hunt and a temple tax paid in wheat and marmot skins.

The women stripped her. Standing naked before the horned altar, Aganippe struggled to stay awake, murmuring prayers she had recited since girlhood, while they painted her body with yellow ocher — the earth color.

To keep alert, she imagined her sainted mother, high priestess and seer, with her dress up, making heel marks in the sod while some passing stranger — perhaps a youthful version of the Cimmerian Hetman — heaved and sweated atop her. It was impossible to picture, particularly on an empty stomach. But that was where she had come from. They had Mother Apia's word on that. Why couldn't an almighty goddess have devised a more dignified way to bear daughters?

They fed her honey cakes and mare's milk, then led her naked out of the womblike shrine. Mother put her finger to her lips, signing for everyone to observe the holy silence.

Knowing what would be needed, Horsetamer had stoked the fire, rolling rocks onto the coals. Using a brass dish, Eohippe and the Enaree carried the red-hot stones into the sweat lodge, a skin wickiup stretched over a willow frame. Entering the lodge, Aganippe lay down beside the glowing stones piled in a central pit. Immediately she began to sweat.

Mother cast big green hemp buds sticky with resin on the rocks. The hemp burst into flames, and intoxicating smoke filled the sweat lodge. Aganippe drank it in through her nostrils. Then came the water, thrown hissing over the hemp. Steam blotted out everything, a white drugged fog, filling her lungs, seeping into her pores.

Thoroughly exhausted, Aganippe closed her eyes and was instantly asleep. The hemp and her lack of sleep had her dreaming almost at once. Everything from the day got mixed together. Her mother was there, as was Horsetamer, and the Cimmerian Hetman. They tried to get her to mount a bedlike funeral bier, making a place for her beside the Hetman's dead son. Mother told her, "Goddess knows, he's not much—but he can give me grand-daughters."

"Grandsons," the Hetman corrected her.

"Twins," suggested Horsetamer.

Aganippe recoiled from the dead son's ghoulish embrace. Leaping from the bier, she ran across the steppe, pursued by a huge shadowy figure. She headed for Hylaea, Apia's wooded home. The Snake-tailed Mother came out of her tree-shaded cave, supported by twin serpent tails in place of legs. She was leading a fine pair of mares and a small herd of red cattle. "Why are you running?" hissed Apia. Aganippe tried to explain, but the Earth Mother merely told her, "Seek the Lion Man," pointing a scaly tail at Aganippe's hulking pursuer. Turning about, Aganippe finally got a look at the man who was chasing her. His body was huge and handsome—but he had a lion's face.

She awoke with an aching head. The sweat lodge was cold and empty. She wormed her way through the entrance flap, then staggered to her feet, blinded by the daylight, her body still yellow and naked, scrawled with power signs.

Horsetamer was waiting, with the Enaree. So were her mother and Eohippe. Had they slept? Only Horsetamer looked rested, but she regularly slept early in the evening, to be up at dawn with the horses.

"Did you dream?" Mother asked, bringing her a basin to wash in.

"More than I wanted to," Aganippe admitted, wincing at the cold wash water, thinking about the part where they tried to mate her to a corpse.

Mother laid out boots, trousers, a shirt, and a red-leather jacket trimmed with horsehair. "What did Apia advise?"

"Seek the Lion Man," Aganippe replied, pulling on the stag-leather pants, hair side in for warmth. She scanned the ring of faces for signs of recognition. No one had a notion who the Lion Man might be—except maybe the Enaree, who smirked for a moment, then got up and left.

Tying off her trousers, she stood half-naked, letting the morning sun warm her wet breasts. "Have Cyme and Phoebe gone out?"

Horsetamer nodded. "They left while you slept."

"Did they take the gazehounds?"

Horsetamer shook her head.

"Then get them ready." Last night's rain had drowned the scent, but gazehounds did not need their noses to hunt. She pulled on the doeskin shirt and the red-leather riding jacket. She had been to the sweat lodge and gotten her dream. Now it was time to act. This killer needed to be brought to bay soon—or not at all.

"I have saddled four horses," Horsetamer told her, then went off to see to the hounds.

Four horses meant two riders. Eohippe got up eagerly. "Take me." The other novices were off with Cyme and Phoebe, searching for Goddess Pride.

Aganippe struggled into her boots, then went to inspect the horses. Eohippe tagged hopefully after her. Horsetamer had saddled Aganippe's favorite mount, a zebra dun, with dark stripes on her legs and withers, also a big claybank gelding, and a pair of roans. The blaze-faced roan was Horsetamer's.

Hanging her bow, quiver, and mirror case on the mare, she mounted the big gelding, meaning to keep her best horse fresh.

Horsetamer returned with the hounds—a half-dozen lean powerful creatures, with long legs and deep chests, bred from Abyssinian wolves, and perfect for hunting in open steppe where prey cannot be stalked and must be caught. Their eyes were as keen as a bloodhound's nose, and they could run down the fleetest prey, turning, dodging, able to outdistance a cheetah if the need arose. She cinched their feed bag behind her.

Taking up the Hetman's spear, she told Horsetamer, "I won't need the roans."

Eohippe's face fell. Horsetamer handed up the mare's drag rope. Their fingers touched. "You should not go looking for this lion alone."

"Oh, I'm not alone." The Moon Maid shook her head. "I have the dogs. And Mother Apia will be with me." Horsetamer looked hurt. So did Eohippe. But Aganippe wanted to face down this lion on her own, with the least amount of helpful interference. An only daughter, she had been brought up to rely on herself—it was too late to change that now.

The Enaree ambled up, bidding her to wait.

"You too?" Aganippe raised an eyebrow. The transvestite's dress was not even slit for riding. She might as well take Mother.

He-she laughed. "Oh, no. The lime bark says this is going to be far too adventurous. But I have something you'll need." The Enaree held up an evil-looking goatskin bag tied together by the hooves. It smelled of wine.

Aganippe tried to refuse. "I won't be drinking."

"All the better," replied the Enaree. "It's not for you."

She shrugged and took the goatskin, wondering how wine was going to help her find her lion. But the Enaree had the far-sight—and was tolerated because of it.

Aganippe called to the lead bitch, a hound named Havoc. They all had fast, easy-to-call names, like Hasty, Blazer, Ripper, and Impulse. Then she set out through the stockade gate, with the pack trotting at her heels. A hot wind blew up to meet her, making it hard to believe that three nights ago it had snowed.

She swung wide to check on the prides. Tawny Pride was scattered south of the Shrine, sleeping off their kill. The dawn sacrifice of a fat bullock had brought Brave Pride in from Lion's Rest. And on the eastern steppe she met up with a pair of lionesses from Dawn Pride, Eos and Daybreak, along with a young male named Helius. Only Goddess Pride had not been heard from—but it was up to Cyme and Phoebe to find them.

When she got to the kill site, the wagon lagger was gone. But the Cimmerians had not headed back to the north country—no such luck. Their yurt tracks went west, toward the Amazon.

She let the hounds run over the blood spoor and lion prints so the pack would know what they were after. Then they set out upstream, looking for some sign of where the lion had come from. Cats are territorial creatures. The lion was apt to circle back. Or Aganippe might get some clue as to the killer's identity.

But all she saw was mile after mile of empty stream mud. Disheartened, she struck out over the steppe. By now the sun was high up, and the vast grassy plain seemed nine-parts sky. Herds of red deer and antelope grazed in the distance. The only lion sign she spotted was a rest, where a traveling pride had stopped to sleep out the day. Which pride it was, she could not say. Suddenly the dogs began jumping about. Havoc loped off, then came racing back. Aganippe loosed the pack, to see what they had found.

It was another kill site. Grass had been torn and trampled in a big irregular circle. At the center lay the remains of a great red cow or ox. Horns, hooves, tendons, hair, and scraps of hide were strewn all about. Lions had been feeding. Hyenas too—their white dung was everywhere. Vultures stalked in and out of an empty rib cage.

Getting down on her knees, Aganippe reconstructed the kill. It was the work of a fair-sized pride. The lions had surprised a small herd of cattle, cutting out a single victim. The terrified beast had spun back and forth, trying to shake its tormentors. Working together, the lions kept the ox boxed in, finally managing to bring it down.

But the pride had paid for its meal. One of the lions was hurt, and lay on its side for some time, then limped off ahead of the hyenas—favoring its left forepaw.

The dogs began leaping about again. Aganippe looked up. A slow lurching movement caught her attention. A two-horse chariot was coming toward her over the steppe, with no horses in the traces—seemingly moving by itself.

Standing up, she saw the chariot was being pulled by a man, plodding purposefully along with the chariot pole across one shoulder. Despite the weight of the chariot, the man kept up a steady ground-eating pace, as though he had come a long way, but would keep on walking until he got where he was going. He was a big black-bearded titan, stark naked from the chest down, carelessly swinging a brass-bound club in one huge hand. He wore nothing but a giant lionskin cloak, with the forepaws draped over his shoulder, and the tail and hindpaws dangling behind him. The lion's mane formed a hood, framing the man's face with its grinning teeth.

## THE LION MAN

Never having seen the like, the Moon Maid watched man and chariot lurch toward her. Her hounds ran out to meet the intruder, but the man barked at them and they came bounding back.

At the edge of the kill site he set down the chariot pole, stepping out of the traces. Fully erect, clad only in his lionskin, he stood over four cubits barefoot. Aganippe had seen taller men—though not by much—but never anyone bigger. He had arms as thick as her thighs, and legs like temple pillars. Eohippe could have lain across his chest and shoulders, with only her head and toes showing. His eyes were light amber, like a lion's.

Giving Aganippe a jaunty greeting, he claimed he was a god-son and that his name was Hercules.

"I saw the vultures circling and came right over." He professed an affinity for vultures. "They are always a lucky omen, being the most pious of birds, never harming anything living."

Aganippe had seen vultures do a good deal of harm to things that had not yet managed to die, but she sensed this was not the time to argue ornithology.

Hercules shook out a short Doric tunic that had been folded on his shoulder to pad the chariot pole. He pinned the simple square of woven cloth at the shoulder, then belted it at the waist with a length of rope, leaving the right side open. The lion tail dangling between his legs was knotted in the middle.

"Have you seen my chariot mares?" he asked. "A matched pair, given to me by Poseidon."

Aganippe told him she had not seen any god-given horses.

"Then how about the cattle of Geryon? Big red shambling beasts — very beautiful?" Without waiting for an answer, Hercules launched into the tale of how he had lifted the cattle from King Geryon of Tartessus, who lived at the far end of the world beside the Ocean stream. Or rather *had* lived. Hercules had been forced to kill King Geryon, along with the king's herdsman and a wondrous two-headed watchdog.

He had been ordered to commit this larceny and homicide by the High King of Mycenae, a Greek with no particular claim to the cattle, who was in the habit of sending Hercules hither and yon to lift or kill all manner of famous wonders. Giant boars to fetch, eight-headed hydras to kill, stables to clean — it made no difference to Hercules. The harder the better.

"All that matters to me is that this is my tenth and last labor. Drive these wandering cattle down to Mycenae, and I'm done — when I find them."

"You've found one." Aganippe held up a scrap of hide from the kill site; long red hair still hung from it.

Hercules swore mightily — not a formal oath, but a string of Greek expletives. Listening to him, Aganippe could hardly believe Mother Apia would saddle her with this ox-sized oaf. But who else could this be but the Lion Man? Fit punishment for clinging stubbornly to maidenhood.

"There is nothing to do but search for the others," Hercules decided. Seizing the drag rope on her gelding, he hauled the big claybank over to his chariot. Without so much as a "by-your-leave" he had appropriated her horses.

Aganippe went along with him, bringing over her zebra dun, and helping secure both horses in the traces. Even on short acquaintance she guessed that quibbling over ownership with Hercules was a good way to end up as dead as Geryon and his two-headed watchdog. Besides, having no notion where her lion had gone, it would be plain idiocy to deny an omen from Mother Apia, no matter how unpleasantly packaged.

Hercules made room for her aboard the chariot, which was loaded with a pair of bows and a collection of oversized armor — gifts from various gods.

"Apollo gave me the bows, and Hermes the sword. The helmet, cuirass, and shield are all Hephaestus's work, totally unbreakable. Can't imagine why they thought I would need them. Sentiment, I suppose. Wanting to see me off well. We gods are greathearted to a fault."

Hercules whipped her horses and they were off, following the cattle trail away from the kill site. The cattle had scattered when the lions attacked, but soon the little herd had bunched together again, plowing a clear trail through the long leaves of grass. If the pride came back for another taste of Geryon's cattle, Aganippe might get a clue to her killer.

As they bounced over the steppe, Hercules regaled her with a description of his last and greatest labor. He had gone all the way to Spain to get the cattle, pausing to set up the pillars that marked the entrance to the Ocean stream — modestly naming them for his favorite deity. "Pillars of Hercules has such a handsome ring," he confessed. Clearly Hercules considered himself the greatest thing since the Hittites sacked Babylon.

He had returned by way of Gaul, Italy, and Sicily — this was all undiscovered country, and Hercules was having difficulty finding his way back to Greece. "At the head of the Adriatic the herd was stampeded by a gadfly. I tracked them across Thrace to here. Then yesterday morning I awoke to find my chariot mares missing as well. A lesser god would have given up."

Or hobbled his horses better — but Aganippe did not say that. Hercules took her silence for mute agreement.

Musing over his lost mares put him in mind of the two horses he had taken from her. "Fine mounts — though not to be compared to a gift of Poseidon. But nice come upon, just when I needed a new team." It was the first time he had shown the least curiosity about why Aganippe happened to be out wandering the steppe. She told him about her lion troubles, ending with her most recent conclusion — that the child-killer with a crooked foot had been lamed by his lost cattle.

Hercules told her she was in luck. "You won't find a mightier lion-killer." He boasted that before he was out of his teens he had killed the lion of Cithaeron—"Taking time out from the hunt to deflower the fifty daughters of King Thespius. A greater task than any ten lions." In fact, he feared he might have missed one of the daughters, lying with only forty-nine, leaving one still a virgin. "The main drawback to mass deflowering is the tendency to lose count. You end up relying on a bunch of giggling virgins to keep track."

He had killed another memorable lion near Thebes, but the pelt on his back came from the Nemean lion. "Whose skin was proof against stone, iron, or bronze. I had to strangle him bare-handed—costing me a finger." Hercules held up his left hand as proof. The little finger was bitten off just above the knuckle. "Lions are nothing."

Not to Aganippe. For all of her life, lions and horses had been just about everything. Now she had lost her horses to this big buffoon—and she still had a lion to kill.

Hercules sensed he had not cheered her. "Really, I will kill your lion. Throughout my labors, I've taken on extra tasks—to show the King of Mycenae he does not own me. I subdued Gaul and Thrace, and sailed with the Argonauts. I would have found the Golden Fleece, if Calais and Zetes had not talked Jason into abandoning me."

The cattle trail led south, past humped burial mounds covered over with wild wheat and blue coneflowers. At dusk, Aganippe made out a thin dark line in the distance. "That is the forest of Hylaea," she told Hercules, "Mother Apia's sacred wood." It was the only sizable tract of woodland along the lower Amazon.

Not even a demigod cared to track cattle through the woods at night, so they set up camp. Unhitching her mare, Aganippe went out with the dog pack, running down several hares and a big ground-dwelling bustard. She rewarded the hounds with treats from their meal bag—dried barley bread dipped in blood—keeping the kills for herself. Hares and bustards are not the best fare for gazehounds. And Hercules showed every sign of being hard to feed.

He started a fire and happily gutted the kills while Aganippe gave her horse and hounds a rubdown. Hercules singed the bustard to get off the feathers, then buried the carcass under the coals to bake. Skinning the hares, he stuck them on a spit, saying, "Today I'm hungry. But normally I do not stoop to rabbit hunting. It is fine to hunt boars and wild bulls, or man-killing lions and wolves—but what harm do little rabbits do?"

Hercules had discovered her wineskin, and pouring it into his empty stomach was making him tenderhearted.

He told her that since crossing the Amazon (which he called the Tanaïs), he was anxious to reach the next river over — "Which runs into the world-circling Ocean. Then I will have gone from one end of the world to the other."

Here she had to disappoint him, explaining that the Volga (which he called the Rha) did not flow into Ocean, but emptied into the landlocked Hyrcanian Sea. Hercules was a long way from world's end.

Hearing this, he grew morose, drinking more and musing about all the people who were jealous of his deeds, or just plain hated him. By his own admission, he had enemies by the score. Hera, his foster mother, hated him. Calais and Zetes got him kicked off the *Argo*. Complete strangers took it amiss when he came to clean their stables, lift their livestock, or just slaughter some wondrous creature that lived nearby. His own cousin, the King of Mycenae, sent him on these impossible labors. "And if I so much as stray for a moment, his herald the Dung Man appears with new demands. Bring me Aphrodite's silver nightie, and a moon rock for my garden, or something equally useful."

Aganippe made the mistake of asking why he was put to these labors. Hercules heaved a sigh, "They are a penance."

"For what?"

"I killed my children. Not all of them — that would be impossible. Just six sons that I had by the King of Thebes's daughter. And a couple of bystanders. I'm not proud of it. I was mad at the time, and mistook them for Minyans."

He took several swallows of wine, which seemed to cheer him. Then he looked her over, his eyes bright and happy. "But I'm much better now. And after we have eaten these hares, we shall enjoy each other and feel even better." Hercules explained that he was partial to Amazons. "I prefer a woman of spirit and have little use for law myself. I fuck when I please, and fight when I must — though gods and men often take it amiss."

Aganippe knew she should slide gracefully out of his clutches, but she lacked the knack for fawning. Instead she said she would sooner mate with one of Geryon's lost oxen.

He laughed. "Don't be modest. I know you've wanted me. Amazons always do. It's my muscles. When I came to fetch Queen Hippolyte's girdle, she was in a fever to get it off. We had marvelous sport, and it was the merest mischance that I had to kill her afterward."

Aganippe did not demand details. She sat in silence, furiously weighing her chances of surviving dinner. It was plainly suicidal to deny him anything. God or mortal. Mad or sober. Death followed Hercules about as diligently as his King's herald, the Dung

Man. He killed people in battles and single combats, as well as in athletic contests, acts of larceny, and simple drunken accidents. He killed to administer rough justice, and in contrite compensation for previous killings, also in fits of madness and chance encounters. And not just people. By his account he had killed lions, serpents, centaurs, bulls, bears, and brazen-winged birds. Not to mention titans, gorgons, three-headed shepherds, and unnamed six-armed monsters. Whole districts had been depopulated, and many marvelous species turned to myth by his arrows and brass-bound club.

Nor was Aganippe under the dangerous illusion that she had half a hope of standing up to him, much less talking him out of it. He was like a force of nature, and his quiver was an open grave. She'd have a better chance of saying no to a cyclone.

Her sole hope was that Hercules was already half shot on the Enaree's wine and would be slow to act. Trust a fortune-teller to know what would be needed.

He tipped back the wineskin, wetting his beard as he drank. She leaped up and ran, sprinting over the darkening steppe like a nomad fleeing a bath.

Aganippe had no notion of where she was going, just aiming to be gone—to get lost in the long grass. It was that or end up as dead as Geryon and Hippolyte. The hounds must have thought it was a chase, because they came bounding up. She yelled for them to be gone, to go back to camp, but they kept bumping at her heels and dashing on ahead.

Hearing Hercules call to her, she redoubled her efforts, damning the stupid dogs. How could she hide with them frisking about? Then she remembered the Hylaea Wood, and made for it, with the hounds pelting after her. Her best hope was somehow to lose him in the dark wood, dogs or no.

Something clipped her foot. She went down, sure she had stumbled over a hound. But when she tried to rise, her leg would not hold her.

"Here, let me help you." Hercules stood over her, flushed with wine, but not even breathing hard. He had easily run her down. Jerking Aganippe to her feet, he twisted her arms behind her, binding her wrists with the rope he used for a belt. "It was foolish to run. Calais and Zetes were sons of the North Wind, but they could not outrun my vengeance."

He hoisted her onto his shoulder, taking up the club he had thrown to bring her down.

She kicked at his head with her good leg—finding it as solid as an oak—calling him a soused clown and a three-legged ass.

"No need to play the coy Corinthian," he told her, striding

back to camp with the hounds at his heels. "If you have the misfortune to be a virgin, you could not hope for a better start. I never resort to rape, since women find me irresistible. Once they see there is no escape, they learn to love it, or at least stop struggling. None of King Thespius's fifty daughters had cause to complain—unless it was the one I missed."

Tossing her into the chariot alongside his bows and armor, he took another swig from the wineskin, then went to dig up the bustard.

Bent double, the Moon Maid massaged her numb leg with her bound hands. A cold dull moon drifted overhead. She prayed to it. Dying to protect her honor would help no one—not the Shrine, not the lions, and least of all her. But giving in to Hercules was no better. Queen Hippolyte had, and ended up as dead as if she had denied him.

She looked frantically about. With her hands tied and one leg lamed, she had no chance to flee or fight. Her weapons were by the fire. So was Hercules's sword. The chariot held only his armor and bows—and his quiver.

Pushing off with her good leg, she edged up to the chariot rail, where her bound hands could reach the quiver. Hercules's arrows were inside.

Back by the fire, Hercules had finished the bustard and was hard at work on the rabbits. Between bites he regaled Aganippe with tales of his conquests—each exploit reminding him of another. Well into his cups, he had trouble telling myth from legend. The Lernaean Hydra now had nine heads, one of them immortal. The fifty nights he spent with King Thespius's daughters became a single dusk-to-dawn debauch.

Her own debauch was moments away—but mention of the Hydra reminded Aganippe that the arrows were dipped in the dead beast's poisonous gall. One of Hercules's regrettable accidents had concerned a thumb-fingered centaur who scratched himself handling Hercules's arrows—dying in unspeakable agony. Muttering a prayer to the All Mother, she slowly drew an arrow out. If Apia meant for her to die, it might as well be now.

Reversing the arrow, her hands crept down the shaft to the point, her fingers closing on the head. Holding it sideways, she sawed at the rope, knowing a single prick would end all her troubles.

A heavy hand shook the chariot. Her fingers froze, and she looked up. Hercules stared down at her, grinning so wide she could count his teeth. "What are you doing?"

"I'm putting myself in the hands of the Mother." She felt the rope part behind her.

"Oh, it won't be that bad," he assured her. "But do eat first, you'll want the energy." Hercules had saved the last hare for her—undersized, overcooked, and badly chewed about by the hounds.

She turned her head away. "I'm hardly hungry."

Hercules shrugged and took a bite himself, spitting out small bones, saying she was not entering into the spirit of the evening. He strolled cheerfully back to his fire and wineskin. Had he not been maudlin drunk, he might already have made swift work of her.

She let the arrow fall, rolling off the tail of the chariot. One leg was still deadweight, but she pushed herself into the grass with her good one, wriggling away from the bright circle cast by the fire. When she lost sight of the fire, she had to take her bearings from the stars. Finding the Great Bear, she kept the North Star over her shoulder, crawling toward the wood, impossibly far off but still her only shelter.

A bellow came from behind her. She dived down beneath the grass stalks. Hercules had found the chariot empty, reproachfully calling her name. Aganippe was not the least tempted to answer.

He strode out onto the grass, braying as he came. "Come, enough of this nonsense. I've eaten and am ready for bed."

She burrowed deeper, down to where the grass roots trap wet warm air. Closing her eyes, she laid her cheek against the earth, listening to his footfalls getting closer. She could hear him thirty paces off. Then twenty. Then ten. Then two.

He was close enough to touch. Holding her breath, she heard him muttering at the unreliability of women—"Always about and underfoot, except when you want one."

Hercules stepped closer, his bare foot coming down between her head and her hand. Another drunken lurch and he would be on her. He sniffed aloud, like a male lion searching for the scent of a lioness. She prayed again to Apia.

His voice boomed over her. "You'll catch your death in this wet grass. Let me warm you."

"Hercules . . ." The answer to his call came drifting on the dark wind like some lost ghost. ". . . Mi-ght-y Hercules."

She felt him stiffen. "What? Where?" he demanded.

"Here, Hercules." The words were somewhere between a whisper and a moan—but it was a woman's voice, as clear as a night bird, with a hint of longing, a touch of anticipation.

"I'm coming," he bellowed. The leg next to her head took off, headed south. His footfalls faded rapidly, along with the voice calling his name.

Aganippe released her breath, daring to move again. Drawing herself into a ball, she began to rub feeling back into her numb leg. Now she was utterly alone. Without food. Or weapons. Barely able to crawl. In splendid shape to tackle a lion.

Nor was that the worst. What came next would be up to the vengeful Hetman and his merry band of Cimmerians. He would sack the Shrine and have her skin for a door flap—if she had not already been beaten to pulp for refusing rape. Night chill crept down the grass stalks, invading her nest. Tired of kneading her leg, she slept.

Near to dawn she was awakened by a stiff warm body nuzzling up to her. She nearly shrieked, thinking Hercules had her. But the body was smaller than she, and another was behind her as well. And at her feet, and above her head. The dogs had found her. They were not used to sleeping without human companionship. At the Shrine, each hound had a girl or novice to sleep with—to keep mange and worms from spreading through the pack. They had cast about in the darkness until one stumbled on her, then cuddled as close to her as they could.

She drifted off again.

"Wake up. The sun is high."

Aganippe jerked alert, giving a strangled gasp. She was still lying in a tangle of dogs, but sunlight streamed down on her. The day was already hot, and Hercules stood over her, like some huge waking nightmare, looking offensively cheery.

"Breakfast is ready. Time to eat and break camp." He was happily holding up "breakfast," a dead cobra, thick as her arm and dangling almost to the ground, with enough venom in its fangs to drop a charging rhino.

Warily she tested her leg, finding it would hold.

Hercules was in his normal asinine good humor. Making no reference to last night's attempt at rape and mayhem, he launched into another of his never-ending stories, telling how the cobra had foolishly crawled under his lionskin as he slept, looking for warmth.

"The snake did not know that I strangled cobras in my crib. When I was only eight months, or maybe a year. Two of them. Sent to kill me by some jealous god or goddess. Or maybe my stepfather." Even as a toddler, members of his family had been hoping to rid themselves of this monster.

Grimly she got to her feet, following him back to camp, her dogs bounding along beside them. Hercules had a fire going and merrily cut chunks off the cobra, sliding them onto his spit.

"Did you hear her?" he asked.

"Hear who?" Snake sizzled on the fire.

"The woman or goddess who called my name. I spent half the

night searching for her. But females can be damned elusive in the dark." He stripped steaming meat from the spit with bare fingers, making room for more.

"It was Mother Apia." Aganippe tasted the cobra, finding it surprisingly succulent, barely remembering when she had last eaten. "Hylaea is her wood." She nodded at the dark line at the southern edge of the steppe.

Wiping greasy fingers on his thighs, Hercules told her, "Cook the rest of this cobra while I harness the horses. We shall see about these woods."

She was no longer surprised by the easy way he ordered her about, not after he had stolen her horses, tried to assault her, and all but broken her leg. What really amazed her was that some irate victim, relative, or stock owner had not put a spear through him ages ago. The answer of course was that hundreds, even thousands, had tried, with small sign of success.

Well, all *she* wanted was her lion. The gods could have the thankless task of putting an end to Hercules, or at very least mending his beastly manners. She whistled up the pack, and they set out, chewing on roast snake.

The cattle trail led straight to the woods. Hercules tethered the chariot to one of the first trees, a dwarf almond at the edge of the steppe, then they entered the holy wood, looking for cattle tracks on the forest floor. Here the rolling steppe had turned hilly, trapping water, allowing the trees to grow. The forest got darker and thicker. Dwarf almond and wild apple gave way to stands of birch and oak. At the brink of a broad stream the hounds stopped and lifted their heads, looking about. Wind rustled the upper branches.

Aganippe heard a low moaning. "Hercules, Hercules, come here. I want you. . . ."

"Hear that!" Hercules boomed.

She nodded, shifting her spear. The words seemed to come from rising ground to the right. They set off after the sound.

Dense thickets along the stream gave way to open parkland, beneath a wide oak canopy. Through the gnarled limbs Aganippe saw two great rounded folds of earth, with a dark cleft between them, topped by a tuft of trees and brush. It did not take any imagination to picture rounded thighs flanking a stone slit, topped by thatched pubes—Mother Apia's grotto.

The wind sighing Hercules's name issued from the gap between the two hilly thighs. Aganippe knew enough of caverns to guess this was completely unnatural. Breezes don't blow out of caves, since the air underground is absolutely still—but then winds don't usually call out to obnoxious god-sons, either.

Telling the hounds to wait, she followed Hercules into the dark stony womb.

The cavern sloped downward past walls smoothed over with plaster, like corridors in an underground palace. The rocky floor turned into flagged stonework. Ahead she could see the glow of lamplight, falling on a fresco of griffins grappling with lions. Along with the light came the splash of water on stone, the whisper of invisible servants, and the strumming of a lyre played by phantom fingers.

The passage opened on a handsome megaron, a temple hall supported by tall round columns. A basin and fountain faced a lively mural of mares giving birth. In the center lay a circular stone hearth, glowing with coals. Otherwise the hall seemed bare, with no stands of weapons, no stools, no cedar chests. None of the gold bric-a-brac great lords display to impress their guests.

At the far end of the hall, Mother Apia sat waiting on an ivory couch trimmed with gold and iron, beside a silver table topped with a jar of wine and a bowl of sweetmeats. Apia looked just like she had in Aganippe's dream. She had the head, arms, and torso of a woman, a strikingly beautiful woman, with wide hips, proud round breasts, a finely chiseled face, and midnight black hair — but her legs from the thighs down were long serpent tails that twined about the flagstone floor.

Behind her stood a stock pen and stalls containing a small herd of shambling blood-red cattle, and a pair of fine chariot mares with speed stamped on every line.

Aganippe prostrated herself before the Mother.

Hercules gave a happy snort, having lost none of his usual strut and swagger. He told the goddess, "I'll trouble you for those mares and cattle," not in the least daunted to take on Mother Apia in her own den.

"You may have them," Apia replied, "if you are man enough. Are you as mighty in the simple things as you are in amazing deeds?"

Hercules laughed. "I can spit straight and fart like thunder, if that is what you mean."

Mother Apia took the tips of her tails and ran them over the curves of her torso. "If you have the strength and daring to get me with child, you can have your cattle and horses."

For once he looked taken aback, staring at her two slithering tails. Apia laughed, mocking him the way he had mocked Aganippe. "Don't be modest. You know you've wanted me."

Hearing his own words thrown back at him, Hercules recovered some of his accustomed bluster, saying, "It is my last labor, and I dare anything."

Aganippe stayed prostrate before the snake goddess, mildly disgusted by the divine flirtation, but glad to see some of the brag and bounce taken out of Hercules. Apia turned to her, touching the tip of one tail to her lips. "Welcome, my wayward maiden daughter—the Moon Maid who never wants to be a mother. You are a disobedient child, willful to an extreme."

With her nose pressed to the floor, Aganippe apologized, telling the goddess she did not mean to be wayward, or disobedient.

"Then you must learn to accept life," Apia warned her. "You grow up. You grow old. And you die. Do not deny it."

"I do not deny it," she replied.

Apia seemed appeased. "You brought me the Lion Man. In return I will guide you to your lion. Follow the stream that runs before this cave, and you will find what you seek."

Aganippe thanked the Snake-tailed Mother, gladly backing out of her presence. She was never at her best underground, and she had no desire to witness the divine mating. As she left the cave, she felt the ground shake with their coupling.

The pack gathered around her, giving her trusting looks, expecting her to make some sense out of what was happening. She told them to wait by the grotto. In dense woods gazehounds would only be a hindrance. She took a deep breath. Her lamed leg started to hurt. Bending down, she gave it a good rubbing, then set out.

She had hardly gone fifty paces downstream before she spotted the first pugmark on the far bank, crisp and recent, hours old at best, and splayed to the outside.

Seeing that crooked pugmark appear again after so much fruitless searching was like magic, as eerie as anything she had witnessed in Mother Apia's cave. The Snake-tailed Mother had brought all the threads together. Her new lover, Hercules. His god-given mares and Geryon's red cattle. And now her lion. Such was the way of the Mother, Aganippe thought, sending us forth from the womb, then gathering us back to her when we are done.

The ground beneath her rippled again, twitching like a horse's pelt on a hot day. Time to stop gawking at fate and get to tracking.

She pushed through the brush on the far bank, parting the leafy tangle with her spear, keeping her body low, eyes searching for lion spoor, feeling the natural claustrophobia of a plains dweller confined by trees and brush. As she advanced, the prints grew fresher. She came upon trodden stems still in the act of bending back toward the light. From up ahead came the low undulating call of a lion.

The ground gave another sideways lurch. Apia and Hercules were hard at work, having a heroic coupling.

A light breeze rustled the branches, bringing the unmistakable smell of cat. Her belly tightened and her heart pounded. The killer was nearby, maybe just beyond the next thicket. She stopped to unsling her bow and peel off her leather jacket, lest it catch on a branch. She had to do her thinking now, because a lion charge from close in was nothing but a tawny blur, over in an eyeblink.

Selecting her sturdiest, straightest arrow, she entered the brush with her bow half-bent, holding her spear in her left hand alongside the grip. That way she could get off one shot just by easing back and releasing. Then she would drop the bow and be ready with the spear.

A sharp warning cough sounded somewhere ahead of her, but she was able to see no more than a pace or two into the bracken. She slid forward, peering over the tip of her arrow, knees bent, keeping low. The best place to hit a charging lion was in the chest.

Two steps. Three. Then four. Nothing. Her leg began to throb again. At ten paces the birch thicket gave way to a grassy glen, filled with shifting patches of shade and sunlight.

Then she saw her. A dozen paces away, a big lioness lay resting in the shady lee of a wild apple tree. Their eyes met. Instantly they recognized each other. Aganippe's heart sank.

Without lowering her bow she called softly to the lioness, "Goddess, where have you been?"

The lioness did not move, calmly staring back at the arrow. Goddess was the lead female of Goddess Pride—a friend and companion ever since Aganippe was old enough to mix with the lions. They had played and hunted together. Kali, the old lioness at the shrine, was Goddess's mother.

The Moon Maid took another step, leaving the shelter of the thicket, saying in a low even tone, "Have you hurt your leg?"

She was answered by a snarl—not from Goddess, but from another unseen lion somewhere to her left. Her bow stayed frozen, the arrow unwavering. At best she would get one shot, and she did not mean to waste it.

Another sinister rumble came from her right. Aganippe kept her gaze fixed on Goddess, taking another step. "Come on, honey, let's see your foot."

She was answered by a low rustle. One by one, members of Goddess Pride came flowing out of the shadows. Aganippe recognized Hera, Rhea, Isis, Luna, Nemesis, and the two males in residence, Eros and Ganymede.

Goddess yawned, stretched, and got to her feet. Shaking herself, she came limping over to greet Aganippe. The wound on her left foreleg was still fresh. Skin and muscle had been ripped almost to the bone by a horn from Geryon's red cattle.

The gaping tear told her whole story. Lamed and separated from her pride, she had swung by the nomad camp to grab an easy meal, picking the child because she was simple to carry. The Hetman's son had been a mere annoyance, neatly disposed of. Neither meant anything. They were strangers to the pride and Shrine. Now Goddess was on the mend and back with the pride. All was well with her world.

Tears welled up. Aganippe had to blink to keep her eyes from blurring. Goddess had merely made the best of a bad business, taking what she needed, then moving on. From her friendly attitude it was clear she did not connect Aganippe with the nomads. The Moon Maid herself felt more kinship with this pride than with a pack of bothersome Cimmerians who treated her sex like dirt. She thought of the Hetman's woeful, winsome daughter-in-law sitting on the death cart, waiting to be strangled just to adorn her husband's funeral. Goddess had killed for food, not for vanity—yet the Hetman would call what he did piety, and what Goddess did murder.

Aganippe blinked again to clear her vision. Heaving a sigh, she pulled back on the intake, releasing on the exhale. Her shaft shot the short distance between them, hitting the lioness in the right eye.

Goddess had no time to dodge, or even to see the arrow coming. She collapsed in a heap, the point driven deep into her brain.

Consternation swept the pride. Lionesses sank down, growling, tails lashing back and forth. With no time to nock another arrow, Aganippe dropped her bow, holding the spear in front of her.

One of Goddess's sisters, a big lioness named Hera, began to slither closer, worming toward her through the low grass. So did Devi, another littermate, advancing from the other side, hugging the ground. Ganymede and Eros, the males, were up on their haunches raising an awful racket—but it was the females she had to fear. In confrontations with humans, lionesses were the most likely to charge.

Aganippe took a step backward, then another, hoping to ease out of the confrontation.

No good. Hera matched her pace for pace, giving off low growls, her tail lashing. Lions use their tails to balance a charge. Hera's tail swayed once. Twice. Like a cobra about to strike. When it went stiff and straight, the lioness would be on her.

Aganippe swung her spear about to point it at Hera. Lions will bluff-charge to chase off humans or hyenas—but even the cat itself cannot always tell when a bluff becomes real.

Out the corner of her eye, she saw a gold streak shooting toward her. It was Devi. She and Hera had cooperated as coolly as they did on a hunt. Hera holding her attention until it was too late. Devi making the classic charge, tail high, claws out, teeth bared.

She swung her spear, but Devi was already inside her guard. For a frozen instant, the lioness seemed to hang in midair while the spear turned slowly toward her. Then the beast came crashing past the point, smashing into her.

"It's over," she thought, as the ground hit her from behind, knocking the breath out of her.

Devi was on top of her, trying to get her jaws past the spear that was somehow wedged between them. Another lion had a hold of her booted foot.

Kicking and struggling, she shortened her grip on the spear, trying to twist the point about—but it was too late. Devi was blindingly fast. Sinking her teeth into Aganippe's left shoulder, she shook the Moon Maid like a hound worrying a hare. Aganippe felt a euphoric complacency, like lying drugged in the steam bath. Being eaten alive did not hurt near as much as people supposed. Numb to pain, she had only a nagging feeling that all was not right.

Without warning the fury subsided. Devi ceased clawing and biting, collapsing on top of her in a kind of limp hug. Half-blinded by her own blood, Aganippe could not see what happened, but the rest of Goddess Pride vanished, their snarls dying in the distance. She lay on her back, bleeding comfortably, with only the limp Devi for company. An utterly unexpected end to the attack.

A huge hand reached down, lifting Devi off her. Hercules again stood over her, looking fit and relaxed after his triple bout of lovemaking. "Which one is your lion?"

Aganippe stared up at him, still in her pleasant dream state, wondering why the big oaf was bothering her.

"Which lion were you *supposed* to kill?"

She looked about. Devi, Hera, Eros, and Demeter were dead, shot down with Hercules's Hydra-poisoned arrows. What remained of the pride had scattered into the thicket. She hardly knew what to think. Someone she considered at best a murderous buffoon had slaughtered her childhood companions, and saved her life.

"Which one?" he demanded.

Shock wore off. Her wounds turned excruciatingly painful. She managed to point at Goddess, lying atop her crooked leg with the arrow through her eye.

Hercules picked up the spear and stuck it into Goddess's chest. The lioness must have weighed as much as he did, but he hoisted her on the spear, slinging her over his shoulder. Then he turned back for Aganippe, who was almost delirious with pain.

She was amazed to see him lift his tunic hem and reach for his prick. Hercules proceeded to urinate long and hard on her wounded shoulder. Aganippe tried to twist away, but she was too weak. Her face and hair were splashed by the stream.

He shook off the last drops, then leaned down and picked her up. She promptly fainted from the pain.

She awoke on the grassy steppe. Her shoulder, bound with strips of fabric, felt like it was on fire. Her horses were hobbled nearby, cropping the grass. Her hounds were frisking about. Hercules had his own mares hitched to the chariot. A snow-white mule and a small herd of red cattle rounded out the menagerie.

There were men around her as well—not just Hercules, but a handsome young man in a travel-stained tunic with a leather bag slung over his back. And an older man in a gold-embroidered gown carrying a caduceus, the herald's winged staff with snakes wound about it. The mule seemed to be his.

Seeing she was awake, Hercules ambled over, showing her a rent in his tunic where he had torn it to bandage her shoulder. "Do you suppose you could sew this?"

Lying there, weak as a hare, having been clawed, chewed, and pissed on, Aganippe managed to shake her head no.

Hercules sighed. "Someday I'll learn to weave and sew. I am sure to make an exceptional seamstress. Did I tell you how I dressed my lionskin—even though it could not be cut with iron or bronze?"

Aganippe shook her head again.

"I used the beast's own claws." Hercules beamed. "Very clever, I would say."

He clapped the young man on the shoulder, introducing him as his nephew Iolaus. "He fell behind when the cattle and mares escaped." The athletic young nephew had not been able to keep up with Hercules on foot, though he had only his kit to carry while Hercules had been dragging the chariot loaded with armor and whatnot.

Hercules turned to the old gentleman with the mule. "And this is the Dung Man, Copreus, the King of Mycenae's herald, who followed the cattle trail from Thrace. He has the effrontery to tell me that I have not completed my labors."

The Dung Man gave a dignified nod. He had tiny gold-thread caducei sewn into his gown. "That is correct. His second and fifth labors are discounted. Iolaus here helped him to burn off the heads of the Lernaean Hydra. And he used the rivers Alpheus and Peneius to clean out the Augean Stables."

Copreus waved his staff to indicate Geryon's cattle. "Did you perhaps help him to either find or herd these beasts?"

Hercules roared in indignation. Ready to kill at the suggestion. "She's been in the way since the moment we met. Teasing and distracting me. Getting lost in the night, then mauled by lions."

The herald insisted on hearing it from her.

Aganippe shook her head, saying she had done nothing. Whatever help she rendered was more than paid for, and she did not mean to be brained for nullifying another labor.

Seeing the Dung Man's disappointment, Hercules turned jovial again, lifting her up into his chariot, saying, "I'll take you to your Shrine. It is hardly out of my way, and I would hate to leave you bleeding on the steppe." He took up the reins, happily making light of her troubles. "Truth to tell, my lot is much worse than yours. I must go back to the western end of the world and fetch the Golden Apples of the Hesperides. What is a measly lion bite compared to that?"

Aganippe did not answer. Goddess's body lay beside her, staring blankly with her one good eye. Flies crawled in and out of the spear holes. Hercules lashed his horses and they bounced off over the steppe. She fainted again from the agony.

Two weeks later her shoulder was still hurting, but on the mend. Aganippe was young, and never slow to heal—though Horsetamer assured her she would have died from septic fever if Hercules had not immediately washed her wounds. The rotting flesh beneath a lion's claws could be as fatal as the claws themselves, but a demigod's urine is pristine clean.

As soon as she could ride, she called on the Cimmerian Hetman, bringing him back his spear along with Goddess's tanned and salted skin, slung over a led horse, ready to go in his son's grave. She showed him the crooked paw, and his granddaughter's remains.

The long-faced Hetman sat her down in his yurt and fed her kefir, saying, "A man must not sleep under the same sky with his kin's killer. You have spared me that shame—whatever I have is yours."

"Anything?" Aganippe asked.

"If it is mine to grant." The old Cimmerian swore by the God of War, literally putting his life in her hands, promising to die in battle if he was foresworn.

"Then I want your daughter-in-law."

The Hetman was taken aback.

"And her child as well," Aganippe added.

"But she must warm my son's bed in Hades." The Hetman seemed shocked by the impropriety.

"Does she go consenting?"

"No," the Hetman admitted. "She is a child, and does not understand why she must die."

"Then it will not be much of a marriage — even for Hades. Give her to me instead."

Remembering his oath, the Hetman shrugged. "Do you want your new thrall blinded?"

"No, I will take her as she is."

When her father-in-law told her what her fate would be, the girl went white as chalk, fearing that being given to the man-killers from the Lion Shrine might be worse than simple strangulation. But Aganippe promised she would not be skinned and eaten. "Nor sacrificed, either — not to the lions at least. My mother wants granddaughters to raise. You and your little girl must do, until I am ready to have daughters of my own."

She helped the girl aboard the led horse and handed up the baby. Then she swung one-handed onto her own mount. Turning her back on the wagon lagger, The-Mare-that-Kills-with-Mercy set off over the Laughing Steppe, with her newfound niece and foster sister in tow.

# Gone to Glory

## THE SAD CAFE

Defoe sat at one of the Sad Cafe's outdoor tables, soaking up gin slings and watching an energetic couple attempting to mate in midair, wearing nothing but gossamer wings and happy smiles. This pair of human mayflies had to be used to the exercise — neither showed a gram of fat or a bit of shame.

The four-hundred-year-old bistro stood in an open-air park on the Rue Sportif near Spindle's main axis, where g forces were low and the fun never slowed. Holodomes and hanging gardens arched overhead. Beyond the mating couple, halfway up Spindle's curve, nude bathers raised slow-motion splashes in a low-g pool. Not a shoddy spot for doing nothing. Defoe ordered his third (or maybe sixth) sloe gin sling from a roving cocktail bar, a barrel-shaped dispenser doing a lazy drunkard's walk between the tables, happily doling out drinks. Never asking for credit or expecting a tip. Human service was rarer than saber-tooth's teeth on Spindle.

Sipping his sloe gin, Defoe listened with mild disinterest to priority beeps coming over the comlink clipped to his ear. The first calls weren't for him, but they were coming fast and close together. Always a sad sign. Hoping not to be dragged too deeply into other people's troubles, he had his navmatrix decode the binary signals. The pilot's navmatrix grafted into the back of his skull was immune to alcohol. Defoe could down a dozen gin slings and still pilot a tilt-rotor VTOL in a blinding sandstorm or rendezvous with a starship—if the need arose. Only the need never arose. Not here. Not now.

First came a distress bulletin, direct from dirtside.

Then a standby alert.

Followed by a formal AID action request.

The final call was for him. Defoe answered in his off-duty voice.

Salome, his section head, came on-line. Her parents had been ultraorthodox Satanists (who believed John the Baptist had it coming), and her strict religious upbringing made Salome controlled and precise, with barely a wayward impulse. Except for her hair, which tumbled in untamed curls and wild midnight-blue ringlets past her hips, almost to the floor. She sounded soft and winsome over the comlink, a sure sign HQ was in second-degree alarm — Salome never courted underlings unless she needed something. "There's an AID team down in Tuch-Dah country. They want us to send someone."

Defoe snickered. "Who's the lucky sucker?"

"AID wants an 'experienced surface hand.' Someone who knows the Tuch-Dah. You've been fortunate with them."

"Fortunate? Not hardly. Incredibly lucky would be nearer the mark." Not the sort of luck Defoe aimed to lean on.

Salome persisted. "But you have come through intact—always a plus—and saved us a lot of trouble." And saved the Tuch-Dah a lot of trouble, thought Defoe, not that the ungrateful bastards ever seemed to notice. "Besides, you're fresh up from the surface; it won't be so much of a shock."

"Right. With four months up-time coming." Up-time as in up here—on Spindle—where it was too perfect a day to contemplate work. Defoe had just done a solid eighteen weeks on Glory. Greataunt Tillie in Alpha C would do duty dirtside before he went back early. "Last time AID lost a team, the problem solved itself— Tuch-Dahs sent their heads back in a leather bag."

"Marvelously considerate. But we can't always count on it. Take a couple of weeks," Salome suggested. "Clear this up, and we'll make it five months." That was double time. A rare offer. AID had to be in a fine panic.

"Make it six months," Defoe countered. *Every* day in paradise is perfect—so one is as good as another. He was demanding four days of up-time for every day dirtside—a splendid deal if he was so awfully essential.

"Find the team first," Salome told him primly. "Four weeks for going down to Glory. Four more for getting the job done." Defoe would get the extra days only if he delivered.

Bargaining with a Satanist was like dealing with the Devil. Centuries of persecution had turned a diabolically carefree sect into overcompensating overachievers. But it was always a comfort knowing that in the bad old days decent folk would have tied his boss to a stake and had her barbecued.

"I'll need a free hand," Defoe told her. "No interference from AID."

"That's your lookout. AID will be there—it's their team that's down. The way to avoid them is to get going and keep going."

"Sure thing." Defoe was already up and moving. "See you in Hell, Salome."

"Not unless you convert." He could hear her wicked smile. Another sign things were serious. Normally, Salome would never kid about religion.

Sloe gin and low gravity made the slidewalk seem to float in front of him. Rooftops and tree-lined arcades curved upward, vanishing into the light streaming down the length of the rotating habitat, reflected inward from mirrors set in the spinning well of stars. Spindle could amaze even sober senses.

Kids flashed past on the slidewalk, tanned young bodies in overdrive. Defoe passed feelie spas and low-g saunas. Happy holos invited him in. No more. Not now. Sorry, guys. Got to sober up and go to work.

Temptation abounded. And it was all free, from gaming orgies to organic feasts. Free as air to anyone who set foot on Spindle. Like an ancient Greek polis, Spindle made its own laws—but without the polis's slavery and infanticide—computers and birth lotteries took their place. No money. No credit. No theft, graft, or taxes. And like the ancient polis, Spindle had only two punishments that mattered. Death and exile. Now Defoe had to face both of these fates, for nothing except the right to return. Hardly fair, but the system lacked honest work.

At Port Orifice—the cavernous lock that let ships enter and exit—he drew emergency rations, heat caps, a thermal parka, bedroll, camp knife, folding mattock, climbing rope, canteen, and medikit. Telling the medikit to sober him up, he ticketed himself for the surface.

A call came through with his clearance. Salome's assistant, a pretty little catamite with painted lids and pierced nipples, purred into the comlink. "Hey, big boy. Is it true the Tuch-Dahs are cannibals?"

"No such luck." Defoe doubted Salome's kept boy had ever seen the surface. "They only eat people." Given conditions on Glory, Defoe thought cannibalism should at least be legal. Maybe even mandatory. If people were like hyenas, compelled to eat everything they killed, dirtside would be a safer place.

Salome's pet laughed wickedly. "Old Battle-ax wants to talk with you."

"Who?" The lock door dilated, cheerily welcoming Defoe aboard.

"Ellenor Battle. Boss dragon lady at AID."

Defoe stepped through the lock into the shuttle. "Tell 'em I've gone to Glory."

The oxyhydrogen shuttle lacked g-fields and cabin service; inflight entertainment was a pair of tiny portholes. Defoe felt the backward jolt of retros. Spindle seemed to leap ahead; the sole fleck of civilization in this very outback system dwindled rapidly.

He had his navmatrix tap into the shuttle's moronic guidance system. Nerve endings merged with avionics — sensors, astrogation, and stabilization became extensions of sight, sound, and kinesthetics. A modest thrill. Pretty dry compared to real piloting. Defoe's previous employer had been an overprivileged idiot who wracked up a Fornax Skylark, stranding Defoe in-system. Delta Eridani was a dead end, producing nothing the wider universe needed. Traffic was all incoming. Subsidized AID shipments came in cosmic packing crates — robofreighters cannibalized at their destination.

Only a knack for steering through trouble (and putting up with Thals) earned Defoe part-time privileges on Spindle.

At the top of the stratosphere, the shuttle shifted her angle of attack. Acceleration gave way to the gentle persistent push of gravity. Through the near porthole Defoe saw the green-brown limb of the planet rising to greet him, edged by a thin corona of atmosphere. Cloud puffs hung over blue splotches — large lakes or inland seas. Knocking around the Near Eridani, he had seen worlds aplenty, some good, some bad, some merely uninhabitable. When humans first arrived, Glory had been an airless husk, pitted with craters. Relentless terraforming had made her almost livable. No worse than New Harmony, Elysium, Bliss, or any of a half-dozen made-to-order worlds. Either a shining success story, or a case of hideous ecocide. As a pilot, Defoe had to believe in terraforming; starships needed places to go.

The shuttle came screeching in for a horizontal landing. Millions of kilometers of steppe, savanna, and lava desert allowed landing strips to be as long as needed. A groundhand undogged the hatch with a gleeful, "Welcome to dirtside, land of enchantment—where falls can kill you, beasts can eat you, and Thals will snap your spine just to hear it pop. Watch your step, you are in two-thirds g."

Defoe nodded. He was used to gaining thirty kilos every time he went down to Glory. The strip was a study in spasmodic activity. Cargo pallets came dropping down from orbit, braked by big silver chutes, raising yellow clouds of dust. Semirigids landed and departed. SuperChimps sat like rows of sad monkeys, ready to help with the unloading. It had been cocktail time on Spindle; here it was early morning. Dun-colored hills stretched north and west of the field. Beyond the electrified perimeter, a solitary male moropus dug for steppe tubers. Hyenas trotted past, giving the moropus wide leeway—behind them, the Camelback Steppe disappeared into endless distance.

Waiting at the bottom of the landing ladder was a uniformed woman. Tall and athletic, with her steel-gray hair cut down to stubble, Ellenor Battle could easily have looked half her age—but she did not go for biosculpt or hair toner. Taking life as it came, she expected the universe to do the same. Defoe had dealt with Ellenor before, finding her as proud as Lucifer's aunt, a nononsense reminder that AID stood for the Agency for *Imperial* Development.

She gave him a liquid hydrogen greeting. "Welcome to Glory. You missed your briefing." Defoe confessed as much. Full-blown AID briefings were full of glaring oversights and ass-backward assumptions—besides, if the problem was solvable from orbit, AID would not have asked him down. But he listened dutifully to the facts as Ellenor saw them. "We have a semirigid and crew more than forty hours overdue. Orbital recon spotted the crash site in the TransAzur, Tuch-Dah territory. . . ."

"How many in the crew?"

"Three."

"All human?" A normal enough question, but Ellenor Battle took it badly, replying with a curt nod. Defoe never knew what was about to bother her. She was very like a Thal in that way—moody and demanding. Salome might worship Satan, but you at least knew where you stood.

A bang and a wail cut off conversation. SuperChimps were refueling the shuttle for her return to Spindle. Boiling LOX filled the collapsed tanks, screaming through the safety valves. With an irritated wave, Ellenor led him away from the ladder. Defoe matched her swift sure strides.

Two huge airship hangars dwarfed the clutter of buildings edging the strip. Outside the electrified perimeter sprawled Shacktown, one of those shameful slums-cum-animal-pens that sprang up around an Outback landing field. Cook smoke climbed lazily over dirty-naked Thal children searching through dung heaps for breakfast. Plastic honeycomb, narrow alleys, and open sewers gave Shacktown the look and smell of a slave labor camp—lacking only the camp's energy fences and city services.

The howl of liquid oxygen faded, and Ellenor went on, "A Thal came into Azur Station with a ship's recorder—hoping to trade it for booze. When the ship crashed, the survivors were attacked by Tuch-Dahs."

It had been a long time coming, Defoe decided, but all hell had finally broken out.

The main hangar was packed with nervous armed humans. Defoe was welcomed aboard by the Port Master, a local worthy who doubled as Mayor of Shacktown, charged with neglecting sanitation and handing out beer and bhang on election day. The hangar canteen had been opened for the duration. Drunk vigilantes brandished riot pistols, pepper grenades, and scoped sporting lasers—as though they could not decide whether they were faced with a prison break or a big game hunt. A Tuch-Dah uprising had the worst elements of both.

The quarter-kilometer hangar housed a giant rigid airship, the *Joie de Vivre*, belonging to a rancher named Helio from the Azur. Ellenor Battle pushed through the jittery throng with Defoe in tow, making for the control car. The gangway was guarded by a brace of armed Thals, meaner than normal Neanderthals, nearly as tall as Defoe, and twice as wide. They wore standard airship harnesses, supporting stubby grenade launchers and bandoliers of gas grenades. A pair of dire wolves strained on electronic leashes.

The liquored-up posse, loudly aiming to take on the entire Tuch-Dah nation, gave the two Thals ample space. It was easier to talk of annihilating ten thousand Neanderthals somewhere out on the steppe than to face down a couple of them sporting grim looks and civilized weapons.

What the Thals thought, Defoe could hardly guess. Heavy browridges hid their deep-set eyes.

A rigger appeared at the top of the gangway—a *Homo sapiens* with dark skin and a drooping mustache trained to blend into trim whiskers. Giving a sloppy sarcastic salute, he led them to the control car's lounge. He had a gasman's easy grace, accustomed to balancing on a catwalk in any sort of wind and weather. Crepe overshoes kept him from raising sparks. RIG'EM RIGHT was scrawled across the back of his bull-hide flight jacket, and he had the veteran gasman's grin—the small ironic smile that said he savored the insanity of making his living aboard a flying bomb.

Helio had that smile too. He sat by an open lounge window, eyes hidden by blue wraparound shades. Broad-shouldered as a Thal, the rancher was reckoned to be a dead shot. Surrounded by a breakfast buffet of cold capon and Azur caviar, he still looked deadlier than any dozen men outside.

Defoe pulled up a handwoven wicker seat, admiring the gold pattern in his plate.

Ellenor Battle tried to decline brunch, but Helio insisted. "It's no advantage to be uncomfortable."

No advantage indeed. Defoe let his host pour him some off-planet champagne. Relaxing under six tons of explosive hydrogen did not stop Helio from doing himself up right. Silk paneling framed slender lacquered columns.

"The first thing," Helio told his guests, "is to see this recorder—and the Thal who found it. We have the transmission from Azur Station. But what is that? A bunch of digital blips." He smiled behind his blue shades, kissing off the tips of his fingers. Electronic evidence was notoriously manipulatable—inadmissible in honest courts.

"So long as we get going." Ellenor Battle glared out the open window at the panicky mob scene below.

Defoe agreed. He too wanted to see the recorder—and the Thal who found it. But most immediately he had to get out of this idiotic atmosphere with its infectious panic. Once underway, things were bound to be better. Helio was supposed to understand Thals—and conditions in Tuch-Dah country—as well as anyone could pretend to. Besides, if there was any answer to the disappearance of the AID team, it was going to be "out there." Somewhere in the endless unknown that lay beyond the fringes of settlement, even on human-made planets. Defoe was fairly at peace with that. Hell, at the moment he made a dubious living off it.

Helio gave orders from the table, speaking through the open window and into the ship's comlink, letting the Port Master's young assistant come aboard, along with a couple of sober gunmen. The rest of the mob would be more of a threat to themselves than to the Tuch-Dahs. A gang of SuperChimps hauled on the ground lines, and the cabin began to move.

As they cleared the hangar, Defoe had his navmatrix lock into the onboard systems. Everything read right. Gas pressure. Wind speed. Elevator alignment. Keel angle. When Helio gave the order to "up ship," the champagne in Defoe's glass did not so much as quiver. The sign of a good crew.

Shacktown and the landing strip fell away to windward. There was a hesitation as the big props started to turn, biting into thin air. Then airspeed picked up and they plowed along, powered by a cold-fusion reactor driving four paired propellers. The Camelback Steppe rolled placidly along a few hundred meters below. Springbok bounded off, alarmed by the airship's shadow.

Defoe decided he should see the recorder transmission from Azur Station, subjecting it to his own prejudices before hearing about it from others. Helio gave an airy wave. "Use my cabin. I have flying to do."

Ellenor Battle followed Defoe to the cabin, bent on seeing the recording again. Helio's private quarters were a sumptuous reminder of the good things to be had on Glory—hand-carved ivory and fine embroidery—luxuries that people on Spindle were too busy enjoying themselves to produce. And there was power to be had as well. Snappy service from human and semihuman attendants. Naked authority over Chimps, Thals, and Shacktown whores who would do nearly anything for next to nothing. Exotic animals roamed the endless veldt, ready to be hunted, killed, and butchered—the cabin was carpeted with a giant moropus hide, its head and claws attached. Defoe knew Dirtsiders who were not even tempted by the tame pleasures of Spindle, who snickered when he boarded a shuttle to go back.

The 3V imager made use of one whole bulkhead, turning curios and tapestries into a stereo tank.

Images leaped out. Defoe saw at once that the transmission wasn't a proper flight recording. The transmission had to come from an AID team member's personal recorder. First came establishing scenes—the semirigid taking off, steppe wildlife, a couple of male team members. Then came a terrible swift pan of breathtaking intensity. The recorder was sited on a small rise, aiming downslope. A low cairn of charred stones poked out of the steppe grass. Defoe flinched as rocket grenades and recoilless projectiles roared right at the recorder, a barrage so real that he almost dived out of his wicker seat, expecting to be showered with exploding shrapnel and shattered bric-a-brac. A ragged line of Thals came screaming out of the long grass, waving steel hatchets and hideous spiked clubs. They were Tuch-Dahs—no doubt there—Defoe recognized the garish paint and blood-freezing cries.

Willungha himself led the charge, atop a full-grown moropus —a tremendous horse-headed, long-necked beast with rhino-sized shoulders and tree-trunk limbs. Like Tars Tarkas aboard a wild thoat, the Neanderthal chieftain brayed commands, wielding a long thin lance. A grenade launcher in his rein hand looked like a tiny toy pistol.

Willungha's mount reared, waving clawed forefeet, and the recorder swung crazily, focusing for a second on the scene atop the knoll. Defoe could clearly make out the crash site. Kneeling among blackened girders and burnt grass was a woman, the third member of the AID team. She was small and brown-haired, in a rumpled uniform, taking painstaking aim with a recoilless pistol. Brown eyes stared intently over the sights, seeming to look right at Defoe. She squeezed off shot after shot as death stormed toward her.

The recorder jerked upward. Swaying grass tops framed empty blue sky. A superbly ugly Tuch-Dah appeared, swinging a hideous curved club. The transmission ceased, replaced by braided hangings and a case of bone china.

Defoe turned to Lady Ellenor, saying, "That was fairly ghastly." Shutting her eyes, she gripped her wicker seat with white knuckles, letting out a short sharp gasp. He had thought Ellenor Battle would be fairly shockproof, especially on a second viewing — but without any warning, her feelings were showing. The woman was full of surprises.

Helio was in the lounge. Any flying he had done had not taken him away from the table. Breakfast had disappeared, but his glass still held champagne. Broken highlands had replaced the Camelback Steppe. Defoe's navmatrix knew the country; beyond these mesas lay the Sleeping Steppe. Then the Azur.

"Enjoy the show?" Helio's eyes were still hidden by blue shades, so it was hard to tell how he meant it.

Defoe nodded. A full-blown Tuch-Dah massacre. No wonder everyone from the Port Master on down was potted and praying. There were a thousand or so bona fide *Homo sapiens* on Glory. Plus maybe twice as many on Spindle who weren't much inclined to come down. Willungha could field twenty thousand club-wielding Tuch-Dah, if he cared to. There were ten million Thals spread over the planet.

Helio twirled the stem of his champagne glass. "Glory might have been a new Eden for ambitious youngsters from the Home Systems — but the task of terraforming was too real for them." Helio did not have to say that *he* had come here, giving up the easy life to raise bison and horses, risking his neck with archaic technology, making the planet not merely habitable but semi-inviting.

He clearly relished the irony of how hard it was to get people just to come down from Spindle. Yet the habitat was built as an interstellar slowboat, launched ages ago to seed the Delta Eridani system. A home for humans while Glory was being terraformed. But by the time Glory had a biosphere and a semibreathable atmosphere, the in-system humans had become perfectly adapted—to life on Spindle.

So AID had to go for Thals. Retrobred Neanderthals were shipped direct to Glory, to do the drudge work, overseeing Super-Chimps, leveling landing strips, digging canals, tending great herds of herbivores. And the brutes had done a sterling job. Hell, they were still doing it. While backward types—like the Tuch-Dahs—bred like lemmings out on the vast steppes.

Defoe glanced over at Ellenor Battle. AID had planned this fiasco, from the first slowboats to the retrobreeding program that produced not just the Neanderthals, but a ready-made Cenozoic ecology as well.

She gave him a defiant glare, daring him to say that AID's multithousand-year program was a disaster. "The first colonists are on their way—ten thousand settlers, headed straight from Epsilon Eridani at near light speed. And a hundred thousand more are set to follow. And a million after that."

Epsilon E was less than twenty light-years away.

"Excellent." Helio emptied his champagne glass with an evil chuckle. "Willungha will have them for breakfast."

The rancher was right. Even a Navy cruiser with antimatter warheads could hardly cope with ten million Thals spread over an entire planet. (Currently the Navy had not so much as a captain's gig in-system.) The colonists could be armed, of course—but the Tuch-Dahs knew all about modern weapons. Dumping an armed mob of city-bred humans on a strange world, outnumbered ten thousand to one, with no way of telling the "good" Thals from the "bad" ones, would be a first-magnitude disaster. They might as well ship the weapons straight to Willungha, compliments of AID.

Ellenor Battle looked angrily out the lounge window, staring stiff-necked and imperious at the endless veldt. "There is room enough for humans and Neanderthals." As she saw it, AID was doing everyone a favor, bringing life to a dead world, making space for settlement, resurrecting a lost race, perhaps partly atoning for some ancient Cro-Magnon genocide.

Helio laughed heartily. "Tell that to Willungha. Maybe there is room. If the wild ones can be tamed, or pushed back. And the colonists kept near the strips. But no one is planning for that, eh?" He clearly thought someone should be.

"We have plans," Ellenor retorted.

Defoe thought of the lone AID woman in the recording, backed against the burnt-out wreck, coolly firing at the oncoming Thals. Whatever plans AID was hoarding had to beat that—in fact, they had better be damned slick.

The great blue-green ink blot of the Azur hove into sight. Azur

Station stood at the near end, a small circle of dugouts and stock pens between the Blue Water Canal and an east-west fence line. All along the canal the Sleeping Steppe had been made to bloom, growing rice, melons, and sugarcane.

Azur's station chief met the airship. She was a big weather-beaten woman named Cleo with flaming red hair, and scoped Centauri Special tucked under her arm — a sign of the times. A caravan was leaving her station, headed west along the fence line. The beasts of burden were low-humped retrobred camels, *Camelops hesternus*, as strong as Bactrians but more docile, with finer wool, also better eating.

Cleo had the recorder, and the Thal who had brought it, guarded by armed SuperChimps. The Thal did not understand Universal, or at least pretended not to — staring dumbly at the ring of narrow Cro-Magnon faces.

Helio tried signs. Grudgingly the Thal responded enough to indicate that he was *not* Tuch-Dah. He was Kee-too-Hee, from the marshes. He had found the recorder in a salt pan and trekked down to the station, hoping to get a reward. Instead he was being held prisoner and insulted. This did not altogether surprise him, but did not please him, either.

Ellenor Battle studied the recorder, then passed it to Defoe with a grim, "What do you think?" The first time she had asked his opinion. Touched, he had his navmatrix go over the recorder. No sign of tampering. But this was an idiot box with sensors, playing back what was put in.

Defoe nodded at the Thal. "He's telling the truth. At least about not being Tuch-Dah. That circle and dot on his cheek is a Kee-too-Hee clan mark. Any right-thinking Tuch-Dah would cut his throat with a dull clamshell before claiming to be a Kee-too-Hee."

"But what was the recorder doing, sitting on a salt pan?" Ellenor sounded unconvinced. Rightly, so far as Defoe could see. "Give him his reward," she decided. "AID will pay. But don't let him go until we come back from the crash site."

The crash site lay across the Azur. Defoe watched the approach from the control car's foredeck, standing before wide wrap-around windows. He felt Helio's firm hand on the elevators, anticipating changes in trim, keeping the keel angle constant. North of Azur Station, the shoreline became a maze of salt marsh teeming with spoonbills and wild boar. Then came the Azur itself, bright green in the shallows, deep blue in the center.

Helio pointed out his plantation, a great green delta thrust out into the sea. On the landward side, a long straight north–south

fence kept his domestic herds from straying into Tuch-Dah country. West of the fence line was a knoll topped with a black smear
left by the burned semirigid. Helio descended, dodging tall columns of vultures. Never a good sign.

Ellenor told Helio to turn out the *Joie*'s crew. "Have them go
through the long grass around the knoll."

"Looking for what?" The rancher sounded skeptical.

"Whatever they find."

On the ground, Defoe was struck by how peaceful it seemed.
This was the Saber-tooth Steppe, a silent mysterious savanna, its
mystique as solid and tangible as a patch of unterraformed
bedrock. The semirigid's small control car was intact, showing no
sign of having come down hard. Blackened girders formed big
looping curves. They might have been spares ready to be assembled into another ship.

Dire wolves sniffed out two bodies. "Burned beyond recognition" hardly conveyed the horror of the charred skeletons, jaws
agape in final agony, held together by shreds of cooked flesh. Riggers watched Ellenor Battle go over the corpses with cool intensity, calling down DNA signatures and dental data from orbit.
"This guy's kinda short," someone suggested. "Maybe he's a Thal."

"I don't know. Might be human."

"Human as you anyway."

"Just bein' hopeful."

Glad not to be needed, Defoe conducted his own search, using
his navmatrix to find the low black cairn and the fold the Tuch-
Dah had burst from. A rigger was down in the grass on his knees,
a strip of gasbag fabric tied around his head like a bandanna
holding his hair back. Defoe recognized RIG'EM RIGHT on the back
of the man's jacket.

Seeing Defoe, he got up. His name was Rayson, which everyone shortened to Ray. He held up a small finned and pointed
object. "There's a mess of these in the grass." Defoe recognized
the spent projectile from a recoilless pistol. The young AID
woman had been firing downslope from up by the wreck. Had she
hit anything? Defoe looked for bloodstains.

Ray glanced upslope to where Ellenor Battle was working over
the bodies, then walked around behind the fire-blackened cairn,
opening his pants.

Defoe called out softly, "That's a shrine."

Taking a sharp step back, Ray zipped his pants. "Shit, I
thought it was a barbecue pit." Just the sort of thing that got people in trouble in Tuch-Dah country—you could get brained by a
Thal and never know why.

Finding no blood on the grass tops, Defoe stood up, studying the shoreline. The colder north shore marshes were thin, broken by shimmering white pans. Wind whipped fine dry grit off the pans, stinging his eyes, settling in skin creases. He licked the corners of his mouth, tasting tiny bits of the Saber-tooth Steppe. It was salty.

A dark object lay between the steppe and the sea, as still as the shrine. Defoe walked toward it, brittle shore grass crunching underfoot. The big still object was a bison, down on its knees. Vultures flapped off as Defoe approached. Tail, ears, eyes, and testicles were gone, but the bison was hideously alive, managing to lift its head, turning bloody sightless sockets toward Defoe.

"Damn." Ray was right behind him, letting out a low whistle. "I'll fix him. " He produced a recoilless pistol with a folding stock. Shouldering it like a rifle, he fired.

The bison jerked at the impact, his head dropping, one horn gouging into the sandy pan. Defoe bent down, examining the dead beast; the tongue was torn out, the muzzle white with salt. There was more salt beneath the sand, where the horn had gone in. Looking east and west along the shore, Defoe saw spiraling columns of vultures.

Ellenor Battle pronounced the bodies to be *Homo sapiens sapiens*. Male. Two members of the AID team were accounted for. Cause of death unknown. "We should start a slow search, standard pattern, centered on the crash site."

Helio nodded and they set off again. As Glory's tight ten-hour day ended, Defoe sat in the lounge, trying to fit together everything he had seen—the mob scene in the hangar, the recording, the silent Thal, the crash site, and the dying bison. Delta Eridani had sunk down almost to the level of the steppe. The *Joie* was making gentle sweeps at less than thirty kph, twenty meters or so above the grass tops. He doubted they would turn up anything. That would be far too easy.

Gathering his things, Defoe climbed up to the keel. Tall hydrogen-filled gasbags swayed in semidarkness. A rigger with CATWALK CHARLIE on his jacket bossed a gang of SuperChimps.

Defoe made his way to the empty tail, unsealing an inspection hatch. Grass tops slid by less than twenty meters below. Unreeling a dozen meters of cable from a nearby winch, he swung his legs through the open hatch, letting the cable drop.

"Hope it wasn't something we said." Rigger Ray was standing on the keel catwalk.

Defoe shrugged. "I need room to work."

Ray sat down on a girder, eyeing the open hatch. This close to dusk, shaded by the giant tail, the hatch looked like a black hole whipping along in midair. "There's room aplenty down there. Just don't end up at the bottom of the food chain."

Defoe nodded. "I'll do my damnedest."

"Well, good-bye, an' good luck." Ray made it sound like, "Hope to hell you come back."

Defoe dropped through, slid down the cable, and let go. He had ample time to position himself. The most charming thing about Glory was the lazy falls at two-thirds g.

Steppe floated up to meet him.

Defoe hit, bounced, and scrambled to his feet. He stood staring up at the big tail of the dwindling airship. The *Joie de Vivre* kept to her search pattern, straining to complete the last leg before nightfall. When she dipped below a rise, he was alone.

Hip-high grass tops ran in every direction, prowled by tawny killers with knife-sized fangs. A cold undertaker's wind sent waves of color sweeping over the twilight steppe—deep blue, rust brown, old gold, and a dozen shades of green. Hyenas chuckled in the deepening gloom.

As Delta Eridani slid beneath the horizon, darkness rose up out of the grass roots, devouring the light. Night birds keened. Whoever said humans were the meanest animals—"the most dangerous game"—undoubtedly said it in daylight. Certainly it was never said at night, alone and unarmed on the Saber-tooth Steppe. Orienting himself by the strange stars of Eridani Sector, Defoe set out walking toward the distant fence line.

# THE SABER-TOOTH STEPPE

Dew clung to the grass tops by the time Defoe found the fence line. He had slept once, to be roused stiff and sore by the cough of a saber-tooth. Throughout the dark morning hours, he heard the catlike predators that gave the steppe its name calling to each other. Dawn wind carried their smell, like the odor of a ship's cat in a confined cabin. At first light the calls ceased; he supposed the pride had made its kill.

The energy fence cut a shimmering line across the steppe, carrying a hefty neural frequency shock. Domestic herds grazed beyond it. Overgrazed, in fact. The far side looked like a low-cut lawn.

Defoe walked along the fence until he found a knot of horses, *Equus occidentalis*, tall as Arabians but heavier, with slender feet, reminding Defoe of zebras or unicorns. The lead mare even had zebra stripes across her withers.

The horses lifted their heads as he approached, staring at him and at the hip-high steppe grass. Defoe told his navmatrix to bypass the fence's gullible software. The air between the nearest pylons ceased to shimmer, but still carried the signal saying the fence was intact. Ripping up some long grass, Defoe stepped through, offering it to the lead mare. They were immediate friends. She took the grass, letting him mount.

Riding bareback, he guided her through the break in the fence. Her little herd trotted after them. Defoe set a leisurely course deeper into Tuch-Dah country. As his navmatrix moved out of range, the fence reestablished itself.

He saw springbok and pronghorn, but no bison or Tuch-Dahs. Steppe thinned into shortgrass prairie broken by black knobs of basalt. Curious antelope came right up to him, heads held high, showing off tiny horns and white throats. Brown somber eyes studied him intently. Defoe doubted they had ever been hunted by humans.

Seeing a spiraling column of vultures, Defoe made for it. It marked a bison kill, a lone bull set upon by hyenas. He got down to study the kill site. Drag marks mapped the struggle. The bison had been hit once and ripped completely apart, probably in seconds. Nothing remained but rags of hide and white bone-rich dung. Hyenas were more to be feared than overgrown cats; their bite was better than a panther's, and they weren't as picky as a saber-tooth pride.

A shadow swept over him, a gigantic condor-sized shape among the vultures, circling downward, parting the smaller birds, boring toward Defoe in a tight spiraling dive, hiding in the orange glare of Delta Eridani. Almost on top of him, the big shape side-slipped, spilling air. He recognized Ellenor Battle, wearing an ornithopter harness—a powered version of the wings people flew with on Spindle. She flew like she had been born with them, doing a low-level stall and landing feetfirst.

Never let down your guard on Saber-tooth Steppe. Defoe had been blissfully alone, sharing the day with vultures and a dead bison. Now without warning Ellenor Battle was standing over him, demanding an explanation. What excuse could he have for jumping ship, cutting fences, and stealing horses?

Defoe shrugged. "No one needed me just to fly around in circles aboard the *Joie de Vivre*."

What fascinated him was her wings. A really fine pair. Falco-form Condors, solar assisted, seven-plus meters of extendible wingspan, with autoflaps and fingertip trim tabs. An energy pack in the small of her back powered the harness.

He nodded at the horses. "These are my tickets into Tuch-Dah country. What's your excuse for being here?" When it came to unwanted company, Glory could be more crowded than Spindle.

Ellenor slowly reached behind her back, taking the AID recorder from between her wings—it must have been strapped alongside the power pack. "I'm here because of this." She weighed it in her hands, then held it out. "It's my daughter's."

Defoe shooed aside some vultures and sat down. So, the woman on the AID team was another Battle. They did not look much alike, except perhaps in the shape of the face. But maybe Ellenor's hair used to be brown. More important, this explained her readiness to listen to reason.

"What *is* her name?" Defoe bore down lightly on the verb; no reason to assume she was dead.

"Lila. It's Hindu, and means the playful will of Heaven."

He took the recorder, turning it over in his hands. "So, why didn't your daughter have this with her during the attack?"

"I've been wondering. There might be some simple explanation."

"Might be." But Defoe doubted it. "That makes another strange circumstance about the crash and recording."

"What are the others?" Ellenor folded her wings, settling down across from him.

"First—no crash. That semirigid landed intact, then burned on the ground. Second, what sort of shot is Lila?"

"I taught her myself." There was pride in her voice and a recoilless pistol on her hip.

"So I supposed." He remembered how cool and unflinching Lila had looked—a lot like her mother. "But there was no blood on the grass. It is hard to believe every shot was a miss."

Ellenor nodded grimly.

Defoe got up, handed back the recorder, and dusted fine grains off his lap. The soil felt thin and silty. "Can you ride bareback?" Ellenor was not his first choice as a traveling companion, or even his fiftieth, but that was Glory for you.

"I was doing it before you were born." She fixed up a loop bridle, selected a mount, and they set off.

The prairie thinned further. Sandy patches showed between tufts of shriveled grass. More buzzards appeared, over more dead bison. More than even hyenas could eat. Defoe reined in, asking, "What do you make of this?"

Ellenor dismissed the apocalyptic scene. "A local die-off. We saw it from orbit. Lila's team was investigating."

Defoe shook his head. "I've been seeing signs of major drought ever since crossing the Azur. And real overgrazing as well. Helio's horses were frantic to cross the fence line."

Ellenor sniffed. "Is that a pilot's opinion, or are you a xeno-ecologist as well?"

"You don't have to be a xenoecologist to know a dead buffalo. The water table is falling. You can see the steppe salting up. Springbok and pronghorns are filtering in from out of the wild, replacing the bison."

Ellenor denied the Azur was in any trouble. "The sea is stabilized."

"Stabilized?" He reminded her the planet was still terraform-ing. "Shouldn't the Azur be growing?"

"A local shortfall," she insisted, shrugging off the buzzards and dead bison. "Another wet season and this will all be forgotten."

It did not seem that local to Defoe. Kilometers north of the Azur he could still smell salt on the breeze. Nor would the Tuch-Dah take a "local condition" so calmly — they had to live here. And they were not the types to forget and forgive. Anyone who endured a two-day Naming Fast knew Thals had god-awful long memories.

From time to time Ellenor took off, soaring aloft to do a turn around the landscape, looking for water. Near to dusk she found a dry bed winding through a sandy bottom. Dismounting, Defoe attacked the damp sand with his mattock. An hour of digging pro-duced a small hole full of brackish liquid. He refilled his canteen, then let the horses drink.

Ellenor alighted on a cutbank, saying a rider was coming.

Defoe nodded. Dusk was when they could expect company. Gathering dry grass and brushwood, he made a bed for a fire. Then he took out a heat cap, a capsule the size of an oral anti-biotic, breaking it and tossing it on the wood. It burned with an intense flame and acrid odor.

He watched the rider trot warily into camp, separating from the red-orange disk of Delta Eridani. It was Willungha, atop a giant male moropus. Thals did not have aerial recon and orbital scans, but not much that went on in Tuch-Dah country escaped Willungha's attention.

Despite rumors about him being a half-breed, or even *Homo sapiens*, the Tuch-Dah chieftain was pure Neanderthal, with bulg-ing browridges, buckteeth, and a receding chin. That chin was the only weak thing about him. Willungha's huge head and shoulders topped a meter-wide chest; arms the size of Defoe's calves ended in hands strong enough to strangle a hungry saber-tooth (a peren-nial party-pleaser at Tuch-Dah fetes). An old scar ran along one gigantic thigh. In his youth, Willungha had been gored by a wounded bison, the horn going through his thigh. Hanging head down, with the horn tearing at his leg, Willungha had clamped his good leg and left arm around the beast's neck. Calmly drawing a sheath knife, he cut the bison's throat. Willungha's mount was an ancient cousin of the horse and rhino, intended to be a browser and pruner—recycling plant material into the soil. AID had never thought a moropus could be ridden.

He grunted a greeting.

Defoe did not attempt to answer. Instead he unhobbled the horses, laying the lead mare's halter rope ceremoniously before the Tuch-Dah. He kept back only a pair of mounts and a led horse for himself and Ellenor.

Willungha responded with a series of snorts. Wild Thals spoke a hideous concoction of clicks, hoots, and grunts, which some *Homo sapiens* claimed to understand, but none could imitate. To the Tuch-Dah, *Homo sapiens* were overwhelmingly deaf and totally dumb, hardly even a thinking species. Powerful and unpredictable maybe, able to tear up the landscape like a mad moropus. But reasoning? Even Willungha reserved judgment. He was tolerably familiar with "man the wise"—which explained his mixed opinion.

Having given gifts, Defoe moved to the next stop in the evening's entertainment, setting up the recorder by the fire so it would play on the cutbank. Using the eroded rock as a 3V screen, he had his navmatrix sort through the recorder's memory for the final images, including the Tuch-Dah attack. When Willungha himself materialized atop his charging moropus, the chieftain gave a hoot and whistle. For all Defoe knew, it merely meant, "Hello." Or, "Handsome fellow, what?"

Lila appeared next, pistol in hand. Defoe froze the image. Walking up to the scene, he stabbed a finger at her, then made as if to look about—hopefully telling Willungha that he was looking for her.

The Tuch-Dah's eyes fixed him from within their deep sockets. Defoe repeated the signs. Wild Thals were not much impressed with off-planet marvels unless they could put them to use. Without as much as a grunt, Willungha headed off into the dark with his gift horses in tow.

Defoe leaped up, telling Ellenor, "We've got to follow." Willungha was the best lead they were likely to get.

They trekked through most of the short night. Badlands gave way to savanna. Tangerine dawn outlined the tops of black acacias.

Twenty-odd hours without sleep had Defoe dizzy with fatigue — wishing to God he could glaze over for a while. From upwind came the smell of burning dung, denoting a nomad camp.

Beneath the acacias stood a dark circle of yurts, surrounded by lowing herds. A crowd of Thals emerged to click and whistle their leader into camp. Defoe and Ellenor got no such cheery greetings, facing stony indifference leavened by the occasional dirty look.

While Ellenor sat with folded wings, Defoe listened to a lively exchange among the Thals, seeing fists waved in their direction. The discussion narrowed to a debate between Willungha and a tall brute with a broken nose and bold red-ocher tattoos. He must have outweighed Willungha by a couple of stone, but lacked the chieftain's sangfroid. Plug-ugly's part in the conversation consisted of low growls and grim looks.

Willungha ended the exchange, turning abruptly and striding over to where Defoe and Ellenor sat waiting. Squatting on his haunches, he made his position plain with signs and finger jabbing. They were free to search for their stray female, with a single exception. Defoe explained to Ellenor, "The only yurt we cannot enter belongs to Mean and Ugly over there." He nodded toward the tall Thal with the broken nose and ocher tattoos.

Ellenor frowned. "Logically that is the yurt we most want to examine."

Defoe nodded. Thals could be amazingly unsubtle. He fished out his medikit, knowing he would need a boost. Strapping the kit to his calf, he told it to give him the chemical equivalent of a week's rest. "I'll see what I can do about getting Plug-ugly's permission."

Stimulants hummed through his blood. The morning got brighter. A two-thirds-g bounce came back to his step. But Defoe hated relying on chemical imbalance; you could fool your body only so long. The Thal stood planted in front of his yurt, a skin hovel on wheels trimmed with camel tails. A bison hide hung over the doorway. Defoe strolled up with a hearty, "How ya doin'?"

The Tuch-Dah merely spat. Since neither could speak the other's language, there was no need for formal insults. Defoe slid silently into migi gamae, arms hanging loose, spine aligned, right foot leading. Out the corner of his eye, he could see Willungha and the boys settling down to watch the fun.

Giving a roar, the Thal rushed at him, arms raised, bent on snapping the spindly Cro-Magnon in half. Defoe was well outweighed, and his sparring partner would be immune to any sort of body blow. He seized the big right wrist with his left hand. Pivoting sideways, he used the Neanderthal's momentum to sling the ogre over his hip, hacking as hard as he could at the immobilized right wrist. Mean and Ugly went butt-over-browridge into a heap against one wheel of his yurt.

Willungha's boys applauded with pant hoots.

The Thal bounded right back up, snarling like a wounded lion. Favoring his right hand, he lashed at Defoe with his left. Defoe parried with his forearm. A bad mistake — the glancing blow staggered him.

Grinning with feral glee, the Thal circled leftward, not even winded. The bastard had probably gotten his beauty sleep. Defoe's right forearm felt numb, and his lungs rasped — a sign the medikit had reached its limits. Much more of this, and the Thal would wear him down. Then stomp him into oblivion.

The Tuch-Dah lunged at Defoe with his left. This time Defoe ducked under the blow, grabbing the Thal's left hand with both of his, ignoring the injured right. Lacking the strength to go the distance, Defoe held grimly to the Tuch-Dah's good hand. He sent the bellowing ogre cartwheeling over his shoulder, letting the Thal's own weight and momentum bend the left wrist until it snapped.

The Neanderthal lay dazed, one wrist badly sprained, the other broken. A firm believer in kicking a fellow when he was down, Defoe brought his boot heel sharply on the Thal's tattooed instep, to discourage the brute from getting up. Mean and Ugly moaned.

Dusting himself off, Defoe glanced over at Willungha. The Tuch-Dah chieftain gave a congratulatory grunt. Defoe was free to search the yurt. He hoped to hell he'd find something.

As soon as he lifted the bison hide, Defoe knew that whatever was in the yurt stank all the way to Spindle. Urine, sweat, and burning dung mixed with moldy leather. Worming his way in, he startled a gaggle of Thal children playing beside the central fire. They piled out past him, terrified by a *Homo sapiens* bogeyman turned real.

The yurt was dank and smoky, walled with soot and skins; aside from body paint and tattoos, Thals did not bother with decoration. What he was looking for sat in the back, amazingly alive. Alert brown eyes ringed with fatigue stared back at him, hardly believing what they were seeing. "Lila Battle, I presume?"

She managed a nod. Tuch-Dah methods were crude and pitiless. To keep Lila in place, a long yoke was fitted around her neck, made from two heavy lengths of wood lashed together with leather. Her hands were free, but the ends of the yoke were out of reach, anchored to the bed of the yurt. She could move enough to feed herself and attend to body functions, but could not reach the knots holding the yoke in place.

As he cut Lila loose, Ellenor Battle came crawling in, dragging her wings. She hurriedly strapped her medikit around Lila's forearm. Mother and daughter were reunited in the fetid interior of a Tuch-Dah yurt, a touching moment lasting about a nanosecond. Lila was clearly Ellenor's daughter, and neither was given to excess sentiment. Before they had finished hugging, Ellenor wanted to know what had happened, and Lila was telling them.

"Helio did it. The bastard flagged us down for a face-to-face. The next thing I knew, I was being bundled up and given to the Tuch-Dahs."

Defoe had suspected something of the sort — it wasn't in Willungha's nature to mix with *Homo sapiens*, either as friends or as enemies. Full-fledged humans had to be behind this. But he was sorry to find out it was Helio. He had liked the arrogant asshole.

Hauling out the recorder, he gave Lila a look at her "last stand." She shook her head. "I wish I had put up that fight, but I never saw it coming." She knew nothing about the fate of her ship and team.

"Dead and burned," Ellenor told her daughter bluntly. Everything else had been digitally programmed straight into the dim-witted recorder's memory. A decent scheme, but not foolproof. The chance selection of Lila's recorder had made her mother suspicious, while Defoe was always willing to believe the worst.

"Why didn't he just kill me?" Lila wondered. Having spent the last few days bound in the back of a Tuch-Dah yurt, she was in many ways the most amazed.

"You are his insurance shot." Defoe set the recorder next to his knee. "A good hunter always has an extra charge handy, to insure his prey is nailed. The crash and fake recording were not enough to thoroughly implicate the Tuch-Dahs. But by the time your body turned up, it would be obvious who had you." Willungha's people probably had no idea why Helio wanted one of his females carted about against her will. But the Thal he had made the deal with fought to keep up his end. Touching in a terrible way.

"But why do this at all?" For once Ellenor looked at a loss. "Why wipe out our team? Why blame it on the Tuch-Dahs?"

"Because Azur is dying." Lila spoke softly. "The sea is overloaded. The steppe is salting up." From the way Ellenor scowled, Defoe guessed this was an old argument.

Lila matched her mother's stubbornness, insisting that, "Sea and grass aren't returning water to the air as fast as the canals are draining it away. The thin layer of soil atop this cinder and bedrock cannot absorb new arrivals. We saw it. Helio sees it. Willungha must know as well. Helio wants the Azur closed off to settlement. So do I. But he apparently thinks it will take a war to do it."

Ellenor gave Lila a sour to-think-I-suckled-you look. But as far as Defoe could see, Helio might be right, even AID wouldn't dump settlers into a war zone. With the colonists diverted and the Tuch-Dah pushed back, Helio would have the Azur to himself.

Hearing hoots outside, Defoe lifted the bison hide for a peek. Thals were looking up. From over the steppe came the beat of paired propellers, announcing more unwanted company. The *Joie de Vivre* was approaching.

Ellenor swore. Her daughter began to gather her strength for a getaway. No one was burning to confront the guilty culprit. Defoe had pictured them sending a signal to Spindle, then lying low until AID organized a rescue operation. Armed and reckless felons should be cared for by the pros.

While Ellenor hustled her daughter out, Defoe scooped up the recorder. Telling his navmatrix to turn the recorder on, he pointed the business end at the yurt fire, getting a long shot of the flames.

By the time Defoe tumbled out, the *Joie de Vivre* was poking her nose over the nearest rise, looming larger as she descended. Mother and daughter were disappearing into the long grass beyond the yurt circle. When he caught up with them, Ellenor had her wings on and communicator out, preparing to punch through a call to Spindle. He grabbed her hand, stopping her from opening the channel. "Wait."

"Why?" Ellenor looked angry, annoyed, and scared. Her recoilless pistol was out and armed.

"Helio will be listening," he reminded her. Ellenor might be absolutely ready to sacrifice everything just to see justice done, but Defoe was not near as determined to die for the law. "Give us a chance to get away first."

"How?" she demanded. Running was ridiculous. Helio would swiftly spot them. Nor was there any reason for Willungha to take their side.

"Start by lying down," Defoe insisted, "so we don't disturb the grass tops. Right now we can see him, but Helio can't see us." He had to make the most of that.

The *Joie* settled down on a hillock near camp, close enough to cover the exits, but not so close as to disturb the Tuch-Dahs. SuperChimps swarmed down the ground lines and anchored the airship to the hilltop. Helio and his gunmen trooped down the control-car gangway, sporting rifles tucked under their arms, fanning out as they approached the yurts.

"Get ready to run." Defoe aimed the recorder at the airship. "I'm going to create a diversion."

Lila nodded gamely. Ellenor remained unconvinced. "What sort of a diversion?"

"Fire and panic." Defoe told his navmatrix to set the recorder on playback, projecting a continuously expanding loop using the most recent image in memory. "No matter what you see, run straight for the *Joie de Vivre*, and up that gangway. Got it?" Both women nodded. "Then go," he hissed, triggering the recorder.

They broke cover as a red glow appeared on the hull of the airship—the image of the yurt fire magnified by the recorder—growing into a terrible circle of fire. SuperChimps hooted in terror, scattering away from the ship. In seconds the image covered half the hull, looking for all the world like a trillion cubic centimeters of hydrogen bursting into flame. The control-car crew dived out the gondola windows.

Defoe topped the hill. Shoving Ellenor and Lila toward the gangway, he began releasing ground lines. Lightened by the loss of men and chimps, the airship strained at her anchors, heaving about above him like a whale in labor.

Someone yelled stop. Without bothering to answer, Defoe leaped on the last line, pulling the anchor pin, letting the line hoist him up and away. The airship tore off downwind, wallowing drunkenly, her control gondola empty. Dangling cables rattled through the stand of acacias.

Seeing he could not clear the trees, Defoe had his navmatrix send a frantic call to the *Joie's* emergency system, releasing the landing ballast. Tons of water cascaded past. The ship shot upward, out of Helio's range and reach.

His navmatrix ticked off altitude increases. One thousand, two thousand, three thousand meters. Savanna spun below him. Time he hauled himself aboard. Holding on with his left hand, Defoe reached up with his right, grasping the taut line. Getting a good grip, he let go with his left.

He fell, steel line sliding through his fingers. His right hand would not hold. Making a frantic grab with his left, he managed to catch the line.

Dangling left-handed, Defoe realized his right arm was useless. It would no longer support him. The medikit strapped to his leg had masked his pain, and the damage done by the Thal. Betraying him into trying too much.

Swinging silently, several kilometers in the air beneath a bucking airship, he pondered his next move. Unable to climb one-handed, Defoe kicked at the end of the line with his boot. If he could snag the anchor loop, he could hang safely until someone hauled him up.

Too far. His foot would not reach. Grass tops whirled dizzily below him. The *Joie de Vivre* topped four kilometers, still rising.

Loosening his left hand, he slid down the line, feeling with his boot for the loop. His toe went in. He gave a silent cheer. He had made it.

Just as his boot settled in, the line jerked—the *Joie* had reached her pressure height, automatically venting hydrogen. Nosing down, she took a drunken dip, porpoising out of control.

Defoe fought to regain his grip. Fatigued fingers weren't quick enough. The line snapped away. Two sleepless nights, the fight with the Thal, the struggle on the line, had all taken too much out of him.

Arms flailing, he fell slowly backward, his booted foot twisting in the loop. Two-thirds g gave him enough time to make a last lunge at the line. And miss.

Dangling upside down, holding on by his boot, he could feel his foot slipping. Doubling up, Defoe made a grab at the boot with his good hand. He got it. Fingers gripped the boot as his foot slipped free and the line bounded away.

He was falling. Holding tight to the useless boot, Defoe shrieked in fright and exasperation. He could see the snaking line above him and the shadowy form of the airship starting to dwindle. Five kilometers away, ground rushed silently up to greet him.

Defoe felt none of the dreamy complacency the dying were supposed to enjoy. Even in two-thirds g, onto soft grass, he knew he would hit hard, bounce badly, and not get up. Ever. His nav-matrix ticked off the fall. Slow at first. A few meters per second—but ever faster. Numbers began to blur.

The horrible silence was broken by the rush of wings. Hands seized him. Primaries beat frantically. He could feel flaps straining against the sky.

Ellenor Battle had him. Pulling out of her stoop, she was trying to brake, wings beating against better than twice her weight. Good shot, thought Defoe. But the wing loading was way too high. He could feel her stalling, about to tumble into a spin—unless she let go.

But she dug in instead, spreading her wings, defiant to the end, her contorted face centimeters from his.

Then came a miraculous jerk, and the impossible happened. Defoe bounded to a dead stop in midair.

A line stood taut between Ellenor's shoulders. She had clipped
a cable to her harness before diving after him. Staring up at the
skyline, Defoe tried to cheer, getting out a grateful croak. The
woman was a pigheaded genius, and he wanted to kiss her. But
then Ellenor might really drop him.

Meter by meter he felt himself being hauled to safety. The
AID woman was grinning.

As they were drawn aboard the galloping airship, Defoe saw
Rigger Ray working the winch. Lila lay full out on the deck,
reaching down to help her mother. Catwalk Charlie was holding
tight to a girder, eyes shut, still waiting for the flaming crash.
Defoe could hear him mumbling:

> Our Satan that art in Hell,
> Damned be thy name.
> Lead us into temptation,
> And encourage our trespasses . . .

Defoe was shocked. Charlie had never *looked* religious. But a
brush with death will bring out the Devil in anyone.

Gingerly sliding his boot on, Defoe told his navmatrix to take
control of the airship. The *Joie* righted herself, turning back toward Shacktown.

Hearing Ellenor put in her call to Spindle, Defoe wondered
how Helio was doing with Willungha. After murdering two AID
workers, trying to frame the Tuch-Dahs, then bungling the cover-
up, Helio had serious problems ahead. But so did everyone on
Glory. And the first ten thousand colonists were already on their
way, leaving Epsilon Eridani at near light speed.

Defoe for one did not want to be there when trouble arrived.
Right now he was headed back for Spindle, to spend long lazy
hours of enjoying himself and looking for a ship headed outsystem. AID could deal with the mess they had made. More people meant more traffic, and one day dirtside and all its dangers
would be a batch of not-too-pleasant recollections. The sort of
memories you were free to file and forget.

# The wagon god's wife

## GUNNAR'S GOOD EYE

A lifeless morning sky spread between the peaks, bringing no fog, no mist, no breath of wind. Birds did not fly. Frost wrung every drop of water from the air. A single ripple lay on the snowfield, a white mound marked by an upright spear.

Snow cracked at the base of the spear shaft. First fingers, then a hand clawed upward, clutching the shaft, dragging an arm behind it. The mound lifted. The bent back of a big man broke through the white shell, snow sliding from his fur cloak and leather jacket. With frost hanging in his hair and beard, Gunnar Helming glared at the bleak morning through his one good eye.

Climbing to his feet, Gunnar greeted the day with a shuffling dance. First he shook one stiff leg, then the other. Flapping his arms about, he staggered in a circle, working life back into tired limbs. He had felt warmer sleeping under the snow.

Dance done, he stood panting, watching little puffs of mist shoot out of his mouth, to freeze and fall as ice on his beard. His good eye saw a twist of smoke rising from a black stand of pines. This thin climbing thread was the only movement in the frigid landscape. Leaning on his spear, he set off, praying for a breakfast fire beneath the smoke.

As he lurched along, Gunnar recalled feasts in King Olaf's hall, wishing now that he had eaten more and listened to the bards less. He had tossed aside bones that might have been split for the marrow, and left behind crusts of bread he would now be happy to chew. Alone in heathen Sweden, he did not hope for royal feasting, expecting that the Swedes were as likely to eat him as feed him.

Thick powdery snow dragged at boots and leggings. Where the drifts were deep, he swung his arms to make a path. The work was exhausting. Without food and warmth, Gunnar would soon have to lie down and die. He clearly heard his Saxon grandfather saying, "Do not wait for ale and old age to carry you off, lying in the straw like a sick cow. A man should die with sword in hand, with Wodan's name on his lips." This speech had impressed Gunnar, though he had been but six summers, sitting on his grandfather's knee and a long way from ale and old age. But going sword in hand to Wodan was a pagan wish. King Olaf Tryggvason had made Gunnar Helming a Christian. He could not follow the Prince of Peace and wish for death in battle. Even now, Gunnar took grim comfort in walking away from a quarrel, fleeing a fight as Jesus would have done.

To die so far from the sea was the real sadness. One summer when the Mermaid's Meadow was fit for plowing, Gunnar had seen his grandfather go down to the sea and not come back. Ever since that summer, Gunnar had set his hopes on the sea death. To be trampled by the white-maned waves and rolled into a seaweed shroud was a decent death for a Christian Norseman. Now he no longer expected to sleep in the Whale's Bed, living or dead. Hemmed in by a bowl of mountains, the only waves that Gunnar's good eye could see were peaks of white-capped stone frozen against the sky.

Buckling at the knees, his legs gave way before he got to the pines. "Get to the trees," his tired heart told him. He crawled toward the dark splotch of wood, frozen fingers locked around his spear—the bit of spar that a drowning man clings to. Pain turned to numbness.

Past the first pines, he smelled woodsmoke. Looking up between the black pine trunks, Gunnar saw a circular mound of sod with smoke rising straight from its rounded peak; an old burial mound tied to heaven by a rope of smoke. Standing stones led straight to a curtained entrance in the tumulus. Fire beckoned from behind that hide door. "I am warmth. I am life."

Numb fingers let his spear slip. Bending his body in the middle, he pushed with his hips; a fur-clad worm wriggling forward, leaving a twisted track through the snow. Collapsing short of the door, chest heaving, he prayed for help. "Lord Christ, do not leave me in sight of shelter." His world dimmed and shrank. Only the mound entrance stayed crisp, the bright circle at the mouth of a darkening cave.

Without a sound, the wide leather door swung aside. A towering woman of supernatural beauty stood in the doorway, tall as a masthead and proud as death. Her hairy calf-skin boots were laced with thick leather thongs, and a beaten silver band circled her stiff waist. Raven hair framed fine ivory features. Deep, dark eyes stared down at him. On her shoulder sat a large hawk, preening silver-and-copper plumage.

This imposing woman stood silent, unmoving. The hawk cocked her head, fixing Gunnar with one unblinking eye. The black cavern closed around him.

Gunnar awoke feverish hot. Heavy furs pressed him into straw that prickled against his naked back and hips. Stirring the straw was another sort of warmth; round, living warmth. Firm, smooth woman's flesh rubbed him, massaged him, kneaded him. Full breasts and strong thighs pinned his fingers. Heaven was every bit as good as the priests had promised.

He opened his eyes. The awesome woman who had stood in the doorway lay atop him, her long hair cascading over them, enclosing their faces in a black tent. Sturdy calves curled around his legs, pressing their hips together. Her soft mouth covered his, breathing life back into his body. Mother-naked; she did not shut her eyes like Christian girls did.

Gunnar's limbs awoke. One hand caught hold of her breast, the other reached up between lanky thighs, pulling on a buttock to bring them closer. The woman lifted her lovely head and laughed, "Have you decided to live?"

"Live? Woman, what you are doing would raise the dead." Gunnar held on as well as he could, trying to twist her over, hoping his whole body would be awake when he had her properly on her back.

Strong and fast as a sow-bear, she slid sideways, still laughing, her long white arm holding him off. "I should be rubbing your feet, working the blood back into your toes. You might lose them."

"Forget my toes. I can count them when we are done."

Luminous eyes studied him with stern amusement. "I can see your blood is working, but we do not even know each other."

"I am a Helming. My Christian name is Gunnar, and I am awfully pleased to meet you." Keeping a resolute grip on her inner thigh, he flung an arm out to pin her shoulders.

The handsome she-troll slipped under his pin, stiffening her arm to keep her distance. "People call me Freyja, and I have no Christian name—but I do have a husband."

Gunnar sank back. The woman was being awkward. A pagan marriage did not matter—unless her man was ill-humored and near at hand—but Gunnar would get nowhere until this beautiful giantess was more willing.

Without letting go, Gunnar looked beyond her. Leather bed curtains were tied back, letting in heat from the firepit. Gunnar saw no man about, no man's things. No boar spear leaned by the door, and the only breeches hung over the fire were his. The mound house was bigger than any he had been in, but beside him was a woman who needed her headroom. Dirt walls, dugout floor, a log roof; all clean work, and the bed showed quality, sturdy, stuffed with fresh straw. Among Swedes, the place could pass for a palace.

"You have an uncommon method of warming a stranger. King Olaf's physicians never cured frostbite so fast, nor made the sick heart so merry."

Freyja nodded, her dark hair spilling over snow-white breasts. "This is the natural way to warm a man. Any woman knows what makes a man's heart merry."

He rolled a bit closer, holding hard to her rump. "It is a poor healer who leaves her cure half accomplished." This time she did not move away, but merely arched a black eyebrow. Gunnar rubbed his free palm softly over a pale nipple, leaning closer and kissing her throat. Again she did not draw back.

"The most important part has been missed." Flinging a leg over her, Gunnar got the leverage to keep her still while he made ready to mount. "Your husband need not concern us. I am an un-married Christian, unable to acknowledge pagan rites. In the eyes of Christ, you have no husband."

Looking serious, almost sad, she said, "I am still bound by my marriage, and if we are to finish this warming, you must do one thing first." Wetting her finger with her tongue, she ran the cold nail down his chest, all the way to the navel.

He squirmed at her touch. "One thing? Is it wood to cut or grain to thresh? I will do a whole week's work when we are done."

She leaned closer. He could feel the long stretch of her body, her breath sighing in his ear. "I want you to kill my husband and brother."

Gunnar sat bolt upright, save one short limb, which went limp. He had forgotten what bloodthirsty heathens the Swedes were. Seeming disappointed, the woman sat up also, pulling furs about her hips and belly, giving him a petulant look. "I thought that since you were a Christian, the deed might come easier. I need a strong, willing Christian to rid me of my husband and brother."

"Lady, you have uncommonly strange notions of Christianity, even for a Swede. Christ forbids murdering strangers and chance acquaintances without reasonable cause."

She shrugged her nude shoulders, the easy movement making her seem tempting again. "Perhaps we see the wrong sort of Christians crossing the Jontun Spine so late in the year. Even in High Summer, Christians hardly come to our mountains. Once snows fill the passes, all we see are outlaws and red-handed killers, fleeing king's justice or clan vengeance."

Her words struck him hard. "It is true that I am an outlaw; but before he exiled me, King Olaf Tryggvason made me a Christian. I try to tread in Christ's footsteps, and I left Norway rather than do violence to King Olaf's thralls."

Freyja asked why he had been outlawed. Gunnar looked up at the log ceiling. "A king is free to call his greed taxation, and his misdeeds justice. King Olaf Tryggvason is a great hero, as great as Ragnar Hairy Breeches or Hrolf Kraki, who tweaked the Pig of the Swedes' snout. It is a fine thing to hear tales told about such heroes, but it is a harder thing to live with one. Being great gives a man an inflated opinion of himself, and makes a king insufferable."

Freyja said the King Olaf must be a great king indeed, to judge by the number of men fleeing Norway these days.

"A man makes his mark as much by the quality of his enemies as by the quality of his friends," observed Gunnar.

She pursed her lips. "If you were to add my husband and brother to your enemies, then I would think better of you."

He was sorry to hear the subject of murder come up a second time. "Woman, I owe you my life, as well as my fingers and toes; but you are making it hard for me to feel happy about it. I will not commit double manslaughter for you, though you are as beautiful a woman as I have ever seen with bedstraw in her hair."

Freyja stood up, saying in a sulky voice, "Who spoke of double manslaughter? My husband and brother are one and the same."

"You are married to your *brother?*" Adding incest to the crimes that the Swedes passed their winters with made even the clean straw feel contaminated.

"What if I told you that my husband-brother delights in the blood of innocents and strangers?"

"I would say that a woman who wants to be rid of an unnatural husband might make up any sort of story." No number of large and beautiful women were worth being dragged into pagan quarrels.

"Come," she said coldly, "and I will show you just how unnatural my marriage is."

Standing, he could see she was a full hand's span taller than he, and Gunnar was not a small man. With great swinging strides, she led him around the paved fire pit and past the shaft of sunlight falling through the smoke hole. Trotting to keep up, Gunnar saw a spacious byre with pens for sheep and goats. Stalls held a milk cow and a beautiful black mare. Herbs, cheeses, and onions hung overhead. Mice scampered between wooden barrels of fermented milk. Gunnar liked the warm mix of smells: drying herbs, cold cheeses, raw dirt, and fresh dung.

In the rear of the mound house was something much less to Gunnar's liking. Wagon ruts in the tramped earth led straight into a heathen shrine as weird and dark as any that King Olaf had burned in Norway. Against the earth wall was the god-cart itself: a light four-wheeled wagon, elaborately carved, and decorated with twisted vine wood. A small alderwood stool served as a seat for the driver. Long ash poles formed the shafts, running all the way to the rear of the carriage and resting on the double axles.

Sitting square in the middle of the cart was a huge heathen idol, rough cut from a living apple tree in the vague shape of a man. All the artist's skill had gone into the wagon, with little to spare for the image itself. Large limbs stuck out below the head, each one ending in five branch fingers. At the base, the trunk was split into two stump legs resting on the wagon. A burst of green growth sprouted from the topped-off trunk, with leaves and small branches hanging down like shaggy hair and a bushy beard. Gunnar imagined that he could still smell the apples. Peering out of the foliage were two knot eyes, on either side of a lopped-off limb that might be a nose.

A helmet made of boar's teeth sat tilted atop the trunk. Its nose guard was a boar's face of beaten bronze, with tiny ruby chips for eyes. A rope twisted around the trunk supported a sealskin bag. At the crotch, where the stump legs divided, a long stone phallus was jammed into the wood. The tree-man had a rock-hard, and permanent, erection.

All this might have been more amusing if Gunnar were not standing stark naked, staring at green leaves growing impossibly from a hacked and rootless tree.

"Here," said Freyja in a husky whisper, "is my twin brother Freyr, who is also my husband."

"Forgive me, Lady, but I fail to see the family resemblance." He stared at the stone phallus and thought to himself that she must have had some wedding night. No wonder the heathen giantess was mad as a jaybird.

Eyes glittering with anger, she said, "He is my twin in life and in death. I am Freyja, Goddess-on-Earth, and I will give myself only to the man who hacks that idol apart. There is a living god in that wood who will resist death in the flesh. To defeat him will require all the strength your God can give you."

As she spoke, Gunnar saw the leaves shake, though there was no draft to move them. Cold returned to his fingers and toes. "King Olaf Tryggvason made me a Christian, telling me to cast aside heathen superstition. Idols are wood and stone; no more, no less. To smash a statue is to admit its power, and in my mind the man who breaks an idol is as much an idolater as the man who bows to one."

She gave him a keen look, full of challenge and contempt. "I had heard that the best of Christians were cowards; now I see it is so." Dropping her fur, Freyja stalked out of the shrine, showing him her long bare back. Shaking his head, Gunnar followed, watching her muscular buttocks bunch and release. If Swedes were not insanely superstitious, where would be the sting in exile?

Freyja put on a white linen shift trimmed with blueberry dye. From the black pot over the fire, she poured him a bowl of stew. Still aloof, she brought bread and a mug of sour milk to go with the stew. As he ate, Gunnar watched her lay out his clothes, dry and smelling of smoke from the fire. He could not tell where Freyja's passion and anger had gone. Perhaps he was just no longer important to her. That thought bothered him as much as her splendid body and proud bearing. He watched her adding to her costume: an amber necklace, bracelets and finger rings, a blue-black cloak with a lambskin hood, finally a pair of catskin gloves. She looked half a witch and half a great lady expecting guests.

Gunnar heard the unmistakable ring of metal on metal coming from outside the mound house, starting far off but getting closer. Glancing about, he wished for his spear, seeing a great shortage of edged metal in the place. No axes or boar spears stood by the door, and the kitchen held no cleavers, not even an iron spit. Grabbing a broom from the corner, Gunnar decided to defend himself with the handle if the Swedes turned ugly.

Voices, like children chanting, grew in volume to something partway between men's and women's singing. Clutching his broom, Gunnar braced himself for an onslaught of Swedes.

In a whirl of skirts, the Swedes swirled into the mound house, clinking tiny cymbals between their fingers. Gunnar thought that the mincing procession must have consisted of Sweden's ugliest women, all singing in squeaky voices. They wore white ruffled dresses, and colored veils hid their faces. Filing past Gunnar, they made erotic gestures, thrusting their hips and waving thick fingers at him. Gunnar was not aroused. He found their movements too oafish to be enticing, and they had incredibly heavy body hair, even for Swedes.

Sitting down, he looked up under their veils to see just how ill-favored these women were. He had to catch himself, to stop from falling down laughing. They were *men*. Their chins were shaven, their lips painted, and silver hoops hung in their ears; but beneath the swaying veils he saw long cheek-beards, and beneath their skirts, hairy calves. He stopped worrying about edged weapons, confident he could scatter this flock of Swedes in skirts with his broom.

Behind these unmanly men walked a lone girl; not buxom, barely into womanhood. The contrast with the veiled men was plain. How could he have been fooled for a heartbeat? She was slim and virginal, with thin hips, small breasts, and a wistful unveiled face. Seeing Gunnar, her eyes went wide. She looked away, then looked back. Gunnar thought he saw puzzlement, hope, and some concern on her face.

Getting up, he followed the file of Swedes into the back of the mound house. There the men danced around the shrine, whirled their skirts, sang in falsetto, and acted foolish. Several times they thrust the young girl toward the idol on the wagon. Though the singing was in Old Swedish, similar to pig grunting, Gunnar understood that the girl's name was Gerd, and that they were offering her to the wagon god.

The god image shook its leaves, sending the dancing men into adoring ecstasy. Gunnar thought that some people are easily pleased. The simple Swedes took a draft down the smoke hole as a sign from their god. If mice ate their harvest offerings, they probably counted it a miracle.

Then the singing, mincing men flounced out of the mound house, leaving Gunnar with the two women and their tree-god. Freyja closed the ceremony by standing straight in front of the idol and spitting on its trunk. Her face was impassive, and Gunnar could not tell if she spat out of contempt or reverence. Perhaps Swedes thought spittle was sacred.

For the rest of the afternoon, Gunnar rested, watching the women do what women usually did: cleaning, cooking, weaving, spinning, and the like. Such tasks normally did not interest Gunnar, but he found Freyja's strong figure fascinating. She did most of the work with easy grace, directing Gerd to the simpler chores such as drawing water and feeding the fire. Gerd was quick at taking up tasks in a new place, and Gunnar thought she would make a hardworking wife for some undeserving Swede. This girl, having never exchanged a word with Gunnar, gave him shy glances and a smile or two. Freyja—who had dragged him from the snow, warmed wild passion in him with her body, and then invited him to kill her husband—ignored him completely. Her hawk, sitting up near the smoke hole, paid him more heed, turning an occasional cold eye his way.

Such contrary and incomprehensible behavior was natural for women, but it bothered Gunnar nonetheless. Freyja's aloofness drew him in. He despaired at how close he had been to having her, picturing every white curve he had seen in the straw, from rosy nipples down to long strong legs. Here was a woman who could squeeze the juice from a man and leave him to die happy.

At dinner, it was Gerd who served him, setting out more good stew, boiled roots, and a generous length of blood sausage. Cutting the blood sausage with a wooden knife, her arm rubbed Gunnar's. Fine gold hair fell against his cheek. Gunnar looked into her large eyes and the girl blushed, shrinking back a bit, but staying within easy reach. Gunnar glanced at Freyja's straight towering figure. She seemed not the least concerned with Gunnar or Gerd, but stared moodily into the rear of the mound house.

Gunnar started to thank Gerd in stumbling Swedish, but stopped. The girl was also staring into the shrine, but with a look of sheer terror. Following Gerd's frightened gaze, Gunnar saw the huge idol stepping off the wagon. If the blood sausage on Gunnar's plate had stood up and started speaking, he could not have been more shocked. His stomach took a heave, and the good stew meat in his mouth tasted like so much straw.

No longer an inert trunk and limbs, the idol was transformed into a striding horror that brushed the ceiling of the mound house. Half-human, half-tree, and completely awful, he shambled toward Gunnar, with long forelimbs hanging almost to the ground. The monster was stark naked, but for the boar's-tooth helmet on his head and the sealskin bag tied about his waist. His rock phallus remained tremendously erect.

The bench creaked as the idol sat down, and the table groaned as he leaned toward Gunnar. Great hollow eyes looked at Gunnar through green hair on either side of a crooked nose. "Call me Freyr," said the idol. "What sort of stranger are you?"

"The sort who wishes he had stayed a stranger." Gunnar's heart raced so fast he could hear it galloping.

Freyr shook the whole mound house with brazen laughter, then asked, "Are you by chance a Christian stranger?"

"Not by chance," he said, "but by order of King Olaf Tryggvason."

"Not the Olaf Tryggvason who knocked Thor from his chariot at Thrandheim and rode my sacred stallion through the holy precinct? Not the Olaf Tryggvason who threatened to maim or kill every Swede living in Norway if we did not adopt the Christian life?"

"The world is not large enough to hold two Olaf Tryggvasons," said Gunnar. He still hoped to get by with mild answers. Freyr seemed to be the sort of troll who broke boulders and wrestled bears for amusement.

"Are you that obnoxious kind of Christian," asked Freyr, "who goes about burning temples and sneering at religion? Nothing puts me in a worse mood than intolerance. I take such atheists and toss them in a bog tied to a heavy stone for company, or hang them from oaks as pious treats for the Black Birds of Odin."

Gunnar shook his head. "No, I am one of those meek Christians you may have heard about, who turns his cheek and tries to live at ease with his neighbors."

Freyr waved a limb that Gunnar could have sat on. "Sister, bring small beer for my meek friend here; but no strong ale that might make him surly." Freyja poured a tankard for Gunnar. Gerd huddled in the pantry, trembling and shaking.

"I neither eat nor drink," said the idol, "but I like to see a man enjoy himself—if that is possible for a Christian. I have only a single pleasure." He lifted Freyja's dress and smacked her bare rump, winking at Gunnar with one great eye. "My sister-wife; you have met her, I suppose?"

Gunnar said that they had met. Freyja said nothing, nor did she wince when her brother-husband hit her.

"Have you had her in the straw yet?" asked the Wagon God with another wink.

Gunnar was now more than happy he had lost the morning's wrestling match. He could honestly say he had not copulated with her.

Freyr leaned closer to Gunnar. "I will wager she tried to warm you up."

Gunnar stammered to find a defense that did not sound guilty, but Freyr shook his hideous head. "No need to deny it. I am not a man that misses a chew or two once the loaf's been broken. I know women, playing at being pure, putting you off when you have the itch, pretending they do not like it. Turn your back, though, and off they go, rutting like she-goats among the bucks. They cannot fool me, and I have my own ways of keeping them faithful." He glanced over at Gerd, hiding behind the milk barrels, and laughed again.

As much as Gunnar wanted to stay on the monster's good side, he felt sorry for the women; especially for Gerd, who seemed in a fine state of terror. He took a big swallow of small beer, hoping it would cheer him.

Freyja refilled his tankard, then turned and went back to the kitchen.

"What a proud bitch my sister is," said the ogre. "I bet when she was rubbing up to you, she did not mention her age. She is older than the pines and oaks, older than the rivers. We were born at the same birth, straight out of Mother Earth, back at the Creation."

"She holds her age well," admitted Gunnar.

"For a long, long time she had it her own way. She bedded any buck she liked, making the best ones into kings. Not that being a king was so special then. Make a few mistakes and her women would start yapping for you to be sacrificed, to make way for new blood. Well, I tamed her and married her. Kings today do as they please, and never need listen to women."

Gunnar said he had seen that was so. "Olaf Tryggvason does not listen to anyone."

"He can thank me for that, bigoted Christian though he is," said Freyr. "Have some more small beer and drink to my health."

Relaxing, Gunnar finished off his second tankard. Freyr was really no worse than one of King Olaf's berserks, bragging over beer about his women. The largest berserk was not half Freyr's size, but Gunnar had seen some just as ugly. Women had run at the sight of Split Nose Hrolf or Sven Rat Face. The fire burned down and starlight fell though the smoke hole. Gunnar's only regret was drinking alone. Freyr kept pounding on the table, demanding beer for his friend. Freyja served the brew with neither complaint nor enthusiasm while Gerd trembled in the earth pantry. Gunnar had been to happier feasts, where everyone shared the spirit of the evening.

At last the ogre stood up, looping a limb around Freyja's waist, saying, "Sister, you can leave the keg. It is time that you entertained your husband." With a nod to Gunnar, he dragged her behind the leather bed curtain.

The thought of Freyja's soft skin and that rock-hard phallus soured the small beer he'd drunk. Sobered, he pushed away from the table and tottered off to the byre to sleep in the hay with the sheep. He was pleased to find that Freyja's ewes were warm and did not wallow in their own dung. Piling straw over himself, Gunnar was also glad that no noises came from behind the bed curtain. If Freyja was being hurt, he did not want to know it. If she was being pleasured, he wasn't sure that he wanted to know that, either. He reminded himself that he had not come over the Jontun Spine to reform the heathen. Nor was it Christian to come between man and wife, even if the marriage did not seem a happy one.

Near to morning, he was awakened by something worming in between him and the sheep. It was the girl, her skinny body still shaking. Gunnar said in halting Swedish, "Gerd, are you scared by that tree-man?"

"No," she replied, "I am not scared, I am not Gerd, and that is not a tree-man. My name is Yusa, Freyr is a god, and I am terrified."

"Well, sleep with me," said Gunnar, "and I will see that you come to no harm."

He could tell she did not believe him, but she curled up with him anyway. She smelled like a Swede and had more vermin than the sheep, but Gunnar was glad for the company. The poor child had probably never slept alone. Hel, this must be her first night away from the hovel.

Gunnar rolled out of the straw the next morning feeling fit as a flea, his frostbite completely cured. He did not need to count his toes to know that none had fallen off. He owed Freyja for that; he wished there were a safe way he could repay her. Gunnar cursed the luck that made Freyja a god's wife. Many men might want their women to be goddesses, but Gunnar was not so fussy. He would have been happier if she were a plowman's wife . . . or better yet, unmarried.

Gerd, who called herself Yusa, was already up and busy with morning tasks. Freyr was back on his wagon, looking no more menacing than a poorly pruned fruit tree. Feeling bolder, Gunnar took Freyja's hand as soon as she came by, asking her to sit with him. "There is no need for you to be cold as a whale's rump, all because I will not fight your husband."

She did not sit, but did not take her hand away, either.

"Does he walk only by night?"

"He walks only when the sun is hidden."

Morning sunlight slanted through the entrance curtain and the smoke hole. He eyed the light, noting, "We could leave now with a full day's start on him. I have seen wives leave happier husbands. A Christian would have a hard time even calling this a marriage."

She stood stock-still, looking disgusted. "This was my shrine, my wagon, and my folk. I will not give them to him. If there are any crimes my brother has *not* committed, it is only out of sheer laziness. I am Goddess-on-Earth and will have a husband of my choosing in his place. Do not expect to have me on the sly, like some pig-keeper's thrall."

Gunnar thought that Freyr's breeches would be big to fill. "It is not my fight. Gerd, or Yusa, the young one, likes me, asking nothing in return."

Freyja drew her hand away. "What does she know? She is a simple child, who supposes you will be sacrificed."

"Sacrificed?"

"Yes, it has become the custom in good winters—when my husband is in a forgiving humor—to strangle Christians and squinty-eyed strangers at the Feast of the Dead."

Gunnar rubbed his good eye and started to rise, thinking that he could be a fair way off by sundown.

Freyja stopped him. "Do not worry. I am not as cold to you as you think. You will not be sacrificed. This winter is too special; the death of a Christian stranger would not do it justice."

Gunnar watched her walk away, feeling both relieved and slighted.

Gerd came over, saying she was between chores. Would he like his hair brushed and braided? Gunnar accepted, not near as pleased as he would have been a moment before. Now he felt like a goat being currycombed for the knife. But the girl did a thorough job, not stopping until his hair and beard were soft and free of lice. Giving her playful thanks with the flat of his hand, Gunnar went out and washed his face in the snow, returning clean and refreshed.

That afternoon, the mincing men returned, still veiled like belly dancers from the Land of the Blue Men. Gunnar hid his laughter, not to taunt the addled; but the sight of their white frocks reduced Gerd to abject terror again. They lifted their veils to blow kisses at Gunnar, then hitched up the god's wagon and rolled their idol out into the open air. Freyja pinned a brooch of gold apple leaves on Gerd, then took the girl's unwilling hand, helping her up onto the cart.

It irked Gunnar to see Freyja going off without a word to him. The fire had gone out. The mound house looked cold and dark, as enticing as an open tomb. He asked Freyja where they were off to.

She looked down from atop the god-cart, as tall and commanding as a housecarl at a king's feast. "It is the Autumnal Procession. We go to the Fall Festival in the market village."

"And to feasting and drinking," added Gunnar.

"It will be a pagan festival, hardly fit for a Christian." Her voice was as crisp as the air.

"Fine," said Gunnar, "I will come only for the food and drink."

How vexing to depend on a goddess's whim for every mortal need.

"The weather may be stormy for such a *peaceful* man," was all she said.

"I will suffer the weather." Even one good eye could see that the clouds still held snow.

"Come along then, you have been warned."

The cart jolted off with the two women riding up front and the men in dresses chanting along behind. Gunnar let them get well ahead, walking in a leisurely way, adopting the air of a disinterested traveler.

Their progress was all up and down, giving Gunnar many chances to rest while the cart was hauled out of one valley and coaxed down into another. The wagon and idol were too much for one horse, no matter how fine a black mare she was. The men in white had to help so often that they trampled on their skirts, tearing and muddying the hems.

Prepared to be appalled, Gunnar was not the least disappointed by Sweden. Each uncouth stone-and-mud farmstead held its sullen knot of Swedes. Many of the women were tall and pleasant to look on, but the men were all sturdy and brooding, an ugly combination. None seemed delighted by their god's progress. In Norway, passing dung carts drew more cheers. Such silent watchfulness made Gunnar uneasy, and the priests' singing had long ago stopped. There was only the occasional sob or sniffle from Gerd to lighten the jolly procession.

At the last pass, Gunnar saw the sun touch the western summits as clouds gathered around the peaks. Frost made the way slippery, and the wagon had a hard time going over the summit. The exhausted priests asked Gunnar to push. He considered, then refused. "As much as I might like the exercise, moving the wagon would be too much like doing homage to your god."

The wagon tottered on even more slowly. Black air boiled above the pass and the storm wind threw hissing sleet at them, freezing into snow. The white-clad priests pushing the wagon groaned and rolled their eyes, as if snow were an especially bad omen. What else did they expect this high in the mountains so late in the year?

Freyja called down to Gunnar. "If you will not push, then please lead the horse. She will slip on the rocky downgrade."

Wind buffeted the wagon. "I will do it," said Gunnar, "but only because I am hungry, not out of any homage to this tree." He was irritable, not having been fed since morning, but felt sympathy for the black mare. Such a horse deserved better than hauling heavy gods through the snow.

Big flat flakes flew straight in Gunnar's face. He had to put a hand up to protect his good eye, or he would have been blinded. The sky covered over, hiding the sun. Hearing muffled screams, Gunnar whirled about, clutching his spear in one hand, holding the bridle steady to calm the mare. The whole flock of priests thundered past him, skirts hiked above their hairy legs, hems flapping in the storm. Like so many frightened swans, they went hooting off down the trail toward the market village. Gunnar thought it strange conduct, even for Swedes.

A brazen voice called out from behind and above. "Why are we not moving?" The idol was alive again, and seemed to have awoken out of sorts. Gunnar did not answer. It should be obvious even to wooden-headed heathen that the wagon was mired in a snowbank.

"Christian," the ogre called down to him, "come back here and push. Being late for festivity puts me in a bad humor."

"Lend a limb," said Gunnar, "or at least get down and lighten the wagon." There were limits to his helpfulness, even for heathen fiends that threatened to snap him in half. Pushing the cart was an impossible task; he might as well push on the mountain. Gunnar would have taken off after the Swedes, but he dared not turn his back on an angered god looking bigger than a barn and uglier than he remembered. Freyja stood statue-still in the front of the cart, her hawk on her shoulder, Gerd gripping her legs. Did Freyja care what happened to him? Snowflakes clung to her lashes and long black mane. She gave Gunnar a cool, distant look.

"If we are to move, you had all best get down," Gunnar said, trying for a respectful tone. "The mare cannot pull anymore, and I cannot push such a load."

"If I step down, Christian, it shall be to hitch you in the horse's place, or slaughter you on the spot."

No wonder the priests had fled. They knew their god was a monster without patience. Helpless as a hog on ice, Gunnar stumbled back, hefting his spear. It felt like a stick in his hand.

Thrashing at the storm, the idol stepped down off the wagon. Aiming at an eye, Gunnar threw, putting his whole body behind the cast. The spear struck Freyr square in the face, hitting so hard that the shaft shattered.

The wound only made the tree-demon more hideous. Laughing, he stomped forward, wearing the spearpoint like a second nose. Gunnar dodged around the ghoul. Grabbing up the longest piece of the broken shaft, he struck the side of Freyr's neck as hard as he could. The shaft snapped again in his hand. He might as well have been beating a tree trunk.

Freyr turned, still laughing.

Gunnar had to keep moving and not let the troll touch him. Ducking beneath a swinging limb, he aimed a kick between Freyr's legs. Knocking the stone phallus loose might give the monster something to moan about. Freyr spun sideways. Gunnar missed his kick, spraining his foot against solid bark.

Toes broken, Gunnar limped crabwise, trying to hobble round behind the tree-god. Crooked fingers snagged Gunnar's cloak, jerking him backward and off his feet. Landing hard, Gunnar felt the ghoul's enormous weight come down full on him. A limb pinned him by the throat.

He saw Freyr loosen his rope belt, making it into a noose. Blood singing in his ears, Gunnar beat at Freyr's mouth until his knuckles were bloody, but the fiend kept grinning down at him.

From atop the cart Freyja yelled. "Call on your God." Flapping with excitement, her hawk hopped down her arm to her hand.

Gunnar opened his mouth, but nothing came out. He could barely breathe. The monster forced the noose around Gunnar's pinned neck.

"Call on your God."

He could not even croak. The rope noose was strangling him.

Freyja threw her hawk at her husband's head, yelling for a third time, "Call on your God!"

The hawk landed screeching in Freyr's hair, knocking off his boar's-tooth helmet, clawing for the tree-god's eyes. Hunks of bark and green hair fell in Gunnar's face. Freyr let go of the rope, loosening his hold, grabbing at the hawk.

Gunnar seized a limb with both his bleeding hands, yelling, "Lord Jesus help me!"

Freyr felt instantly lighter. Leaping up, pushing the god off him, Gunnar called on Christ again. The tree-god staggered back, with Gunnar hanging on one limb. "Christ help me!" said Gunnar a third time, and the limb he was holding snapped.

The torn idol twisted about, swinging his remaining limb and roaring in anguish. Then he bounded off into the storm, with the hawk still tearing at his hair.

Leaning on the broken limb, trying to keep weight off his bruised foot, Gunnar gasped for breath. Freyja descended from the wagon. "I told you it was a task easier done by a Christian."

Gunnar said nothing, needing his half-crushed throat for breathing. He stood swaying, his chest heaving, knuckles torn raw by Freyr's bark, the rope hanging from his neck. Freyja placed the boar's-tooth helmet on his head. She took the noose from around his neck, then knelt down and belted the rope and sealskin about his waist.

Gunnar got his throat working. "What are you doing, woman?"

She helped him onto the cart. "Ride here. When we get to the market village, you will enter as a god."

"This is silly," said Gunnar, too tired to step down. "I hurt in a dozen places and do not feel in the least godlike. How can I be a god when I am not even a heathen?" He did not know the Swedish penalty for impersonating a god, nor for pruning sacred idols without permission. Was it burning, flaying, or something *really* nasty?

"I am Freyja," she said, "Goddess-on-Earth. My husband *has* to be a god. The simplest child knows that."

Husband? Gunnar thought this over as her hawk fluttered back to land on her shoulder. She nuzzled the bird, then looked Gunnar over. "Please remember in the festival hall that gods stand tall. They do not slouch about, or pick their noses, or pass wind and belch to show satisfaction at the table." She took the reins of the black mare.

"I hardly speak Swedish."

"Fine," she said over her shoulder, "we prefer our gods aloof, not troubling us with wise words and bothersome commandments." Her glance turned wild and wanton. "We think it enough if our gods enjoy themselves."

The wagon jolted forward, skidding on the snow and slick stones. Gunnar gripped the rail and leaned on his tree limb. Seeing him riding in the god's place, the Swedes were certain to laugh, or at least tear him to pieces.

Deathly silence greeted them in the market village. Gunnar's cart lurched past people and thatched cottages, up to a high hall with its ridgepole shaped like the prow of a ship. Carved trolls' faces peered at him from under the low eaves. The shamefaced priests appeared, throwing open the doors to the hall, dragging the wagon inside. Standing high on the cart, Gunnar saw rafters black with woodsmoke. Swedes crowded into the hall, those in the back standing on benches and tables along the wall, watching Gunnar and Freyja in uncanny silence.

Too scared to quiver, Gunnar was sure his only salvation was to stay as still as an image. The priests pulled them up an earthen ramp to the high table at the back of the hall.

As long as he could, Gunnar stood erect. The Swedes heaped a platter with meat and turnips; the priests placed it before him. When he could no longer support himself, he sank down onto the small alderwood stool at the front of the wagon.

The Swedes all drew breath at once. Freyja seated herself at his side.

In the hush, Gunnar could smell the steaming pigs' trotters

and half-burnt roast. Food was everywhere, but no one ate. If he was to be chopped and burned himself, he might as well make the best of it. Selecting a rich joint, he stripped off a meaty mouthful with his fingers.

The Swedes cheered. Then they sat down at their own tables and began to eat. Amazed, Gunnar lifted his tankard to wash down the meat. That brought on more cheers, and general drinking.

How strange to have his body functions provoke adulation! Gunnar guessed that if he dropped his breeches and pissed on his platter, the Swedes would have stood for a frenzied ovation, then urinated in unison. He did not put that notion to the test.

A memorable feast followed. Gunnar had never seen men and women drink like porpoises without a combat or a killing, since the presence of women always provoked men to brag in their cups and paw each other's wives. And yet the Swedes acted as if it were the most natural thing in the world for the sexes to sit together without mayhem or bad feeling. Gunnar studied the female diners. They were tall, handsome women, with proud lips and long limbs — utterly wasted on Swedish men. He was surprised to find them returning his stares with frank interest and imagination, as though they were picturing their new god in the nude.

Gunnar kept comparing them to Freyja. Marriage was a serious thing. A Goddess-on-Earth would be used to having her way and would by no means make a docile wife. She sat at ease beside him at the high table, laughing freely, head held high by her swan-white neck. He mortally wanted her — more than any other woman before — but could he give up every other woman for her?

Graybeards and village matrons laid gifts at his feet: honeycombs, fox furs, fleeces, sea ivory, and the like. The pile grew so sizable that Gunnar hardly noticed new additions. Then the priests thrust forward their gift, and the hall fell silent. It was Gerd. She looked as shy and fearful as when he had first seen her. Gunnar turned uncertainly to Freyja.

"This is Gerd," she said, "offered for your enjoyment." She said it stiffly, as if the words were from a ritual.

Gunnar looked back at Gerd, who now seemed quite pretty, scrubbed and brushed, with burnished gold circling her arms and fingers. "Thank you for the offering," he said in halting Swedish, "but this is not the woman I want."

The Swedes cheered, and Gerd seemed overjoyed, smiling wide at him. Gunnar sat back, feeling deflated. In his days as a mere man, young women had not been so happy to be passed over by him.

Freyja leaned close, asking if the pork was sitting poorly, or if his ale was sour. "No," he whispered, "the pork and ale are doing well. I just thought that the girl liked me. She could at least have looked a little downhearted."

Freyja smiled. "Do not feel so bad. This is the Feast of the Dead, when Freyr sent messengers to the Underworld. If we had no suitable stranger for him to sacrifice, Freyr demanded that the men bring him a young girl instead. All these girls were renamed Gerd. When Freyr was done with his Gerd, he strangled her, using the rope and sealskin, then tossed her body in the bog. Naturally enough, no girl is eager to mate with my husband."

Gunnar yelped and leaped up, ripping off the rope as though it were a viper, tossing cord and bag straight into the cooking fire. The Swedes looked stunned, then leaped to their feet, beating out an ovation that shook the smoky ridgepole.

Shaking, Gunnar sat down, demanding, "Why did you not tell me sooner what the rope and bag were for?"

"I wanted everyone to see you tear it off. A goddess must think of what will please her people, even ahead of what will make her happy."

Glumly, Gunnar watched the evening progress until the last Swedes had staggered home or collapsed senseless on the straw. He turned to Freyja. "There is not much that I like about being a god. I cannot get roaring drunk, nor eat until I slump beneath the table, and even young girls are wary of me. All the manly pleasures are missing."

She stood up and took his hand, whispering, "All but one." Freyja took two cups of dark honey wine and led him to the curtained marriage bed. Gunnar was only moderately happy to follow her. She'd never asked him if he wanted to be married, to foreswear all women for her. She'd just arranged things to suit herself. How like a goddess! Gunnar could not decide if, as a Christian, he really *was* married. But then, if he were not married to Freyja, he was not a god—and the Swedes might take that amiss.

In the blackness behind the curtains, her hands slipped inside his tunic, stroking, pulling, and imploring. Soon he was contentedly plowing away atop her, not caring that he could hear his worshipers snoring outside. Sweden could have been worse.

Spring comes late to the mountains. As the world warmed, Freyja's belly began to swell. Gunnar was pleased that his winter's plowing was bearing fruit, but between her growing belly and the shortening nights, he had fewer chances to improve on previous work. Then, at spring sowing, a white procession approached the mound house. This time the procession was made up of real women, not men pretending to be priestesses. They did not mince or chant, but stood in a smiling row with flowers in their hair, giving Gunnar those frank looks from under their lashes. He asked Freyja what they were here for.

"These are the unmarried women of the district," she said, "here for the god's spring blessing."

"Being a god is bad enough," said Gunnar, "but how could I give a heathen blessing? The words would lodge crossways in my throat!"

"Oh, they are not here for words. A god that eats and drinks is nothing compared to one that fathers children." She stroked her round belly. "Now they have a god that gives life instead of taking it. *That* is the blessing they wish to sample."

After a full winter among the wild Swedes, Gunnar was still astonished. "Would you be happy if I did that?"

"A goddess thinks first of her people's happiness. What would please these women is plain . . . but you are a Christian. Can a Christian do what these women want done?"

Gunnar looked at the scrubbed, beaming faces. Yusa was not among them, but there was a stout blonde who might have been her big sister. With knit brows, he turned to his wife. "It is hard to know," he said, "what the Lord Jesus would do, were he put in my place. . . ."

With the corner of his one good eye, Gunnar studied the line of young women, his smile returning. "All I *do* know is that King Olaf Tryggvason made me a Christian—but he never made me a fool!"

# The other magpie

## MEDICINE WHEEL

*A true description of the aboriginal American Indian dare not be put in print. Novelists of the future will give him a new character; like the Spanish Cid Campeador, the Indian will be knighted and put on horseback after his death. But as the Buddha says, "Amid the brambles a lily may bloom."*
—Capt. E. F. Ware, Seventh Iowa Cavalry

The Other Magpie knelt on a dusty knoll, sharpening her knife against a flat rock, her heart beating like a rabbit's. Spring starvation stretched her dark skin taut. Ribs and hips poked at her doeskin dress; cheekbones stood out beneath eyes hollow from crying. She mourned her only brother—scalped and killed by the Sioux.

Spread around her were the contents of her weasel-skin Medicine bag: an antelope's tooth, a breath feather, two stone shells from the days when the prairie was a sea, the bright body of a stuffed woodpecker—all the power she had gathered in her fifteen winters. It seemed small and pitiful, pitted against the Faceless Destroyer. Dead eyes on the little woodpecker watched as she sharpened the knife—the slick scrape of iron on stone hid every other sound. Above her rose the black-white tops of the Big

Horns; below the knoll stood the tall hourglass tipis of the Kick-Belly Crow.

She stopped. The shining blade was silent. From out of the woods came the drumming of a live woodpecker—the bird's fearless pounding shouted out to her, "Be brave before the world!"

Listening to the living bird, she told herself, "I will cry no more. I will not fear pain, or give in to death." Reaching up, she hacked at her black braids. Feeling the rough fringe of hair brush her shoulders, she promised, "I will mourn my brother as long as my hair is short."

She pressed her left hand hard against the flat rock, splaying her fingers. The butcher knife had been her great-grandmother's; decades of women's sharpening had worn the blade down to a steel sliver. Laying the bright edge against the little finger of her left hand, just below the first joint, she struggled to control her fear, trying to feel only grief for her dead brother. Belly muscles tightened as she tasted coldness in the air. There would be more snow before Sundance time.

She pulled the blade back in a single convulsive stroke. Her grandmother's knife sliced skin, then bone, as easily as it carved grizzly meat. Shock shuddered down her spine. Half a finger lay next to the severed braids. She told herself, "As long as I have a left hand, I will remember him—if I grow old and gray, grandchildren will know I lost a brother."

Horrified by what she had done to her guiltless hand, the Other Magpie thought how weak she was—"But with my brother beside me, I was strong. I was everything, brother and sister, man and woman, the two halves to the hoop of life." Now the hoop was cut, like her finger.

Using teeth and her right hand, she tore a thong from her half-sleeve, tying it around her finger to stop the bleeding. Working one-handed was awkward, but that too reminded her of her lost brother. Refilling her Medicine bag, she placed the braids and fingertip in with her antelope tooth, breath feather, stone shells, and dead woodpecker. Light-headed with grief and loss of blood, she got up to look for Finds-and-Kills, the only person in the Kick-Belly camp likely to help her. Her hurting hand left red stains on everything it touched.

Afternoon shadows stretched out from the tipis. She found Finds-and-Kills at the edge of camp, sitting on a cutbank by Rotten Grass Creek, humming a Medicine song as she mended a moccasin with a long steel needle. Finds-and-Kills had big hands, big feet, and other body peculiarities that separated her from most women. This separateness was why the Other Magpie sought her out; the Magpie needed a woman who had men's Medicine in her, who knew the Sundance and understood death in battle. Finds-and-Kills had the Medicine to open the Way Between the Worlds, the trail that led to the Camp of the Dead.

Sitting down next to her friend, the Magpie trailed her hand in the tumbling water, cleaning and numbing her aching finger. "My brother is dead," she declared, "killed and scalped by Sioux."

"This is so." Finds-and-Kills used a high piping voice. Her coarse features were hardly even feminine, but she had done her damnedest to improve them, tattooing circles on her forehead and a line from lips to chin—painfully determined to look more womanly. "That is why they call them Sioux"—she made the slash across the throat that means *Sioux* in sign talk.

"I must do something for him."

Finds-and-Kills looked up, shocked by the sense of urgency that went beyond mourning. She nodded toward the Other Magpie's cropped hair and cut finger. "You have done what a sister should."

"I must do more." The Magpie meant to have her brother back, even though Death stood between them.

"You cannot be more than a sister," Finds-and-Kills reminded her. The brother-sister taboo was not strong among the Crows, but everyone had a horror of sexes reared in the same tipi becoming too close. "The dead are dead. We tell them, 'Go, do not come back.' " Crows were convinced that death could be catching—no one, not even the Magpie, dared use her brother's name now that he was dead.

"I miss him," the Magpie insisted. "I do not care if he is dead. I must see him again, if only to say good-bye." Coming from a Crow, this was dangerous blasphemy—like a drunk Baptist damning salvation.

"Nah, nah, nah, nah." Now Finds-and-Kills sounded like an old woman. "The Other Magpie cares for nothing but herself and her brother. She is the girl who closed the smoke flaps on the council lodge, who chased a buffalo cow into camp. She is the young woman for whom no man is good enough. The dead go to the Land Beyond. We do not ask them back."

The Other Magpie made the "no" sign. "You have the power to help me. You have the Sundance Medicine. Last spring the men dragged you out to cut the Sundance tree. I have cut off my hair, and cut off my finger—but I cannot cut off my *brother*." She could not stand to think of him lying scalped and naked on the prairie, feeding the coyotes—she could not let their life together end like that.

Finds-and-Kills asked politely if she had gone insane, telling her, "You are far too extravagant, even in grief."

The Magpie smiled, "I am far too extravagant in everything — that is my charm." She had a wild beauty that the big woman both loved and envied, the beauty of a strong brown foal with dainty feet. If it were in Finds-and-Kills to love another woman, she would have loved the Other Magpie, and the Magpie counted on that attraction. She could be merciless in love. Dozens of men had brought ponies to her tipi, only to be turned away: chief's sons with round arms, seasoned warriors with many wives — all had been sent home with their horses.

Finds-and-Kills sighed. "Your skin smells of pine and sage. If I were a man, I would be outside your tipi, waiting with a blanket whenever you went for wood or water. But one day this wildness will kill you."

"Better to die young and wild, than old and sick in a winter lodge."

No Crow could argue with that. Finds-and-Kills got up and put on her moccasins. "Wait here. I will help you." Watching the big woman walk off toward camp, the Magpie noticed that one moccasin was still unmended — Finds-and-Kills left two different prints in the dust, one torn and the other whole. Sitting, waiting, soaking her finger, the Magpie knew that she was pressing her Medicine. But what else could she do? She would not give in, even to Death, the Faceless Destroyer, the striding terror whose war club is raised over all our heads.

As the sun set behind the Big Horns, Finds-and-Kills came back, carrying what a man would take to search for power: a bone pipe, a plug of short tobacco, and a buffalo robe tanned with the hair on. Wrapped in the robe was her rifle, a Sharps Sporter chambered for half-inch shells — her shooting bag held two-dozen .50-70 centerfire cartridges, stamped out at the Frankford Arsenal.

The Magpie cut her brother's trail ponies from the herds, two sorrels and a gray. They had always shared horses, and he had been an only son, indulged in everything. His ponies were all fast and strong, but not fast enough — now his favorite war pony was picketed beside some Sioux lodge. In bright twilight, the two women rode up the Big Horn river, past the ghostly remains of Fort C. F. Smith, burned by the Sioux under Red Cloud and Crazy Horse. Chorus frogs sang by the water, trilling like a thumbnail run over the teeth of a comb. Owls hooted, filling the burned timbers with the cries of lost souls. Mournful hoots meant that the Magpie was on the path to the Beyond, the way she wanted to go.

Dawn found them deep in the canyon of the Big Horn. Here, half-mile cliffs towered over the river like giant painted lodges, striped with sandstone. For a time, four ravens flew behind them. The Magpie could tell by their calls that the birds hoped that the women were buffalo hunters.

The land tilted up under their ponies' hooves. By the time they reached the timbered slopes of Medicine Mountain, atop Porcupine Creek, even the ravens had turned back. Blue peaks rose one above the other, like the backs of giant buffalo. Now the Magpie could hear the Beyond calling in the cries of eagles and in the wind whistling off black pine tops, between the mountains and the sky.

Near the tree line, they hobbled their ponies, walking the rest of the way. On the rocky shoulder of Medicine Mountain, the Magpie saw the gateway to the Spirit World. The spokes of a great stone Medicine Wheel poked up through the windblown snow — twenty-eight spokes; the number of nights in a moon, the number of days in a woman's cycle, the number of poles in a Sundance Lodge. A stone hub stood in the center. Six cairns marked the midsummer sunrise and sunset, and the risings of Sirius, Rigel, and Aldebaran.

Finds-and-Kills gave her the pipe and tobacco, telling her in a low deep voice, "This is as far as I will go. Stay here. Seek a vision, mourn your brother, but remember that you are letting go. Do not say his name. Do not call him back." The Magpie did not answer, already observing a holy silence. She wrapped her buffalo robe about her, hair side in, planting herself beside the Medicine Wheel, feeling the sacredness of the place. Her brother would come for her here if she waited long enough. Finds-and-Kills lit a fire and then left.

Darkness crept out of the earth, swallowing the light. Watching the first and brightest stars come out, the Magpie felt her frailty. She smoked to greet the stars, lighting Finds-and-Kills's pipe, holding it aloft, letting the winds fan the flames, sharing her smoke with the sky. Between puffs, she stared at the Medicine Wheel, waiting for a vision. Her fire was fixed up Crow fashion, logs laid with only their ends touching; every so often she pushed a little more of one log into the fire — making the wood burn longer, giving her something to do.

Stars wheeled overhead. Sirius and the Seven Sisters set. The Hanging Road shone like a band of frost in the sky. She could see how the world moved in circles, with the great stone wheel matching the spinning heavens overhead. Her mind rolled with the night, but her brother did not come. Finally a great square of four stars rose in the east; behind it came the light, blotting out the night.

At noon, the sun beat down on the snow. Finds-and-Kills came with fresh wood for the fire and gave the Other Magpie a sip from her water bag. The Magpie was thankful, but said nothing that might break the Medicine. The next nights were worse. Her fire went out. No stars kept her company—the Magpie was blinded from staring all day at the gleaming white blanket covering the Medicine Wheel. Numb to the cold, she could only hear the night birds and smell the mountain scent of pine pitch and bear grass. Her stomach felt small and empty. Her body was lighter than a breath feather, but the barrier between here and the Beyond is not easily broken.

Strength ebbed. In the cavernous darkness, she lost track of days and nights, no longer knowing how long she had gone without sleeping and eating. Dreams invaded her blindness, bright flashes and moving shadows. Defeat closed in. "I have lost," she thought bitterly, but she did not have the strength to leave. Death had claimed her brother—now she felt the Faceless Destroyer coming for her. Tears fell from snow-blind eyes. Unwilling to die alone, the Other Magpie whispered her brother's name, the name that no one had dared speak since the day he died—calling on him to come for her.

A spirit wind swept over the Medicine Wheel, opening her sightless eyes. She saw neither night nor day, but a strange in-between where the snow was black and the sky was white. Raven's-wing clouds hung overhead, and the Medicine Wheel was a great gray web, stretched over black snow. Out of the center of that web staggered a wraith in worn moccasins and ragged leggings. Death came for her wearing her brother's stricken face—ash-white skin stopped above his eyebrows, black naked bone shown through the circle made by a Sioux scalping knife.

"*Sister*," he moaned, opening his hands, showing the ragged wound in his chalk-white chest. "*Why have you called me?*"

She reached out. Their hands met but did not touch. "I could not say good-bye without seeing you again."

"*You called me back. I am lost. I cannot enter the Camp of the Dead. Do you like what you see?*"

The Magpie hated what she saw. She wanted to look away, ashamed to have called him back, but you cannot shut your eyes to a vision. "I did not do this to you."

"*You called me back. Now I wander, without a robe against the cold, without hair to cover my head.*" Her brother's voice rose, filling her with the shrill force of his suffering. "*I cannot enter the Beyond without some token of honor.*"

"What do you need?" She was ready to give anything—her hair and fingertip seemed trivial compared to his loss. "What token of honor?"

"*I must have a Sioux scalp.*"

The Magpie wanted to tell him how impossible that was, but her tongue was twisted from thirst. She was trapped by her own Medicine — having called him back, how could she dare deny him?

He started to shrink and recede, saying, "*Help me, sister. Help me go whole into the Beyond.*" She tried to rise, to go to him. Tottering, she stumbled and fell.

At noon on the fourth day, Finds-and-Kills found her stretched out beside the high Medicine Wheel.

# THE ROSEBUD

> Men won't tell about the woman who rode with Three Stars to the Rosebud battle, because she was a wild one, with no man; bad and brave. People called her the Other Magpie.
> —PRETTY SHIELD, CROW MEDICINE WOMAN

By starving her body and staying awake, the Magpie had pushed her spirit into the Shadow World. She recovered slowly, lying in a wickiup Finds-and-Kills had made out of bent boughs. The wickiup fire made her limbs burn. The least light sent sparks flying into her eyes. She heard Finds-and-Kills shuffle about in the blackness like a mother bear, and felt her friend's thick fingers flick snow into her eyes, moistening and soothing.

When the Magpie had eaten and slept, and her eyes could stand the burning daylight, the two women rode back down the Big Horn. Chickadees called out to them, saying, "Summer's near."

At the Kick-Belly camp, the Magpie's parents saw her shorn hair and missing finger joint, and assumed that she had been in the hills mourning her brother. As their daughter grew older and wilder, they'd learned to put the best interpretation on her wanderings — what could be worse than having a grown daughter hanging around the tipi, refusing to marry and behaving like a boy? Asking no questions, her father collected his son's ponies and gave them away, to show the family's grief and to give his ghost no reason to return.

It was already too late. The Magpie had ridden his horses to the Medicine Wheel and called his name. Her family's cut-down tipi, short hair, and deliberate poverty were constant reminders of her brother's wretched condition. Unless she avenged him, he would never be the strong handsome man she remembered from life.

But freeing him was a crushing obligation. How was she to get her hands on a Sioux scalp? Wife Stealing Time was over, and the first war parties had gone out. The Yellow-eye soldier chief, No-Hip-Bone, had come upriver in a Fire Boat, asking for Crow wolves to help the Long Knives find the Sioux. Two boys barely older than she, named Curly and Grandmother's Knife, had gone with No-Hip-Bone, to meet Son of the Morning Star on the Yellowstone. They had no brothers to avenge, but they went because they were boys. The Magpie complained at the unfairness of this.

Finds-and-Kills had no sympathy. "You have done too much already. Stay in camp. Mourn your brother. You have no gun, and no horse. You are no Woman Chief, to slip into Sioux Country with a skinning knife and come back with a scalp."

To prove her point, Curly and Grandmother's Knife came trudging back into camp a few days later, saying that the Crow who went with No-Hip-Bone had lost all their horses—"Sioux swam the Yellowstone and came right into camp. The Long Knives could not tell Sioux from Crow, and let them have our ponies." The horseless Crows had been cold and miserable, with no women to cook or pitch tipis, lining up every morning to be counted by the Long Knives. The Magpie could see that there was no profit in joining No-Hip-Bone's Long Knives—but at night she still heard her brother's cries in the hoots of owls and in the wind howling between the tipi ears.

In the Moon When Leaves are Full, at Sundance time, a strange Snake rode into camp. She knew at once that he was a Snake, because Snake men are short and shabby but make a tremendous show. Soon the Magpie heard a Caller going around. Rattler, the Great Snake himself, had invited the Kick-Bellies to join a war party against the Sioux. Rattler's invitation was bound to be accepted. Unlike the Long Knives, Rattler did not dither about, or do things backward. If Rattler said that he would fight the Sioux, he would fight the Sioux. He would not waste mornings lining up and counting his warriors. And if Rattler's Snakes went alone against the Sioux, the Crows would never be able to forget it. Snakes would see to that.

Late that night, the Other Magpie sat in the family lodge, listening to her parents sleep, and watching sparks fly up from the fire, following the spiraling lodgepoles into the Beyond. The moon was nearly full—perfect for pulling smoke poles out of tipi ears—but she was not that sort of wild girl anymore.

Her wildness must now have a purpose, even if it meant joining Rattler's war party with just a skinning knife. Lifting the lodge cover, she slipped out to where Finds-and-Kills picketed her ponies. Taking two trail ponies, a black mare and a paint, she left a bloody braid tied to a picket pin, so her friend would know who had the horses.

Men had gathered near the ruins of Fort Smith, stripped for war. Their muscles stood out in the half-light like the humps on a buffalo herd. The Snake was not with them, but a half-breed named Grabber told them that Long Knives were waiting for Rattler south of the Tongue. The Magpie went with them, crossing the headwaters of the Little Big Horn by moonlight.

Day dawned hot and dry. Men looked her over. She hoped that her shorn hair and cut finger spoke for her—telling them that she was not just tired of being a virgin, looking for education and excitement. By dawn light, she saw how few they were.

There were famous warriors among them, like Flathead Woman and Alligator-Stands-Up. Plenty Coups had brought his Burnt Mouth Crazy Dogs, and Bull Snake was leading some Lumpwoods Without Sweethearts; but she saw only three chiefs —Old Crow, Medicine Crow, and Good Heart. Up ahead, the Sioux would be gathering in their thousands—Sitting Bull, Crazy Horse, Crow King, Red Top, Lame Deer, Big Road, and Runs-the-Enemy would be waiting with their bands, along with hundreds of Cheyenne.

Bull Snake dropped back to ride beside her—his broad forehead painted white with clay. He was as near perfect as a man could be, tough as teak, not too short, not too tall, with a straight nose and smooth face. His hands and feet were small as a woman's, smaller than Finds-and-Kills's. He was everything a woman could want—with four wives to prove it; his gaze charmed females as easily as a snake charms a chickadee.

He gave her a cool glance. "We need no nervous virgins. This is Sundance time. The grass is thick in the bottoms, and the Sioux come together like buffalo in rut." He was half boasting, half hoping to scare her.

She made the sign that means, "I know that."

"Go back," Bull Snake advised. "When your brother was alive, no man's horses were good enough to win you. He turned aside every offer. But now he is dead, and you know nothing about battle or scalp taking."

"I can learn," she retorted, twisting her drag rope around her hands, refusing to be turned aside.

Bull Snake snorted and kicked his pony, going back to be with his Lumpwoods. It was unseemly for a handsome war chief to argue with a silly virgin.

Crossing over a series of ridges, they descended the bluffs and forded the Tongue. There were no Long Knives on the south bank. Men spread out to look for sign. Near the mouth of Prairie Dog Creek, they found iron-shod prints and mounds of firewood—showing that the Yellow-eyes had camped there—and also several arrows fletched with turkey feathers. Long wavy lines snaked down their shafts, and they were not poorly notched like Sioux arrows—the men all agreed that they were Cheyenne. Hostile Cheyenne had met the Long Knives on the Tongue, warning them away, or challenging them to come over—either way, the Long Knives had turned and headed back in the direction of their forts along the Platte Road.

For most of the men, this meant that the war party was over. Old Crow said he would go south with Grabber and look for the Long Knives. Men agreed that this was fine for Old Crow, who did not have many moons left and was clearly senile to trust a guide like Grabber—a half-breed who promised much and delivered nothing.

The Other Magpie sat on her borrowed horse, watching the war party melt in the morning sun. She was torn between duty to her brother and fear of being left alone in incredibly dangerous country.

Bull Snake declared that Crazy Dogs and scared virgins could run away—"I will do some hunting." He made a nonchalant show of crossing the Tongue to look for breakfast.

That decided her. Death could not be worse than coming home shamefaced and hearing the Lumpwoods sing about her. She dismounted and watered her ponies, rubbing them down with bunches of bluestem.

The war party dwindled to a dozen nervous young Lumpwoods Without Sweethearts, sitting in a circle, playing cards, and laying bets on who would return first: Bull Snake, Old Crow and Grabber, or the Cheyenne and Sioux. None supposed they would see any Long Knives.

They kept looking at her and laughing, then one got up and walked over. He wore pink body paint with silver zigzags, and she could smell the sweat on his limbs.

Loosening the blanket about his waist, he dropped it at her feet, nodding toward the low willows by the river—"Virgin, come into the bushes. You can keep the blanket when we are done." He told her that he had the virility of a rutting bull, and that any girl could count herself lucky to begin with him.

She replied politely that she would not even defecate under the same bush with him. Raising her voice so that the others could hear, she held up her shorn finger, "I do not want your blankets, or what is beneath your breechcloths—I want one of you ready-to-die Lumpwoods to avenge my brother! The man who gets me a Sioux scalp may bring ponies to my parents' lodge." She doubted that a dozen Lumpwoods could come up with even a lock of Sioux hair, but it was worth a try.

The Lumpwoods laughed, making the pinwheel motion beside their heads to show that she was crazy—the Other Magpie was a well-known man-hater. The smiling brave picked up his blanket and went back to the card game.

From the bluff above came a Coyote call that meant that a rider was approaching. Lumpwoods scrambled up to see who had won—but the arriving rider was not Cheyenne or Sioux, and not Bull Snake or Old Crow. It was Finds-and-Kills, riding down from the north with her Sharps Sporter across her lap.

She dismounted, thanking the Magpie for taking care of her horses, then saying, "It was silly of you to slip off on the vague hope of meeting the Long Knives." She reminded the Magpie how poorly things had gone for the Crows who went with No-Hip-Bone.

"This war party is with Rattler's Snakes," the Magpie insisted. "It will be different."

"Different does not always mean better—with Snakes, it may mean a whole lot worse. Besides, I see no war party"—Finds-and-Kills nodded toward the card players—"just a handful of Lump-woods Without Sweethearts playing Red Dog for pony stakes."

Before the Magpie could reply, the Coyote call sounded again. Bull Snake came splashing back across the river, a dead buck slung over his horse's withers. Without a word he dropped the deer between the arguing women, then dismounted to smoke with the Lumpwoods. The effect on Finds-and-Kills was magical. She stopped haranguing the Other Magpie, drew her hatchet, and began to cut kindling for a cook fire.

The Magpie was disgusted. She told Finds-and-Kills that she would rather be yelled at than see a friend so eager to be used. "He treats us like we are his, here to clean his kill and fix his breakfast."

Finds-and-Kills was unashamed. "Of course, what woman can resist him?" The big woman took a percussion cap from her shooting bag, twisting it in a rag with some black powder. She laid the rag atop the kindling, hitting it with a hatchet until the cap burst and the rag caught fire. "They say he has an elk-bone whistle, and when he blows it, you just have to go with him into the brush—to find out why he is called Bull Snake."

"I have heard his whistle, and I would not go with him if his name was Pole-in-the-Crotch." The missing part of her finger hurt, and she could not scratch it.

"Nah, nah, nah—no man is good enough for you."

"Not true. Remember Kills Good, the wife of Chief Long Horse—the woman who had such long lovely hair?"

"Who could forget her hair." Finds-and-Kills sounded wistful.

"Every morning, Long Horse brushed and braided her hair so that the whole camp would know how much he loved her. *That* is the kind of man I want. Not the kind that takes me in the bushes so that he may sing my name to the Lumpwoods."

"I wish Bull Snake would just hum *my* name." Finds-and-Kills looked up at her. "You can be free and virtuous, with your straight face and small feet. Is it a wonder people talk? You menstruate, but you are not married."

"You talk like my mother." The Magpie knelt down to help gut the buck. "Besides, it will be a long time before I am married. I told the Lumpwoods I would only go with a warrior who avenged my brother—if I even look at another man, think what they will sing about me."

A pair of Coyote calls came from the bluff. Two Yellow-eyes came splashing across the Tongue and into camp. The lead rider whistled through a gap in his teeth, letting the Crows know he was coming. He was a bear of a man with long filthy hair, wearing a battered felt hat, woolen leggings, and a raffish scalp shirt shining with grease. Worn moccasins were thrust through huge wooden Mexican stirrups. Across his saddle horn lay a Springfield .45-75 "Long Tom" infantry rifle—a bone-handled Bowie knife and two dead rabbits dangled from his belt. Beneath the wild hair and whiskers, the Magpie recognized the squaw man Crows called Plenty Good.

Behind Plenty Good came a completely different sort of Yellow-eye: a young Long Knife dressed in blue, clean-faced as a Crow, wearing a neatly creased white hat. Not too tall, not too short, he did not have the blue watery eyes that made many Yellow-eyes look like spirit persons. Long stripes ran down his pant seams. Army rank was a mystery to the Magpie, but leg stripes meant a Long Knife chief, a "Captain," to use a word the Crows borrowed from Spanish.

Plenty Good's rabbits landed right beside Bull Snake's dead buck. The trapper swung out of the saddle, pulled a pipe from his hatband, and asked the Lumpwoods if they wanted to smoke— every movement was lethargic, meant to put the Crows at ease. The Long Knife with him moved quicker, brimming with barely contained energy, dark eyes flicking back and forth as he dismounted. Even squatting on his heels, he seemed half in action, holding in his Medicine. The Magpie guessed that this handsome Yellow-eye could not speak Crow. Every so often, the trapper had to turn to him to translate. By listening closely, she caught some of what the Captain said. He called Plenty Good "Très Bon," or sometimes "T-Bone."

Suddenly the Long Knife leaped up, hitting his gloved hands together, saying, "Jesus!" She knew that he was praying. Jesus was a Yellow-eye name for the Great Mystery.

He started kicking the dirt, like a Mandan doing the Buffalo Dance, saying, "My God, Très Bon, all Grabber got was a dozen warriors, an old man, and two women?" God was another name for the Great Mystery — but the rest was meaningless to the Magpie. Still, she was pleased to find him so pious. She liked his voice, and the funny-serious face he made when he prayed. There was something far-off yet appealing about him.

Plenty Good cocked his head to indicate the Lumpwoods. "Those bucks claim beaucoup Crow were here not long ago."

"But what in Heaven are we going to do now?" He swung his arm, taking in the camp, the stream, and half the Big Horns in a single sweep. Heaven was a name for the Beyond.

"Nothin' much," Plenty Good shrugged, "not till the breed gets back with the ole chief." He gestured toward Finds-and-Kills, bent over the buck, tearing back the skin, scooping out steaming entrails. "I'm gonna get myself some rabbit 'n' venison, an' maybe some Crow for dessert."

The officer glanced at Finds-and-Kills, then at Plenty Good, giving both of them a queer look that the Other Magpie could not interpret. She got up to find more firewood, watching as she worked.

Plenty Good took her place, tossing his saddle down to use as a backrest, giving Finds-and-Kills a gap-toothed grin. "Howdy, pretty," he addressed her in pidgin Crow. The big woman laughed at Plenty Good's insolence, but the Magpie could see that her friend was pleased to be getting male attention, even from a Yellow-eye.

The Magpie had gotten about a dozen sticks when the Long Knife Captain bounded up without warning. She stood stock-still, unable to guess what he would do next. The man smiled, bent down, and began *to gather wood!* She could barely believe it, but there he was, working like a woodchuck, grinning all the time, gathering up one load, dumping it by the fire, then starting on another. Crows say, "Yellow-eyes keep warm by gathering fire-wood" — and soon the Captain had stacked enough wood for a

week. She could hear the Lumpwoods laughing. To hide her confusion, the Magpie sat down, drawing her knife to skin and gut the
rabbits.

"What's so funny, T-Bone?" asked the Captain, standing beside
Plenty Good, breathing hard, looking about for something else to
do.

"Yew'r the show," drawled the squaw man. "No Crow gathers
wood for a woman unless he's got the itch to lift her skirt."

The Captain looked flustered. "I only wanted to help." Plenty
Good gave him a leathery grin, "Hell, help yerself. This hoss has
got his own hindsights set on the big 'un."

"Surely one is too young and the other married." The Magpie
heard irritation in her Captain's voice. She wished she could
thank him for his flattering attention, but explain that she could
hardly copulate until her brother had been avenged.

Plenty Good shook his head. "Ain't any such thing as too
young among the Crow. If a girl is ready, she is ready. An' I saw
no husband sign. This hoss guesses these women are here to
avenge a killing—an' maybe see a little man-action on the side."

The Captain stood with his mouth hanging open. "Well, I
mean, I merely. . . ."

Plenty Good laughed. "Sir, say what yew please. It's a free
country an' these coons don't hear American." He gave Finds-and-
Kills a friendly grin, saying in English, "As good as deaf, ain't yew,
sister?"

Finds-and-Kills blushed, bending down, hiding her face in her
work. The Captain shrugged, "I thought it terrible to see a girl
working while men loafed—I certainly had no designs on her."

"That's good," Plenty Good studied the Magpie, " 'cause this
girl is one of yer high-toned, high-strung, Crow virgins. Pretty to
look at, but wild as a peck o' panthers. See her shorn hair and short
finger? Probably lost a father or a brother, and she is out to get
some of her own back from the Sioux." Magpie recognized the
word *Sioux*, and guessed that Plenty Good was talking about her.

"No, the older doe's fur *this* coon," Plenty Good concluded.
"She's a big'un, but I wager I can wrassle with her. Two falls in
three anyway. That young 'un's pretty, but lookit her handle her
knife. If yew don't come onto her just right, she'll feed you yer
pecker on a plate."

"I'll remember that," replied the Captain dryly, seeing the
Magpie strip the bloody skin off the second rabbit, then drape
their pink bodies over the flames. She was secretly happy to have
him watching. Despite being a Yellow-eye, he had shown his
desire to copulate in a refined but energetic way—not like the

insolent Lumpwood who had thrown his blanket at her feet.

While the men breakfasted on venison, the women shared Plenty Good's rabbits. Finds-and-Kills leaned over, whispering to the Magpie. "The big hairy one likes me." The Magpie agreed that Plenty Good had done everything short of dragging Finds-and-Kills into the brush.

Her friend hastened to add, "The one who wants to copulate with you is handsome."

"Yes," the Magpie eyed her Captain carefully, "he moves like a man with much Medicine." Her own Medicine felt shaky. The handsome Long Knife had shown his interest at the worst possible time. She was duty-bound to avenge her brother, and likely to be dead and scalped when the Sioux were done with her—in poor condition to attract a man.

"But he cannot speak." Finds-and-Kills spit out a pair of small rabbit bones. "I could not love a man I could not talk with afterward."

"True," admitted the Magpie. "He does not talk, but he has a strong friendly voice, and he carried wood for me." No man needed words to show his desire.

Plenty Good entertained the women by telling them how the Long Knives had gotten lost, mistaking Prairie Dog Creek for Little Goose Creek. "They stumbled onto the Tongue, bumped into some Cheyenne, rebounded, an' came to rest by the Forks of the Goose, where they had meant to be in the first place."

The Magpie could not understand how hundreds of men and horses could lose themselves, mistaking one stream for another.

"Weren't hard," replied Plenty Good, half in Crow, half in English. "Army's a lot of ex–railroad clerks and Bog-Irish coolies, led by coons that wouldn't know a goose from a prairie dog if it flew overhead an' shat on 'em." His explanation made no sense to the Magpie.

He treated them to cups of Black Medicine and handfuls of white sap. Yellow-eyes food is not like real food—the Black Medicine was bitter and bracing, and the white sap looked like sand but tasted sweeter than honey. Plenty Good shrugged off their thanks, saying something nonsensical about "catching more flies with sugar." Licking sweet grains off her fingers, the Magpie wondered why the Yellow-eyes caught flies—perhaps they ate them too.

When the sun had moved the width of a small pine, Grabber and Old Crow returned, saying that the Long Knives were indeed camped at the Forks of the Goose. Everyone mounted up to gallop after the retreating war party. Collecting stragglers as they went, they caught the main body loafing through the fat country above the Greasy Grass and got them turned around. The Other Magpie rode back beside her Captain, who looked splendid on his big American horse. He smiled at her, gesturing at the landscape and making meaningless comments. Around them rode a barbaric retinue of tall Crow braves on painted ponies, carrying guns, bull-hide shields, and sharp-bladed war clubs—the Magpie understood now why men so loved the warpath.

At the Forks of the Goose, they found the Long Knives lined up to greet them, neat and straight on their huge mounts, sitting stirrup to stirrup for nearly a mile. Behind them was their huge square cantonment. A Crow went to war with weapons, blanket, breechcloth, and a pair of ponies, but Yellow-eyes would not even take a piss that poorly equipped. Their camp was stocked with wagons, tents, bedrolls, cots, kegs, barrels, cookstoves, packs, mules, horses, cattle, pigs, and pets—it was as big as the Main Band's camp at the Crow Agency, and overflowed with Yellow-eyes—sleeping, cleaning, cooking, running footraces, cursing and hectoring each other with no sense of privacy or restraint. Everything was done by men, which worried the Magpie as much as the Sioux ever had.

Plenty Good and the Captain took them to see the only woman in the cantonment. She sat under guard, wearing a man's shirt and a makeshift skirt fashioned from a striped Mackinaw blanket. Plenty Good introduced her as Calamity Jane. She was plainly bored with being a prisoner, saying "How" and smiling at the Captain. The Magpie was not jealous—a man like her Captain must have many sweethearts; besides, she could see that the Calamity's attention embarrassed him tremendously. He tipped his hat to hide his blushing face.

The Magpie asked why Jane was not allowed to cook or gather wood. Plenty Good grinned, "Calamity was caught posing as a teamster. She did a man's work, but acted overfriendly to the mules—didn't cuss 'em enough. Now she's suspected of being overfriendly with the men too." When Finds-and-Kills understood that Calamity's crimes were wearing pants, helping with the packing, and wanting to copulate, she was horrified—and insisted on leaving. The Magpie tried to comfort her, pointing out, "They are Yellow-eyes. We are Crow." Finds-and-Kills did not feel safe until they were back in the Crow camp, working on a wickiup.

The Magpie kept looking back toward the cantonment, hoping to see her Captain. Bugles blew. The Long Knives lined up to count themselves. Then Rattler arrived. His Snakes galloped up to the line of Long Knives, waving glittering lances, neatly turning left-front into line. Rattler employed Texans, former Confederate

officers, to teach his warriors how to parade, but he had brought
even fewer braves than the Crows.

She did not see her Captain again until evening council. There
she spotted him sitting among the Long Knife chiefs by a huge
bonfire of crackling boughs. She realized that his restless Medicine was natural—all the Long Knife chiefs were staring about,
wide-eyed and inquisitive, unable to sit still like warriors. The only
movement among the Crows was the slow circulation of pipes.
Even the Snakes managed to look dignified and attentive.

Half-breeds and squaw men had to repeat each word in three
languages, so that the Magpie had plenty of time to dwell on what
was happening. She saw death all around her, in the ghostly white
of the wagon covers, in the intense blackness of the night. Crows
and Snakes were horribly few, less than three hundred, and the
night hid thousands of Sioux warriors. Out beyond the firelight
was Sitting Bull with his deadly visions, and Crazy Horse with his
never-miss Medicine gun. She imagined the avalanche of arrows,
and the hideous cry, "Hwoon, hwoon," as Sioux war clubs thud-
ded into flesh. The thousand-odd Long Knives in the cantonment
were scant comfort, considering how easily they got lost or confused. Determined to meet her fears head-on, she got up, walking
away from the circle of men, straight into the darkness. Either
powerful Medicine protected her, or she was going to die; there
was no middle way. No one seemed to notice her going.

The night was covered by clouds. The only light came from
the huge campfires lit by the Yellow-eyes—the dark plain burned
in a hundred places, as if all the stars in the sky had fallen between
the Forks of the Goose. Turning her back to the fires, she called
out into inky void, saying to her brother, "Come, guide me, protect me, or I can never do as you ask."

Buffalo grass brushed her ankles, nodding in the night wind.
She heard the hoarse chirp of a Mormon cricket, followed by the
yips and laughter of Old Man Coyote. Then from far off came a
low eerie call.

Whooo! Whooo!

She pictured the huge shadowy bird of death, with his
speckled body, powerful wings, and heart-shaped face, his round
eyes looking almost human. From out of that ghostly face, the call
grew louder, coming closer.

Whooo! Whooo!

The last mournful note broke into harsh screeching directly
overhead. Darkness parted behind the bird of death, and her
brother strode toward her. He lacked color and substance, but
stood upright, with a proud look on his hideously mutilated head.
In his hand, he held a long coup stick, wrapped in buffalo hide and

trimmed with hair. A single breath feather fluttered at the base of the shaft.

His mouth split in a skeletal grin. *"Sister, take this coup stick against the Sioux. Take it and count coup for me."*

Shaking, she reached into the Beyond, taking the coup stick. Wind howled. Rain started to fall. Her brother shrank back, vanishing into the night. She found herself holding an ordinary length of cherry wood—cold, hard, familiar. It had no hide, hair, or feather.

Drumming rose up from the Crow camp. Men's hands beat on taut parfleche, pushing back the night. She followed the drumming back to camp. The council was over. Flickering light came from the cracks in the wickiups. Yellow-eyes wandered about looking amazed, including Plenty Good and her Captain. Plenty Good nudged the officer, "Take a peek into one of those lodges. It's a peephole into Hell."

The Magpie watched her Captain lean over, looking through a crack in the covering of a men's wickiup. She pictured the men huddled inside, half-naked, crouched around a small fire, moaning and chanting, making Medicine for the coming fight. He straightened up, shaking his head. "I thought they would be resting after riding all night and half a day."

"Resting?" Plenty Good chuckled. "They figure they'll sleep enough when they're dead."

Unable to understand what they were saying, the Magpie sat down before her own wickiup and began to wrap the cherry-wood staff in buffalo hide. Rain pattered down. Winding the hide as tight as she could, she trimmed the staff with tufts of hair, fixing her breath feather to the bottom, making it match the stick in her vision. As she worked, she stole glances at the Captain's boots, shining in the firelight.

Plenty Good stood over her, saying, "Bet she lost a brother. Now she's making herself a coup stick."

"She'll be going into battle with only that?" The Magpie heard incredulity in her Captain's voice.

"Damn straight," declared the squaw man, "and you are gonna need to be one eager beaver to stay ahead of her."

The officer shook his head, saying she looked young and helpless.

"Sure she is. But that's how the Crows make war—the cussedest mix of cruelty, calculated idiocy, and raw courage you are ever likely to see."

At dawn, the Long Knives put on a ridiculous display, mounting two hundred soldiers on pack mules—they had not brought enough horses. Neither mules nor riders liked the idea. All morning, the Magpie saw mules bucking off riders and breaking saddles, or charging about with cursing Long Knives clinging to their backs. Yellow-eyes never lost their ability to amaze. The mule rodeo made them a day late leaving the camps at the Forks of the Goose. Without her handsome Captain beside her, there was nothing romantic about the ride. Rattlers snaked through the buffalo grass, emerging from their winter holes to rejoin society.

Shots made her sit up, staring wildly about, but it was only some Lumpwoods shooting buffalo for the thrill of seeing them fall over. The men's antics angered her. So did her own fear—here she was, trying to part a warrior from his hair, but frightened by men shooting buffalo. She told herself bitterly, "Silly fool, you better get used to guns going off." Riding a strange pony, surrounded by armed and nervous men, the Magpie realized that she might never live to see the Sioux. Already a Long Knife had managed to shoot himself dead while chopping wood.

At sundown, they pitched camp near the headwaters of the Rosebud. Horses, happy to be free of their saddles, rolled down grassy slopes strewn with blue phlox and prairie clover. Bull Snake strode over to their fire, bringing some tripe and tongue. Finds-and-Kills made the meat into sausage, threading it on a ramrod and rolling it on the coals until it was cooked.

Neither woman got to taste it. Bull Snake took the sausage back to his fire, where Lumpwoods, Fox Warriors, and Crazy Dogs were "Naming Married Women." This naming was something the Other Magpie had heard of but never seen, because it only happened on the warpath in enemy country. Men passed the buffalo sausage like a pipe, each man biting off a bit, saying what he would do in battle and then naming a married woman he had copulated with. Bull Snake started off, "I will take a pony for my sweetheart Pretty Bottom." The Crazy Dogs laughed, and each named several women. Crazy Dogs are so wild and reckless, most husbands let them have their way.

The Other Magpie studied the husbands' faces. Each tried to show no emotion, but she could tell by their eyes which of them expected to hear their wives' names, and which did not see it coming. The sausage came to Pretty Bottom's husband. He bit off a big piece, saying he would count coup, calmly naming Bull Snake's youngest wife. Foxes snickered. Crazy Dogs howled. A man who swore by buffalo meat staked his life on his words— Pretty Bottom's husband was either telling the truth, or risking death just to take Bull Snake down a notch.

Having no one to name, she wrapped herself in a buffalo robe and lay staring at the starless sky. As she fell asleep, it began to rain again.

At half-light, she was awakened by a hand on her shoulder. Rain had stopped. Finds-and-Kills's huge silhouette knelt over her. "Our wolves found a Sioux campfire in the hills." Men at the next fire were admiring a blanket brought back by the scouts, made of rubber, useful for keeping the rain off. Who knew the Sioux had such luxuries?

"I am afraid," whispered Finds-and-Kills.

"So am I," the Magpie admitted — she only hoped that her coming death would be creditable enough to set her brother free.

"I am worried by more than death." Finds-and-Kills's voice was low and hoarse.

The Magpie told her that death was enough of a worry.

"I am afraid of disgrace as well."

She found this hard to imagine; Finds-and-Kills was as straight and stalwart as anyone she knew.

"I am afraid of what will happen if the Sioux kill me, and then strip my body. I know how they will laugh when they see me naked."

The Magpie was not looking forward to that, either. She did not expect to cut much of a figure sprawled naked and bloody on the prairie. Her friend produced a bundle of men's clothes wrapped in a blanket, saying, "Help me change. Hold up this blanket so the men will not see."

The Magpie got up and covered the big woman as best she could. By dawn light, she could see what Finds-and-Kills was hiding. Her friend's body was not like other women's bodies — no breasts, just a broad chest, and men's private parts hanging down between hairy thighs. Finds-and-Kills was not a woman by birth, but by choice. When she stepped out from behind the blanket, she did not look like a woman at all, except for her tattoos. The blanket shirt, leggings, and breechcloth fit naturally — and must have belonged to Finds-and-Kills before she became a woman.

"If I am killed in my dress, the Sioux will laugh, saying, 'This Crow was hiding in a dress.' Now they will merely think I am a man."

The Magpie stood glumly, holding the blanket. "If I am killed, there will be no surprises, nothing for the Sioux to even smile at."

"Yes," her friend agreed, "you are lucky."

The Magpie did not feel lucky. Preparing her Medicine as best she could, she painted her forehead yellow and took the stuffed woodpecker from her Medicine bag to tie in her hair. Everyone mounted up. Setting off over sodden ground, following the south fork of the Rosebud, the war party was amused by the "new man" among them. The Magpie did not find her friend's transformation funny. The new man next to her seemed half a stranger—and her Captain rode with the Long Knives. She felt abandoned, going into battle very alone.

The south fork of the Rosebud corkscrewed through thickets of wild roses and sweetbriar. At the big double bend where the forks came together, the ground rose up—benches by the river blended into low bluffs topped by conical hills, forming a natural amphitheater, alive with menace. Her brother whispered to her on the wind, *"This is the place."*

Yellow-eyes straggled along the bottom in a line stretched all the way back to last night's camp. Their leaders called a halt for the rear to catch up before plunging into the wooded defile where the bluffs came within a long bowshot of the river. The Magpie saw Medicine Crow in his buffalo headdress making signs, saying that the Long Knives should stay mounted while scouts swept the hills for Sioux. The Yellow-eyes ignored him, dismounting to smoke, talk, and play cards, moving like men in a dream.

Finds-and-Kills looked grim in a man's clothes and a man's paint, saying, "Sitting Bull has made Medicine over the Long Knives. They cannot see the bluffs. They see only what the Sioux want them to see."

Morning turned to noontime. Hot air shimmered like water. The Magpie scanned the hills, too scared to speak or spit. She had not seen a single Sioux or heard a shot in anger, but the way the land rolled up toward the bluffs was enough to set her heart racing. Fear crawled down her spine and dug a pit in her stomach.

Shots rang out, followed by a wild ululation. Crow wolves poured down from the bluffs, whipping their ponies into a run. Shock made each detail impossibly sharp. A wounded wolf rode past the Magpie, swaying in his saddle and holding his side. His eyes were glazed. Flecks of spittle flew from his lips—red blood welled up between his fingers, like in a Medicine man's trick.

Strange riders spilled out of the draws, demons springing straight from Grandmother Earth, wearing war bonnets or half-masks with the faces of animals, waving lances and eight-foot tomahawks. For all her fear and anticipation, she did not understand who they were until men cried out, "Sioux, Sioux!"

Mesmerized, she sat helpless on her borrowed mare. Long Knives darted about like blue butterflies drunk on locoweed, chasing their horses and mules, trying to mount. Others stood stockstill, wanting someone to tell them what to do. Crows and Snakes charged straight up the benches to meet the oncoming Sioux, waving their weapons and making horrid noises in their throats. It seemed that they must be swallowed up by so many enemy. Masses of men and ponies met with a sickening crash—a terrible amalgam of shots, yells, and screaming mounts. The Magpie saw Long Knives scramble up onto the benches in the wake of the Crows and Snakes; mostly on foot, shooting as they went. She hoped they were firing high. Yellow-eyes could never tell one warrior from another.

Not happy to be targets for both sides, Crows turned and galloped back. As they returned, she expected to see empty saddles and slopes littered with the fallen, but the Crows came back carrying no dead and leaving no bodies behind. It amazed the Magpie that hundreds could meet thousands—fighting hand to hand—without losing anyone. Sioux came pounding down from the bluffs on either side of the Crows, whooping and shouting, "Hoka hey." Again she expected a massacre, but they turned about as soon as the Long Knives formed a firing line. The fight dissolved into private shows by single braves attempting to draw the troopers forward with feigned retreats and feats of daring. An enemy rider would break from cover, hanging behind his mount with only a leg showing, firing from under the pony's neck or trying to touch the troopers. As that warrior dashed off, another would emerge to put on his own display of devil-may-care riding at breakneck speed. The cavalry's continuous firing deafened the Magpie, but did not seem to disturb the Sioux.

Shaken and weak, terrified almost to tears, she had done nothing to avenge her brother. She had not gone up the bluffs. Her coup stick had not touched the enemy. She could not even claim to have been close to death, since there had been so little killing.

A band of Long Knives rode up, with chief's stripes on their pant legs. Among them was a tall old man with a funny braided beard who wore plain pants and a battered slouch hat—the Magpie thought the silly man in the shabby coat was a mule skinner until men said this was Three Stars, the Long Knife big chief. A squaw man rode over to tell the Crows it was time to turn their backs on the Sioux, to continue downriver into the canyon where the bluffs came closest to the stream. Warriors made the pinwheel motion beside their heads—the Long Knife leader was mad or crazy drunk. If the firing line opened up, thousands of angry Sioux would swarm down from the bluffs like hornets from a broken hive. The Crows and Long Knives could never negotiate the thickly timbered canyon with Crazy Horse hanging on their heels. This was the worst possible moment for Three Stars to get lost in the woods.

Crows flatly refused to move. A Snake boy who had been holding the horses ran up to Rattler, begging to be allowed to fight. Rattler agreed, and the boy ran off to paint himself. There would be no safety anywhere if the Long Knives opened the line. The Magpie realized that she too was going to be thrust into battle, brave or not.

Long Knives mounted up, pulling out of line, heading downriver, leaving a yawning gap. If Sitting Bull himself had commanded the Long Knives, he could not have done more to wreck their line. With a whoop and holler, Sioux streamed toward the opening, blowing their eagle-bone whistles and firing from the saddle. Crows braced themselves. Men around the Magpie sang their death songs. As she resigned herself to death, she saw her Captain ride up with Plenty Good at his side. The Captain was wild-eyed, waving his arms like he had a wasp in his pants, yelling orders in English. From his excitement, the Magpie guessed that he too was disobeying Three Stars. She was proud to see him act like a thinking man.

Plenty Good had the sense to speak Crow, "Come on, you Crazy Dogs, an' ready-to-die Lumpwoods, don't let Rattler get ahead of you!" He pointed to the Snakes, already catapulting themselves at the onrushing Sioux.

The Magpie kicked her pony and rode over to her Captain. Nothing could stop the Sioux from coming through, and she wanted to die beside him. He smiled at her, saying, "Howdy, ma'am," looking shocked and shy, oddly formal given the havoc around them. "That's a girl," yelled Plenty Good. He had lost the pipe he carried in his hatband. "Get moving! No Sioux can hit nothin' smaller than a buffalo from horseback. Crazy Horse hisself jumps off to shoot." The squaw man turned in his saddle to shout at the Crows, "Let's go, Lumpwoods! Gonna let girls an' Snakes get ahead of you?"

Sioux were swarming out of the draws, gaining momentum, singing their own death songs. Her Captain led the Crows right at them, firing his revolver, shouting more meaningless commands. The Magpie was shouting too, but she did not know what. Every word, every thought, was swallowed by the inferno of buzzing bullets, rearing ponies, blinding dust, and multicolored horsemen. Sioux slammed into the Crows, screaming, "Hwoon, hwoon," swinging tomahawks round their heads, trying to beat them from the saddle.

Somehow they broke through to the Snakes. The Magpie saw Rattler stripped to the waist, wearing a feathered bonnet that swept all the way to the ground. The Great Snake had seen seventy winters, but fought like a warrior in his prime. Long

Knives were with the Snakes, fighting in isolated groups against terrible odds. She reined in her black mare, breathing dust, her heart beating like a bird in a snare. She had lost her Captain. Was he hurt? Killed? Her coup stick had still not touched the enemy, and she certainly did not have a scalp. Sioux were all about her, shooting and showing off their trick riding. None were offering up their hair.

A Long Knife leader rode back and forth, trying to re-form the firing line. Suddenly he reeled in the saddle, shot through the face. His jaw dropped against his chest, blood gushing out of his mouth. For a moment he stayed mounted, then he toppled. Long Knives around him broke and ran.

She rode anxiously up to him, but the wounded man was not her Captain.

Bull Snake burst past her, painted black and yellow like a real bull snake. He jerked instantly backward, somersaulting off his mount in an absurd display of horsemanship — not until he hit the ground did she realize that he'd been shot. The Lumpwood chief flopped like a fish on land, his handsome features twisted. Sioux came storming up to count coup and take scalps from the fallen. She felt helpless to stop them.

A big figure dashed forward, dismounting beside Bull Snake. It took a moment for the Magpie to recognize Finds-and-Kills, still disguised as a man. Standing over the fallen warrior, she fired her Sharps Sporter as fast as she could work the breech.

The Magpie had to decide. She could run with the Long Knives, or die beside her friend — there were no other choices. Kicking her pony, she felt a sudden surge of courage. The Sioux could do no worse than kill her, and they had already done that to her brother. For the first time that day, her mouth ran wet with saliva. Having no weapon, she spit at the charging Sioux, showing how she did not fear them. Circling in front of Finds-and-Kills, she shouted, "Spit is my arrow. I dare you to face it."

The lead Sioux took her up, nocking a wicked war arrow — its barbed head fixed flat to slide between her ribs. He dropped down on the far side of his horse where Finds-and-Kills could not hit him, showing nothing but his left foot.

The Magpie charged forward, putting all her fear into her lungs, screaming as she swung the coup stick around her head. Her yell startled the man's pony, a beautiful bay with dainty white stockings. The bay turned sharply, not willing to play toss-the-pony with a wild-eyed woman.

Hanging by his left foot, holding both bow and arrow, the Sioux struggled to stay with his horse. His foot slipped and he fell. The white-stockinged bay bounded off.

Scrambling upright, the man took aim at the Magpie — she saw the big barbed point, and behind it the man's eye, sighting on her breast.

Finds-and-Kills's buffalo gun boomed. The Sioux flipped over, bow and arrow flying in different directions. Finds-and-Kills was a formidable shot, who could place a bullet as carefully as a stitch — her shells were painted yellow and blue to add to their Medicine. The Sioux did not so much as twitch.

The Other Magpie dismounted and gingerly whacked the man with her coup stick. He was sure-enough dead. She drew the steel sliver that had taken off her finger. Bending down, she made a neat cut along the man's hairline, running across his forehead and above his ears. She grabbed the man's hair and pulled back. There was a gruesome ripping. A lifetime of skinning animals made the task easy, if not pleasant. She slashed through the last flap of skin, and the scalp came off in her hand.

She stood up with the man's bloody skin and hair in her hand. He was her enemy, who had tried to kill her, but her hate evaporated into vast emptiness. A warrior would be taking his bow as well, but she could not even look at the corpse. She swung back onto her mount.

Finds-and-Kills was still firing, keeping the Sioux back. Two tall Snakes, one wearing a jaguar-skin headdress, stood over the fallen Long Knife chief, a pair of panthers holding the buzzards at bay. Lumpwoods were hauling Bull Snake away by the heels. Her Captain came up, rallying the Long Knives, forming a new firing line.

She had the hair her brother needed. Her fight was over — but the battle was still on. Sitting on her horse, chest heaving, she saw two dismounted Long Knives running in terror for the safety of the re-formed firing line. A pair of Cheyenne split off from the Sioux, tearing after the two men.

Crows mustered for a countercharge. The Magpie braved herself to go with them. But then a squaw man came riding up, yelling in Crow — Three Stars wanted everyone to fall back. Anxious as she was to leave, the Magpie was disgusted. She saw the two Cheyenne catch up with the running soldiers. The frightened men raised their hands in surrender, offering their guns to the Cheyenne — who took them eagerly, turning them on the terrified soldiers, shooting them down with their own weapons. Then they leaped off their horses and began to prune body parts in typical Cheyenne fashion.

The Magpie felt mortified. Glittering piles of cartridges marked the line they were leaving. Soldiers had spilled the shells from their pouches to have bullets ready at hand. Now they were abandoning the ammunition, to be scooped up by the Sioux and someday fired at the Crows. Long Knives seemed to care for nothing, leaving their bullets and weapons, their comrades dead and living.

Three Stars himself came up, looking more than ever like a load of old clothes flung on a post. He signed that the Crows should get ready to ride downriver into the wooded defile—not satisfied with his original blunder, he was hell-bent to repeat it. White Feather swept Three Stars's suggestion aside, signing, "What is the use of going farther, if you will not fight here?" Completely obsessed, Three Stars acted like an old man with only one idea left in his head, pointing at the canyon, claiming Crazy Horse's camp was somewhere downstream.

White Feather laughed. He turned his chin toward the Sioux swarming on the heights, practically encircling them—"Here is a petty war party, a thousand, two thousand; I had no time to count. Go downriver to their camps; you will find more Sioux than there are leaves of grass." He rubbed his palms together, imitating a woman grinding seeds between two stones. "They will rub you out." After seeing the ridiculous show Three Stars had put on, no Crow was about to ride into a blind canyon looking for Crazy Horse.

Ashamed for her Captain, the Magpie rode slowly back to the little stream where they had left the led horses. They were gone. The Snake boy who had been watching the ponies lay by the brook, his face half painted, his bare skull white and bloody. When Three Stars opened the line, Sioux had ridden through, shot the boy, and scalped him.

Three Stars kept threatening to ride into the canyon, looking for Crazy Horse. But when he counted his men, he found that he had scores of wounded whom he could not take into battle, or leave behind for the Sioux. So he changed his mind, and everyone trooped back to the Forks of the Goose—not a moment too quick for the Crows. The next day they rode off up the Tongue. Sioux country was no place to blunder aimlessly about. The Magpie had avenged her brother, taken a scalp, and fought beside her Captain, but it all tasted of ashes.

# LITTLE BIG HORN

*The little soldier chief [Maj. Reno] ran away, knowing how the fight would end. My man, Goes Ahead, rode down Medicine Tail Coulee with Son of the Morning Star. He heard the Sioux shout, "Go back, go back. You are dead men."*
                                                    —PRETTY SHIELD

Dawn sky on midsummer's day was the color of a newly cast skillet. Snow lay in the shadows between the trees, but the great Medicine Wheel was blown completely clear. The Other Magpie sat by the northwest cairn, watching the sun rise over the stone hub, her face painted black to show that the fires of revenge had burned down to embers. She laid her last hank of Sioux hair on the flames of a small fire—the rest of the scalp had been cut up so important members of the war party could all have a piece to dance with. Bull Snake was shot through both hips, in no shape to scalp-dance or strut before the women, but even Old Crow, shot in the kneecap, managed to hobble about with the dancers.

The smell of singed hair and burning flesh filled the air, and her brother's spirit appeared, striding purposefully out of the hub of the Wheel with the dawn behind him. For the first time she saw his ghost in daylight, fully fleshed out, hair restored, no longer a wraith. Each time she saw him, he seemed to take on substance, becoming the strong young man she remembered.

*"Sister, see what you have done for me."*

The Magpie felt whole as well, able to look straight at him, sure she had earned forgiveness. "Brother," she told him, "I must ask something of you." Crows considered ghosts troublesome, but able to be helpful—if they wished.

*"Ask, sister."*

"I want my brother's permission to marry."

*"You have my permission, even if he is too poor to give ponies."* Her brother was not near as proprietary as when he was alive—no longer needing horses to ride, or women to tend his tipi. *"Just so long as he has not shamed himself in battle, or taken back a runaway wife."*

"He is the Yellow-eye Captain who rode beside me at the Rosebud. We know he is brave in battle, and he must have ponies, since all Yellow-eyes are rich. I do not know how many wives he has, or if any have run off."

The ghost looked grim. *"Sister, you must choose another."*

"Why? I have earned the right to pick my man." Would no one let her have her way?

"*You have,*" her brother agreed, "*but this Long Knife Captain will soon be dead.*"

"Dead?"

"*Already they are making a feast for him in the Camp of the Dead.*" Her brother turned his chin toward the rising sun. "*The Long Knives have lost themselves again. Right now this Captain and Plenty Good are in the Wolf Mountains, trying to slink past Crazy Horse's village, which they think is on the Rosebud. Three Stars has sent them to find No-Hip-Bone and Son of the Morning Star—but the Sioux have left the Valley of the Rosebud and crossed the Wolf Mountains to camp along the Little Big Horn. It is Son of the Morning Star and his Long Knives who are headed down the Rosebud.*" Three Stars's confusion was complete—Son of the Morning Star was where he thought Crazy Horse was; the most foolish Lumpwood Without a Sweetheart knew more of war. And her Captain was on an idiot's errand, going the wrong way around the Sioux camps.

"We must help him." The Magpie had no faith that the two Yellow-eyes could find their way through Sioux Country on their own.

"We must?"

"Yes, you owe me that."

Her brother's smile turned benevolent. "*Yes, you have earned this. Before I go into the Beyond, I will unite you with your Captain and help him find Son of the Morning Star.*"

Finds-and-Kills waited below the shoulder of Medicine Mountain, wearing women's clothes again. When the Magpie walked into camp with her brother, the big woman said nothing and did not seem shocked—the Magpie guessed that her friend could not see the ghost. Just as well. She explained what had happened on the Medicine Wheel, and how she had to find her Captain.

Finds-and-Kills listened, then sighed, seeing yet another insane venture ahead—"You have a brave and foolish nature that leads you into mischief. But you stood by me when I fought as a man. If you must do this, I will do it with you." The Magpie added that Plenty Good was with her Captain, so they both had a man to look forward to if they were so lucky as to get through Sioux Country alive.

Even though they were guided by her brother's spirit, it still took them days to track Plenty Good and the Captain through deep ravines crisscrossed by Sioux trails. They finally found the two men holed up in a cottonwood draw, afraid to travel by day or make a fire, drinking cold coffee with their guns in their laps. Plenty Good saw them first, slapping her Captain on the knee. "Hot damn, sir, it's our honeys!"

The Captain responded with one of his short vehement prayers. "Jesus, what are they doing here? How'd they ever find us?"

Finds-and-Kills was suddenly shy in the squaw man's presence — so the Magpie spoke for both of them, telling Plenty Good as much as she considered safe. She did not want to scare him by mentioning her brother's spirit, though the ghost was standing a few feet away, studying her Captain. A spirit person could stare all he wanted without seeming impolite.

Plenty Good turned to the Captain, shaking his head. "Got any of that bacca left? This needs a smoke."

The Captain fished out a pouch of pipe tobacco.

"Appears these women have come to lead us to Custer." Custer was what the Yellow-eyes called Son of the Morning Star.

"Did General Crook send them?" The Magpie could hear disbelief in her Captain's voice — Crook was their name for Three Stars.

"No." Plenty Good took the pouch. "Crook's still sittin' by Goose Creek, his head up his arse, fishing for trout an' wonderin' where Terry and Custer might be. But these women say Custer has cut hisself loose and is coming down the Rosebud alone."

"Do you believe that, T-Bone?"

Plenty Good got out a bit of paper and rolled a *cigarrillo* from the pipe tobacco. "Yew askin' me if I believe General George A. Custer would cut loose from Gibbon and Terry an' go riding off on his own, to take on half the Sioux Nation with nothing but the Seventh Cavalry and a pair of bulldog revolvers?"

"I suppose it was a silly question," the Captain grimaced. "Custer will kill his horses to be in at the death."

Plenty Good licked the *cigarrillo,* taking a long look toward the Rosebud. "But yew can bet your pants bottoms ol' Son of the Morning Gun don't know Crook ain't comin' north to meet him."

"Then it's our duty to tell him."

The trapper tapped the white tube against his thumbnail. "Suppose that's what we're paid our four-bits-a-day for."

"Do you think these women can find Custer?" The Captain gave the Magpie and Finds-and-Kills an uneasy look. "I hate to drag them into danger."

"They found *us* easy enough, and I thought we were damn well cached. Besides, they are already in danger. We all are. I'll tell you plain, I don't take to traipsing after Custer. That man has killed more cavalry than the cholera. If we pitch into beaucoup Sioux, I'll figure I've earned my fifty cents, an' Son of the Morning Star can look out for hisself." He stared down at the *cigarrillo* in his hand, "Got a locofoco to light this?" The Captain handed him a match, and they passed the burning paper like a pipe.

Plenty Good was dead against moving during daylight, saying there was way too much "sign" around, so they rested until the sun went down, leaving a red streak of war paint above the western hills. Mounting up, the Magpie managed a private conference with her brother. "*Do not worry,*" the spirit assured her, "*I see with the eyes of an owl. I can guide you as well in the dark as in daylight.*"

"We will not miss Son of the Morning Star?" The Magpie knew how easy it was for Long Knives to get lost.

"*I will lead you right to him.*"

But about midnight, descending a plum-choked canyon, the Magpie heard Plenty Good mutter, "I smell woodsmoke." All four froze atop their horses. The Magpie strained to see over the plum bushes.

Tipi ears showed against the sky. Shots rattled from the thicket. She realized they had ridden right into a Sioux camp. The trapper yelled, "Cache yourselves," grabbing Finds-and-Kills's bridle, leading her up a bank, crashing through the brambles and plum brush. The Magpie tried to follow, but Plenty Good soon outdistanced both her and the Sioux. She "cached" herself and her Captain in the dense thicket, waiting for dawn, no longer trusting her brother's owl eyes.

"How could you have missed those Sioux?" she whispered. Spirits are supposed to be superhuman, above stupid mistakes.

"*I did not miss them, they missed us,*" her brother chuckled. "*It was like when we chased the buffalo through camp.*" It was hard to get a ghost to take life seriously.

"But now we have lost Finds-and-Kills and Plenty Good."

"*No harm will come to them.*"

The Magpie stopped arguing, afraid her whispers would wake her Captain, making him think she was crazy. How could she explain her spirit brother to a Long Knife who did not know Crow? Instead she curled up and slept, saving her strength for the long morning.

In the Moon of Midsummer, there is hardly any night. First light edged over the rim of the world. The Magpie fed her Captain pounded meat, mixed with berries and kidney fat, along with a rather tasteless root that grows in the Big Horns. Etiquette called for them to eat apart, but the Magpie decided that was absurd. Her man was properly thankful, nodding his head, smacking his lips, saying, "Not Delmonico's, but it beats hardtack and uncooked bacon." Tipping his white hat back, he looked right at her, the way a Yellow-eye will. "You know Delmonico's, don't you? Steak house in New York?"

She could see by his smile that he thought they were alone and enjoyed being forward. She returned the smile, though it was hardly the time to copulate—not when the mosquitoes were up and half the Sioux Nation might be watching.

A little encouragement went a long way. The Captain's idiot grin grew wider, "No, I guess you don't know Delmonico's." He shook his head, saying a short morning prayer. "God, how do I get myself into these things—all alone with a girl I can't talk to, and a few thousand Sioux!"

Her brother stepped between them, acting as ghostly chaperon. *"Son of the Morning Star is stirring; by midday he will be moving."*

The Magpie made the sign for Morning Star, holding her hand up toward the star itself, still visible in the predawn.

"Venus?" Her Captain nodded vigorously. "Sure, the Morning Star, that means Custer, right?"

She crooked her finger to show him the sign for agreement. Then they mounted up and headed for the Valley of the Rosebud, with her brother riding her led horse, the black mare she had ridden at the Rosebud. It was strange to have the two men she cared most about riding beside her—only one of them able to see the other. The valley was silent, smelling of roses and crab apples. No smoke hovered in the morning air. Her brother led them across to the west bank, where the wind blew the mosquitoes away. Then he turned south. Her Captain's impulse was to collect the straying mare and head downstream, where No-Hip-Bone would be waiting. The Magpie had to dismount in the half-light and show him the ironshod hoofprints headed upstream. Hundreds of American horses had passed not long ago, going south.

"Son of the Morning Star?" asked her Captain, making the sign she had shown him: holding up his hand, thumb and forefinger forming a circle, tapping the two fingers together to indicate twinkling.

She smiled, turning his arm about until it pointed to where the dawn had been. Then she crooked her finger.

"Have to say I'm learning quickly," her Captain smiled, plainly enjoying the finger play and physical contact. They headed up the Rosebud, following the ghost-ridden pony. Where the valley widened, the Magpie saw the remains of tipi rings, surrounded by skeletal wickiup frames. Grass was cropped to the roots and covered with pony droppings. She made the cutthroat sign, saying "Sioux," opening and closing her hands many times so the Captain could know there were more than could be counted.

The Captain turned in his saddle, looking around. "Right, beaucoup Sioux. But where is Custer?"

Upstream, they found a giant twenty-eight-pole Sundance

Lodge, laid out like the Medicine Wheel. Everywhere were signs that the Sundance had been cut short, with rituals half-completed. Axheads and cooking pots lay hastily abandoned. A scalp hung from the Sundance Lodge. If that were not enough of a warning, some Sioux had drawn a row of men head down in the sand, ringed by horseshoe prints to show that they were Long Knives.

"Primitive art." Her Captain smiled at the sand drawing. "The guy wasn't Rembrandt. He got it upside down."

Head down meant dead. The Sioux were supremely confident—with good reason, so far as the Magpie could see. Where the trail mounted the divide, headed for the Little Big Horn, the ironshod tracks were surrounded by thousands of pony prints and travois ruts. So many lodgepoles had been dragged over the divide that in places it looked like a plowed field.

They followed the trail west, into the direction of death and sunset. By late morning, they found the first body, facedown in a dusty alkali draw, circled by turkey vultures. Her Captain dismounted, turning the dead person over. He was a Sioux boy, shot through both lungs; buzzards and magpies had already been at him. Her Captain remounted, showing her something he had found under the body. "It's hardtack." He crumbled the slab in his hand. The Magpie did not want to touch either the dead boy or the Long Knife bread—both looked to be very bad luck.

He paused, pointing his thumb toward the creek. "That boy back there. Is he Sioux?"

"Hunkpapa Sioux," replied the Magpie, signing as she spoke. "Maybe Sitting Bull's band."

"I suppose all that means yes. He is not long dead."

A rising sun baked the trail. Near to noon, they reached the watershed and climbed a tall spire called the Crow's Nest, to get a good look over the dry arroyos and grassy mesas. A thin haze from hundreds of cook fires hung over the Valley of the Little Big Horn. Through the haze, the Magpie saw pony herds blanketing the prairie, wriggling like brown worms in the sun. From the size of the herds, the village had to be immense.

Her Captain saw nothing but haze, so she pointed to dust trails moving through the badlands closer at hand, signing, "Son of the Morning Star."

"Custer? Really?" The Captain shaded his eyes. "Great, I'll get the horses." He clambered eagerly down the spire. When he was gone, she asked her brother if there were Crows with Son of the Morning Star, not trusting Yellow-eyes to see how many Sioux lay ahead.

*"Oh, yes,"* he assured her. *"Half-Yellow Face is with him, also White Swan, Hairy Moccasin, Goes Ahead, White-Man-Runs-Him, and the boy Curly."*

Farther off, she saw the white flash of pronghorns fleeing from smaller dust devils, little whirlwinds moving north and south of the Long Knife columns. She asked what his spirit vision made of them.

*"Sioux,"* he pointed with his chin, *"and Little Wolf's Cheyenne."*

"You can get us through them?" She looked back at the huge pony herds crawling over the benches along the Little Big Horn. They had to move fast before the Sioux got angry.

*"I will get you to Son of the Morning Star,"* the ghost promised.

"In daylight? No more owl eyes nonsense?" She was not forgetting the fright he had given her.

*"By midafternoon, before he reaches the big village by the Little Big Horn."*

Descending the spire, she found her Captain in an agitated state, trying to make coffee over a tiny fire, anxious to press on. She explained with words and signs about the hostiles around them, but assured him she would get them through to Son of the Morning Star.

"Right," he nodded, "beaucoup Sioux, but we can get through to Custer." He took a sip of his half-brewed coffee, and spit it out.

"Bad water," signed the Magpie, cupping her hand to drink, then making a throw-away motion — streams trickling down the divide were shallow and alkali.

"Bitter as a mule's behind," her Captain agreed. He poured the coffee into the ground, and they mounted up.

The bleak sameness of the badlands hid sharp turnings and sudden folds in the earth. The Magpie watched the winding trails of ironshod hooves diverge, a smaller trickle of horseshoe prints turning southward, but her brother led them straight on, following the greater stream. Sage and buffalo grass gave way to ash and cottonwood as they entered a shallow canyon. The bottom was mostly dry, with a few swampy mud holes surrounded by red-tipped paintbrush. Smoke drifted up the canyon.

At each turning, the Magpie tensed, expecting to see Sioux. Instead they came upon a second scene as ghastly as the dead boy in the draw. In the middle of the wash was a burning tipi, a burial lodge with its hide cover consumed by flames. Tongues of fire climbed the burial scaffold, which was collapsing under the weight of the body wrapped in buffalo skins.

The Magpie looked quickly away. Here the tracks of the Long

Knives split again. And again her brother followed the larger path, but the stream of hoofprints had shrunk almost by half. She told her Captain, "Son of the Morning Star scatters his men like sparrows before a storm."

"Custer?" He looked puzzled. "But where is he?"

She nodded toward the empty slopes ahead, where short-grass bluffs ran parallel to the river, like the spines of long-dead animals. Dust hung in the air, and summer flowers were trampled by the passage of hundreds of horses.

As they mounted the bluffs, the Magpie heard firing coming from the Valley of the Little Big Horn. She turned her horse to get a look.

Her brother tried to stop her. *"Do not turn aside, sister. We can get to Son of the Morning Star before he reaches the village."*

"I must see for myself," she shouted.

*"The trail goes straight ahead."*

"There is fighting in the valley," she insisted. The firing grew, sounding like a ripping blanket.

The Captain looked surprised by her burst of loud one-sided conversation, but he turned his horse to follow. Climbing the back of the bluffs, she saw her first Long Knife, standing over his fallen horse, hitting the tired beast, trying to get his mount to rise. Man and horse seemed half-asleep until her Captain stopped to shout, "Where's Custer?" The man waved toward the head of Medicine Tail Coulee.

Reaching the ridge, the Magpie looked down into the Valley of the Little Big Horn. Slopes dotted with bunch grass danced in the heat. Blackbirds with bright red-wing flashes flitted between wild sunflowers and patches of buffalo beans. Beyond the redwing blackbirds, a white sea of tipis stretched downriver, camp circle following camp circle, until the lodge tops were lost in the haze of cook fires—each circle had hundreds of lodges: Hunkpapas, Minniconjous, No Bows, Oglalas, plus the Cheyenne, Santee Dakota, and smaller bands. At the near end of the village, she saw a small knot of Long Knives fleeing for their lives, trying to reach the bluffs. Warriors rode in and around them, whooping and killing.

Shaken, she turned to her brother. "Is Son of the Morning Star down there?"

*"No, he is ahead, descending Medicine Tail Coulee."* Both their horses dripped sweat, nipping grass tops in the windless heat.

"But he will be rubbed out!" A handful of Crows, a few hundred Long Knives, facing thousands of Sioux and Cheyenne—what other result was possible?

Her brother looked grave. "*Yes, he will be rubbed out.*"

"Then why are you taking us to him?"

"*Sister, I must go into the Beyond; so must Son of the Morning Star. Now you and your Captain can come with us.*"

The Magpie stared at her brother, hardly believing. One look back into the valley took the mist from her eyes. She saw where he had been leading her. No ghost can ever be trusted — they are of the dead. "Go," she told him, "you are dead. We don't want you."

Her brother looked hurt and anguished. "*I love you, sister. I do not want to go into the Beyond without you.*"

She saw stems of wheatgrass appear behind him, showing through his body. "Go," she repeated, "you belong in the Beyond. We do not want you back."

"*Sister, I fear to go alone.*" He faded, his smoky image reaching out to her, imploring. A gust of ghost wind wrapped him up and whipped him away.

Sadness replaced anger. She whispered, "Someday I'll join you." But not now — she leaped onto the black mare, who had carried only a ghost all day, dashing down the hill.

The Captain pointed to where Medicine Tail Coulee split the bluffs. "That trooper claimed Custer went that way." Whatever he was saying was utterly unimportant. The Magpie did not pretend to listen. Grabbing his reins, she dug her heels into her mare's flanks, making the signs for many Sioux, turning him toward the pine ridges to the east. They pounded down the bluffs and up a snake-headed draw.

"Well, yes," her Captain gasped, "there are many Sioux, but Custer's command is right here." He waved toward Medicine Tail Coulee. From the top of the draw they could see a line of troopers waiting on big bay horses. She had no time to pay polite attention and tugged harder on his reins, dragging him toward a line of pines. He kept turning his head, trying to see what was happening on the bluffs above the Little Big Horn.

The column waiting by the coulee advanced along the crest, becoming enveloped by dust and gun smoke. Soon the only riders they could see were Cheyenne and Hunkpapas whirling around the cloud of dust, darting in and out like swallows. "Well, damn," he complained. "We'll never get to Custer now!"

Pines closed around them. For a time, they could still hear the gunfire — it lasted for as long as it would take a leisurely man to load and smoke a pipe.

In the dry bluffs above Tulloch's Fork, a lone Crow in war paint came over the crest, riding with deliberate haste, his tired pony taking the slope in slow motion. Seeing the oncoming brave, the Captain clawed at his holster. The Magpie stopped him before he got his pistol out. The rider was Curly, the boy who had gone with Grandmother's Knife to scout for No-Hip-Bone.

Curly was exhausted. His face, sharp and handsome as a hatchet, looked pale and drawn. His pony's flanks heaved.

"You are tired," the Magpie told him.

The boy gave her weary agreement. "We rode for half the night and most of the day behind Son of the Morning Star. No-Hip-Bone sent us to guide him, but he would not be guided."

"So where's Custer?" Her Captain inserted English into the conversation.

Curly did not understand, but the Magpie knew what her Captain was asking. "Where is Son of the Morning Star now?"

Curly ground his hands together, like a woman crushing seeds. "Rubbed out. He would not listen. He called us women. He was like a breath feather, blown to his fate. They are all dead men now."

Magpie had no signs to express the magnitude of what had happened, so she signed to her Captain, "Come, No-Hip-Bone will have someone who speaks." He seemed to understand, and they headed downstream toward the Big Horn, with Curly lagging behind on his tired horse. Dusk settled, and they lost the boy in the darkness.

By dawn the next day, they had reached the Big Horn. Finding a cold stream, she drank, inviting her Captain to do the same. "Thin your blood," she told him. "Our bodies are water." He drank, then turned politely away while she washed, showing that he was a man of feeling.

When she was done, she handed him her porcupine-tail brush, showing him with hand motions that she wanted him to brush her hair. Smiling, he sat behind her, using long even strokes on her wet hair. It was wonderful to sit, hips against his knees, feeling him stroke her hair, watching morning light shine on the water. Yellow butterflies sat on black-eyed Susans by the bank, opening and closing their wings, warming themselves in the sun. Every woman's day should begin this way.

By the time her hair was shining, she saw a Fire Boat churning its way upstream beneath a pillar of smoke, and she knew that her delightful morning would end here. The Captain stood up when he saw the boat, handing her back her brush, looking embarrassed. She turned to face him, having important things to say. If he could not understand her words, he might at least see her feelings. "I am sorry that we will not copulate. You are a good man, you gathered wood with energy, and you brushed my hair beautifully, but it is hard to be a Crow — being pretty, brave, and helpful is not enough. Each year the Yellow-eyes crowd closer, and the buffalo go away. I cannot live my life looking out for you, keeping you out of danger, finding you when you get lost. It is better for us if that Fire Boat takes you to your own people."

Her Captain stared at her, seeming dumbfounded by the speech. From the brush above came the "Yak, yak, yak," of someone imitating a magpie. Finds-and-Kills and Plenty Good descending the draw, leading their horses. They too had seen the smoke from the Fire Boat. After an enthusiastic reunion, the Magpie turned her chin toward the Fire Boat, saying, "They will take you to No-Hip-Bone. You do not need us anymore." Plenty Good reckoned that was so, slapping Finds-and-Kills on the back and offering his hand to the Magpie. She shook it. Then both women took their horses and headed west.

On the far bank of the Big Horn, they turned to take a last look at the Fire Boat — fine and impressive with its white woodwork, black-belching stacks, and its huge wheel whacking the water. The Magpie felt wistful, but Finds-and-Kills looked happy. Seeing her friend's smile, the Magpie asked, "Did you have a good time?"

"Oh, yes," replied Finds-and-Kills. "Plenty Good is as good as his name."

On the deck of the steamer *Far West*, moored to a cottonwood at the mouth of the Little Big Horn, the Captain told his story to Plenty Good. "She led me almost to Custer — then, when we got to the bluffs by the Little Big Horn, she started acting crazy, talking to herself, holding loud conversations with the air. She got angry, turned around, and brought me straight here. It was almighty strange, even for an Indian."

Plenty Good agreed that you could never tell what a Crow would do.

"Then she had me brush her hair. I thought I did a damned good job too — but when I was done, she gives me a long lecture in Crow, and rides off. Can't figure out why. I thought she liked me."

"That's yer high-toned Crow virgin," Plenty Good laughed. "Yew were lucky to come away with both balls."

The Captain raised an eyebrow. "Well, how did you do, T-Bone?"

The squaw man smiled. "Well enuff. Hell, I knew right off me an' that big'un had itches in common. When I got her in the brush, this hoss was almighty surprised to see just how *much* we had in common. But I'd say our itches are well scratched."

The Captain called Plenty Good a sly bastard, clapping him on the back, saying that he wished he handled women half so well. The steamboat's tall stacks continued to draw stragglers—a sleepy Crow rode up on a tired horse. The Captain pointed him out to Plenty Good—"Hey, here's that boy we met."

The trapper took a look. "Damned if it ain't Curly, Gibbon's scout."

"Well, good, call to him. Find out where in the hell Custer's gone to."

Hell, of course, is a Yellow-eye name for the Beyond.

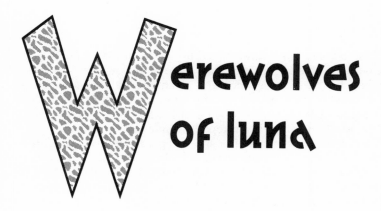

# Werewolves of luna

## DOWN AND OUT IN ORBIT

*It was a unique, almost mystical environment up there.*
— EDWIN E. "BUZZ" ALDRIN, JR.

Ian was lost, listening to the last of his air hiss away, when he saw the moon faerie — a silvery form flitting on gossamer wings among the slumped peaks and scree slopes. He snapped his head about, trying to hold the glimmering light in focus. Lunascape reeled and tilted, but his battered tourist helmet couldn't turn quick enough. Horizontal reference is haphazard on Luna — limited field of vision and the short horizon made local features lean alarmingly. Before Ian could compensate, the faerie had slipped from sight.

Hallucination was his first thought. Oxygen starvation. Hypoxia. Rapture of the Void. He had been stretching the last of his air (heaven knows why), cranking the intake valve down to a whisper, letting blood oxygen dip into the danger zone, ignoring seductive warnings from his suit. "Do not lower your airflow," advised a husky come-hither voice, whispering into his left ear. Even idiot suit computers knew that young males paid more attention to sexy voices. This throaty whisper had swaying hips, pert nipples, and a neck like Nefertiti. Ian could hear the willing smile. "Time to renew your air supply — please return to your vehicle."

"Fine advice, but I *cannot find* my goddamned vehicle!"

Unless the faerie returned, Ian was going nowhere. The surrounding bit of moonscape seemed familiar—a low saddle between two slumped peaks, littered with pebbles, talus, and house-sized boulders. But so much of Luna looked the same.

And all the while, his air kept hissing away.

No natural complainer, Ian still resented this slow measured extinction. He was near to thirty, with three advanced degrees, a solid career in mass conversion maintenance, a dry Scots humor, and even decent judgment—when he deigned to use it. Cosmetic medicine gave him trendy unblemished features, and he owned a thatch-and-stone bothy in the Hebrides. Damn it, he played the bagpipes too—"Practically a lost art, for Christ's sake! What a waste!"

On the moon less than forty hours, his death had to set a record for nonimpact fatalities—fastest tourist kill since a load of Zen sightseers aboard the *Dharma Bum* completed their current incarnations by carving a fresh crater inside Tycho. Barely two hours before, Ian had been atop a peak, able to see the goddamned rover, sitting on the mare—a shining silverfish on a basalt plate. That's when he thought he'd take a new route back. "No sense seeing the same moon twice."

The suit's mapping program was supposed to project an optimum route onto his visor, using broken yellow lines. But the dotted lines had not taken him back to his rover. Instead the lying yellow brick road only led him deeper into the Montes Carpatus, the Lunar Carpathians, part of a highland arc forming the southern shoreline of the Sea of Rains. (The montes were named for a range in Poland or Hungary—Ian was not sure which, and never likely to know now.) He was lost amid the protruding bones of the ancient moon, blunt peaks and scree slopes older than the surrounding mare. Older than life on Earth. A bouldered moonscape, saturated with impact craters, filled with stark shadows so solid he couldn't see into them.

Halo comsats and Lagrange navigation stations were supposed to instantly locate anyone, anywhere on Luna. But the same suit-flu that infected the mapping program had locked his comlink on Radio Ganymede. Upsun rockabilly jammed the wavelength. Right now he was listening to a folksy refrain by Jolly King Jove and the Red Spots, accompanied by mouth harps, guitar, ceramic jugs, and an electronic washboard:

> Us gud ole boys ahn Ganymede,
> Got us ah gee-tar an a band . . .

Amateur night in the Jovian moons was drowning Ian out. He

could see Jupiter, eight-hundred-million kilometers away, a yellowish disk among the hard sharp stars. He shouted for Jolly King Jove to "Shut the hell up!" A futile gesture. At light speed, the signal would take forty-five minutes to reach the Jovians—Ian would be dead long before Ganymede could reply. He reached up and gave the suit antenna a vicious jerk, snapping it at the base with an armored gauntlet. That did not solve his communications glitch, but at least he could hear himself think.

Suddenly everything was as quiet and cryptlike as only the Lunar Highlands could be. Silent and spooky beyond belief.

Softer sounds filled out the silence. His suit and helmet formed a compact little coffin, whirring with life, holding back burning daylight and freezing night. Air hissed in at the nape of his neck. He had water in his helmet tank. By turning his head to the right or left, he could pop pills onto his tongue—glucose and vitamins on one side, hard drugs on the other—synthetic opiates to block out pain and fear, powerful amphetamines to pump him up. Readouts on his visor told him his pulse and respiration rate, blood oxygen, air supply, radiation exposure, interior-exterior temperature, even the time of day in Greenwich, England. When the hiss of air gave out, his treacherous friendly-faulty suit would continue to hum for months—maybe years. Micrometeorite erosion takes eons, a millimeter every ten million years. His body would be there for good, a grotesque little warning for future tourists.

The faerie came back, a silver form leaping between bright sunlight and black shadow, its gossamer wings shot with rainbow colors. Why wings on an airless world? "Ian, old son—you are not just dying, but flipping your set switches as well." (Suit tapes of hypoxia victims were full of fanciful imaginings, mirages of home, mother, and rescue ships that weren't there.) The first faerie was joined by a second.

Just as quickly, they were both gone, disappearing into dense shadow. Ian had the impression that they were playing with him.

He gobbled several white stim pills, washing them down with tepid water from his helmet tube—long-term addiction was not an immediate worry. Drugs snaked through his veins, snapping the moonscape into sharp, crisp focus, like a 3V negative of some brilliant desert scene where sand and sky are black and shadows glaring white.

Ian pushed off, full of drugs and anger, dizzily determined to find the dancing lights and force them to take him to the rover.

"Warning, you are now on 120-second reserve—kindly return to your vehicle."

Reaching around, Ian clamped his helmet intake valve down

tight, cutting off the hiss of air, saving his last breaths for when he really needed them. He still had the stale air in his suit and helmet, sweaty as a jockstrap, but breathable. He shuffled forward. Short steps. Shallow breaths. With no rush of air to cool his sunlit helmet, perspiration collected in the suit's itchy plastic collar. Suffocating closeness dulled his sense of self-preservation. Even before he'd started seeing moon faeries and talking back to his suit, Ian had noted an insane desire to tear off the confining helmet and breathe the pure, cool vacuum. Catastrophic decompression might rip his lungs out, but it would save him from dying in a slobbering brainless stupor. Ian did not look forward to lying facedown in the regolith, drowning in his own sweat and $CO_2$, while sultry recordings told him he was in trouble.

With his air shut off, he actually felt better. No annoying little hiss reminded him of his troubles. Best of all, the faeries came back. Ian admired their low gliding leaps, touching down every ten or twenty meters—barely making contact—skimming prima donnas with a million years' practice. They had no faces, just gentle hollows where the mouth and eyes should be.

Ian's blood oxygen blinked red. He ignored it. The sensuous voice in his suit pleaded, "Please open your helmet intake valve." The brute mechanical valve could not be overriden by his suit computer. He told the sexy synthesized voice to "Put ah sock in it." Ian was not ready to take his next-to-last breath. The faeries did not seem to bother with breathing.

He started to step off again, meaning to meet the hallucinations halfway—but his legs were locked. Looking down, Ian found that he was kneeling. He had fallen without knowing it. Fine cohesive sand, produced by eons of micrometer impacts, had softened the impact, sliding and caking, spreading the force outward.

Blood oxygen blinked angrily. Time to obey that sweet persistent recording—"Please, open your intake valve." Reaching back, Ian fumbled about, finding the intake tap—but he could not make it turn. He struggled to close his gloved hand. Numb fingers no longer had the strength to work the tap, to get at those last breaths. He pitched headfirst into the lunar dust.

Dust falls gently in one-sixth g, like a slow-mode damask curtain. Through the falling motes, Ian could see the highlands tilted sideways, butted against stark cosmic night. *What a stupid way to die!* Ian loved life, loved it so much that being on the moon had made him want to climb mountains. Cold emptiness crept through the sweaty heat of his suit, descending his spine, balling in his gut. He had gone too far. Fucked up once too often.

As Luna faded, Ian felt himself rising, cradled in silver arms, borne up by gossamer wings. The faerie's silver-clad face did not look the least bit human—it was shaped more like a wolf's snout. Not that it made an angstrom's difference to Ian. The dead don't care who gets them.

Nothing beats going to bed dead and waking up alive. Ian lay on his back, eyes closed, feeling the moon's feeble pull. Air moved in and out of his lungs. Somewhere, water was dripping. In a burst of panic, he realized that his helmet was off, his suit unsealed, exposing face and chest to vacuum. Groping wildly, he tried to close his suit.

"Human, quit batting the air and *breathe* it."

Ian lowered his arms. Shadows flickered against stone high overhead. He lay in a huge cave lit by hundreds of stubby wax candles. Dark air tasted cool and musty. A caninelike humanoid crouched next to him. Ian's first impression was "wolf," then "hyena," but the beast was not nearly so close akin to him. It was a xeno—an Eridani Hound, human-sized, vaguely baboon-shaped, with dark beady eyes and tufted audio antenna set on either side of a short snout. Twin rows of white fangs showed through parted lips. The Hound's body was hidden by silver fabric; a hooded mask hung to one side; rainbow wings covered with solar cells sprouted from the beast's shoulders. A standard speakbox rested on the Hound's silver chest.

Lounging beside the Hound was a human, a man with the face of a blond, blue-eyed faerie king—handsome, devil-may-care features that screamed biosculpt. His silver body suit showed off nearly sixteen stone of muscle and bone to stunning effect. Neither of them was a Loonie. Loonies looked like the "before" holos advertising a cheap health spa—the man was too well-built, and the dog came from the far side of Human Space.

"Clive Barrow," the muscular faerie said, giving Ian a relaxed two-finger salute. He jerked a thumb at the wolf. "A Hound. He doesn't figure he needs a human name."

The xeno's six-digit hand keyed his speakbox. "Howdy, human," drawled the box, "welcome to the Wolf Pack." The speakbox repeated, "Wolf Pack, Wolf Pack . . .," echoing the refrain from *Best of the Beasts.*

Ian looked around. The gravity felt right, but everything else was wrong. He was lying in a vast limestone cavern—Tom and Becky's cave, transported from Hannibal, Missouri, to the moon. Stalactites hung down from the cave vault, and massive stalagmites rose up from the floor, some meeting halfway to form tremendous flowing columns, like pillars of half-frozen ice cream.

From far off came the drip, drip of falling water and the high, faint squeak of bats. The leather-winged rodents flitted back and forth in the candlelight. Little blackish-brown vampire bats — Ian could picture their evil beady eyes and bright fangs.

"Where the hell am I?"

"Luna." The Hound hit a dictionary key: "Earth's largest natural satellite, thirty-five hundred kilometers in diameter, surface grav . . ."

Clive cut in, "And your name is Ian MacNeil. From the Outer Hebrides — Earth. Today is Tuesday, Greenwich time. Does that help?"

Aside from the short personal bio, none of this made the least sense. There were no vampire bats on the moon. There was no air for them to fly in. No mammalian blood to feed on. Nor did lunar caves have stalactites or stalagmites, which are caused by water seeping through limestone — the moon being bone-dry. Mare Imbrium was a sea in name only. Luna does not even have limestone, which is formed from the remains of ancient marine creatures pressed to stone.

Ian's senses were plainly on a drug-induced holiday, but that did not stop him from feeling better, overwhelmingly better — on top of the world. Or at least, on top of the moon. Instead of worrying over where the bats came from, Ian marveled at how really superb life was, picturing summer afternoons off the Hebrides. White sails on the water. Sea turning sunset colors, copper-red and deep lilac. He remembered the devilishly beautiful stewardess who had served him dinner aboard the shuttle. Ian felt as happy as if she had whispered, "When we land, let's rent a futon and fuck," instead of merely saying, "Have a nice stay."

Insanely thankful for his second shot at life, Ian babbled on about how glad and grateful he was. . . .

"How grateful?" asked the Hound.

"Could you put it in money terms?" Clive suggested.

"Well, really, really grateful. I feel like an absolute fool. . . ."

"Humans often are," observed the xeno. "Did you know that your intake valve was clamped down?"

Ian gave a guilty nod. "I was saving air."

The Hound's speakbox chuckled. Clive wagged an admonishing finger, "Boy, ya gotta breathe *now*, not next week!"

Ian laughed with them, looking off into the deep recesses of the cave — the gallery above seemed to go on forever. "Where do these bats come from?"

Clive looked at the Hound. "Bats? What bats?"

"Human's hallucinating," concluded the Hound.

Okay, I'm cracking up, thought Ian. Can you blame me? The

last few hours had been enlightening. Ian now knew that humans were never meant to leave Earth. Since his first ancestors wiggled free of the anaerobic slime, they had been adapting to live in the open air — and nowhere else. The ease with which Luna could kill you was eerie. You could suffocate in vacuum, drown in $CO_2$, be bent by nitrogen, OD on oxygen, freeze in the shade, or fry in the sun. Slow falls could puncture your suit. Flash fires could turn you to toast. Or a tiny lapse in shielding could let in a particle of hard radiation, carrying the seed of inoperable cancer that would cream you twenty years down the line, when *la Luna* was merely a memory.

Outrageous. Unfair. Such casual deadliness made staying alive cheerless drudgery; checking and double-checking, looking before each step, always having healthy margins of everything. *Being good all the time.* With no slack for daydreaming, or just enjoying the moonscape.

Nothing had properly prepped Ian for this, not 3V, not the shuttle ride, not the stewardess's "Have a nice stay." Instinctively, he reached into his open suit for the return ticket, wanting to touch the plastic promise that there was a shuttle berth set to take him home.

The ticket was gone. Ian sat bolt upright. His sweat-soaked pocket was empty. No ticket. No ID. No credit key. He glanced about. Neither of his rescuers was looking his way. "Where's my stuff?"

"Stuff?" Clive lifted an eyebrow. "What stuff?" The Hound's evil grin broadened a millimeter or two. Xenos have a beast's ability to observe without making eye contact.

"The stuff in my pocket. My ID. Credit key. Shuttle ticket?"

"We took 'em." Clive patted a small packet adhering to his silver ribs. It was no great admission. Who else could have emptied his pocket? Ian calculated furiously. Weird as these two were, they had saved his life, and he hated to tangle with them. Clive had height and weight on him, and the Hound looked inhumanly strong. The ID was replaceable, he could spare the credit, but he had to have that prepaid ticket.

"You're sort of like salvage," Clive explained. "Unwritten law says we get half — and unwritten law's got to be strictly obeyed, since there's no one to enforce it."

The fare home was more than Ian made in a year. If anyone cashed the ticket, or used it to disappear dirtside, he might as well never come back. "Hey, I don't mind splitting with you — you deserve some reasonable reward — but I have to have that ticket home."

The xeno set his speakbox to extraharsh. "Human, a minute

or two more, and we wouldn't be dickering. We'd have had that ticket, along with a slew of body parts and valuable bio-implants, while the rest of you did dust to dust in an organics dump."

Clive grinned amiably, "Absolutely—you can't thank us enough. Without air, you don't have a ticket nowhere. Not even out the door. If you think you can do better, then get up and go. Just reseal the lock when you leave."

What lock? Ian saw no sign of a cave entrance.

"Look," Clive reflected, "what real use is half a ticket? Shuttle's not going to take you halfway to Earth. The only way for a fair and even split was to make you a full, one hundred percent, voting member of the Wolf Pack."

"What's the Wolf Pack?"

His ignorance provoked pitying looks. Clive turned to the Hound. "Claims he never heard of the Wolf Pack."

The Hound gave his shoulders an exaggerated shrug, as if to say, "Your stupid species."

"*We* are the Wolf Pack," Clive explained. "What's left of her."

The Hound stared up between the hanging stalactites, looking past the limestone roof. "Would say the jumpbug is just about due."

Clive produced Ian's helmet from behind him. "There's a motion on the floor that we suit up and meet the jumpbug. All in favor?"

"Opposed," objected Ian. "I vote you give me my stuff and show me the way back to my rover."

Clive shrugged. "Sorry, I got to go with the xeno. That's a two-thirds majority—motion passed and veto-proof. Want a recount?"

"No. This isn't fair."

"Hell, no! It's *democracy*." Clive pulled his silver hood over his head, handing the helmet to Ian. "You're gonna love being a Loonie."

The Hound thumbed a switch set incongruously on a stalagmite, and the cave vanished, bats and all. Ian found himself sitting in a transparent half-bubble, pitched under an overhang at the edge of an extensive mare.

Clive pointed a silver finger. "Gotcha!"

The whole cavern had been a 3V holoprojection. The air holding the bubble taut no longer tasted cool and musty, turning flat and metallic. The 3V had been good. Feelie quality.

The Hound pulled on his own hood and unplugged a seal. Air spilled into the void. As the bubble collapsed, Ian set an amateur indoor record for donning a helmet and sealing a suit. Untangling himself from the deflating shelter, he stepped out onto the Sea of

Rains, the vast lava plain connecting the Oceanus Procellarum to the Sea of Serenity—carved out four billion years ago by the Rhode Island–sized rock that gave the Man-in-the-Moon his right eye.

Earth hung overhead, nearly full, bigger by far than the fullest moon. White cloud torrents streamed across blue seas. So much air, so much life! You never knew what a blue-white jewel Earth was until you saw her from the surface of her dead sister.

Ian had a full million complaints, questions, and accusations —none of which could be voiced. His comlink was still out, and there was no point shouting into vacuum. Clive and the xeno were a few meters off, wings full extended, pulling in afternoon sunlight, the collapsed shelter tucked casually under Clive's arm. Neither of them looked his way. Ian could hardly run off. He had to stand anxiously checking his oxygen—with his helmet valve wide open, pouring final seconds of air into the suit.

A point of fire appeared overhead, growing larger, outshining Jupiter, then Earth. Waiting on an open mare for an incoming lander can be uncanny. The jumpbug appeared to be coming down right on top of them, aiming to grind them into the regolith.

At the last instant, the angle of descent steepened and the jumpbug came down a short ways off, raising a fiery red cloud of dust and exhaust gases. The lander looked old and boxy, a three-legged spider with porthole eyes. LITTLE DEUCE COUP was stenciled in white across the lock door.

Ian hustled for the lock. Hustle did not mean run, but sort of a fast shuffle, leaning far forward—in Luna's light gravity, it was always a long way to the ground. The others beat him easily. Clive let the xeno cycle through, then made an "after you" motion. Ian took the rungs two at a time, diving into the lock. The outer door closed behind him.

As the little chamber filled with air, Ian tore off his suffocating helmet, happy to breathe whatever the jumpbug offered. Through the tiny square window on the hatch cover, he caught sight of Clive backing off—Ian's first hint that he and the Hound were making this jump alone.

He felt the soft shudder of paired oxyhydrogen engines, muffled by insulation and lunar vacuum. Acceleration replaced gravity. Too much had happened too quickly. Too much was *still* happening. Ian watched Luna drop away—taking his ID, his credit key, his ticket home, and the rented rover he had no hope of returning. Meanwhile, he was sealed in a hurtling metal box, headed fast for who-knows-where. Music rattled out of a pair of scratchy speakers—Radio Ganymede again. Jolly King Jove had given way to the Callisto Tabernacle Choir, coming in a cappella, with "Higher than the Angels" and other hits of the last century:

*Flying higher than the Angels,*
*In the heavens so free,*
*I hear the sinners a-sighin',*
*"Why me, Lord? Why me?"*

# LITTLE DEUCE COUP

HOUSTON: *Watch for a lovely girl with a big rabbit.*
APOLLO 11: [Static] *Say what?*
HOUSTON: *Legend says a beautiful Chinese girl named Chango is living on the moon. Been there four thousand years. Should be easy to spot.* [Static] *Companion is a large Chinese rabbit standing on his hind legs in the shade of a cinnamon tree.* [Static) *Name of the rabbit not recorded.*
APOLLO 11: *Check. Keep a lookout for the bunny girl.*

Prying open the inner pressure door, Ian wormed his way between blue propellant tanks into the jumpbug's command cabin, a cramped metal closet, old and awkward. Modern shuttles and mass conversion ships hid their guts behind hardwood paneling and plush carpets, but here tubing snaked around vents, electronics bays, and indicator boards. Two huge trapezoidal viewports dominated the clutter, showing bright slices of Luna's sunside. Glare and interior lights blanked even the brightest stars, and the sole feeling of flight came from the double throb of oxyhydrogen engines.

The Hound was in the far couch, half-hidden by the combustion chamber cowling. The near-acceleration couch was empty. The command couch sat atop the cowling, with the primary axis of thrust running straight through the seat of the pilot's pants—if the pilot were wearing pants. From where Ian stood, the pilot seemed to be wearing nothing. A smooth, bare leg sprawled alongside the high-definition screen, relaxed and professional, heel nestled comfortably in a crook of the optical alignment mount. Nearest to Ian was a nude shoulder, and a head of short-cropped hair, dark as the starless night outside. The pilot was saying something to the xeno, so Ian could not see her face. He stood there feeling hugely overdressed, swathed in layers of nylon fabric and spun silicone.

She turned abruptly. "Welcome aboard, stranger. Where ya headed?"

Ian was too struck to answer. The pilot's face had deep natural lines, untouched by biosculpting. It was not an ugly face—merely the face of a woman who had lived long and worked hard without the benefit of chemosurgical cosmetics—something you seldom saw on the dirtside dating circuit. But what hit him was her tattoo. A diamondback rattler covered the right half of her face, rattles touching the corner of her mouth, body coiling up her cheek and arching over her eyebrow—the gaping mouth and thin curved fangs filling her right forehead, ready to strike. Not another pretty face.

"Name's Angel O'Ferrall." Her upsun accent was smooth as cream and honey. Looking down at her bare body, she laughed, "Well, pardon my tits. I didn't know I had to put on panties to pick up a pecker-headed Hound." She nodded toward the far seat. "Xenos don't give a damn what you wear—or look like. Ain't got human feelings."

The Hound's speakbox made noises of grateful agreement.

Angel bent forward, snagging a black top draped over the doppler hood. While she struggled into the synthetic fabric, Ian managed to introduce himself, finding it easier to talk to her bare back and shoulder blades than to that rattlesnake tattoo. Angel straightened up, pulling the black top down to her waist. "Hound and I are headed for Lagrange Farside," she explained. "Sure hope you were too."

Lagrange Farside was an empty point in space teetering at the edge of the Earth-Moon system—farther than ever from where Ian needed to be. "Good God, no! Why the hell would . . ."

She silenced him with a snaky look. "We got business, there. Private business. If you're not headed for Lagrange Farside, why are you tagging after the Hound?"

Private business? Ian could easily believe it. He did not want to know more, hoping to stay as clean and innocent as possible. Angel would hardly be burning reactant mass merely to give some canine ET a get-acquainted look at the Earth-Moon system. Clive and the Hound had larceny punched all over them—having offhandedly robbed Ian of everything worth taking. Angel looked only an angstrom more honest. It was hardly in Ian's best interest to know the details of whatever criminal alien-smuggling enterprise he had tumbled onto.

He felt nervously compelled to assure Angel that he was exactly what he seemed—a hapless law-abiding tourist gone astray. He hastily told his whole story. How he had come up from Terra to do an on-site inspection of a new-style mass conversion furnace—then set out on some private lunar exploration. He had rented a suit and rover from a tourist shop in Copernik North—in retrospect, a ghastly mistake—but, "My God, I was on the moon!"

Ian had wanted to do a Neil Armstrong, heading off into the unknown. Or at least the unvisited. The Lunar Carpathians had scores of unclimbed peaks. He merely meant to stand on a virgin summit, mentally naming the mountain for himself. Where else in the Earth-Moon system could you put your footprint where no fool had ever trod? Luna made Antarctica look grossly overpopulated—a bubbled tourist trap with polluted ice and hordes of tiny panhandlers in tuxedos. But the vendor had been your typical Loonie, a spindly little weasel—sending him off in a terminally defective suit with a smile and a hearty clap on the back. (That got a chuckle of sympathy from Angel.) He had gotten lost (outright laughter). And rescued (applause from the Hound's speakbox). And *robbed* (mixed laughter and applause).

"Sounds like Luna." Angel shook her head. "Always pays to see Lady Selene at a distance. I surely do want to hear the finish of this really funny story, but I got to do a bit of piloting." Angel cut her throttle, reaching down for the attitude controller between her legs, playing with her thrusters. Roll. Yaw. Then counter-thrusts. Farside swung into view, filling the jumpbug's ports. She cut her thrusts. They were in free fall. Farside was in half phase, and they were falling past the sunlit half, seeing the pockmarked plain in maximum contrast. Craters lay on top of craters. No dark maria here. The broad ancient lava seas were all on Nearside, facing Earth's pull, created by tidal action. Farside was a tortured moonscape of secondary and tertiary impacts, dominated by the big bull's-eye of Orientale Basin.

"Gorgeous, isn't she?" sighed Angel. The Hound's speakbox pounded out a rolling crescendo, the intro riff from "Great Wall of Galaxies" by Gas and Dust.

He saw Angel's features soften, the snake relaxing—charmed by music and moon magic—no longer about to strike, becoming merely a bizarre and intricate design inked into a woman's face. She gave her shoulders a wistful shake. "*La Luna* and Big Blue are the best reasons to come downsun."

Ian shrugged. "I'd trade my next ten-dozen looks for a ticket to Earth." With each passing second he slid farther from his home in the Hebrides.

"Can't take you to Earth," she told him. "Not if Big Blue still has that steep gravity well and soupy atmosphere. My bug would fuckin' fly apart before we hit bottom."

Angel considered for a moment. "I *could* drop you off in low orbit, at a factory or research station—wouldn't be hard to hitch a ride dirtside from there."

Ian calculated. The jumpbug might make it down to low orbit, stripped and carrying only two people. Definitely not the way he wanted to return—Ian far preferred the shuttle's air cushion couches, elixir bar, and in-flight entertainments (feelies, 3V gaming, and maneuvering nimble flight attendants into semiprivate berths). But . . .

"It'll cost," Angel added. "Have to burn like hell to get there, then refuel in low orbit. Give you a straight freight deal—fuel plus ten percent trouble and overhead. Course, it'd be cheaper to drop you on Farside, or even to take you around to Tycho or Armstrong Station."

Cheaper maybe, but any return to Luna was a step backward. Ian hadn't half a chance of finding Clive, and without his ticket, he'd be at the mercy of the Loonies. The scrawny bastards would be thrilled to send him home, charitably billing his agency double or triple for room, board, travel, damages to the suit and rover, use of the lavatory, and for every deep breath he took. Loonies were adept at wringing a living out of visiting Dirtsiders. Going back down to the moon dead broke, with no ticket home, would be like slitting his wrist in a shark tank and ringing the dinner bell. Much as he might enjoy a chance at force-feeding his virus-ridden suit to that Copernik shopkeeper—Ian needed to get home. On Earth, he could file a claim for the lost ticket and credit, suing the tourist shop in a dirtside court, charging fraud, punitive damages, and outrageous pain and suffering.

Angel looked him over. "I'd have to know how you planned to pay."

Ian hedged. "I can pay. But I would need to contact my agency, arranging some reasonable compensation . . ."

She cut him short. "This bug does not run on promises, reasonable or otherwise." Angel patted a panel with affectionate intimacy. "Only solid reactant mass is gonna change your vector."

Ian glared at the Hound lounging in the far couch. The xeno knew he was good for the nut, but was saying nothing. Not taking sides.

Angel bent forward. "Got more flying to do." Main thrusters burped. The jumpbug pitched and yawed. Ian had to grab a handhold to keep from rattling about like a bean in a box. Farside slid back behind them. Their destination swung into view. Lagrange Farside is the farthest libration point in the Earth-Moon system, a spot where a ship's fall around the Earth exactly balances its fall around Luna, leaving the ship at rest relative to those two bodies. (Nothing ever stops relative to everything.) Even this limited stability is an illusion—the least displacement gives the Earth or moon an advantage, causing the ship to fall away from the libration point. It was an inherently unstable location that Ian had never dreamed of visiting.

There was a lone ship orbiting the Lagrange point, looking like a three-bladed exhaust fan, slowly rotating in space. Judging size is difficult against a dimensionless black backdrop, where even the stars seem small, but Ian figured the ship had to be fairly big, and quite old, powered by solar collectors married to a fusion reactor. The one- or two-rpm rotation was a rube goldberg gravity simulator, using circular motion to create internal acceleration.

Angel did a neat job of docking, sliding the jumpbug's stubby lock into a port on the ship's main axis. Ian felt a slight bump. Locks opened automatically and they were joined. Free fall returned. Through the cabin ports, Ian could see kilometers of slowly rotating solar collectors, their flat surfaces pitted by micrometeors.

Angel kicked off the control console, flipping with knees tucked into a tight back somersault, ending up in demi-plié at the lock entrance—a neat bit of zero-g gymnastics, proving she knew every millimeter of the cabin. The tight black top came only to her waist, dividing her neatly in half, adding to her mystery—half of her was dark and remote, topped by her menacing tattoo, the other half of her was unclad, open, even enticing. Unembarrassed by seminudity, she slid past Ian, entering the big ship through the open lock, vanishing into the revolving hatch of a de-spin system —not bothering to look back.

Ian dived after her disappearing rump, unwilling to be left aboard the jumpbug with only a big ugly xeno for company. As soon as he had joined her in the de-spin system, Angel reached up and banged the inner hatch shut, saying, "Room for two. The Hound can take the next drop."

They began to fall toward the tip of the solar panels. Weight built up. Angel looked him over, head cocked, deliberately showing the profile not disfigured by her tattoo. By now, Ian was used to this trick. She would flick the snake back toward him whenever she wanted to shock. "You're really damned cute," she decided. "Do you have a body to match that face? Earth men usually do." This was all challenge and bravado. She knew there was no chance of Ian taking advantage of her at close quarters, not when he was suited up tighter than Sir Galahad.

The capsule thumped to a stop at somewhere near two-thirds standard gravity. Angel kicked open the deck hatch with her heel. Humid misty air steamed into the capsule. She swung her bare legs over the lip and dropped through the hatch. Ian followed, struggling to compensate for Coriolis effect, and his bulky suit.

He landed in a photosynthetic greenhouse. Vines clung to the bulkheads. Wavering illumination and light gravity made Ian feel like he was standing on the bottom of a weed-choked pool. A brown pygmy goat stared curiously up at him from amid the undergrowth.

"Mind the goat shit." Angel pushed aside some creepers, exposing another pressure hatch. "And take off that suit. You'll be so much more comfortable." She slipped through the hatch, again without a backward glance.

Ian unsealed as quickly as he could, opening the pressure suit down to one knee like a pair of kid's pajamas. Stepping free of the suit, he stuffed it into the open hatch above him, to keep the elevator lock from closing. With the hatch held open, tons of air pressure kept the elevator capsule from returning for the Hound. The xeno might as well be back in the Eridani.

Proud of his ingenuity, Ian swaggered after Angel. Now it was him and her. No clumsy suit. No free-fall antics. No superhuman Hound. Earth-trained muscles in two-thirds g made him feel strong and agile and very much in control. For the first time since getting lost, things would go his way. Angel had her bold talk and brash habits—but he had the law behind him (or what passed for law on Luna). She had to cooperate—and at least punch through a call to Earth—or be an accessory to robbery and kidnapping. He opened the pressure hatch, prepared to be firm but reasonable.

The inner cabin was free of vines and creepers. Instead a great stone eye stared sideways at him. As Ian stepped through the hatch, the bulkhead behind him turned into sand dunes, rising and falling beneath a cloudless sky. He saw that the eye belonged to a colossal face, half buried in desert sand. Ian recognized the face at once. It was Ramses II. Beside it stood two tall trunkless legs of stone.

It was, of course, a projection, hiding the real decks and bulkheads behind a 3V image of the broken monument of Ramses II. Not a true image, either. (Ian had seen the real thing, flanked by a ruined temple complex, rent-a-camel stands, and tourist shops.) It was a projection of Ramses's fallen statue as Shelley pictured it in his poem "Ozymandias":

> Nothing beside remains. Round the decay
> Of that colossal wreck, boundless and bare
> The lone and level sands stretch far away.

But it was every bit as good as the bat cave. He could taste hot barren air and hear the sirocco moaning off the dunes. Flecks of illusionary sand struck his face.

Beneath Ian's feet was a brightly colored Persian carpet,

stretched flat. Angel sat cross-legged on the big embroidered rug, filling china cups with tea from a brass samovar. Ian guessed that only the rug and tea set were real; everything else was sensory illusion. Determined not to be impressed, he sat down, taking an offered cup.

"So, you cannot pay for a trip home, or even the drop to Farside?" As Angel spoke, the rug began to rise. Ramses's face and legs sank out of sight. Dunes dwindled. The carpet took off, winging over sunlit waste.

"I cannot pay for anything," Ian admitted, trying to ignore the desertscape unrolling below.

"A lot of us up here are in that income bracket."

"Come on, how much could it cost to punch a signal through to Terra for me?"

Angel considered. "If I did put a signal through, would they come to get you? And arrest the Hound?"

"I hope so." Ian heard caravan bells tinkling on the wind. A line of camels plodded nose to tail beneath them, casting dramatic shadows over the plain.

She shook her head. "No good. I need that xeno. Right now there is a Gypsy Mother Ship in a decaying orbit around Neptune, in terminal need of repairs. Everyone aboard is in desperate trouble — and that xeno is my link to enough credit to fix that ship, saving them from a nasty fall."

Jesus, a Gyp. It made a sick sort of sense. The antique equipment. Angel's brash talk. And the *Arabian Nights* 3V show. Gyps lived their whole lives between cramped decks. Illusions like this kept them just this side of being psychotically claustrophobic. They were as witless as Loonies, and twice as wild, with a fine disregard for the rights and opinions of Dirtsiders. Ian was going to have to work hard to get her sympathy. "Look," he protested, "I can't think, flying about like Ali Baba. Land this rug."

The carpet picked up speed. A double line of palms poked over the horizon, marking a pair of rivers. Harun al-Rashid's Baghdad hove into sight. The carpet descended, just clearing the huge circular walls. Banking between tall minarets, they flashed over sweating porters at dockside and crowds haggling in the bazaars, making straight for Harun's domed and turreted palace at the heart of the city. Swooping into the palace precincts, the carpet slid under an ornate portico, coming to rest in a sunlit harem court.

Women and girls lounging under citron trees beside a rosewater fountain played with dwarf deer and an ape with a gold collar. Tough-looking eunuchs guarded the pointed doorways.

Angel's fantasies had casts of thousands and vivid detail. Ian could hear the deer's tiny silver horseshoes clicking on the tiles. She set down her teacup. "You're a Dirtsider. Check?"

"I thought I said that?"

"Got a job?"

"Yes, I told you . . ."

"Pension, paid vacations, health plan . . ."

"Well, sure."

". . . and dental plan?"

"I don't see . . ."

"Clearly not a charity case. I got *none* of those. My problems are all cash-and-carry—yours don't impress me much. People depend on me. Oldsters and babies who don't have agency grants or pension funds. If their ship isn't fixed, they will all die when the orbit decays."

"That sounds harsh, surely. . . ." Ian groped about for a solution, but no easy one came to mind.

"Harsh? Hell, it's just *gravity*. And gravity's the *law*—it keeps the system together. Can't bitch about that. But with that Hound's help, we can afford to fix the ship."

"Why is this Hound so precious? They are more obnoxious than rare."

"We mean to enter him in the Great Games at Tycho."

*Gamers*. My God! Why couldn't Angel and the Hound have been into something sane and sensible, like credit fraud, or hijacking interstellar liners? "No one wins at gaming," he protested.

"The Wolf Pack does!" Angel's rattlesnake seemed to leap out, reminding Ian how often gaming addiction went with disfigurement—a deep-seated distaste for mere flesh, even your own.

Despite being a 100 percent voting member of the Wolf Pack, Ian hadn't the least faith in this phantom organization. "From what I've seen, I wouldn't stake a microcredit on them, much less my sanity." Gaming was the most insidious, dangerous addiction ever invented. Ian liked his brain undegraded.

"They've won before." Angel's eyes glittered with the gambler's fallacy—because something had happened once, it had to happen again. "Turning that Hound over to the law is a null program. No payout. He's a xeno. No clothes. No pockets in his moonsuit. The only way he could have your ID and ticket is if he ate them."

She leaned forward, putting her whole body into her plea. "Forget your crummy little job. We're going to hit a sweepstakes jackpot! Getting rich by doing good. Saving you, and saving my ship. I'll see you fly back to Earth in style. A private shuttle. Your own orbital yacht!"

"And if we lose?" Addicts never considered that—they were hooked on the game itself. Earth had millions of feelie addicts, but there the disease was more or less under control, with clinics to help you kick, cut back, or live with the addiction. On Tycho, things were wide open. Addicts were soaked until their credit went sour, and the gaming casinos owned them—body and soul. "God, why can't you guys earn an honest living!"

Angel laughed. "This is absolutely the most legal thing Clive has ever done. And win or lose, I'll personally make it worth your while."

No need to ask how. The fountain was pouring out some hell-ish pheromone, jacking his hormones into overdrive—reminding Ian why the caliphs built these perfumed harem courts. In case he somehow missed the message, the houris began to strip and bathe, splashing rose water over each other's breasts and thighs, engaging in erotic play, while caged birds broke into a song from *Scheherazade.*

Ian fought to shake off the spell. "This is mad. And illegal. And I am not going near Tycho."

"Look, I'm giving you a hundred percent free choice." Angel leaned back, letting him look her over. "You can come with me to Tycho. Or I'll have Tiny sit on you until the Hound and I come back rich and happy."

"Tiny?"

She pointed her chin, flashing the snake, indicating the gold-collared ape in the garden, the only male member in the lesbian garden party. This was the problem with gamers, they found it impossible to tell illusion from reality. It would take more than a 3V gorilla to terrorize Ian into obeying. "I'm going to insist on you bouncing a call to Terra off one of the Lagrange stations."

Angel smiled and snapped her fingers. The ape shambled away from his playmates, stepping onto the carpet. A moment later, Tiny was towering over Ian, looking like the colossus of Ramses come to life. Clearly this was a real three-hundred-kilo Super-Chimp, able to stuff Ian into his teacup. "Tiny or me, take your pick." Angel looked him straight in the face, half woman, half snake. "Either way, I promise not to be insulted."

The lady or the behemoth? Ian had little choice. Tycho might be a first-class brain-fuck, but it beat hanging about Lagrange Far-side with Tiny for his keeper. There was no way he would stay here, not even if Harun's harem were real and ready to indulge him.

He threw up both hands. "Okay, let's take Tycho apart!"

Angel's congratulations were interrupted by an insistent rapping on one of the harem gates. A bored eunuch drew his scimitar and opened the cedarwood door, revealing a plastimetal airlock, full of EVA gear and deflated pressure suits. The Hound stepped out in full silver suit, having obviously just climbed several kilometers of solar paneling to reach the living quarters. "The capsule did not come back," his speakbox complained. "Some witless human jammed the elevator lock."

# THE GREAT GAMES

*Hail Caesar, we who are* not *about to die salute you.*
—MOTTO OF THE CIRCUIT MAXIMUS

Smack, crack, crank, speed, booze, acid, hash, bhang, poppies, and belladonna; none of the above (or all of them taken at once) had even half the addictive power of gaming. As proof of that, all these drugs (and a hundred others) were offered free or at cost to customers by the gaming palaces in Tycho. Not to compete with gaming—which could never be done—but to provide a relaxing comedown between sets, taking the edge off tattered neurons.

Angel set the jumpbug down just inside Tycho's massive ringwall, amid long afternoon shadows. Like a lot of inhabited Luna, the landing field looked really low-rent, tramped-over, scarred by blast craters and crawler tracks. Posh automated pressure vehicles scuttled out to greet them, like giant scavenger beetles competing for a fresh cadaver. Each sported the logo of a different gaming palace. Angel picked the one marked CIRCUIT MAXIMUS, and they were piped aboard by a corny full-orchestra version of *Also Sprach Zarathustra.* Ian pointed out that this was pure hype, to impress the marks, setting them up for plucking.

Angel waved off his sour attitude. "Of course it's a shuck—so lie back and enjoy it."

He gave in, settling back on a plush sofa facing the forward viewport. Angel snuggled next to him. The Hound sat hunched on the deck, visibly bored by human luxury. Tiny wedged himself into a plastic seat, like King Kong trying not to fill a small living room. Through crystal vacuum, Ian could count the notches on the crater's central peak. Tycho was only a couple of billion years old, blasted out by a flying mountain somewhat smaller than the one that had carved Copernicus. The gaming palaces were perched on the central massif. The surrounding crater floor was graded like a giant Japanese rock garden, covering over centuries of crawler tracks. A massive pillar-and-lintel shrine stood over a small black depression, dedicated to the *Dharma Bum* and her passengers.

The crawler rolled right up to a private lock, to keep Circuit Maximus from losing customers to another casino. They disembarked directly into the autobar and gaming area, done up to resemble a Roman forum. Holos made the place look huge, throbbing to the beat of "Nero's Treat," by Smug and Insincere.

A tasteless neon triumphal arch opened onto a 3V arcade blazing with simulated life. "Come this way!" it shouted. "Choose from HUNDREDS OF ALIEN WORLDS—fight WILD BEASTS in the sun-scorched ARENA, win the SLAVE MAIDEN caged overhead—TAKE HER on the burning sand!" Ian could tell by the frantic appeal that the arcade booths must be nearly empty. Such synthetic vice was amusing enough in its own robust way—especially if you lacked the energy and imagination to jerk off on your own—but it could never compare to the Great Games. The real action did not begin until you plugged in.

Demigods in tights and togas and women with impossible tinsel-wrapped figures were having such a raucous good time that they had to be shills or holos. As soon as Ian passed up the penny-ante arcade, a suave majordomo stepped forward with a wave and a bow. He was a Loonie, with spindly limbs and the distant unflappable smile of a feelie addict. Minor employees were almost always virtual-reality junkies, endlessly working off their debts to the casino.

Ian ordered up a room, only to find Clive had already rented them a suite. Angel's bold tattoo, Tiny the SuperChimp, and the outlandish xeno did not get so much as a blink. Clearly nothing happening in the here-and-now could possibly compare to this Loonie's off-hours. Ian suspected that he could have spit in the majordomo's face, and the smile would not have wavered. It was impossible to annoy someone who was merely going through the motions of life—in his spare time he could easily be Caligula or Kublai Khan, lord of some synthetic Xanadu, with a seraglio of nubile young houris and painted boys waiting for him to plug in. Greeting the public was so many hours of humdrum, endurable so long as it paid for his pleasure. It would have taken a plasma torch between the man's toes to get more than a polite, "Right this way."

Angel took Tiny to their suite. Ian went with the Hound to inspect the gaming arena, a steep high-tech pit smelling of blood and sand, surrounded by pillowed couches and low tables. Two towering holos rose out of the center of the pit, ten meters tall, and sweating under an indoor sun. A huge retiarius, armed with fish net and trident, stalked an Amazon Samnite in half armor, defending herself with an oblong shield and Spanish short sword. The female holo limped from a leg wound, and a ribbon of blood cut across the retiarius's muscular chest.

The phantom combat got scant attention from prospective gamers crowded around the pit, huddled in groups and pairs, striking deals, debating tactics, or going over map displays of nineteenth-century Africa and medieval Transylvania. Tables were spread with a typical Loonie tourist buffet: curried bulgar and garbanzos, a three-fungus salad, peppered leeks, champignons farcis, and edible pond algae. Every so often, someone would look past the giant gladiators, glancing at the hexagonal display floating overhead, getting a readout on games in progress.

Ian noted that most of the games were now closed competitions, of interest only to touts and gamblers. A Renaissance Italy team elimination was down to a dozen pairs, stalking each other with stilettos and poison cups through the back alleys and banquets of fair Verona. In the Arthurian tourney, Lancelot looked to be mopping up. Gawain and Galahad trailed in the standings. Tristram and Mordred had been eliminated by a bad fall and a broken lance. Bedivere remained a long shot at twenty to one. Of the open heats, the Cape-to-Cairo Rally had yet to begin, and attention focused on the Grand Luna Sweepstakes, still accepting latecomers at bargain rates. A timer showed that the moon over Dracula's Castle was waxing, nearly full.

The base of the hexagonal display bore a cheery warning—ALL OUTCOMES ARE FINAL.

Clive came strolling through the crowd, dressed as a blond Alcibiades in a gold toga, its purple border trailing behind him. He paused several times to listen in on strategy sessions, exchanging comments, sometimes aloud, sometimes in a stage whisper. When he got to Ian, he clapped him on the shoulder. "Perfect timing— I've entered us in the sweepstakes. We go in at oh-seven-hundred."

A gawky sharp-faced Loonie with slick black hair and a spade beard slid up, looking furtively from side to side. Clive introduced the Loonie, saying, "This is Philaemos, but you can call him Phil—he's on our side, I think."

Phil nodded eagerly. "Until the Castle."

"Until the Castle," Clive said, and laughed.

Ian knew that alliances and conspiracies were an integral part of team competitions. But once you plugged in, anything was fair; surprise, duplicity, and betrayal were standard tactics. The sweepstakes competition had a single prize, "The Vampire's Heart," a blood-red ruby hidden away in the heavily defended tower of Dracula's Castle. Each team could increase its chances by cooperating with the others—until the Castle was breached, or an advantageous double-cross presented itself. But whoever seized the ruby was sole winner of the accumulated credit—minus the casino's cut.

Phil looked warily about. "The White Company has put out a call for allies."

Clive looked up at the display. "Of course. They got waxed in the opening rounds. Well, tell 'em the Wolf Pack's back."

Phil scuttled off, happy to have a confidence to betray. Clive lowered his voice. "Philaemos hangs around the pit, talking up games he hasn't the credit to enter. People call him Phil the Shill, but he's pretty harmless, unless you happen to trust him."

The White Company did not look much like Conan Doyle's band of chivalric adventurers; clumped together at one end of the arena, their casino togas haphazardly arranged, they looked more like a load of soiled laundry. The only thing *Roman* about them was the hollow-eyed Romulus and Remus look—abandoned at birth and suckled by wolves. One of them growled at the Hound, "This table's for humans."

Clive flashed a smile. "He's not fussy."

According to the readout above, the White Company had already been overrun by Tartars in the early innings. Ian recognized the nervous brooding of gamers at the losing end of a bad run. Several sat hunched on couches, staring past their eyebrows at the timer ticking overhead.

"Brilliant, absolutely brilliant," muttered a big blonde Amazon in a man's toga. "You sure gave 'em hell, Gertrude. Screaming for mama until they slit your throat."

"No shit, Sheila. You weren't so fuckin' slick yourself." Her companion, small and dark, was dressed more like a woman in an ill-fitting Ionian chiton.

"What was I supposed to do? Those Tartars just creamed us, coming out of nowhere. It was hardly fair." Sheila's appeal for fairness got a grim laugh. "I mean, how can they bring in a fuckin' Kipchak killing machine from out of Central Asia just to roll over us?" There was no answer, except for the obvious one: so long as the casino stayed within the game parameters, Circuit Maximus could tilt the play any way it pleased. It was up to the gamers to beat the system or go away broke.

Ian looked over toward the readout, to get a fix on the time. Almost 2200. He should be resting. Or better yet, in bed with Angel.

The Hound got into a spirited argument with the Circuit Maximus management, absolutely refusing to go into the game in human guise, citing several treaties and insisting that his rights as an extraterrestrial were being violated—threatening to sue. If the casino had no provisions for ET players, he could at least go in as a dog. Any sort of human would be too degrading.

Sheila took a sharp bite out of a peppered leek. "Well, next time out, I hope to see all you fuckers dying *hard*."

A man protested. "You think it was fun getting feathered with iron-headed arrows? Feeling yourself bleed to death?"

"Right," Sheila snorted. "Want to hear what the Kipchaks were doing to us while you were lying on your backs, restfully bleeding to death?" She nudged the smaller woman, "Gertrude, tell 'em about it." Gertrude merely grunted.

Phil the Shill took the chance to cut in. "Hell, one time I was tortured by Hurons, for days."

"Hurons? This was the bloody Balkans."

White Company members blinked at him, staring as if he had lost his wits. "It was another game," Phil admitted. "But it was real bad—they had red-hot tomahawks."

"Shit, that's nothing."

"God, I hope they hacked you in the crotch!"

The White Company tried to go back to their argument, but they had lost the thread. Soon everyone was comparing their most gruesome, horrendous deaths—burning, impaling, crucifixion, flaying, and dismemberment. It seemed that every form of violent, bizarre extinction had been suffered by someone at the table. Hollow eyes lit up. A false bravado seized hold. Whatever else had happened, they were still the goddamn White Company, and they could sure as hell take it!

Ian got up and looked around. Sicker than the stories themselves was the way they were told, full of verve and energy—*as if it actually mattered*. He hated to hear gamers spilling their guts, trying to sound bad. All it showed was how totally delusional they were. The most elemental rule of gaming was that if you die, you lose—your original stake is gone. You have to give up, or buy your way back in. This tough talk amounted to a bunch of chronic losers bucking themselves up by boasting about how badly they had lost. Somehow he had to *win*.

Disgusted by the whole show, he went to look for Angel, to get what he could out of the game—up front. The Wolf Pack's suite was immense—three bedrooms, two baths, a full galley, a salon, and an autobar. Tiny had his own room. One of the salon walls was 3V, tuned to show an in-depth surface projection of Kikku, Chi Draconis III, with its planetary ocean rolling under china-blue skies. Twin moons hung low on the watery horizon. All charged to Ian's line of credit.

Angel was wearing a green silk casino chiton and snacking on dishes brought up from the buffet downstairs. "Try the curried bulgar," she suggested. "Come tomorrow we're likely to be living on it—along with this edible pond scum."

Ever since he'd agreed to go to Tycho, she had shown him nothing but her good side. Now was the time to take advantage of that. He sat down next to her, resting his hand on her thigh. She did not flinch or draw back. Her leg felt strong and warm through the thin fabric. His fingers slid inward. Hardly suave, but he was in a hurry.

"Save it for the games," she told him. "At seven A.M. sharp, we've got to cut our way to Dracula's Castle, storm the sucker, then steal a ruby out from under some mean opposition."

Ian assured her that he'd be better able to wrestle Bulgars in the morning, if she would loosen up a bit now.

Angel turned slightly, showing only the fangs and tail of the snake. "Come morning, we are going to be in a megacredit sweepstakes competition. Bulgars will be the least of our worries. We have to beat the House. Beat the White Company. Beat *everybody* —you know what the odds on that are like?"

"Not good."

"Bad enough that Circuit Maximus is willing to bet a thousand-to-one on us fucking up—and feel sure of winning. Look around you; none of this was paid for by backing bad bets."

She held up her hand edge-on in front of her face, defining an invisible plane dividing her face down the middle, an eye on either side. By moving her hand forward, she indicated that the plane extended outward, as far as the mind could take it. "We have to walk it tight if we aim to win. No missteps, no mistakes. Our energy has to be on-line. We better damn well *hum*, or my people orbiting Neptune will die. And we'll all end up losers, like those sad fuckers downstairs."

"Sure, sure, but . . ."

"No buts. Did you see that duded-up corpse that greeted us at the door? Talk about your undead, that was a goddamn zombie! Give the casino a week or two, you could be him. Totally glazed-over in some electronic Neverland. In a gaming casino, you check your sanity at the door. So don't blow it. You've got to promise me that you will never think it's not real."

"I promise." Ian would have promised her the whole god-forsaken moon at this point. What did he have to lose?

She gave him a swift kiss on the lips. "Good. Now get some

sleep. In a day or two, we'll be dodging vampires in the dark — if we're real lucky."

At 0600, the crowd in the gaming pit was gearing up for the start of the Cape-to-Cairo Rally. Tarzan wannabes were poring over projections of German Tanganyika, swearing in Swahili. Clive was there to prep Ian on plugging in. "Remember — go light. The Board is going to offer you all kinds of weapons, armor, and parapher-nalia — tempting you to turn yourself into a walking arsenal."

"What's so bad about that?" Ian was having second and third thoughts about the whole business.

"First, you have to lug it about, and edged weapons weigh a lot. Have you ever hefted a halberd or a broadax?"

"Not lately."

"Would you know how to use one when the time came?"

"Maybe . . ."

"Most likely, you'd never get the chance. The casino wants you to load up on weapons and spells, figuring you'll be blindsided before you can ever use 'em. Going in overarmed is worse than being bare-assed — if you're naked, you at least feel *exposed.* You'd know to take cover and keep alert. All an arsenal does is lull you into making mistakes — it can even give you away. Have you ever heard someone walking in plate armor? It sounds like a conven-tion of drunk tinkers. Are you ready to take on every Turk and Tartar who hears you coming?"

"Probably not. So what's best?"

"Dress like a peasant," Clive advised, "with a dirk or dagger — and one distance weapon. How are you with a bow?"

"I don't know." Except for the bagpipes, Ian had never handled anything that could be called a "distance weapon."

"Try a light crossbow. They're easy to aim and can be fired from hiding — always the preferred position."

"What about magic?"

"Way too expensive. That line of credit you came here with wasn't endless. It took your ticket and most of that credit to get this far."

"Next time, I'll do better." *Next* time, he would stay on Terra. "So if we lose, Circuit Maximus will be expecting me to pay up?"

Clive grinned. "Sounds too perfect to be true."

"Could only happen on Luna," added the Hound. He had won his tussle with the casino — happily going in as an ugly black mastiff.

Ian grinned back, secretly wishing he could flatten them both — but they easily outmassed him. Besides, he was trapped.

Back out now, and Circuit Maximus would present him with an absolutely unpayable bill. Somehow the Wolf Pack had to win.

Clive patted him on the back. "Just remember the Pack motto."

"What's mine is yours?"

"No," Clive laughed, "though that's a good'un. It's 'All for One and One for All.' Punch French Crusader so that we can go in together—and never think it's not real."

Circuit Maximus had a whole phony ritual connected with plugging in—part of the casino hype, delivered at no extra charge. Servants stripped off Ian's toga, leading him down marble steps to a subterranean Roman bath. Light streamed down from stone vents onto pale steaming water. Here he was washed, toweled, rubbed, and scented, then escorted to his gaming compartment, as though he were a gladiator going into single combat, the casino's champion, instead of its chump.

Gold letters decorated the Roman arch above the entry vault —DACIA, the name of Trajan's Romanian province.

Inside, lying on slabs, were rows of high-tech coffins, plastimetal cocoons covered with tubes, circuitry and instrumentation. Inside his was a tiny human-shaped space, adjusted to Ian's size and physique. Casino flunkies helped him in, tightening the seals until the chamber fit like a surgical glove, with dermal transceivers touching every centimeter of skin. Then the chamber was screwed shut, light-tight.

He was in total darkness, silent and disorienting. Then the Board appeared. The display floated about half a meter in front of his face, listing identities, physiques, languages, arms and armor, spells and countermagic, mounts, pack animals, and special equipment, each item paired with a price in credits. All had tiny red dots beside them. He could make selections by reaching up and touching the dots, turning red settings to green. His hand would not really be moving, any more than he was actually "seeing" the Board. Movement and sensation were already wired in. The Board was a projection onto his retina. Blinking made it go away. Opening his eyes brought it back. The decision to lift his arm and touch a setting triggered complex feedback loops that registered his choices, while stimulating his kinesthetic and pressure receptors, making him feel touch and movement.

All contestants came into the game from outside Transylvania. Identities ranged from the Khan of the Golden Horde or Osman Sultana (both hideously expensive) down through Prince Philip of Artois (merely overpriced) all the way to Crippled Beggar (the casino was willing to give credits to anyone who thought he could win with one leg and spastic shakes). Under French Crusader a double column of entries included:

| | |
|---|---|
| Jean the Fearless | Chevalier |
| Marshal Bouciquaut | Esquire |
| Admiral de Vienne | Hospitaller |
| Comte Jacques de la Marche | Courtesan |
| Enguerrand de Coucy | Monk |
| Henri de Bar | Gross Valet |
| Gendarme | Crossbowman |

And so on, down to Common Whore and Scullery Knave.

The titled nobles all came with armed retinues (handy, no doubt, but way out of his price range). Ian skipped over the various forms of men-at-arms, concentrating on the lowly and affordable personae at the bottom of the list. He doubted his abilities to perform as a Monk or Courtesan, but Crossbowman seemed to fit, and supplied him with the distance weapon Clive had suggested.

There was a whole list of physical features—height, weight, hair and eye color, and so on. A makeover cost nothing. He could go in as handsome as Clive and hung like a god *at no extra charge.* Or as a woman, if he wanted that thrill. Something told him he would do better as he was.

The first couple of languages came cheap. French was free with the character. Magyar, German, Romany, Turkic, Yiddish, and so on could all be had at reduced prices. But the ability to plead for mercy in Mongol did not seem all that much of an edge. He selected the local Romanian dialect, which would at least let him know what the poor folks were saying.

The list of edged weapons read like a grotesque military museum catalog:

| | |
|---|---|
| Broadsword | Halberd |
| Brown Bill | Mace |
| Claymore | Poleax |
| Double Ax | Rapier |
| Falchion | Saber |
| Flamberge | Scimitar |
| Gisarme | and so forth . . . |

A dirk came with the costume. The only other piece of cutlery that tempted him was a silver stiletto, for dispatching loups-garous and vampires, but it cost more than all the rest combined.

He lingered over the lists of spells and magics—not because he could afford or use them, but to get an idea of what he was up against. In general, any sort of central Balkan ghoul or beastie seemed to be allowed, everything from werebitches to bottled djinn. God, what a disaster this was going to be.

He punched ENTRY. Let the games begin!

# THE UNDEAD

Ian stood on a gallows hill. A narrow rutted cart path at his feet wound down the knoll toward an almost treeless plain, dotted with villages, each with its domed church. In the near distance, a gaily colored pavilion stood by a silver stream. Farther off was a walled town with leaden roofs, and an outlying Byzantine tower. A crossbow and quiver dug into his back.

The gaming compartment, tons of rock, Tycho, and all of Luna had vanished at the press of a button. His sole companion on this place of punishment was a mummified body, impaled from pelvis to collarbone. The half-rotted head lolled to one side, wearing a wide toothy grin. Whatever software ran the scenery had a perfectly macabre sense of humor.

None of this is real, he reminded himself. He was *really* back on Luna, in a plastimetal womb, being force-fed sensations. But it damn well felt real. Open skies and Earth-normal gravity seemed totally natural, a relief from the tunnels of Luna. Rough homespun itched against his skin. The clink of chains on the gibbet and the moan of the wind through the spokes of the tall breaking wheel raised hairs at the nape of his nonexistent neck. Ian smelled horse leather, and heard the clank of armor.

Spinning about, he saw a knight on horseback, framed by the flogging post and burning stake. Fear and amazement shot through him. He had been caught flat-footed, mooning over the reality of the setup, his crossbow uncocked and untested, leaving him nothing but a dirk to save him from this armed apparition on a war-horse.

"Yo, villain," the knight called down, couching his lance. "Give my regards to Beelzebub!"

Ian ducked behind the gibbet to keep from being ridden down in the first rush—all the time thinking, this is impossible. Unreal. Grossly unfair. The knight bearing down on him was armed with a lance, mace, broadsword, and even one of those thin silver vampire-killing stilettos. Right out of the chute, he was somehow supposed to gut and kill this heavily armored horse and rider, with nothing but bare hands and a sliver of sharp steel that did not even exist. There was no way this could happen. Not even in a feelie.

Sir Asshole rattled right up to the gibbet, taking a couple of lively stabs with the lance, laughing as Ian jumped from one side to the other. Then he lifted his visor, "Gotcha!"

It was Clive. Ian cursed, calling his teammate every rude anatomic name he could come up with on short notice, ending the string with "You bugger-headed bastard, you lied! 'Go light,' you told me. 'Dirk and crossbow.' Then *you* terrorize the shit out of me, dressed like a steel scarecrow!"

Clive shrugged, letting his shoulder armor rattle. "Your line of credit was nowhere near long enough to arm us both. Besides, just moving in a suit like this requires training." Clive did a swift mounted pirouette, showing off his costume, which was that of a *gendarme de la Garde,* a Scots Archer armored cap-à-pie, à la Quentin Durward—gorget, greaves, and back-and-breast over chain-link hose and hauberk. Ian recognized the Robertson coat-of-arms in Clive's shield, three wolf's heads on a red field.

"Look, I'm the one who's disappointed"—Clive brought his lance down, resting the point against Ian's chest, pressing gently—"finding my teammate thumb-up-the-butt, gawking at the landscape. That ain't the Wolf Pack way. This is an elimination sweepstakes, not a goddamn sightseeing contest! You're a French bowman far from home, on an incredibly suicidal quest." Clive pushed harder with his lance. "Start fuckin' acting the part. Or you are going to be dead. Gone. Out of the game. Explaining to Circuit Maximus why you can't pay up."

Ian wanted to groan, or mayhap scream. Instead he grimly unslung his crossbow and took a few practice pulls at cocking it. The bow came with a stirrup, goat's foot, and spanning belt, so that he could use his thigh and back muscles to bend the steel bow. Slip the goat's foot over the bow cord, put his foot in the stirrup, then straighten up. The bow was cocked. Stick in a wicked-looking quarrel, and he was set to do damage. The immediate impulse was to test the bow's effectiveness by sticking it under the skirt of Clive's hauberk and squeezing the trigger. Only the threat of being left alone stayed his hand.

He unstrung the bow, and they set off, leaving the gallows hill behind. The gray mud and the dour medieval landscapes were supposed to match Transylvania, the Land Beyond the Trees—not as it was, but as it might have been in the days of Dracula. The white peaks of the Southern Carpathians poked through blue haze. How long was it since he had been lost among the Lunar Carpathians? Hours? Days? It seemed like centuries.

Fields and vineyards butted up against the blue mountains. The undead live more or less forever, so game time was tele-scoped. Anything from thirteenth-century Kumans to Ottoman Timariot cavalry could come out of the Carpathian passes — Transylvania had been threatened or overrun by nearly everyone. In actual fact, the doomed crusade of Jean the Fearless had gotten no closer than Nicopolis, seventy or so leagues to the south, but considering how totally botched that crusade had been, ending up on the wrong side of the Transylvanian Alps was no more unimag-inable than the actual disaster that had engulfed the cream of French chivalry on the Danube.

The cow path dipped down to ford a stream. On the far bank, a knight's pavilion stood planted in a field of stubble. A slim raven-haired damsel lounged in the shelter of the tent fly, black eyes shaded with kohl, bare feet peeping out from under a blue flounced skirt. Diamonds sparkled in her dark hair. She gave Clive a languid smile. Foot-slogging crossbowmen did not even rate a glance.

The knight himself came trotting round from behind the tent, a gruff bearded giant on a black charger, face flushed and beaded with sweat. He challenged Clive for "the right to cross the stream, and the hand of yon fair maiden."

Clive tipped his lance. "You may keep your fair maiden — hand, tits, toenails, and tiara. As for the stream, we will gladly back up and go around."

But the knave in black armor made it plain that his challenge was mere formality; Clive would not get away without a fight. Ian hurriedly cocked his crossbow, doubting the light bow would even dent the big man's armor, but in a crude setup like this anything could happen. The "knight and lady" had to be part of the pro-gram — real villains with posh pavilions, and pretty maids at their mercy, had better things to do than camp by a brook, hoping to break lances with some stalwart stranger.

Clive grinned, then lowered his visor. He and the behemoth cantered to opposite ends of the stubble field. The black knight lifted his bridle; his lance came down. Clive did the same. Ian swallowed hard, no longer grudging Clive the horse and armor. Let Mr. Handsome go in and take the whacks. Ian would not have traded places for all the maidens in Transylvania.

The lady let fall her kerchief, and the two cavaliers in sheet metal launched themselves at each other. Hoofbeats shook the stubble as chargers chewed up the turf. The galloping pair came together like a combination anvil chorus and ground-car collision. Ian flinched.

An instant before contact, Clive leaned in, angling his shield, throwing his whole body into the impact, a move that called for incredible concentration and timing. The black lance struck Clive's tilted shield and was tossed outward. Clive's point caught the inner edge of the black shield and skidded off, slamming into the man's breastplate at belly-button level. The lance bowed on impact, but Clive was braced for the shock, his body angled into the blow.

His opponent rose up out of the saddle, stirrups flying. He hung for a moment in midair, arms splayed, as his war-horse ran out from under him—then he came crashing down, bounced, and lay prone. Clive reined in directly in front of the pavilion.

The dark-eyed beauty in the blue dress raised her diamond-crowned head a notch higher, giving Clive a haughty so-you-think-you've-won-me look. Clive answered with a jaunty salute, turned and trotted over to poke at the prone man with his lance. The fellow refused to respond. Clive lifted his visor, calling to Ian, "Get his purse and broadsword. I'll go after the horse."

The black charger had come to a halt by the brook, saddle empty, drinking nervously. Before Clive got there, Phil the Shill emerged from the weeds by the bank and seized the bridle, bringing the horse over to Clive. Phil was dressed in a jester's outfit, with three thin juggling knives thrust through his belt—acting as helpfully inoffensive as ever.

Ian frisked the Black Knight, finding the man's purse full of aspers and his broadsword a bit heavy. Clive called to him, "Finish the fucker."

"What?" Ian looked up.

Clive tapped the silver stiletto with his gauntlet, then made a swift stabbing motion. "Use your dirk. Through the eye slit." Ian stood rooted. Clive sighed, and waved to the jester. "Phil, show him how."

The tall scrawny jester ran up, bells jingling on his cap. Drawing a juggling knife, he tilted the man's helmet and slid the thin blade between the bars of the visor. Leaning forward, Phil put all of his weight behind the knife. The prone man shook till his armor rattled, then lay still.

"Good job," Clive called down. Ian felt like having a virtual vomit. Phil beamed, saying he knew where the White Company was rallying. Clive lifted an eyebrow. "Can you get us there?"

The jester nodded eagerly. "A few leagues farther on, this path crosses an irrigation ditch at a proper bridge—ignore the bridge, but follow the ditch until you come to a cherry orchard. Through the trees you can see a farmstead with a walled court. That's where the White Company will be."

Clive leaned down, took the black purse from Ian, counting out five silver aspers and giving them to the jester. Grinning his appreciation, Phil cocked his head toward the pavilion. "And what about her?"

Clive laughed. "Feel free. But give her half a chance, and you'll be joining him." He tapped the dead man with his lance.

Phil tucked the aspers in his purse, looking longingly at the pavilion.

"Some kept women will thank you for killing their lord and master, others might take it amiss." Clive handed Ian the reins to the black charger. "Between here and Dracula's Castle, we're going to be offered enough virtual tail to kill you out of sheer exhaustion." The French crusade's riotous progress through the Balkans was infamous for murder and debauchery. Beautiful concubines. Spearmen drowned in butts of wine. Monks scandalized. "It doesn't cost the casino a thing to jerk you off. Feelie-fucks are part of the programmed obstacles. Hell, a half-dozen gamers are coming in as eunuchs, just to avoid temptation."

The dark-haired damsel laughed at Clive, a high musical laugh, light and inviting. Her hand rested on a silver table set with wine and sweetmeats. Ian mounted up, not tempted in the least. The early morning entry meant they had been sent off before breakfast; Ian's stomach was already inquiring about lunch—soon the sweetmeats on the silver table would be more seductive than the perfumed bed within.

They passed more pavilions, and more women. Also some lumpy-looking peasants, who did not appear happy to have bogus French knights tramping about. Crusaders had earned an evil reputation, even in Transylvania.

Clive hardly gave them a glance until well into the afternoon when he stopped before a golden tent with a well-upholstered blonde seated by the entrance. Here Clive dismounted. A towering djinn in Turkish armor with boar's tusks and a wicked scimitar stood guard over the woman. Ian expected him to square off with Clive, but the damsel merely told the muscular demon to see to the horses. Then she gestured toward a low table decked with wine and fruit.

Clive rested his armored seat on the table, reaching for a wine goblet. The woman poured. She had big blue innocent eyes, lips soft as a child's, and a friendly open smile.

"Is the food safe?" Phil asked.

"The wine is," Clive told him. "The fruit might give you diarrhea."

The blonde woman laughed and washed an apple in wine, offering it to Ian. "It's not poison," she promised solemnly, sounding like a girl determined to do good, whatever her natural impulse might be.

"But how do you know?" Phil whined nervously.

"I know." Clive and the blonde exchanged mischievous looks. He would not say more—but they ate and survived.

As they rode on, Clive kept joking with Phil, going over old games, refusing to say how he knew the food was safe. Finally they found the bridge and irrigation ditch, and after that, the cherry orchard. Phil leaped the ditch and disappeared beneath the trees. Clive paused to pluck and eat some cherries. He handed a few down to Ian, saying sotto voce, "Cock your crossbow."

Ian did as he was told, wondering what had made Clive suddenly wary. Phil called out to them from under the trees. Clive spit out a seed, saying, "Phil is going to come running back—when he does, shoot him."

"Say what?" Ian stood holding a square-headed armor-piercing quarrel and a handful of cherries.

"When Phil comes back, shoot him. Through the heart, if you can. Point your bow at his chest and pull the trigger."

"My God, *why?*"

"A head shot's too hard. And a gutshot would be cruel."

"Why shoot him at all?"

"Why do you think you brought that bow? You're going to shoot people. Might as well start with Phil. We don't need him anymore, and this is an *elimination* sweepstakes, remember?"

The jester leaped the ditch again and came jogging back. "What's taking you guys?"

Clive shook his head and started fumbling for something on the far side of his saddle. Ian stood mesmerized, clutching the cocked bow, telling himself it was all a hideous game and no one was really going to die. But he still could not just put a quarrel into Phil's chest.

"What's wrong?" Phil demanded.

Clive nodded toward Ian.

The jester turned to him. "Well, what is it?" Clive rose up in his stirrups. The arm on the far side of his high saddle was holding his heavy flange-headed mace. Swinging it through a tremendous arc, he brought it down with a wet smack on the back of Phil's jester cap. Ian saw Phil's eyes go wide and his jaw drop. The jester crumpled face forward, the back of his head a bloody mess.

Clive tried to flick the blood off the mace, with not much success. Hair and skin clung to the steel flanges. "See what you made me do? The crossbow would have been so much neater." He tossed the mace to Ian. "Clean it off."

Feeling numb, Ian knelt, trying to clean the mace in the orchard runoff while Clive rolled Phil into the ditch with his lance. The cool green shade of the ditch smelled heavily of cherries. He handed back the mace, and they set out again.

Halfway through the orchard, Clive reined in, saying, "At least the little shit wasn't lying."

Sheila and Gertrude came riding up, looking like Britomart and Amoret fresh out of the *Faerie Queene*. Sheila wore full armor and rode a big chestnut war-horse, carrying her lance half-couched to fit under the cherry branches. Her surcoat and shield bore the red lion of the White Company. Gertrude wore a ball gown and rode a dapple gray palfrey. Both looked wary.

"Where's Phil?" Sheila leaned forward to see under the lanes of trees.

Clive answered with an armored shrug. "He went his own way." Flecks of gore still clung to the mace.

Sheila and Gertrude were not totally taken in, but seemed willing to let Phil fend for himself, asking, "We still have a truce, don't we?"

Clive smiled cheerfully. "Until the Castle."

Ian marveled at the man's ability to lie. Some truce. Sure, it was a *game* — and he had never much liked Phil. But the pain was as real as the smell of ripe cherries. Ian could hardly stomach what he had seen so far. And worse was sure to come. At any moment Clive could start hacking at these two women — shouting happily for Ian to lend a hand.

As they rode on, Sheila and Gertrude started ribbing each other to keep up their spirits. They had gone through grisly deaths already, and bought their way back into the game. But at least these two hopeless addicts had a lively good humor. Already Ian liked them more than he cared for Clive.

Trees thinned. Through the branches, Ian saw another ditch and the white walls of a farmstead. "Load your bow," Clive whispered.

The bow was still cocked. Ian looked about, seeing no sign of trouble. No one but Sheila and Gertrude, riding just ahead.

"Load your bow, damn it!" Clive demanded.

Ian hesitated, hating to reach for the quarrel.

Gertrude turned to see what the commotion was. Her curly dark hair framed a round, pleasant face. Not plain. Not pretty. Just pleasant. She had not bothered to make herself beautiful — but Ian still felt moved. He was damn well not going to shoot her, even if it cost him the game. He smiled, trying to set her at ease.

Clive cursed and couched his lance.

Ian saw a flash of color over Gertrude's shoulder. A line of men rose out of the ditch. The nearest man wore a sleeve-shaped turban and a short flashy green jacket over baggy maroon pants. Ian smelled burning sulfur, and realized the men were pointing big crude matchlocks at them. Janissaries, elite Turkish infantry.

With a hideous crash, the whole line exploded in flame and smoke. The black horse beneath him screamed and jerked. Instinctively, Ian turned his mount about — neither he nor the horse wanted to face that hail of lead.

The beast stumbled on for a dozen yards before going down in a thrashing heap. Ian struggled free of his dying mount. For a moment, he lay amid fallen cherries, mouth open, his jerkin smeared with horse blood. Janissaries swarmed out of the smoke, howling with glee, waving scimitars and short curved daggers. Sheila was down. She and her horse both looked dead. Clive was down too. A Janissary tore off the knight's helmet, and Ian caught a glimpse of Clive's cosmetic features grimacing in agony. A neck wound pumped blood onto his blond hair. Gertrude's horse was down, but she was up and running, trying not to trip on her gown.

Ian bolted, knowing he had no chance against a platoon of Turkish musketeers. None of this was real, but he aimed to be gone before they reloaded. Ducking branches and stumbling over furrows, he risked a panic-stricken glance back. Gertrude was pinned against a cherry tree, holding three colorful attackers at bay with a dagger. A dozen more stood around her, laughing and loosening their harem pants. Another pair was busy sawing off Clive's head. Janissaries were slave soldiers, raised from boyhood under rigid barracks disciplines, trained to take out their urges for sex and aggression "in the field." Murder, mayhem, and rape were as fundamental to them as the manual of arms.

He did not stop until he was huddled in the irrigation ditch. Ian could clearly see how insanely idiotic the whole business had been — thinking that they could beat Circuit Maximus at the casino's own game. He and Clive had gone up against a perfectly integrated program that suckered players in, then ground them up. The Wolf Pack, the White Company, Phil the Shill, and God knows how many others were all being dealt with swiftly and efficiently. It was only a matter of hours before the program hunted him down and finished him off in some painful dramatic fashion.

With no future worth worrying over, Ian decided to attend to the present. Cold and miserable, he lay in a clammy ditch. Virtual hunger gnawed at his gut. The need to eat was hardwired into the program, to keep him from just lying low and waiting for an opening. Well, he might as well die comfortably. Getting up, he followed the ditch back the way they had come. He knew he was nearing the cart path when he came on Phil's body, head down in the ditch. Corpse beetles crawled over the back of his broken skull.

Dusk was descending on the virtual world by the time he came upon the line of pavilions. He sought out a cloth-of-gold tent lit by tall burning cressets and guarded by a huge djinn in Turkish armor. If the demon wanted to do him in, the monster had the strength to do a quick, neat job of it. Otherwise, Ian was determined to eat.

The silent colossus with the gleaming scimitar looked him over and let him in. As the silk tent-fly closed behind him, he saw the blonde was waiting, wearing the same good-girl, bad-girl smile that she had seen him off with. Her table was set with cous-cous and stewed chicken, sprinkled with saffron. Ian set at once to eating, too hungry to care what the meat might contain. Love potions. Sleeping drafts. Slow poison. Whatever kept him from getting to Dracula's Castle was fair game.

She watched, blue eyes alight with amusement. "Where are your friends?"

"Couldn't make dinner," Ian replied. He gave a brief brutal description of Phil's murder and the Turkish ambush. She looked sad and offered more cous-cous.

Maybe there *was* a love potion in the saffron chicken because the more he ate, the better the blonde looked, with her upturned nose and infectious good humor. There just had to be a computer-perfect body under her golden robe.

She stood up, taking him by the hand, heading toward her curtained bed. What the hell. She was clearly programmed to please. If she was also programmed to slip a stiletto into him, he only hoped she'd let him come first; anything else would be cruel.

The bed was lit by a single candle suspended in a slotted brass ball, a sort of orb-shaped censer giving off shafts of light. A golden haze filled the curtained chamber. Somewhere in the gaming software, there was a real artist at work. She knelt beside the perfumed coverlet, hands clasped in her lap. "Would it please milord if I undressed?"

Ian grunted and sat down on the bed, kicking off his boots. He'd never thought much of virtual sex. Programmed partners always seemed so slick, so perfect, so ready to please. Real women did not eagerly submit to every semisordid act the male mind could imagine and then come at a touch—just when you wanted them to. Not all the time anyway.

She let her robe fall and leaned forward, helping him with his pants. As he pulled his homespun shirt off over his head, he felt her go to work, first with her hand, then with lips and tongue. Letting out a little gasp, he lay back on the bed. This was more like it.

Without warning, she bit him. He yelped, struggled up onto an elbow, and looked down at her. The virtual bitch had *bit* him, hard, in the soft hollow of his thigh. He could see the red teeth marks.

"Why the hell did you do that?"

She looked impishly up from between his legs, all smiles and innocence. "To show my Master that this is real."

Then she rose up and kissed him, covering his face in a cascade of golden hair. "This is Transylvania," she told him, "land of the love bite." To prove it, she nibbled on his neck.

It seemed to work. What followed did not feel like virtual sex. To Ian's intense surprise, he found himself really fucking, in a perfumed bed with an utterly real woman that he had met that afternoon over lunch. She was wild, winsome, and headstrong, with her own ideas about pleasure, playfully unpredictable. By the time they were done, he was exhausted, and utterly pleased.

"Was it worth waiting for?"

"Waiting?" Ian stared at her. How do you properly thank a program, especially one with soft curves and an impish grin?

"Doesn't this beat a Circuit Maximus guest suite?"

He sat up in bed. "Angel?"

She rolled her blue eyes. "Who else?"

"But how?" He gestured at the tent and bed.

"Protective coloration." She started to redo her hair. "Mobile hazards are programmed to avoid the line of pavilions. Can't have Mongols messing up the casino's honey trap."

Seeing her lift her arms up to redo her hair was too much. He reached over to slide her closer. "It was worth waiting for. You feel ungodly wonderful."

She laughed, not resisting, letting him run hands over her. "That's just programmed hormones. The casino jacks up your testosterone, to keep you virile and distracted. And we have serious work to do. With Clive out of the game—you, me, Tiny, and the Hound are the only ones left to tackle the Castle."

Ian did not like the odds. "Shit—I think I'll take my testosterone to the tent next door."

She gave him a peaches-and-cream pout. "Please don't be such a mark. So Clive is out. He served his purpose."

"The only purpose Clive served was to get his head planted on a virtual pike."

"He got us here. He's the one who infected your suit."

"My suit?" He stopped, thinking back to the *Lunar* Carpathians and the convenient virus in his suit programming.

"I mean, what were the chances of Clive just finding a ticketed tourist lost in the highlands? A zillion to one — right? He helped out the odds."

"Fuck." Ian shook his head. "I've been screwed from the beginning."

"And you'll keep on being screwed until you learn to get going and take control." She stamped her foot, blue eyes blazing, beginning to look like the old Angel — minus the rattlesnake tattoo. "I for one can't wait forever. I've got my people around Neptune to worry about — and a sweepstakes to win. This is real. No one's going to rescue you. Not Clive. Not your agency. No one but you and me can do it."

He had been made into a total mark. First by Clive. Then by the casino. "Okay, okay, I'm in. Just one thing."

"What?" Angel went back to fixing her hair.

"How much is this virtual virility good for?"

She grinned. "Near infinite."

A bright, full summer moon turned the Transylvanian plateau into a velvety landscape, half blue moonlight, half dense shadow. It was near to midnight, but Ian kept feeling it was neither night nor day, but some weird in-between world, cloud-racked and peopled with ghouls and bloodsucking phantoms. The Hound led, loping ahead, sniffing out snares and sentries. Tiny's dark bulk loomed behind Ian. Angel was at his side, warm and comforting.

Since the Hound retained his nominal intelligence, the Wolf Pack got a werewolf without having to pay the steep prices attached to any sort of magic. The xeno lost his speakbox, but he'd never been much of a talker. He continued to radiate his usual superhuman confidence, slipping past one dark obstacle after another, until Dracula's tower loomed ahead, huge and lonely, rising straight out of the plain, casting a deep immense shadow. It was a twelfth-century keep, copied on Byzantine works, seven stories tall, pierced by nothing but loopholes. The inner floors had to be as black as the devil's basement, even at noonday. At night, Ian found it utterly uninviting.

The remnants of the White Company were laying dilatory siege to the place, having beaten back the Janissaries. Too weak to storm the tower, they were merely patrolling the approaches, killing or turning back any gamers who refused to join them. They hadn't enough players to picket the entire tower, and posting sentries in the Transylvanian darkness was semisuicidal, so they relied on strong roving patrols, which the Hound artfully avoided.

Crawling from one moonlit hummock to the next, Ian edged after the Hound. The xeno led them right up to the base of the tower—a massive battered plinth, topped by blocks of dark stone rising toward black battlements blotting out the stars. Here the Hound faded and Tiny took over. The djinn disguise was all tusks and muscle; no magic came with it, but he still had the innate talents of a SuperChimp—including balance and climbing ability. Taking out a pair of pointed hooks tied together by a couple of fathoms of rope, he went straight up the wall.

Standing in the dark shadow of the tower, Ian could hardly tell how Tiny did it. Using the hooks as both grapples and pitons, the SuperChimp swarmed up the side as easily as if he were walking on all fours. In a matter of minutes, a line snaked down.

The werehound yipped a warning.

Angel whispered, "Let's go," seizing the line and starting to walk up the wall, almost as freely as Tiny had. Living in spin ships had stripped away any inborn fear of heights. Ian grabbed the dangling line, planting his feet against the wall, doing his best to imitate her. Bats brushed past, squeaking in the blackness. He could feel the rope jerk as Angel went hand over hand above him. Strangely enough, he was not scared. Everything was tinged with a virtual invincibility. Probably part of the trap, like his height-ened testosterone—a hormone rush that would carry him up the wall into who-knows-what.

The outer battlements were bathed in moonlight. Ian pulled himself through a narrow embrasure, sliding softly onto a stone guard walk between the parapet and inner wall. Angel crouched in the shadows, her hand over his mouth. Her thin fingers felt warm and fresh, absurdly sexy. She pointed silently down the walkway.

Ian saw empty, curving stonework. He nodded. Angel took her hand away, and they set out together. Less than a quarter of the way around, they came on a pair of bodies in plate and mail armor, their necks bent at odd angles. Tiny's work.

Farther on, they found Tiny himself, looming over a third body at the head of a dark stairwell, his djinn fangs shining hideously in the moonlight. They had breached the tower. No other team had gotten this far. Win or lose, the Wolf Pack was liv-ing up to its dubious reputation. What came next did not look so inviting. Aside from the scant light filtering down the spiral stair-way, and the odd moonlit loophole, there appeared to be abso-lutely no interior illumination. Dracula did not need light.

Angel tied the rope around her waist, signing that she would go first. Ian took the rope end, passed it around his middle, tied it tight, then handed it to Tiny—glad that Angel had volunteered to lead. Nothing could have convinced him to go first into that darkness, where the undead had every advantage.

Flint scraped on steel, and a thin sliver of light appeared, shining down the back stairwell. Angel had the brass candle ball in her hand, the light that had hung above her curtained bed; by holding the ball in her gloved hand, she let only a thin shaft fall on the stairs. They descended.

Ian held tight to the rope, feeling each step with his toes. Moonlight ended at the first turn in the spiral stairs. There was nothing beyond but the dark castle odor of cold wet stone. The stair wound counterclockwise, antisunwise, so that defenders retreating up the stairs had their left hands free. Vampires were notoriously left-handed.

At the bottom, Angel paused, motioning for him to stop, then stepping over something in the blackness. She spoke for the first time since coming into the tower, "Watch that last step, it's a baddie."

By the thin light of her candle, Ian could just make out the shining jaws of a man-trap, lying on the last step, set to snap shut on his leg. The jagged teeth would tear through muscle and break bone, leaving him to writhe in very real agony until the game ended or some softhearted ghoul came along.

As he stepped over, Angel caught him, keeping him from coming down where he naturally would have. As she set him down, he saw the outlines of a second man-trap, right at the foot of the stairs—blackened and sprinkled with straw, making it nearly invisible. He was supposed to see the first one, sitting on the last step—then step over it onto the second.

Angel whispered softly, "A good sign."

Ian nodded. Not your normal stairwell. The passageway led where no one was supposed to go. You could not have sentries losing legs as they went on and off duty. Angel called to Tiny, and the apish djinn leaped over both traps, landing next to his mistress.

They set out. Bats squeaked overhead. Clumps of the little beasts hung from cobwebbed stonework. Ian had his crossbow out, expecting to see guards or worse. The passage curved, following the contour of the tower. Ian silently counted steps. He calculated that they were about halfway around when suddenly Angel's light vanished.

The rope at his waist snapped taut, jerking him forward. He let out a muffled squeal. His boots slid on straw, then the stone flags beneath his feet disappeared. He fell into blackness.

For a horrible moment, Ian pictured himself splattering on a stone floor or crashing down on top of Angel in some spiked pit. Then the line about his waist jerked tight. He caught the rope above him, pulling himself up, taking the strain off his waist, which had to support Angel's weight as well, keeping himself from being cut in half. Swinging in the dark, he realized that they had fallen into an oubliette, a wide mural chamber several stories deep, with no exit except the hole at the top.

Once you stumbled in, you were lucky if the fall killed you, since the alternative was to lie broken on the floor below, waiting in utter blackness for thirst or internal injuries to put you out of the game. A fine way to go mad.

Between labored breaths, Ian felt himself moving. Bit by bit, the rope was rising. He bumped against the domed ceiling of the oubliette. Tiny was pulling them out. Ian let go of the rope. When his waist was flush with the stone lip, he scrambled back into the passage, feeling absurdly "safe." Another nanosecond to catch his breath, then he and Tiny drew Angel up out of the dark pit.

The only way to get past the oubliette was to brace feet and back against the stonework—like climbers in a rock chimney—and inch across. On the far side was another man-trap, waiting for anyone incautious enough to try to leap over the opening. Ian hoped these hellish entanglements showed that they were headed in the right direction.

Beyond the oubliette, he saw moonlight at the end of the tunnel. Ahead was a wide recess, with a tall window niche opening onto an inner court topped by bare battlements. Ian could see windows running around the inner wall, turning the enclosed court into a vast air shaft that brought air and light into the tower. Bats fluttered by the window. Next to the niche was a heavy wooden door, reinforced with iron bands. From the placement of the windows, Ian guessed that the door led into a series of mural chambers spaced around the upper floor of the tower. Tiny tried the door. He might as well have tried to move the tower.

The window niche was too cramped for a battering ram, but there had to be a way in. Game rules required that obstacles be prodigious, but not absolutely impossible. Angel stuck her head out the window. Blonde hair shone in the moonlight. She grabbed Ian by the shoulder. "Look, we can go around."

Ian gauged distances between windows and silently shook his head. The windows were well spaced, and the inner shaft was faced with small flush stones. It could not be climbed the way they had gone up the outer wall. "Tiny can do it," Angel assured him.

She told Tiny to stop grunting over the door and take a look out the window.

The SuperChimp in djinn disguise stuck his head out, nodding eagerly. Angel played out more rope, then she and Ian braced themselves against the stonework. Tiny swung out the window, cutting an astonishing arc, just catching the stone sill of the next window. Tiny did not seem perturbed by height or distance, reminding Ian of Poe's pitiless killer ape in "Murders in the Rue Morgue"—monstrous and unstoppable.

Tiny pulled them after him. The neighboring window opened on a mural chamber, and another ironbound door. So they tried the next window, and the next, swinging silently over the stone court six stories below. Bats flew back and forth, excited by their passage.

Finally they came to a window sealed with leaded glass. Angel peered through one of the dim little panes. "Bingo," she breathed softly, signaling to Tiny. The djinn took off his Turkish helmet, using it to shield his hand, giving the window a ferocious tap. Panes splintered. The sash buckled. Shards of glass tinkled against the stone, falling like snow crystals into the court below. They were in.

The trophy room was a cross between some *ancienne noblesse* dining hall and Kublai Khan's rumpus room. Curved and pronged weapons lined the walls, along with Gothic armor and silk tapestries. Turkish battle flags and the heads of weird steppe antelope hung over a huge hand-carved table surrounded by Roman-style cushioned stools. A silver table service glittered in the light from the broken window.

The only door was a brass monstrosity, bolted on the inside, that looked as if it could not be cracked with a tactical nuke. But what they wanted sat right at the far end of the banquet table. A tall barred cage contained an emir's ransom—gold chains, jade rings, big bevel-cut emerald necklaces, silver Orthodox crosses, a diamond coronet or two. Perched atop the heap was a ridiculously large blood-red ruby. The Vampire's Heart.

Angel bounded down the length of the banquet table and went to work, picking at the lock. Tiny shambled after her to lend a hand. Ian stood by the window, thinking that it all had been too easy.

He was right.

A bat flitted by, looping between the candlesticks, sideslipping into a neat split-S, and coming down behind Angel. As the beast descended, it started to grow, extending its legs, lengthening head and torso, assuming human form. Wings became a great billowing cloak. Ian stood rooted. Too late he realized why the tower had so few human defenders.

As the face formed, the vampire's features took on a familiar cast, showing a sharp spade beard, thin smiling lips, and slick black hair. It was Phil the Shill. There was no sign of the mess Clive's mace had made. The undead could not be daunted by normal means.

Tiny leaped at him. It seemed to be no contest. Vampire or not, Phil was still a Loonie, with long spindly arms and legs, looking barely able to stand in a one-g field, much less put up a fight. The djinn-cum-SuperChimp outmassed him handily.

And it was no contest. Tiny lunged. Phil batted aside one outstretched hand and grabbed the other one, grinning. He twisted the hand sideways. Through Tiny's wounded bellowing, Ian could hear the bone crack. Phil twisted more, all the way around, until the hand came free, separating from the wrist with a bloody snap. Tiny howled and staggered back, swinging with his sound arm. Phil seized it with both hands, planting a foot in Tiny's chest and yanking. The arm came off at the root.

Tiny dropped to his knees, screeching in pain. Phil leaped at his prey with fangs and nails; when he was finished, Tiny lay dismembered and half-decapitated. White cervical vertebrae poked through bloody flesh.

Ian was horrified and sickened. Not just by what he had seen, but by the gruesome unfairness of the game. All this time, Phil had been tracking them, letting them think they were winning while Circuit Maximus laughed up its collective sleeve.

Phil wiped gore from his lips. "Don't look so shocked. Any decent Greek scholar would have known that Philaemos meant 'blood-lover.'" Ian could see Angel working furiously at the lock. He raised his crossbow. Fighting was hopeless, but if he could hold the vampire's attention, Angel had a chance to open the cage, grab the Vampire's Heart, and end the game.

Laughing at the antique weapon, Phil advanced. Ian took a step back, keeping the corner of the table between him and the vampire. The window was open beside him—but that was no escape. Without Tiny, Ian would splatter on the black stones.

Phil glided around the table. "Give my regards to Clive."

Angel gave the lock a last twist. It snapped open with a hideous click that could have been heard in Constantinople. She threw open the barred door.

Spinning about, the vampire sprang the length of the table, slamming the cage shut, holding it closed with superhuman strength. With his free arm, he backhanded Angel, sending her flying across the table. She landed in a heap against the wall, taking a velvet stool and sterling place setting with her.

Ian could only think how horribly, monstrously unfair it all was. There *had* to be a way to win—it said so in the goddamn casino contract. But he had no hope, nothing to fight with, not even Clive's silver stiletto. In a second, the vampire would be on him, tearing at his neck, twisting his head until it came off. He wanted to cry.

Phil looked down at Angel, huddled behind the stool. He blew her a kiss. "Don't bother to get up, girl. I'm saving you for last."

Then he turned back to Ian, trapped against the window. Ian saw Angel scoop something long and thin off the floor, tossing it to him. It turned and flashed in the moonlight. "Shoot him!" she shouted.

Instinctively, Ian caught the object, it was an oak-handled silver-bladed knife. He knocked the iron bolt from his crossbow, slipped the knife in its place, and took aim.

Phil screamed in baffled rage, leaping forward. Ian shot him straight through the heart.

They brought him out of the vaults and hoisted him onto a chariot. Touts dressed as nymphs and satyrs dragged him onto the casino floor. Holos thundered overhead.

And not just Ian, either. The whole Wolf Pack was on chariots, even Tiny, who was not much of a burden in one-sixth g. Clive flashed him a grin of triumph. It was weird to see them alive and ecstatic after being decapitated and/or dismembered. Sheila and Gertrude were in the throng, as deliriously happy as if they had won. Half the White Company was there to cheer someone else's triumph. Addicts to the last.

Casino shills crowded around as Circuit Maximus broke out the cheap champagne; gaming palaces loved to record mob scenes around a big winner. It was their best advertisement. A life-size animated holo, done up like a slave in Roman leather, held a laurel wreath over his head, whispering in a sexy synthesized voice, *sic transit gloria mundi*—passing are the glories of the world.

So enjoy them now. He looked over at Angel. She was no longer blonde and bouncy, but by God, she had guts, and purpose and enough credit to save her people orbiting Neptune.

A crisp, smartly dressed Dirtsider, with an outdoor tan and earthbound muscles, shoved his way through the crowd. Easily parting the Loonies, he asked if Ian was really who he claimed to be. Short of a chromosome match, Ian no longer had any proof of identity—but what the hell. "Ian MacNeil at yer service."

The fellow demanded to know why he had cashed his ticket in. Didn't he know that gambling with agency credits was a termination offense, possibly a felony? This had to be a casino touch. No one could be so obtuse—but Ian was ready to play along. He yelled down from the chariot, "I quit."

Loonies cheered, laughing at the ridiculous groundhog, trying to bully someone who had just won several lifetimes worth of credit. Casino beauties in body paint and moonstone G-strings climbed aboard the chariot, happy to start helping him spend it. A newsie from some Tycho-based casino network thrust a recorder at him. "Ian MacNeil, you have just won a Circuit Maximus grand sweepstakes! What are you going to do next?"

Angel smiled over at him—showing only the good side of her face. Ian grinned back, "I'm going to Neptune."